A CAUSE MOST SPLENDID
THE BATTLE FOR THE BIBLE

PRAISE FOR MARK ALAN LESLIE'S NOVELS

TORN ASUNDER

I read about 20 Christian novels a year, and Mark Alan Leslie and Buck Storm are my favorites of the last decade or more ... Get ready for a roller-coaster ride with *Torn Asunder*, an apocalyptic thriller. Leslie opens with scary, soul-stirring landslides, tsunamis, earthquakes, famine, and a weird disease. It is the epitome of the genre—'end times thriller.'
—**Randall Murphree**, editor, Former longtime Christy Award judge, *AFA Journal*

THE LAST ALIYAH

This could turn out to be a definitive book, from the shame of replacement theology to the Christian involvement in the rescue of the Jews.
—**Frank Eiklor**, president of Shalom International

The Last Aliyah is one of the most intriguing stories written about the plight of the Jewish people in the End Times. What makes it memorable is the author's resurrection of the use of the Underground Railroad that originally brought the slaves to freedom in Canada, and now used to bring Jewish people home to Israel. A must-read for Christians who stand with Israel.
—**Mitch Forman**, vice president of Chosen People Ministries

[*The Last Aliyah*] is a compelling, fast-moving and timely story, and unfortunately begins with a very scary, but very plausible scenario. I enjoyed the book and kept wondering how [Leslie] was going to get out of the corner he had painted Omri into. Very clever using the sci-fi version of 2 Kings 6:18.
—**Neil Lash**, co-founder of Jewish Jewels

CHASING THE MUSIC

A gripping story told with the maturity of a seasoned wordsmith. I'll put this one in the class with John Grisham

or other secular novelists touted for producing today's best fiction ... Readers can't go wrong with the intricately woven plot, intriguing characters, and crisp writing style.
—**Randall Murphree**, editor, *AFA Journal*

One word to describe *Chasing the Music*? ADVENTURE! ... This was *Indiana Jones* wrapped up in *Romancing the Stone* overlaid with *National Treasure*—all my favorite action movies between the covers of one book ... It definitely reads like the best action-adventure movie I've ever seen ... I definitely recommend that adrenaline junkies read this book."
—**Pam Graber**, *BookFun* reviewer

I was blown away at the many scientific connections and historical ones in *Chasing the Music*. The extensive depth of information was exceptional. Well done!
—**Lynda MacDonald**, Heart to Heart Ministry, Nova Scotia, Canada

Fast action and high suspense ... The read was exciting, following clues and moving from place to place. I loved it.
—**Randy Tramp**, freelance writer and author of *Night to Knight*

THE CROSSING

Mark Alan Leslie includes a meticulous attention to historically accurate details with respect to the KKK's presence in Maine and their attempt to target Catholic immigrants, Jews, blacks, and illegal alcohol. With a genuine flair for compelling, entertaining, and deftly crafted storytelling, *The Crossing* is very highly recommended, especially for community library Historical Fiction collections.
—*Midwest Book Review*

THE THREE SIXES

Leslie's insights into world politics and contemporary culture are staggering and frighteningly realistic. He and his co-writer, son Darek Leslie, will make readers think they're living too close to catastrophe.
—**Randall Murphree**, editor, *AFA Journal*

TRUE NORTH: TICE'S STORY

Leslie vividly describes the plight of runaway slaves ... Tice exhibits a deep religious confidence that will endear him to readers of inspirational literature. While the main plot is a work of fiction, the well-researched historical elements make it believable and even, at times, educational.
—**Publishers Weekly,** naming *True North* a Featured Book

MIDNIGHT RIDER FOR THE MORNING STAR: FROM THE LIFE AND TIMES OF FRANCIS ASBURY

In a world of namby-pamby Christianity, along comes a story of a man who played no games with God. The life and exploits of Francis Asbury read like the biblical Book of Acts. Mark Alan Leslie did not write 'just another book.' I couldn't put *Midnight Rider for the Morning Star* down. Neither will you. This one is a 'must-read.'"
—**Frank Eiklor,** president, Shalom International Outreach

An exciting, exhilarating story that challenges the reader in an intense way.
—**Dr. Dennis E. Kinlaw,** dec'd., past president, Asbury College, founder, The Francis Asbury Society

Again and again it spoke to my heart.
—**Merlin R. Carothers**, founder, Foundation of Praise, author of *From Prison to Praise*

A stimulating and imagination-provoking book.
—**Patch Blakey**, executive director, Association of Classical and Christian Schools

A CAUSE MOST SPLENDID

THE BATTLE FOR THE BIBLE

A HISTORICAL NOVEL

MARK ALAN LESLIE

PUBLISHING THE POSITIVE
Plymouth, Massachusetts

Copyright Notice

Cover and Interior Design: Derinda Babcock

Editor(s): Mel Hughes, Deb Haggerty

PUBLISHED BY: Elk Lake Publishing, Inc., 35 Dogwood Drive, Plymouth, MA 02360, 2021

Library Cataloging Data

Names: Leslie, Mark Alan (Mark Alan Leslie)

A Cause Most Splendid: The Battle for the Bible / Mark Alan Leslie

372 p. 23cm × 15cm (9in × 6 in.)

ISBN-13: 978-1-64949-428-3 (paperback) | 978-1-64949-429-0 (trade paperback) | 978-1-64949-430-6 (e-book)

Key Words: Revolutionary War; Congressional Congress; Philadelphia; Boston; British Redcoats; Patriots; Patriatism

Library of Congress Control Number: 2021950148 Fiction

We cannot read the history of our rise and development as a Nation, without reckoning with the place the Bible has occupied in shaping the advances of the Republic ...

Where we have been truest and most consistent in obeying its precepts, we have attained the greatest measure of contentment and prosperity. Where it has been to us as the words of a book that is sealed, we have faltered in our way, lost our range finders and found our progress checked."
President Franklin D. Roosevelt

Those who do not treasure God's Word might some day lose it.
Anonymous

I rejoice in your Word as one who finds great spoil.
Psalm 119:162

I have not departed from the command of His lips; I have treasured the words of His mouth more than my necessary food.
Job 23:12

DEDICATION

This book is dedicated to all those who—despite the danger of torture, prison, and even death—smuggle Bibles into China, Muslim countries, and everywhere else the Holy Scriptures are outlawed. May the Lord be their front and rear guard and the Holy Spirit their guide.

ACKNOWLEDGMENTS

This book is a memorial to Robert Aitken, the Scotsman who immigrated to America in 1769 at the age of thirty-five and shook his adopted home by daring to break England's laws and the royal family's personal edict to publish much-needed Bibles. Bibles were in scarce supply but needed by military troops, churches, schools, and homes at a time when Scriptures were used to teach reading, writing, and history and to spiritually nourish children and adults alike.

Thanks to my wife, Loy, for first unearthing this story and for her continued help with molding the characters.

I'm also indebted to Donald Pauley, an industrial engineer whose degree from Boston University was a simple jumping-off point that took him around the country as an expert in waterpower and design. It didn't hurt, either, that Don's a Boston boy, a Boston Latin graduate, and knows the North End particularly well. His help with this manuscript was invaluable.

Thanks to my friends and fellow encouragers in the American Christian Fiction Writers (ACFW) writing loop.

Thanks also to my master editor, Mel Hughes; my publisher, Deb Haggerty; cover designer Derinda Babcock, and others who have been essential to this work being published into a world needing the inspiration of those people, like Robert Aitken, who put their lives and fortunes at risk to share the God of Abraham, Isaac, and Jacob.

FOREWORD

With the Bible being outlawed in a number of countries around the world today—and even in the classrooms in many American schools—with some even calling for a ban on Bibles as "vehicles of hate," we face an ominous future. Perhaps our time is akin to what the American colonists confronted in the 1770s, when only one company, certified by the king of England, was allowed by law to print the Bible. Any who defied the king disobeyed British law and faced the consequences.

Let's pray against a sequel. But if such does occur, I implore that we, as Robert Aitken in 1777, are bold enough and fearless enough with our treasure, talent, time—and expertise—to stand for the truth.

CHAPTER 1

POPE NIGHT
WEDNESDAY, NOVEMBER 5, 1777
BOSTON, MASSACHUSETTS

Elsie de La Borde, trying to get her bearings in this confusing city, brushed aside a curl from her eyes, lifted her petticoat to her ankles, and skittled across the muddy Boston street. In Paris, the lamplighters would have lit gas streetlamps by this time of day, but here, dusk ruled.

Where was she, anyhow? Boston Harbor's dark waters were at her back. To her right flowed a narrow expanse of water—the mouth of the Charles River, perhaps—and beyond the waterway, flicks of light revealed a tiny point of land.

Moments ago, the stores lining both sides of the street had shuttered, and this without her finding the haberdashery for which she was searching. Before she could ask for directions, shoppers had unexpectedly disappeared like spirits off the streets and alleyways that spiderwebbed everywhere.

"Make haste, make haste," a woman called somewhere, a tremor in her voice.

Closer by, a man barked, "Shut the shop door."

Elsie shivered and pulled her fur coat tight around her, shuddering against the early-November cold. She was reminded of being lost in the forest on her family's estate outside Lyon, and her throat constricted. If she'd only allowed her handmaiden to accompany her, she might not be so anxious.

Shouts broke out some distance behind her. She looked in that direction.

Torchlight flickered around a corner about fifty yards away, and she breathed a sigh of relief. But the breath caught in her throat when a second and third torch appeared, and a crowd five or six people wide stepped onto her street. Yelling and singing, their voices metamorphized into a collective roar, a belligerent assortment of bellows and barks battling with what sounded like lyrics.

She watched, bewildered. Walking forward, the throng grew longer, and in its midst—what? A wagon. And atop the wagon? A scarecrow. No! The scarecrow wore a tall, white-peaked cap like that worn by the Roman Pope.

The mob surrounded the wagon, marching along, some holding torches aloft. Then a second wagon, or farm cart perhaps, turned the corner, and on top was a huge effigy of Satan with oversized horns, eyes blazing, and massive bulbous nose and chin.

The devil? What's this?

The entire entourage was growing closer. Forty yards away? Thirty?

Elsie looked about to spot any gendarmes. Oh, in America, they were called constables, *non*?

She shrugged at her own question, quickened her step toward the sidewalk. But, no, her ankle-length baroque boot stuck in mud and her foot slipped completely out.

Cold muck on my new silk stockings.

The crowd grew closer. Shouts grew louder, rougher. Coarse jests. Was she witnessing a cheerful anger? Or an angry cheer?

Fear wrapped tendrils around her spine.

Trying to stand on one foot, Elsie reached down to pull her boot out of the mud. She tugged. Her foot didn't budge.

She yanked harder. Mud slurped and the boot wrenched out of the ground, but the force of her pull sent her sprawling.

She cried, "Oh, no!" and fell to the wet earth. But she grasped her boot.

Now twenty yards away, the multitude swarmed ahead, unflinching, unheeding this helpless French girl on the ground.

She pushed herself to her knees and looked. The crowd, all of whom appeared twice her size, was ten yards away, not slowing, its roar so loud she could no longer hear her thoughts.

Five yards! Close enough to distinguish the buckles on their boots. Elsie envisioned being trampled to death.

Out of nowhere a strong pair of hands grasped her right arm and snatched her off her knees, into the air, out of harm's way.

Elsie shrieked.

Those hands pulled her close to a broad chest, their owner wrapped her in protective arms, and pulled her into the alcove of a store. She felt like a rag doll. *Une poupée de chiffon.*

She looked at the handsome young face of the man and said above the din, "*Mon sauveur.*"

"No savior," he replied. "There is only one Savior, the Christ, Jesus."

"*Tout à fait*," she said, and took notice of his English. "I mean, of course. You're a colonist, yet you speak French?"

"*Un petit*," he replied, his smile mirthful. "I only—"

His next words were drowned out by the passing throng, singing:

> *Remember, remember*
> *The fifth of November*
> *Gunpowder, treason, and plot.*
> *I see no reason*
> *Why gunpowder treason*
> *Must ever be forgot.*

The words meant nothing to Elsie. November fifth? Treason? Gunpowder? But the timbre of the chant was disturbing. Forgetting her normal reserve, she huddled closer to this stranger with the strong arms.

Ill-dressed teenagers and young men were pulling the first wagon past them. Their lyrics suddenly transformed into declarations she'd never learned from her English tutor, but she was certain they were vile, derisive, disparaging words against the Pope.

Her Papé, or a representation of him. Pius the Sixth., ambassador for Christ, reduced to a few arms-full of straw and a white robe and pointed hat. *Oh, non!*

The rabble marched along, the clamor ear-splitting. Clutching her boot in her right hand, she covered an ear with her left to lower the din. Next came the second wagon, resembling the flower cart she'd passed earlier in the afternoon. Aboard was the bizarre likeness of Satan, apparently made with papier-mâché.

Répugnant.

Elsie turned away in disgust and peered into the store beside them. A dim light burned near the back of a spacious room. Books lined shelves from floor to ceiling along the walls.

She leaned back and asked her rescuer, "Did you come from here, sir?"

He nodded. "Would you like to go inside, away from this, this ..." He swung his arm toward the crowded street. "Mayhem."

Yes, escape!

"*Oui.*"

He knocked on the door and an older, bald man appeared from a room beyond the lamp. In a moment, the man had crossed the room and opened the door, ushering them inside.

"Please, Alec. Please, young miss," the man said in haste. His accent was strong, full of tongue, foreign. "Come, come."

"Thank you, Calum."

Her protector was Alec, then. And this man, Calum, appeared kindly, his eyes wide and welcoming.

Alec placed a hand to the small of Elsie's back, but she needed no exhortation to enter. She darted inside, her bootless left foot wet and cold.

"Best stay awhile here before venturing out into the storm," Calum said. "What with Pope Night bonfires, burning effigies, and other shenanigans."

"Pope Night?" Elsie's voice was edged with fear.

"Guy Fawkes Night," Calum said. "England's and America's grand celebration of catching a gang of Catholic conspirators bent on killing the king and his sons and blowing up Parliament."

"Oh!" Elsie's hand shot to her mouth. "This just happened?"

Calum laughed. "If by 'just' you mean ..." he hesitated and thought for a moment, calculating ... "one hundred and seventy-two years ago."

"Ah."

Gunfire sounded outside. Several volleys worth of noise.

Elsie recoiled and turned toward the street in alarm.

Alec put a hand on her shoulder. "Don't fear, miss. No one will be shot, but people may be badly beaten. Those volleys signal the beginning of a furious fight between the North Enders and South Enders. You see, there're not one but two parades—one here in the North End, another in the South—and in both places they've built their own pope wagon, and both have headed for a point up the street." He pointed outside. "Now the two mobs will fight to see who'll have the honor of burning the pope and the devil."

Elsie could only manage, "Oh, my ..."

This was all news to her. She knew of Bloody Mary, of course, and other Catholic kings in England who had burned Protestants at the stake. And the favor had been returned by Protestant kings and queens.

Dare I say? I must.

Elsie turned to Alec and frowned, weighing her decision. "I'm Catholic," she whispered.

Alec tilted his head as he appraised her, his eyes sparkling in the darkness, and asked, "You're not armed, are you?"

Elsie grinned sheepishly at his jest.

Calum chuckled and said, "You'll have no troubles with us, Miss. My problems are with that mob."

Elsie felt relief on one hand and anxiety on the other. "Oh?"

"They're the reason we shop owners closed up a bit early. I'd like a sixpence for every pound I've paid to those blackmailing thugs."

Elsie shot him a questioning look.

"Oh, those who make the effigies pound on our doors 'asking' for donations acknowledging their creativity. If we give not, they break our windows. Give and we're granted reprieve until next year."

He shook his head in apparent repulsion and continued, "Young Miss, you find yourself in a city that is a nursery for dangerous tumults. We've had twenty-eight riots here since 1700. Pick a reason and Bostonians have rioted against the insult. Besides the Tea Party and Stamp Act, there've been grain prices, price-fixing by butchers, merchant hoarding, riots for not enforcing laws against brothels and, most of all, the Brits impressing colonists into military service."

Alec chuckled ruefully.

"Boston's is a recreational rowdiness," he said. "Violent, yes, sometimes. Riots are a political tool for us commoners. Sorry to say, but the anti-Catholic sentiment continues to be kindled here."

Elsie wondered now about her father's wisdom having her accompany him to the colonies just days ago. Certainly, she was the woman of the house now that her mother had passed away. Surely, she had learned the art of the hostess from her mother. And undoubtedly, the experience would heighten her suitability as a marriage partner for a member of France's aristocracy. Perhaps she'd even find a gallant young suitor here, though she held no high hopes.

She thought fleetingly of her coming-out at the debutante gala in Lyon, the young noblemen falling over each other for her hand at a minuet or allemande—her mother, then alive, gushing over Elsie's marital possibilities.

But now, she emphatically questioned her father's necessity for a female presence at his side here in the colonies, especially in this dark city. She had heard countless good reports about Boston. How could trusted adults be so wrong?

True, her father's job as Pierre Beaumarchais' chief aide was to supply covert support from France to the revolutionaries, including field guns, arms, ammunition, and money.

And true, when the Continental Army defeated the British at the Battles of Saratoga two months ago, most American soldiers carried French arms fired with French gunpowder. Arms her father had secured.

But she need not be involved even in a peripheral way. Need she?

Pourquoi? Why?

Alec interrupted her reflections.

"Here we are, going on and on and haven't yet made our introductions," he said. "I'm Alec Craig, at your service, and may I introduce you to Mr. Calum Cameron?"

Elsie held forth her gloved right hand which, despite its mud stain, both men dutifully took. At least there was a semblance of manners on this abysmal continent.

Should Elsie reveal her true identity to these two strangers? The men eyed her with anticipation. The moment lingered.

They must wonder if her tongue had been tethered. Or was that the correct English idiom?

Were they truly on the side of the Revolution? Or were they Loyalists, pledging devotion to England's King George III?

Living in Boston, they were likely revolutionaries, no?

England's eleven-month siege of the city had ended a year and a half ago, in March 1776, when the colonists' militia drove General William Howe and his troops out of the Province of Massachusetts Bay altogether. If these men were Loyalists, they would be long gone, would they not? Sailed off to St. John, New Brunswick, or with the British soldiers to Halifax, Nova Scotia.

She made her decision. Smiling, she said, "I am Elizabeth de La—"

A sudden crash stopped her. She looked.

A man had fallen into the bookstore's door. Several others scuffled in the entryway. With the streetlights still unlit and dusk turning to darkness, the scene outside was in silhouette. One man punched another in the stomach, doubling him over halfway to the ground. Another struck a foe on the jaw, sending him sprawling and his shoulder cracking into the store's outside wall.

"Some of the Northsiders and Southies have decided to continue the, ah, 'game,'" Monsieur Cameron said. He hurried toward the front door, perhaps to protect his property.

"I'm so sorry you should be forced to witness this violence, Miss Elizabeth," Alec said. Even in the dimness of the room, his eyes and the firm set of his jaw confirmed his concern.

She glanced back at the spectacle and nodded.

"Not your fault, Monsieur."

"Alec," he corrected.

"Alec," she repeated. "And my friends call me Elsie."

Fisticuffs and kicks continued outside. What looked like a big stick appeared in one person's raised hand. A whistle blew and all the figures stopped, stood upright, looked to the right, eastward, and turned to run to the left.

Within seconds, three constables appeared—whistles between their lips, billy clubs in hand—and ran off in pursuit.

Elsie breathed out in relief. Calum turned to face her and shrugged.

"Boston," he deadpanned.

A figure carrying a torch emerged behind the constables. And the face its light illuminated? Her father!

"*Mon père!*" Elsie exclaimed and rushed from Alec's side.

Her father—tall, upright—noticed the movement and peered through the window. His eyes grew wide, his face broadened from fretful to excited, and he cried out, "Elsie!"

Her father started toward the entrance, and Calum threw the door open wide. Elsie met her father at the threshold and leaped into his arms.

One hand holding the torch, her father held her to his chest with the other.

"*Ma chéri!*" he said, his voice soothing, filled with relief. "*Ma petite fille!*"

In French, he told her he'd been searching since Lisette, her handmaiden, had informed him Elsie had gone shopping on her own. When light turned to dusk and Pope Night carousing began, he'd truly become concerned and had enlisted the constabulary's help.

Noticing Calum, he turned to the bookstore owner.

"Papa," Elsie said, "please meet one of the men who saved me from the mob: Monsieur Cameron."

Her father gushed over the bookstore owner and introduced himself. "Charles de La Borde—at your service, dear sir."

"You can call me Calum." Simple, direct, and neighborly.

After a moment, Elsie's hand sweeping toward Alec, she added, "And *mon savior*, Alec Craig."

Alec shook his head. "No savior, sir. A humble printer's assistant from Philadelphia."

"Young man," her father said, "humble or not, if you ever, ever need assistance in anything, anything, please call on me."

"Thank you, sir," Alec said and shook her father's hand.

"We have rooms at the Green Dragon tavern," her father said.

"*Oui, s'il vous plait, Papa,*" Elsie said. "Can we have them to dinner soon?"

Her father smiled. She hadn't seen him this happy in far too long.

"Sans doute, *ma coeur,*" he replied and squeezed her shoulder. He looked at Calum and Alec. "Could you join us tomorrow evening, gentlemen? At the Green Dragon?"

Alec looked a question at Calum, who nodded.

"Your supplies shouldn't arrive for a day or two, Alec."

"All right," Alec said.

Calum extended his hand to Elsie's father. "We'd be honored, Monsieur de La Borde."

CHAPTER 2

Hustling from his ground-floor print shop and bindery, situated in temporary hiding behind Pope's Head Coffee Shop and Pub, Robert Aitken peeked out the front door. Philadelphia had become every bit as modern as Edinburgh or London. And Market Street was bustling with shoppers on this market day. From appearances, for every ten shoppers there was a Redcoat, rifle at the ready across his chest, eyes alert.

They were searching for someone in particular.

Probably not Benjamin Franklin, whose home was a block away near Fourth Street. Mr. Franklin was abroad in France, no doubt regaling King Louis XVI and his court with wit and wisdom, waging his own battle to negotiate continued support from the colonists' allies on that side of the Atlantic.

Not Thomas Jefferson. He'd long left Graff House on Seventh Street, where he'd boarded while helping to draft the Declaration of Independence.

Nor Robert Morris, whose manse was near the corner of Sixth Street. Because he'd financed much of the Revolution, Robbie's life was at high risk and he was in deep hiding with his wife, Mary. The couple would be mad as an angus bull if they knew General Howe had confiscated their home for his headquarters.

And the Redcoats clearly had a twenty-four-hour presence in Independence Hall two blocks away down the street. Robert had observed their silhouettes prowling around inside and out the last six weeks.

Perhaps the search was for Robert himself. Although his wages were fiddler's pay, he was the official printer of the *Journals of Congress* for the fledgling Continental Congress and, therefore, a prime enemy of Britain. Howe would love to lock Robert behind bars, or simply shoot him on sight. Robert shuddered at the thought.

When the Redcoats' imminent conquest of Philadelphia became obvious, Robert had moved his press to this spot, semi-hidden in the back of the building, where he hoped and prayed he wouldn't be discovered. At the same time, he'd transferred his wife, Janet, the four *bairn*, and Alec to a small home between North Third and North Bread streets.

Robert had tried to leave no bread crumbs for the Brits to track him down, and the new home's mundane appearance left the place inconspicuous.

Arriving from Scotland in 1769, Robert had opened a bookshop and bindery, choosing Market Street for its busyness. But that bustle was now the problem, dangerous since the Brits had savaged their way into town six weeks ago. September 26, to be exact. A day of infamy, sending the Second Continental Congress into panicked flight.

That momentous turn in the war came just fifteen days after the leadership decided that a locally produced New Testament of the Bible was not viable because of the risk and cost of procuring the necessary materials.

Robert had locked arms with William Marshall of Robert's own Presbyterian, or "Seceders," Church of Philadelphia; Patrick Allison, the chaplain of Congress and pastor of Philadelphia's First Presbyterian Church; John Ewing, provost of the University of Pennsylvania; and

Francis Alison, a founder of the University of Pennsylvania and University of Delaware.

You'd suppose such prestigious colleagues would persuade Congress. Once the war began, England had banned shipments of all sorts of goods, including King James Bibles, to the colonies.

The group related Bibles were "growing so scarce and dear that we greatly fear unless timely care be used to prevent it, we shall not have Bibles for our schools and families, and for the public worship of God in our churches ..."

Congress's response?

"The proper types for printing the Bible are not to be had in this country, and the paper cannot be procured but with such difficulties and subject to such casualties as render any dependence on it altogether improper."

Folderol.

Robert possessed the types and press. All he needed was the proper ink and paper, a special fibrous blend, and both were available from Holland and Italy.

In fact, six months past he had messaged an ally in Scotland to negotiate a shipment of both the specialized ink and paper.

The problem was getting shipments through British blockades entering and exiting Philadelphia and New York City. Not so much of an obstacle in the free city of Boston, so that was where he'd sent his apprentice, Alec. If all went well, the shipment would arrive soon.

Congressmen, perhaps the loss of the colonial capital was God meting out justice for your weak-kneed frailty and lack of faith.

Indeed, the day of the vote, General Washington's troops were pummeled at Brandywine and driven to Valley Forge.

Since then, Robert had decided to remain in Philadelphia, to try to remain anonymous, and to pray no traitors or Loyalists who had not sailed off to Canada would turn him in to General Howe.

At least he could trust Jake Tremble, who operated Pope's Head and owned the building. Jake was as steadfast as Hawk Mountain.

But Robert fought off nightmares of being caught and tortured for what he knew of Congress's intentions. As a Scotsman, he knew well the Brits were expert at torture. Anyone who drew the ire of the king could suffer William Wallace's fate of being drawn and quartered.

Meanwhile, the Lord's will was for Robert to print and distribute Bibles, regardless of breaking British law. And when the Lord gave a person a calling, he provided the means—regardless of the foe.

And especially this foe. King George, the head of the Anglican Church, England's "official religion."

Pshaw!

George, the incorrigible, dogmatic pedant. The mumpsimus, declaring the English Crown owned the copyright of God's Word—King James Authorized Version or not—and printing a Bible was illegal unless you had George's personal permission as "Royal Printer."

Balderdash. Twaddle. Bunkum.

Robert's hands balled into fists. Containing his Scottish temper was sometimes like climbing the summit above Fort Douglas back home in Dalkeith.

George! As bad an enemy to God as the Roman Catholic Church, forbidding congregants from reading Scripture in their common language at risk of being burned at the stake.

And here history had been laid at Robert's doorstep.

When the entire American Congress fled the city, Robert considered his options.

Thank the Lord for Ben Franklin enticing Thomas Paine to immigrate to America last year. And the unheard-of one hundred and fifty thousand copies of Thomas's *Common Sense* Robert had published and sold. Those proceeds— along with those from *Philadelphia Magazine*, which Thomas had handled as managing editor—had been a godsend, despite the lengthy arguments with Thomas over the divinity of Jesus and the importance of relationship with him.

Robert looked again out the door but in the other direction—toward the tall edifice of Christ Church, a simple block away. A quick hop, skip and a jump to meet with the church's rector, William White.

Whether Loyalists or revolutionists, at least the city's clergy agreed on the need for more Bibles.

Robert could hear Francis Asbury's voice ring out, calling Congress to action. The only British-born Methodist to refuse John Wesley's command to return to England once the war broke out, Asbury had stood tall and adamant for the publication of God's Word. Now Asbury, too, was hiding out to avoid jail. Such was British justice.

As Robert gauged the time to walk the six hundred feet to Christ Church, a voice came from the hallway behind him.

"Da. Da?"

Robert turned. His daughter Jane, not a wee *bairn* any more but an attractive young lassie of thirteen, stood midway down the hall from the back room where she and her younger brother did their studies.

"Aye, darlin'," he said.

"May we play with the press?"

Ten-year-old Robert Jr., "Robbie," stood behind her, enthusiastically nodding. "We've finished our studies," the boy added.

"Play?" Robert shook his head. Chagrin filled their countenances, and Robert held up an index finger. "But you may create a page with your new poem, Jane. And Robbie?"

"Yes, Da?"

"You act as your sister's helper."

"Yes, Da."

Robert looked at his daughter. "Is that all right with you?"

Jane was Robert's apprentice without title, a brilliant lass, and would no doubt take over the business when the Lord called him home.

Her face brightened, her eyes twinkled, and she looked back over her shoulder. "You have to do what I say, Robbie."

Robbie's mouth twisted in acquiescence.

"Okay," Robert said. "I'll be back in an hour or so."

"Where're you going, Da?" Jane asked.

"To Christ Church, but you shan't tell anyone who asks. Understand?"

"What about Ma?"

"Her, you can tell. In two hours you two go on home out the back door and through the alleyways so as not to be detected."

The children nodded, their faces flush with excitement, and Robbie careened down the corridor, his sister hurrying behind. A large bookcase at the back wall opened on hinges, revealing a hidden room where the press was housed.

Robert tugged his tricorne hat down tight over his forehead, buttoned his wool overcoat to the top, and stepped out alongside Market Street. He pointed his nose toward Christ Church, his eyes locked on the toes of his boots to ensure he would not stumble on the cobblestone, and made haste. Along the way, all two hundred and twenty-three steps, he prayed no soldier would spot and stop him.

What a way to live a life!

After a few steps he passed South Bank Street to his right and, a hundred meters further, two alleyways to his left. The church rose before him. He cast a glance at its austere and cold stone face. A line of trees, their limbs bare to the upcoming winter, edged closer, bordering this west side of the church.

Robert scurried alongside the edifice to a door near the back, knocked twice hard, twice softly, then twice hard. Moments later, the door creaked open a sliver. A blue eye belonging to William White peered out at him and the door opened thirty degrees. William beckoned him inside.

"Perhaps we should've met at your house," Robert offered, imagining fewer soldiers would be patrolling Walnut Street a quarter mile to the south from this main fare.

"Six of one, half dozen of another," William said. "I'm afraid they're as much looking for Robbie Morris as they are for Mr. Franklin or anyone else."

William occupied a most unusual and tickly, if not dangerous, position. Not only was Robert Morris his brother-in-law, but William was also publicly supportive of illicit Bible printing, despite the king's edict. Not a safe position for a priest in the Anglican Church. A third degree of jeopardy was that his father was retired Colonel Thomas White, who—despite his distinguished career with the British Army—was an outspoken supporter of the Revolution.

What a lark for the Redcoats if they caught all the Morrises and Whites together.

"I wanted to give you an update," Robert said.

William nodded, anxious.

"I expect Alec back any day but also realize he could be arrested, or he may have already been seized if the goods are discovered and a smart soldier figures out their destination."

William's brow knitted in concern.

"I know this," Robert said, "I'd trust Calum Cameron with my life, and if the ink and paper have arrived and if he does not make the delivery himself, his prayers will inhabit heaven all day and all night to secure the material's safe delivery."

William blew out a deep breath as in relief.

"But," Robert said, "I fully expect Alec to avoid the Brits' inspection of his cargo. He'll have my wagon loaded with yard goods for Henry Hinckle and rough iron and such for Douglas Bradford. We hope all that cargo on top of the wagon will deter further inspection beneath."

Robert's voice became hoarse. "If anything happens to me, William, Alec's instructed to hide the wagon in Maurice Brackett's barn and ride the horse into the city. If he finds me jailed, he'll get word to you about the shipment."

"But who would do the printing?"

"If the press hasn't been confiscated, Alec will. I've trained him well and he's a bright young man. Jane can be his apprentice and Robbie will collate the pages."

"What about Mr. Paine?"

"My resident heretic?" Robert offered a faint smile. "I trust believers only, my friend. True, without Thomas's *Common Sense* we might never have fought beyond the first volley, but he believes in his own reasoning above God's Word."

Robert cocked his head and added, "Besides, Thomas has put aside his pen for a sword—for now at least. He obtained a post under Washington."

"Ah-h."

Robert shrugged. "My life and death lay in God's hands. The Bible comes first and foremost."

William nodded, his eyes thoughtful, his voice firm, said, "Yours is a cause most splendid, most noble. May angels watch over you."

"But if I slip through their hands and am caught, Alec's my proxy."

"Alec." William's face formed a crooked smile. "Well, he's made of good Scottish stock."

"Indeed. I knew his parents well." Robert fought back a tear, his gaze distant. "Both survived the famine only to die of malnutrition when Alec was a lad. Gave their lives for their *bairn*."

"I know you paid dearly to bring him to America and live with you." William shook his head. "Born and raised here in Philadelphia, I never faced what you and other Scots had to struggle through. We in the cities have no notion what fights the folks in our own countryside have endured. Fat and fancy-free, many of us."

"Aye. But we're all in the same boat now."

Robert pondered his next step, disclosing his update to their co-conspirators. That's what the Brits considered them: conspirators—lawbreakers intent on sticking their fingers in King George's eye.

Finally, he said, "I need your assistance disseminating this information. Can you reach Bill, John and Patrick?" Being colleagues in the struggle to print Bibles, Marshall, Ewing and Allison all needed to know. And while Second Presbyterian was close to Aitken's home, the Seceders and First Presbyterian churches were about two miles distant.

"Maybe Patrick will be able to get the information to Dr. Rush, James Wilson and Thomas McKean. They all attend First," Robert added. "I can contact Francis Alison and the new pastor at Second Presbyterian."

"Hmm." William put his thumb and forefinger to his chin. "Dr. Rush, Wilson and McKean all signed the Declaration of Independence. Their faces are on the wanted notices, for certain. Not easily traced—even by us."

"Try your best and I'll do the same."

"'Let us not be weary in well-doing: for in due season we shall reap, if we faint not,'" William said.

Robert nodded. "Galatians 6:9." And with a tip of his tricorne, he slipped back out of the church.

General William Howe stood behind his desk, fingering an ear and holding a communique from King George III. Howe slammed his powerful fist on the table and peered down his narrow nose from his six-foot height at the lieutenant who'd delivered the message.

Yes, Howe had to flush out propaganda and already had men hunting down the sources of rebellious vitriol. And, yes, he agreed with the king's orders to keep the rebels harassed, anxious, and poor until the day when "discontent and disappointment is converted to penitence and remorse."

But he was in no mood for this merry chase on which George was now sending him. He peered again at the dispatch and growled.

As commander-in-chief of the British army in North America, he'd sent his letter of resignation on a ship to England three weeks prior and was left to wait for London's acceptance. He'd probably have to linger five or six long months before he and his brother Richard, an admiral in the Royal Navy, could return home to defend their strategy in the Battle of Saratoga. The support they needed for that fight was meager, woeful.

Not our fault!

The British government and newspapers had pilloried Richard and him. Had Westminster forgotten his successes? The Seven Years War two decades ago? His capture of Quebec and Montreal eighteen years ago? His succeeding years of service in Parliament? And then a return to battle and more triumphs?

Yes, the victory at Bunker Hill in 1775 had cost heavily, but then came Brandywine two months ago, followed by the gemstone: Philadelphia.

Some buffoon had complained of Howe's "destructive confidence." What military leader shouldn't be confident? And destructive? Men were lost in war. It was called "war" for a reason. Would they prefer the "American Feud"? The "Colonial Competition"?

And now Howe's foul mood was made nastier by this new demand from the king. A whispered profanity escaped his lips and he squinted again at the handwriting, double-checked the king's seal.

In the midst of a war, the sovereign wanted him to deploy forces to discover colonists conspiring to print the Bible. What?

Howe stewed.

Deploy manpower I can better array elsewhere.

But the last thing he could do was dismiss the order and have George find out. Moreover, as he further ruminated on the command, he thought this could be a good thing, a grand occurrence.

Yes! A gift from on high.

Find the plotters, flog them mightily in the public square, leave them there to be pelted with rotten fruits, then hang them high for the world to see what happened to rogues and traitors who flaunted the king's will.

As a broad smile crossed his face, Howe gestured for the messenger to wait. He dipped his quill in the inkwell and composed a reply.

Absolutely, he would seize the task to personally root out the adversaries. Without doubt, he would publicly scandalize the very idea of publishing the King James Bible without the royal family's approval. Unapologetically, he would visit mayhem upon friends and family of any would-be plagiarists. Villains, copycats and collaborators would be scourged.

General William Howe, the son of 2nd Viscount Emanuel Howe as well as Charlotte Howe, a regular in the king's court, would not disappoint the royal family.

His troops would scour the country for any scoundrels daring to break royal law. He would purge them from society in a memorable public display.

Blowing fine sand onto the letter to dry the ink, Howe folded the paper, inserted the message in an envelope, sealed the flap with wax with his family crest, and handed his reply to the lieutenant.

"Be quick—on the next vessel to London," he pronounced, narrowing his eyes at those of his subordinate. The young man saluted and hurried off.

Howe's mind turned to more pleasant matters. First and foremost, his impending tryst with his mistress, Elizabeth Lloyd Loring, was far more stimulating. If, indeed, she could escape for a few hours from her husband. The bore, assuming that being a Loyalist would win Howe's esteem.

How about winning over your countrymen, sir? Let alone your own wife? We stormed into this city expecting ... What did you promise? "Friends thicker than woods," you said. And what did we find? Women, children, and scores of empty homes.

At least those uninhabited houses included this one. William glanced around the lavish confines of Robert Morris's manse. Nice. Exceptional. Well-appointed beyond his expectations—certainly beyond that hovel he'd lived in while posted in Boston.

CHAPTER 3

The Green Dragon was impressive by Boston standards, though in Paris or Lyon the establishment would be considered a bit common. The place served Charles de La Borde's purposes well.

Situated in the city's North End on the length of Union Street that led from Hanover to the Mill Pond, the public house was strategic. Its three-story brick structure proved well-appointed enough that he, Elsie, Elsie's maidservant, Lisette, and his valet, Malcolm, could all quarter on the second floor. He could have reserved rooms near the third landing, but with windows at three gables offering the only natural light up there, he'd chosen the much brighter second story.

The Freemasons used most of the first level for their meeting rooms now steered by John Hancock, since Grand Mason Joseph Warren had been killed in the Battle of Bunker Hill two years before.

Indeed, although St. John's Inn would have been more comfortable, the lodge lacked one main ingredient present at the Green Dragon: Benjamin Burdick.

Burdick, who owned the establishment, was proud to declare to anyone who'd listen that his basement tavern was the oven in which the Sons of Liberty had conjured, incubated, and baked plans for the Boston Tea Party on Griffin's Wharf back in 1773. Even Paul Revere had been dispatched from here for his famous ride to Lexington.

The Green Dragon was the epicenter of all things American.

And, revolutionaries being Charles de La Borde's friends in arms meant that Burdick and the Green Dragon possessed the Frenchman's esteem and trade.

All this and no harm done by the fact the food was substantial even during these lean war years. Tonight's dinner was a time to thank Calum Cameron and Alec Craig for saving his daughter from certain harm.

A gentleman would do no less, and Elsie meant more to him than all the treasures of heaven.

When her father stuck his head in the doorway to check on her, Elsie was undergoing one of her favorites of life's moments: styling her hair. She had dressed in an elegant midnight-blue gown over a stylish gold-colored petticoat, and now Lisette was braiding her long, curly, molasses-colored locks in a flowing fashion unlike back home.

In France, as in England, women's hair styles were so elaborately artificial, teased into an inverted pyramid or a balloon a full one-and-a-half times a girl's head height, ornamented with ostrich feathers or such, with full scenes in miniature. Insane, she thought. Here in America she felt free to be natural.

Her father smiled, winked, twice unballed his fist and flashed his fingers—*ten minutes*—and closed the door behind him.

Elsie checked the mirror and breathed deeply, satisfied. She'd never felt so beautiful, so mature, so satisfied with her appearance. She must resemble her mother at this age. Alec would be impressed. That was the goal.

"I'm gut-foundered," Alec said to Calum. "I could eat an entire cow and come back for seconds."

"Mutton, most likely," Calum said with a poker face.

Alec elbowed the older man. He'd become close to the Scotsman through a couple of earlier visits and especially the last several days living in Calum's apartments above the bookstore while waiting for the ship to land with his materials. No one could replace his ma and da but Calum had become like an uncle. So now he had two "uncles," Mr. Aitken and Calum.

They walked along Snow Hill Street. To their right, embers still smoked from the Pope Night bonfire on Copp's Hill.

Calum shook his head. "Bad thing, that."

Alec shrugged. "Boys will be boys."

Calum chuckled. "And how old are you, son?"

Alec's smile went silly. "You got me. The answer's nineteen."

They walked along, putting Mill Pond on their right.

"Amazing thing, that," Calum observed, pointing toward the low walls holding back a mammoth body of water.

"Always wondered how it works," Alec said.

"A tidal mill pond," Calum said. "They store water in the pond when the tide comes in, then shut off the gate when the tide goes out. That done, they release what's stored to turn the water wheel and power the millworks."

"I'm impressed."

They crossed Bridge Street, then Croft Street, and Calum pointed to two large brick buildings. "The mills."

Alec nodded, wondering if a mill wheel could power a printing press.

A moment later they came to Union Street and turned right, walking closer to Mill Pond.

After a minute, Calum pointed to a large, three-story brick building with three dormers on the top floor. Five oversized windows on the first floor and six on the second gave light into the place. To the left of its front door two flags billowed in the breeze.

Alec recognized both. One was the New England flag and contained three sets of red, white, and blue horizontal stripes with an additional red stripe representing the thirteen colonies, and in the top left corner a white square with a green fir tree. The flag had been released two years before.

The other was the Continental flag, revealed last year, boasting thirteen horizontal red and white stripes, with thirteen five-pointed stars in a circle centering a blue square in the left top corner.

A small sculpture of a dragon overhung the entrance. Ah, the Green Dragon.

"The place used to be called Mason's Arms," Calum said. "The dragon was ornamental. But the beast is copper and kept turning green, oxidizing in our salty air. And the owners got so maddened by continually cleaning the darn thing that—when even Revere gave up on the quest to keep the dragon untarnished—they renamed her."

Alec chuckled. "Good story."

"The pub's in the basement. Meeting rooms and dining hall are on the first floor," Calum said and motioned toward the front door. He noticed Alec's hesitation. "What?"

Alec waved a hand over his clothing. "I feel too common for dinner in such a fine place and with such a fine young woman and her father."

"They'll understand you're far from home," Calum said.

This was the rare moment in Alec's young life when he felt deficient, inadequate, embarrassed at his poverty. The notion of "position" had never occupied a place in his thoughts. Mr. and Mrs. Aitken always treated him as an equal, as a son even. They'd become his second parents. And their children were like his brothers and sisters.

Calum grabbed Alec's elbow and pulled him to a stop. "Put all those thoughts aside, son. I've got something to tell you in regards to the Green Dragon's manager, Benjamin Burdick."

Alec cocked his head. "Go ahead."

"As captain of the watch for the middle part of town when the British controlled the city, Benjamin was one of several constables embroiled in legal and real fisticuffs with British army officers."

"Fisticuffs?"

Calum nodded. "British officers are all from the genteel class," he said, "and regard any of our constables unfit even to hail them. Our watchmen and the selectmen who employ them want all the people in Boston, including gentlemen of the army, to answer to the law. But the Redcoats felt themselves above the law."

Having heard his father's stories in Scotland and seen the Brits terrorize several women and children in Philadelphia whose menfolk were rebels away at battle, Alec believed this.

"Benjamin was forefront in demanding that Redcoats, officers or not, received—ahem—colonial justice." Calum's smile was one of satisfaction. "For that, Mr. Burdick owns the esteem of every respectable rebel."

Alec smiled and nodded.

Calum loosened his elbow and motioned him forward over the cobbled sidewalk. Alec tipped his cap to an elderly woman obsessed with clinging to an armful of yarn, and nodded to a large farmer pushing a cart filled with potatoes, its wheels clacking along the uneven stones.

Alec arrived first at the entrance, which was slightly off-center on the building. He took a deep breath, squared his shoulders, and opened the hefty door wide for Calum to step through.

They faced a large open room filled with long, narrow tables and benches, each of them able to seat six or eight people.

A sign over an open doorway to their right said "Pub" with an arrow pointing down a short flight of stairs. Noises escaped up the stairway. Loud. Jocular.

At that moment a large, burly man ascended the stairs two at a time. Reaching the top, he stopped short.

"Calum!" He extended his hand.

Grabbing it, Calum said, "I want you to meet a special friend of mine from Philadelphia."

Turning to Alec, he said, "Benjamin Burdick, meet Alec Craig. Alec, meet the owner of this establishment and possessor of the hearts of all who know him."

Benjamin chortled and waved off the praise.

"Honored, sir," Alec said and stretched out his hand.

"Honored? Ha!" Benjamin's eyes sparkled with mirth. "You do me too much favor, my boy. I'm one man in a"—he waved to the room around him—"world of gentility."

Alec laughed. "Not so much gentility downstairs, you mean?"

Benjamin chuckled and looked down the flight of steps where cacophony transcended into a howl of joviality.

"An astute fellow," Benjamin said. "A few of our Sons of Liberty-to-be are toasting their own decisions to join the fray. That bookseller friend of yours, Calum, you know, the one Washington assigned to bring the heavy artillery captured at Fort Ticonderoga back in January last year."

"Henry Knox." Calum obviously didn't have to guess. "If not for those cannons stationed on Dorchester Heights, the Brits would still be here."

"Well, Knox is now Washington's chief of artillery, but he strolled in with a couple of his men looking like they'd crawled out of a swamp. Every man here took stock, every ear was turned Knox's way, and he didn't disappoint. That young man fired up the coals of disgust in this place like you haven't seen since Sam Adams. That soliloquy of his would rattle a dead man's bones. Convinced the gang downstairs who hadn't taken the colors to do so."

"Henry was always reading books on military science as a boy, and now look at him," Calum said. "Is he here now? I'd like to see him."

"No, no, no. He chugged a pint, we loaded a wagon with as much food goods and blankets as we could spare, and he and his men headed out a half-hour ago. Back to Washington."

Calum turned to Alec. "When General Howe saw Knox's cannons, he knew his supply lifeline was in danger and Boston was indefensible, so he withdrew his troops."

Benjamin nodded. "All the way to Halifax, Nova Scotia, we're told."

"Philadelphia, actually," Alec said.

Benjamin turned to Alec. "Oh?"

Alec nodded. "Six, seven weeks ago."

"So, Knox is a bookseller-turned-soldier. Might that be a mirror on your future, son?"

Alec mused, then responded, "Yes, but I'm afraid my immediate battle is one more spiritual, sir."

Benjamin's eyes narrowed, a question on his brow.

Alec looked at Calum to gauge whether he could tell his mission to this man.

Calum nodded a go-ahead.

"Printing New Testaments for the troops and the colonists," Alec said.

"Illegal." Benjamin placed hands on hips.

"Highly," Calum said.

Benjamin stepped forward and slapped Alec on the shoulder, his smile cheek to cheek. "Your victuals are 'on the house' as long as you're here, my boy."

"Why, thank you, sir."

"Benjamin," he corrected.

"Benjamin."

Calum broke in, "We're actually here to dine with Monsieur de La Borde."

Benjamin took a half-step backwards as if stunned. "*You're* the guests."

Calum's smile widened, his eyebrow raised.

"Do you know with whom you're dealing, Calum?"

"A wealthy Frenchman is all we know."

"He's chief aide to Pierre-Augustin Caron de Beaumarchais," Benjamin said.

"Who's Beaumarchais?" Alec asked.

"The man who saved our soldiers at Saratoga, son," Calum said.

"And may indeed save the colonies," Benjamin added. "De La Borde stood at Beaumarchais' side in lobbying the French and Spanish governments to supply us with arms and finances."

Alec's eyebrows leaped.

"When Gentleman Johnny Burgoyne, the British general, gave up the fight at Saratoga," Benjamin said, "our men were largely clothed and armed by the supplies Beaumarchais and de La Borde provided."

Benjamin lowered his voice to a whisper and continued, "De La Borde is operating an imports business, Rodrigue Hortalez and Company, down on the docks to secretly funnel in French munitions, money, and supplies."

"I've never heard of Rodrigue Hortalez," Calum said.

"Fictional," Benjamin said. "King Louis wants to keep his support secret—for now."

The news swirled like a whirlwind in Alec's head, discombobulating his notions of how things stood. He had to completely rethink who this Frenchman was, who his gorgeous daughter was, why they were in Boston, and for how long. His apprentice-level station in life seemed all the more lamentable, his esteem in Elsie's eyes more diminished. His dreams of any relationship beyond mistress-servant crashed into broken bits of ego.

The de La Bordes were high-class; he was low. They were near nobility; he was, in the king's eyes, "rubble." She was exquisite; he was common.

Make that "ordinary."

But the counterthought struck him. Why had Monsieur de La Borde happily invited them to dinner? Because of Elsie's enthusiastic pleas. Her joy was obvious, palpable, when her father made the offer. And he was now fulfilling his generosity at an establishment obviously the epitome of American patriotism.

Think on things that are true, honorable, just, pure, lovely, of good report. The counsel from Philippians rattled around in Alec's mind.

A sudden smile curled his lips as the rapid changes in outlook leveled off at a high point. He was young. He was strong. He had an apprenticeship and prospects of a bright future. He'd overheard young ladies call him handsome, even ruggedly good-looking. Maybe he had a chance. Just maybe.

In his ruminations, Alec didn't hear the rest of the discussion between Calum and Benjamin. Not until the inn owner said, "I'll take you to them."

Benjamin motioned them forward and led the way to a door at the northeast corner of the building. He opened to a twelve-by fourteen-foot room with floor-to-ceiling walnut paneling disparate from the rest of the building. Windows on either wall were shuttered to keep the cold out. Logs burned brightly in a hearth on the inside wall to their right. A large dining table, with four settings lit by three tall candles equally spaced and centered, stood in the middle of the room.

Standing with his back to them, looking out the northern window toward Mill Pond, stood Charles de La Borde, his hands clasped behind his back. He seemed lost in thought, but he turned at the sound of the door swinging open.

His brow was knit in concern. Something was vexing him.

"Your guests, Charles," Benjamin announced. "Dinner will be served in fifteen minutes." He spun on his heel and disappeared through the doorway.

Planting a smile on his face, de La Borde stepped around the dining table and extended his hand.

Alec and Calum shook the Frenchman's hand, and Calum asked, "Is this not a good time, sir? You seem disturbed."

"No, no. Just business." De La Borde took a breath and added, "I'm so glad you were able to dine with us so I may thoroughly thank you for protecting Elsie. She is my life."

"Boston can get rowdy," Calum said. "Especially on Guy Fawkes Night."

The door opened behind Alec. He turned at the sound and there was the most splendid female he had ever set eyes upon. Elsie de La Borde stood before them, a demure smile playing at the corners of her lips. Her molasses-colored hair draped over her neck, a lock curled on her forehead. Her chocolate-brown eyes, with specks of gold, caught his and sparkled in delight.

Helen of Troy, step aside. Peggy Shippen, your match has been found.

Robert Morris's beautiful wife, Mary, came to mind—but only briefly. Alec dug deep to catch his breath.

This was the same young lady he had pulled from the mud on Snow Hill Street the day before. She was pretty then. She was magnificent now.

Alec knew nothing of shifts and petticoats and shortgowns and jackets. Gowns and caps and bodices and aprons flummoxed him. But what he did know was he had never laid eyes on anyone so ... so ... so captivating.

He was mesmerized, tongue-tied. He felt the fool for being so, but could do nothing to solve the affliction.

He stammered but Calum strode to his side and bowed at the waist, saving him from further embarrassment. That set the example and Alec followed suit.

He expected Elsie to half-curtsy, to extend a hand, palm-down, to be kissed, or some other lady-in-waiting response.

Instead she flew through the air—certainly her feet did not touch the floorboards—and wrapped her arms around his neck.

"Alec!" she exclaimed. And the world was in perfect order for Alec Craig.

An eternity later—though it was in reality a few seconds—Monsieur de La Borde *a-hemmed* and Elsie released her hold and drifted away, lowering her eyes, her cheeks pink.

CHAPTER 4

Minutes later, the four were seated about the table. Elsie's father asked Calum if he would like to offer the Lord's grace upon the food. He had told her this afternoon that he might do so, since so many in this country were uneasy around Catholicism.

Elsie loved how easily this shopkeeper—wearing no collar or priest's vestments, nothing special to call attention to himself—spoke of and to their heavenly father. Familiar, conversational, not stilted, not read out of a prayer book. The words were so sweet they even captivated Malcolm and non-believer Lisette, who stood by ready to serve the meal.

Minutes later, linen napkins in laps, silver knives and forks in hand, they were eating a meal worthy of the finest establishments in Lyon or Paris. Candles instead of candelabra, *assuré*. Assuredly. And drinking glasses like beakers instead of goblets, *vrai*. True. But the beef? *Savoureux*. Tasty. The carrots? *Exquis*. Delicious. And the cream of broccoli, *agréable*. Nice.

Her father was seated to Elsie's right and Calum to her left, and, thankfully, Alec sat across from her.

So handsome.

While she and Alec exchanged smiles, the older men shared news and commentary. She listened peripherally; she was the mistress of the house now, after all, and couldn't seem aloof to adult conversation. But distractions of a certain order defied best intentions.

Her father was waxing on about France's adversary, the English king.

"George wants to keep the rebels anxious and poor," he said. "Naturally and inevitably. He wants your fighting men disappointed and discontent, emotions that will grow into penitence and remorse. He wants all of you on your knees in submission and repentance, kissing his ring, singing his praises, seeking his singular acceptance for your atonement. That done, you can slink away, ever facing the crown, in utter defeat."

Calum shook his head in disgust.

Her father continued: "Even if Lord North were to retire, Lord Chatham to accept defeat, and Lord Weymouth to resign and move to his country estate, King George would stand his ground. He is obstinate, determined to never acknowledge American independence."

Alec smiled at Elsie. She returned her own, wider.

But so quiet.

"The crown is, above all, prideful," Calum said.

"George wants the rebels hungry, too." Elsie's father held up a forkful of beef. "And that is why we're shipping salted beef from Spain and goat meat and cheese from France here to America."

"Wonderful," Alec said.

And, so, he has been listening with his ears to the men, not to his heart? Elsie mused. But she caught herself and felt a touch of shame at her selfishness. She was not the center of the universe. But, yes, she wished Alec thought she were.

Calum's heavy brogue interrupted her contemplation: "The British people and Parliament, do you hear one way or another whether they're in favor of this war?"

36

"Recruitment is running high since their defeat at Saratoga," her father answered. "If there are opponents to the war, they're a small minority and afraid to speak out."

Calum shook his head in disappointment. "Will France ever officially voice public support?" he asked.

Elsie's father nodded. "Yes, and soon, two or three months perhaps, and Spain and the Netherlands may not be far behind. But I'm no politician, simply a businessman hoping to help the colonies against a common enemy."

Listening to the exchange, Alec had to tear his eyes away from Elsie. Her beauty was so distracting he couldn't concentrate on the conversation. Yet the exchange was important. He wished Elsie and he were alone, but he wanted to absorb every smidgeon of insight this Frenchman had to divulge.

He glanced at Calum and locked eyes with Monsieur de La Borde.

"Calum and I probably have kin fighting *for* the Redcoats," he said. "Odd, since our ancestors have battled *against* the Brits for generations. Men from the Highlands joined ours from the Lowlands—well, except for the traitors among us."

"Alec's father and I fought side by side for Bonnie Prince Charlie in the Battle of Culloden in 1746," Calum explained. "A grand fight, but a losing one. Hurried me on my way to America."

Calum tilted his head and pointed to a long scar starting behind his ear and arcing backward.

"That close to walking through the gates of heaven, I was."

Alec knew the story behind the injury, so he watched Elsie's response. Her eyes went wide and she shivered. She was indeed stunning no matter her expression—from joy to fear to whatever this was. Dismay?

"You're fortunate," Monsieur de La Borde said.

Calum nodded and poked his fork into the few remaining carrots on his plate.

"A musket ball or bayonet?" the Frenchman asked.

"A bayonet. And when my foe was about to finish me Alec's da came to the rescue."

"Oh, my!"

"Hand-to-hand combat," Calum said. "The most frightening time of a man's life. Eye to eye with someone who wants to kill you. Doesn't matter what you see in those eyes—fear or fury. That man wants you dead."

"You must have nightmares."

"I do, I'm not ashamed to say."

"You're so brave," Elsie said, her voice sounding like she'd had an awakening.

"Brave's nothing to do with the matter, Miss Elsie," Calum said. "Love of your country, loyalty to your neighbors, securing a future for your family."

"Your family?" Elsie's father asked. Alec cringed, knowing the answer, and prayed for Calum.

Pain filled Calum's face as the moments passed. Finally, he said, "The Redcoats burned down my barn with all our animals inside. What they may not have known was my wife and three *bairn* were hiding there. So ..."

Alec hung his head. He'd wept for Calum, cried for the death of his own father and mother, and now found difficulty fighting back renewed tears of grief, even if the death of Calum's family was more than two decades gone and that of Alec's own ma and da a dozen years in the past. He was able to keep his emotions in check ... barely.

Tears ran down Elsie's face and she dabbed at them but the flow continued. Monsieur de La Borde reached to put a soothing hand on her arm.

Calum spoke up. "Dear girl, please don't cry. My dear wife and *bairn* are in a far better place than us right now. No, no, don't shed one tear, young lass."

Still dabbing at tears, she appraised him and managed a half-smile.

There was a knock and Malcolm, standing behind Monsieur de La Borde, strode the few steps and opened the door. A boy stood before him, raised a small letter, and spoke in French. Alec understood just four words, "Monsieur de La Borde."

Malcolm shared a look with his master, who nodded his assent and motioned for the boy to deliver the scroll.

"Excuse me," the Frenchman said to Calum and Alec. He broke open the seal on the envelope. As he read the message, his face turned to surprise, then astonishment. He shook his head.

"This cannot be," he murmured.

"Disturbing news?" Calum asked.

De La Borde nodded. "A Dutch ship bound for Boston has been captured and appears to have been escorted to Newport, Rhode Island."

Alec sat forward, alarmed. "Any idea the name of that ship, sir?" he asked.

"*Gouden Adelaar*. The Golden Eagle."

"No!" Alec's stomach turned to stone.

Calum turned to face him full-on. "Easy, son." Then he turned back to de La Borde. "Sir, how did you come by this information?"

"The captain of one of my own ships landed in Boston Harbor moments ago. He sent this message." The Frenchman held up the letter. "He himself saw *Gouden Adelaar* boarded by British sailors, muskets at the ready. Then watched the vessel sail off south, the British cannons on HMS Ariel at broadside keeping aim at her all the way."

"But, Father," Elsie said, "does that mean Monsieur Ward was mistaken?"

De La Borde looked at Alec and Calum. "Elsie's referring to Major General Artemas Ward."

"Who commands Boston and Charlestown for our militia," Calum explained to Alec.

The Frenchman nodded. "He dined with us the other day and said the British have mainly left the New England colonies alone since evacuating Boston. In fact, the English now control New York City and Philadelphia, a bad omen for the Revolution."

"Surely the Golden Eagle must have sailed off-course," Calum said. "The Brits haven't blockaded Boston Harbor since we drove them out."

This changed everything. What would Alex do now? What would Mr. Aitken say? A dark numbing defeat scared away the giddiness of moments ago.

"Why are you so concerned?" de La Borde asked.

"*Oui, pourquoi*?" Elsie added. "Yes, why?"

Alec threw a look at Calum. He'd shared his mission with Benjamin Burdick, but to reveal such information to these people neither he nor Calum knew? He considered the idea. Well, of course revealing his mission would be all right. Maybe letting them know would even be helpful. But the valet and maidservant?

Reading his mind, Calum asked, "The de La Bordes can know, Alec. As sure as Artemas Ward sharing such information with them. I've known Artemas and his wife, Sarah, for years. Used to send them books for their general store in Shrewsbury."

Alec cast glances at the servants. De La Borde caught his apprehension and said, "Malcolm and Lisette, will you give us a few minutes? Have yourselves a glass of milk or ale in the pub downstairs and ask them to bill me."

The two left the room and Alec told his story, including that the Golden Eagle carried the desperately needed supplies.

"You want to print—" de La Borde gulped and inhaled, "Bibles for *public* consumption?"

Alec wondered at the question. "Why, yes. And it's against King George's law. He owns the rights."

"He owns the rights to God's Word?" Elsie asked.

"King James the Sixth had the Scriptures translated into English," Calum said. "The royal family owns the copyright."

"Gentlemen," de La Borde said, "you realize we are Catholics."

Alec and Calum nodded.

"Since the Council of Toulouse in the Thirteenth Century, the Holy Roman Church has forbidden the open use of the Bible. In fact, the Council of Trent two hundred years ago pronounced a curse upon anyone daring to oppose this decree. Many popes have issued declarations forbidding Bibles in the common language of the people. Our religion has burned alive those who translated Bibles and the books as well."

"So has the Anglican Church," Calum said, shaking his head. "William Tyndale is an example—himself burned at the stake after declaring church authorities wanted to keep the world in darkness, intent to satisfy their proud ambition and exalt their own honor even above God himself."

The Frenchman sat back in his chair, crossed his arms, closed his eyes, and nodded several times.

Silence descended. The candles seemed to flicker, in need of oxygen. What was left of the beef and carrots and broccoli grew cold. A clock standing against the wall behind Alec ticked and tocked.

Finally de La Borde opened his eyes, looked directly at Alec and Calum, and declared, "Then I myself will get your supplies, young man."

"Papa!" Elsie exclaimed.

Was her cry an objection or dismay? Alec wondered.

De La Borde raised an index finger asking for silence and gazed at his daughter.

"My love," he began, "does our God truly want his people to live without having his Word in our hands? This has always troubled me about the Holy Father's decrees. Must I agree with him, always? Is our pope unerring, infallible?"

Elsie blanched.

Alec rocked back in his chair and stifled an exclamation.

"Does God want his children only to hear his Word on Sundays from the lips of a priest?" de La Borde continued. "Doesn't our Savior want all his followers to have instant contact with his wisdom, his directions, the stories of glory from the Old and New Testaments? Have you never wondered why they say we parishioners, although we might study Latin, are incapable of understanding and interpreting the Bible—that only they can?"

De La Borde was speaking in English for his and Calum's edification, so they would know his reasoning, of this Alec was certain.

De La Borde reached a hand across the table toward his daughter's. "As your father," he said, "I want the best for you, no?"

Elsie hesitated and replied, "*Oui, certainement.*"

"So, if I write a set of rules and recommendations for you to live a full life, will I say to you, 'Ask your teacher,' or will I say, 'Read my writings and keep them close to your heart'?"

Alec studied Elsie's reaction. Her face seemed to transition from alarm and disbelief to restraint, then reassessment and, finally, agreement—as if lightning had struck. The Holy Spirit kind of lightning.

De La Borde turned to Alec. "What do you need, son? Ink? Paper? Typeset?"

Alec shared a dumbfounded look with Calum.

"Tell the man," Calum urged.

In the span of a minute Alec's emotions had tumbled to the depths and risen to the heights. Some Bible verse—a psalm, a proverb?—about God working in wondrous ways, occurred in the back of his brain. Could this man who had been instrumental in the Americans' military victories also be vital to the publishing of Bibles? And contrary to the commands of the head of his own religion?

"Sir," he said, holding de La Borde's attention, "we are well-fortified in most all our needs. Until Congress left Philadelphia, Mr. Aitken and I were printing the *Journal of Congress* ... and my, those gentlemen can *talk!*"

Calum and de La Borde both chuckled, and Elsie joined in.

What a sweet laugh.

Alec smiled and added, "Therefore, we have the letterpress, the paste balls, all two hundred and seventy characters in abundance." He hesitated, considering Mr. Aitken, Jane, little Robbie and himself. "And we have the manpower."

Alec wiggled two fingers of his left hand. "But we would be ever so grateful, eternally, if you could provide two things. First, black, oil-based ink in paste form, made from the soot of lamps mixed with varnish and egg white. Three twenty-gallon barrels should do."

De La Borde nodded. "Yes, and ...?"

"A major supply of cloth-rag paper."

"Cloth-rag?"

"Most likely from Italy or Holland," Calum interjected, "though you may have a supply in France, or know of another source?"

De La Borde shook his head. "Of these things I have no knowledge," he said, "but Pierre Beaumarchais and I have contacts in Italy and Holland as well as France. First, I'll try to get both the paper and ink from France. If not, I'll go elsewhere, but I foresee several months to get your materials."

Alec blew out a breath.

So much time!

"What do you imagine will happen to the *Golden Eagle*?" he asked.

"I have no idea. But if they get their shipment to you, my company can always sell the ink and paper somewhere."

De la Borde's eyes went wide and he snapped his fingers. "I have a faster way—a mail ship. Speedier than any frigate, any schooner, any Sphinx-class ship. "*Élan* sets sail tomorrow morning and will be carrying my urgent request for ink and paper. She'll land in Port de Calais, which is near Holland, be stocked as immediately as possible, and return with your supplies here in Boston. My guess: eight weeks, twice as fast as other ships.

"Aha!" De La Borde beamed. "*Élan!* Dash. Sprint."

Alec released a sigh of relief, gratitude and amazement filling his chest.

God makes a way when there seems to be no way. And from sources you'd never imagine.

Elsie scrutinized her father. She had watched him for years in business situations. Always courteous, refined, charming. And, of course, he was knowledgeable and sophisticated, effusing self-assurance.

But at this moment she discerned something else, something more. He was animated, exuberant over the possibilities of this new challenge. His volunteering for this test, a cause so unique and unusual, surprised her.

Certainement, her father had faith in Christ, but to be an accomplice to an act outlawed by Rome? What would be the repercussions if he were successful, if Alec printed Bibles for common consumption, and if their priest were to discover they were accomplices in this defiant contravention?

Would her papa be excommunicated? Would she? Or worse? She imagined herself seated before a tribunal of priests. Cardinals, dressed in red from head to foot, their faces stern, teeth clenched, jaws set, arms crossed.

The cardinal at the center pointed at her. A long finger. A crooked digit.

"You've broken our rules, child."

"But your Eminence—"

"But nothing!" The cardinal turned his attention to someone standing beside her. She looked. Her parish priest, Father Bellerose, stoical and indifferent.

"Send her to the outermost," the cardinal said, "where no eyes can be lain on her, where she can contemplate an eternity in perdition."

Elsie's eyes pleaded with her beloved Father Bellerose, but he nodded agreement, satisfaction written across his face.

"And so it will be." Elsie's father's words jolted her from her fantasy.

Energized. That was the English word to describe her papa here at this moment.

Elsie gulped, then directed a question to Alec. "Who exactly will get these Bibles?"

"The common people, the soldiers and schools and churches, mostly," Alec said.

Calum added, "Our school teachers here in New England use the Bible for English grammar and composition, history, geography—"

"And religion?" Elsie interjected.

"Of course." Alec's eyes twinkled at her, and she was sure she blushed.

She lowered her eyes. "I see. Admirable."

She offered her papa a brief smile. He nodded, accepting the gesture as approval, if only tacit at the moment.

"I know one place alone that needs as many Bibles as we can provide," Alec said. His eyes widened as if he had received a particular inspiration, and he exchanged a glance with Calum.

"Yes?" Calum said.

"The meeting hall Mr. Franklin built for itinerant preachers in Philadelphia."

"You're talking about Benjamin Franklin?" Elsie's papa asked.

"Yes, sir," Alec said. "Mr. Franklin was so affected by the eloquent preaching of George Whitefield that he constructed a building the size of Westminster Hall. Any preacher of any religious persuasion can speak there. I heard Mr. Asbury preach there once. Unforgettable!"

Elsie caught Alec's enthusiasm. Next, she caught herself. *Don't act like a schoolgirl.*

She was the mistress of the house—her father's house—and she must act mature. Not matronly but adult, not aflame but mellow, not fake but genuine, not animated but subdued.

"We met Monsieur Franklin, didn't we, Papa?" she asked.

"Hard to forget such an acquaintance," he replied.

"Mr. Franklin wrote about Pastor Whitefield," Calum said.

All eyes turned to him, and Calum put his napkin to his lips, folded and laid the material on the table, and continued, "Mr. Whitefield wanted to build an orphanage in Georgia. Mr. Franklin said he'd support the plan but only if the orphanage were built in Philadelphia. Whitefield resisted. Franklin persisted. Next, Mr. Franklin attended one of Mr. Whitefield's sermons, after which Whitefield planned to take a collection for the orphanage."

Elsie joined her father and Alec leaning forward to hear the story.

"Mr. Franklin later wrote he'd silently resolved to give nothing. He had in his pocket a handful of copper money, and several silver Spanish coins. As Whitefield proceeded, Franklin began to soften and concluded to give the coppers. Another stroke of Whitefield's oratory made Franklin ashamed of that, and he determined to give the silver."

A smile of expectation filled Elsie's face.

"Whitefield finished so admirably," Calum said with a flourish, "that Franklin emptied his pocket wholly into the collector's dish."

Laughter exploded and Elsie's father pounded the table so hard the dinner plates tossed into the air with a clatter.

CHAPTER 5

Darkness and a chill ruled the evening as Robert Aitken slid along North Bread Street between two houses and toward the rear door of his modest home next to North Third Street.

Back in Scotland they'd say the night was "black as the Earl of Hell's waistcoat."

Robert was returning from clandestine visits to the Reverend Patrick Allison at First Presbyterian Church and to John Ewing of the University of Pennsylvania. The clergy were on tenterhooks, nervous about British troops who swarmed the city—their looks haughty and menacing. So much for fostering sympathetic rapport with the colonists. Even the Loyalists ought to be discouraged by the heavy-handed legions.

General William Howe was no one to tinker with, but Allison had insisted he would never abandon his "flock," and Ewing promised Robert total support even if threatened with the gallows.

As Robert approached the back entrance into the kitchen, Robbie opened the door. Seeing his father, the boy jumped, startled.

"Da!" he exclaimed.

"Where're you going, lad?" he asked.

Robbie pointed at a wall of firewood stacked beneath the eaves of the house.

"Let me help you."

Father and son loaded up their arms and went inside. Robert put his load next to a large black stove that stood as a sentry in the small kitchen, while Robbie continued to the center room and wide, five-foot-high fireplace.

Robert opened the little side door to the Franklin stove. Warm air escaped and he rubbed his palms together. Embers were red-hot, but only one log burned. He took a log off a stack that had been indoors for two days and positioned it atop the coals.

"Is that you?" his wife's voice rang out from the front room.

"Indeed."

"I've news." Janet Aitken appeared, wiping her hands on a dark-blue apron, concern pasted on her face.

"Yes?" *Expect the best, prepare for the worst.* A good rule of thumb that was being tried by his wife's restless appearance.

"Milly broke her leg," Janet said. "She fell from the barn loft."

"Oh, no!"

"Oh, yes, and she's asked if I can come and help her tend to little William and the house chores." Janet held out a letter to Robert.

Milly and Abner Linnell farmed a large tract of acreage north of Reading, a good distance west of Philadelphia. Abner was fighting in the artillery battalion of the Pennsylvania militia. Robert and Janet were godparents to their one-year-old, who was weaning and teething and who-knew-what-else.

"So you're going," Robert said. He shut the stove door and walked toward his wife, his brow knit. "What of the children?"

"I can take the wee *bairn*," Janet said, "and Robbie and Jane can stay with you. They're old enough."

Robert was quiet, pondering the alternatives.

"Besides," Janet added, "Margaret will get a thrill having someone younger than her in the house."

Robert nodded. Sounded logical. Euthen was eight years old, Margaret three. They and their mother would be out of harm's way. Milly obviously needed help, and she and Abner were new to Reading; probably hadn't made a lot of friends—none closer than Janet and himself.

They were as close as family. Closer than some family members.

He nodded agreement.

Yes, the print shop was moved from its storefront. And yes, thus far the few people who knew its whereabouts and the Aitkens' new place of lodging had kept the secrets. But what did the future hold? Only God knew, and he hadn't seen fit to make Robert privy to that information.

Robert had fasted, he'd lain on the floor praying for hours, facedown. He'd talked up a storm to the Lord and listened for hours for his voice. Nothing. Not yet. And now he was stressed from waiting for Alec.

Where are ya, laddie? Halfway here? In Connecticut? Still in Boston with Calum? Captured and conscripted into the Royal Navy?

He caught Janet's eyes in his and knew, although he desired her at his side, her decision was best.

The words of Methodist John Wesley came to mind:

> *Do all the good you can*
> *By all the means you can*
> *In all the ways you can*
> *In all the places you can*
> *At all the times you can*
> *To all the people you can*
> *As long as ever you can.*

Robert opened his arms and Janet walked into them.

"I'll miss you," she said, her face buried in his chest. "*We'll* miss you."

I'm sure I'll miss you more.

Moments later, resigned to the decision, he said, "I can get a wagon from Douglas's livery to take you."

"You can't be leaving. You have to be here when Alec returns. That's the most important matter."

"Then what?"

She looked at him, her eyes moist. "I thought you might hire Angus to take us there in his wagon."

Angus Rayford. Right. He was trustworthy, the grandson of a famous Covenanter and a staunch member of the Reformed Presbyterian Church.

The Covenanters were among the most vocal agitators for independence from Great Britain and had imported their ways from Scotland, volunteering in large numbers, taking the colors in the Continental Army. Angus's eldest son was among them, fighting who-knows-who who-knows-where in this hodgepodge war.

"Angus, then, my love. And may angels watch over and protect you while you're there."

She squelched a sniffle. "May angels guard you and Robbie and Jane, too."

Robert pulled the love of his life close to him and prayed this would not be their final farewell.

Monsieur de La Borde had been magnanimous in his praise for Alec and Calum's boldness in rescuing Elsie and in his vow to obtain the printing materials. Alec wondered if the Frenchman's generosity would extend to allowing him to escort Elsie about town before returning to Philadelphia.

Alec still had to pick up the yard goods for Mr. Hinckle and rough iron for Mr. Bradford, whether or not he possessed the secret supplies of his own to hide underneath. Mr. Aitken had struck the deal with the two men, and Alec didn't want to doubly disappoint him.

Getting those materials would take a day. Alec knew his class of people didn't normally connect so intimately with that of the de La Bordes, but these were no ordinary circumstances, were they? And this evening had gone so well, he held higher hopes than beforehand. He might have only a one-percent chance, but one percent beat zero, no?

As Charles de La Borde neared the door to escort them out, Alec put a hand on Calum's elbow to delay him.

"Monsieur de La Borde," he said, trying to calibrate his voice to hide his anxiety, "I wonder if you'd be so kind as to allow me to escort you daughter about Boston tomorrow?"

De La Borde hesitated. Tension was evident. Alec had made the Frenchman uncomfortable. But he grabbed the silence to add, "I'll have only one more day here before heading home, and I'd love nothing more than to show her the other side of the city—her Commons, the Charles River. To erase the memories of Pope Night."

De La Borde chuckled, nodded ever so slightly, and caught his daughter's eye. Elsie smiled a "Yes," and he replied, "All right, my boy. You have my daughter's approval and my permission."

Alec fought to contain his elation. He eyed Elsie. "Ten o'clock?"

She nodded, her delight obvious.

"I will gather you here?"

She nodded and the warmth of her smile buckled his knees.

Was the girl speechless? He knew he couldn't manage many more words himself. There was a frog or something caught in his throat. He now realized that was not simply an expression but a creature with which to wrestle.

Once Alec and Calum were gone, Charles de La Borde turned to Elsie. She read apprehension in his face.

Speaking in French, he said, "About helping to print Bibles, my darling, I know you're hesitant. But I cannot agree with Rome in all things. You know I subscribe to St. Augustine and St. Thomas Aquinas and Madame Guyon's interpretation of God's Word. That is, our salvation is the result of grace, not works. And by God alone, not the church."

"*Oui, Papa.*"

"I also believe Bibles are for all people to read and decipher, not only priests and theologians."

Elsie bit her lower lip, keeping her contrary thoughts to herself.

"Of this I am sure," her father said. "The disciples worshiped and shared God's Word with each other and from house to house, not from cathedral to cathedral."

She had heard this argument before from her father in the privacy of their home. And she was afraid he would one day slip and say such a thing in the hearing of the clergy.

"One other thing," he said, "about tomorrow."

She regarded him directly, knowing what was coming and more so now that her mother had passed. The look on his face was firm.

In a voice he was struggling to keep calm, he said, "Beware, sweetheart ..."

"Papa?" Her tone urged him to continue.

"Hold dear your heart, Elsie. Young men of grand stations are at your feet in France. In Lyon, Paris, Versailles. But with a printer's apprentice? In America?"

Oui, perhaps.

She started to protest, and he cut her off. "Even if we agree with them, young men hostile to British rule may become a risk for those close to them. This liaison with Alec?"

She frowned.

Do I want to hear this, Papa?

"It would be irresponsible for me to encourage attachment—beyond friendship. If America loses this war, if we lose this war, the ramifications could be wide-ranging." He raised an eyebrow. "And personal."

Elsie balked at this. She knew her father was correct, but didn't the heart rule over danger? At last she said, "I will beware, Papa."

He leaned in and kissed her forehead and she turned and scurried off, up the back stairway to the second floor, fending off a tear at the warning with one hand and yet hiding her jubilation.

A whole day with Alec!

As Alec walked through the dining area, loud cheers arose from the pub—full and boisterous. No wonder people said the Green Dragon and other public houses fueled the fervor behind the revolt against British rule. Combine alcohol with anger and you served a concoction for confrontation.

In this case the serving was a righteous potion, spawned by the king's greed and arrogance, blended with condescension toward his colonial commoners and the certainty of his troops' superiority. What King George wasn't taking into account was the fact suppression bred an elevated magnitude of scorn and contempt.

To Americans, this was no trivial matter. They were to play no insect to the king's fly swatter.

CHAPTER 6

The day broke bright and cold. Too cold for General William Howe. But at least he wouldn't have to break ice in his hand bowl to splash water on his face and start the day. He shivered at the thought of his time in Canada and the far northern reaches of New York as a young general during the French and Indian War twenty years earlier.

Foolish war! Oh, for the foresight to see the results of your actions.

England might have won land in Canada, the Caribbean and the deep south of this continent, but the upshot? The upshot was this horrid rebellion.

To pay the French and Indian War's enormous financial cost, Parliament had imposed taxes on the colonists. "Resentment" was too shallow a word to describe the response. Americans saw the taxes as a further attempt to expand British imperial authority, not to mention hard-to-fathom parliamentary attempts to prevent colonists from expanding westward. Howe himself couldn't argue against colonial expansion. Why not?

Foolish Parliamentarians! If Howe had only been a member of the House of Lords at the time, he could have advised this: King George's subjects in America needed to count themselves friends, not foes, of those they left behind in Britain. Weren't they from the same stock? Sharing the same fathers and forefathers? Disputes needed discussion and resolution, not autocratic (almost flippant) decrees from those who had not even set foot on American soil.

Foolish Montagu! Where did you learn tactics of war and earn your command as lord of the admiralty? Did you hear, and was your mind engaged, when Lord William Barrington revealed the simplest, least costly strategy for victory?

Barrington's solution: blockade America. Such a tactic would have cost neither side precious lives nor the vast fortune that was every day slipping from the British treasury.

The scheme was simple. Use the army only as auxiliary manpower. The colonists had no navy, so place British navy ships outside every harbor and seize incoming and outgoing vessels and their cargo, financially strangling the colonists. Stockpile the treasury back home with the American plunder and wait out a peaceful surrender. Even be magnanimous and present the colonists with the compromise that Howe had, in fact, brought with him into the fray—a measure of American autonomy within the empire.

But, no, John Montagu, 4th Earl of Sandwich, possessor of vast brain power, you had to declare that British military could easily subdue the revolt. Battles and bullets and death. Not in your vocabulary, sir. Stay home, ensconced under your own roof, on your own cushy chair, a tumbler of whiskey in one hand, cigar in the other, feet up before the fireplace.

Howe fingered an ear and looked about him at the luxuries of Robert Morris's manse. Well, he himself wasn't in actual danger this wintry November day. But he'd been close enough to the battlefield to hear musket balls whiz and cannonballs land. Near enough to have the fear of death rattle his heart.

Howe made his way to the den and checked his pocket watch. 07:54.

Six minutes until his meeting. He stepped to his desk, picked up the most-wanted list, and read the names again.

The order of the people of infamy might be arguable, but not its entirety. Benjamin Franklin's name, of course, sat at the top, but he was least likely to be caught because he was in France, the pompous old jollocks, the ratbag, the … Howe caught himself and continued down the list.

As surely as he would want all these men in shackles, paraded down Market Street *sans* knickers, next to Franklin, Robert Morris was the one Howe most wanted caught. And here he was, standing at Morris's own desk; how appropriate to appropriate the man's property.

Ha!

Again, to his list. Thirteen names and one "Unknown." All but one were Pennsylvanians, though Howe's intelligence report stated some were born in England (Morris), Scotland (James Wilson), and Ireland (George Taylor and James Smith). *Reprobates.*

The list contained a gaggle of lawyers: Francis Hopkinson, Thomas McKean, George Ross, James Smith, and James Wilson.

Howe thought of the one-liner: "Where can you find a good lawyer? At the city morgue."

He chuckled and continued. The signers included one physician: Dr. Benjamin Rush. *Charlatan.* Three merchants: Robert Morris, George Clymer and George Taylor. *Profiteers.* A farmer: John Morton from someplace called Ridley Township. *Muckshoveler.*

And there was the non-Pennsylvanian, the Reverend John Witherspoon in New Jersey. *Traitor.* Witherspoon, why not stay in Scotland where you were born? Instead, you immigrate to become president of the College of New Jersey and poison young minds with revolution.

When Howe's soldiers took Princeton a year ago, they hung in effigy two men: Washington and … wait for it … Witherspoon.

When Howe's troops reported they'd killed Witherspoon's eldest son, James, in the Battle of Germantown in October, he'd shed no tears.

And then there was "Unknown"—the person expected to print illegal Bibles—listed third only below Franklin and Morris.

Confound this king so singular in his focus.

But, again, all the more motivation for Howe to grab the culprit and win a permanent station in George's court.

Howe narrowed his focus on "Unknown" and squeezed an earlobe.

What should he call this particular felon? Hmmm.

A boisterous bevy of officers entering the house interrupted his thoughts. The men were led by his second in charge, Major General Henry Clinton, a thirty-seven-old whom Howe was sure would succeed him once he returned home.

"You saw an apparition?" one officer asked another.

"A ghost? No."

"You say she looks like your dead aunt?"

"Exactly."

"Can't be."

"Well," a hesitation, "you've heard of doppelgangers?"

"Look-alikes? That's more likely than a dead aunt."

A third voice entered the conversation, "Or a ghost."

"Yes, Shanks, you going delusional? Seeing ghosts?"

Bible Ghost. That's what Howe would call him: Or *Biblio-Ghost.*

Howe gathered Clinton and the dozen mid-level officers about the room. Standing. At ease, but standing. He didn't want anyone sitting, comfortable.

Each man was given a copy of the Most-Wanted list. Howe's aide-de-camp, Lieutenant Vance Brown, held up drawings of several of the men in question and paraded them before the officers.

"I want each of these men found," Howe began. "Found and flogged, and then we'll decide what to do with the scoundrels."

"I know of Franklin and Morris, but who are the others, sir?"

The question came from a colonel.

"Signers from this region of the colonists' Declaration of Independence. There are others, but we have reason to believe, except for Franklin, these men may be in Pennsylvania. Soldiering or in hiding, perhaps. What confounds me is the number of children they've taken with them. How could Robert Morris secure seven of his spawn, or Clymer his eight little scallywags?" Howe shrugged. "Maybe we'll find none of them, but the two I truly dream about strangling? Morris and the third man on our list."

"Unknown?" another officer asked, sounding baffled.

"Yes."

The officer chuckled. "Fellow might be hard to find."

Others joined the laughter.

Despite himself, Howe managed a smile.

He shook his head and explained about the royal family owning the copyright to the King James Version of the Bible, about King George being God's representative here on earth, and therefore, his ire at the thought of God's Word being spread by traitors, ragtag colonists, and ne'er-do-wells, and about Howe's own desire mirroring that of their sovereign.

Finally, Howe pulled a large wooden box from the desktop and opened the lid, revealing a stack of paper money.

"Incentives, gentlemen," he said. "Twenty-five pounds sterling to the man among you whose troops capture anyone on this list. Fifty pounds and a medal for Unknown, or as I shall call him, Biblio-Ghost."

"Biblio ..." began a lieutenant.

"Ghost. Biblio-Ghost," Howe finished, detecting some mirth in the minds of his troops. "Do you have a better name?"

They collectively shook their heads.

"Biblio-Ghost, he is then," Howe said.

Clinton asked, "Any leads as to who the ghost is?"

"Think, General," Howe replied. "Who would have the wherewithal to print Bibles? And where could a press be located? New York? Boston? Possibly here? Maybe more probably here, since this is where Congress has been operating, and those men will have wanted a press to record their deliberations.

"Someone somewhere must know these things, must have an idea, a recollection, a suggestion. A prophecy would be acceptable."

"Can we offer rewards to anyone who gives us information leading to the ghost's capture?" a lieutenant asked.

"You may," Howe replied and thought over the idea. "But the amount comes out of your own compensation. One place you might start—interrogating the Presbyterian pastors here in Roger Penn's *phileo adelphos*, City of Brotherly Love. These ministers are of the one denomination that is, more than others, driving this rebellion because they want to stop King George from establishing Anglicanism as the official religion here. They've been preaching religious freedom can only be secured through independence.

"Make them," he added with a smirk, "*feel* your love."

Guttural cheers around the room buoyed Howe's expectations. *Ha! Esprit de corps.*

And Clinton? The perfect state of mind for the endeavor.

Alec Craig checked his reflection in the front window of Tales of Yore. As best as he could tell, he looked presentable. How he wished he could afford to hire a fancy carriage to carry Elsie around town in fashion. He thought of his horse and wagon housed in Wilder's Livery, but that was no coach for a lady. Better to stroll. And, after all, though convoluted, Boston was flat and walkable.

He looked down. He'd polished his black boots, obscuring their true age. His breeches were clean if not new, his coat worn but not frayed, his dark-brown tricorn the single new, fashionable article of clothing he owned. His hands were clean, no dirt beneath his fingernails. His breath was fresh from the mint herbs kept alive on a south-facing windowsill in Calum's upstairs quarters. All in all, he passed muster—in his own eyes at least.

"Handsome and tall can't be taught." Calum's voice behind him, tinged with cheer, caught Alec by surprise. "God gave you those attributes. But, son, what'll win a girl's heart is your own heart. If your heart is pure, if it's godly, if it's sensitive, if it's selfless. Be yourself, not someone you *imagine* she'd like. And, most of all, be chivalrous, be the young man of honor you are, and treat her like the princess she is in God's eyes."

Alec turned to Calum. "You must have made your wife a happy woman."

"She was. We were." Calum paused, a sadness spreading over his face. After a moment, he allowed a faint smile and said, "I try not to bemoan the things I no longer have, but to be thankful for the time I had them. When you do find true love, hold on, treasure every moment, water that relationship to overflowing with all the kindness you can pump out of the well. That's my advice."

"And good advice, too, Calum. Thank you."

Alec spun around, opened the door, and left with feet that felt six inches off the ground.

At ten o'clock in the morning, the Green Dragon was quiet. No one in the dining area, no noise from the pub. A pleasant-looking, middle-aged lady stood behind a counter, checking a ledger filled with names and times. A prosperous place, this.

Alec smiled at the lady, introduced himself, and asked if he could go to the rooms housing the de La Bordes. Extending her hand and introducing herself as Mrs. Sally Burdick, she motioned him toward a stairway.

"Take the corridor to your right and knock at the middle door halfway down."

Alec double-stepped to the top of the stairs, straightened his hat, breathed deeply, and stepped down the hallway. The door he faced was sturdy oak with the framework of the cross. A small brass plate to the right at eye level read: "1A."

He knocked and Malcolm opened the door.

"Mr. Craig." He motioned Alec inside.

An attractive room spread before him. Comfortable. Inviting. The furnishings were embroidered in bright-colored flowers and swirling designs. He'd seen such in Mr. Morris's and Mr. Franklin's homes.

A happy mood, like a joyful hymn, infused the place. He could sense the ambience, the absence of tension, unlike the feeling during last night's dinner when Monsieur de La Borde agreed to ship the printing supplies. He wondered about the private father-to-daughter conversation that must have followed his and Calum's departure.

Elsie entered through a door from the south side of the room, and Alec knew straightaway that whatever friction existed had been dispelled. The gleam in her eyes, the bounce in her step, her whole demeanor elevated the mood. Her joy was palpable, and Alec's heart leapt.

Elsie swept aside the ringlets from her eyes, beamed a smile as broad as the morning sky, and curtsied ... as though he, not she, were the royalty in the room.

Alec cleared his throat. "Miss Elsie, you look glorious this morning."

"*Merci.*" A smile curled her lips.

"It's a beautiful day for a stroll."

"*Oui.*"

"I wish I could take you by carriage."

She made a face to dismiss such a notion. "To walk is fine for me."

Lisette appeared out of the room from which Elsie had come. She held a shawl in one hand and long fur coat in another. Again, Alec was reminded of the class divide. But, again, Elsie's disarming smile as she put her arms through the sleeves—not taking her eyes off him—dismissed the inner turmoil.

She stepped right up next to him, slipped her left arm behind the crook of his right elbow and nodded toward the door to the hallway.

"Sir?" she said.

"*Mademoiselle,*" he replied. One of only a half dozen French words he knew. *Oui, non, monsieur, mademoiselle, bonjour,* and *ferme la bouche.* That was his repertoire.

Malcolm held the door for them and just before they stepped outside the room, Elsie said something to her father's valet in French.

"Bien sûr," Malcolm replied.

Boy, I have to start studying the French language. Maybe Calum has a book for me.

CHAPTER 7

Alec was certain every person they strolled by took special attention to "an unlikely pair." But he commanded himself to disregard each crooked look or second glance.

After walking a short distance, he turned toward the Charles River, a half mile away. Should provide a quiet and pretty stroll.

Alec fumbled through various chambers of knowledge as they ambled along. What topics would interest this girl of the world? What did he know that she didn't? Little, considering the schooling she must have experienced.

He turned to her and pointed about sixty degrees to their right. "Have you seen the Mill Pond?"

"I've noticed this big, ah, body of water, this lake," Elsie said.

"Do you know its purpose?"

"Purpose?"

He nodded.

She shook her head, and Alec went on a grand explanation, repeating Calum's account. Her eyes widened.

He sprang the question he'd asked himself: "Could such waterworks generate power to run a printing press?"

"*Your* printing press?" she asked.

"Well, ours operates on muscle power. I'm envisioning a contraption with gears and levers and pulleys and such. If such an apparatus were to exist, that is."

"I don't know. If so, would you only be able to operate for certain hours of the day?" she asked.

The question flummoxed him. He stuttered and replied, "I suppose that would depend on how much water was in the pond and how strong the flow."

"You want to know what I believe?" she asked mischievously.

Alec stopped and considered her face-on. "Always."

"You ought to build such a machine." She hesitated a moment and with a flourish added, "And you'd be famous the world over."

Alec laughed. "You know, you're right. I'm going to meditate on that."

"Meditate?"

"Deliberate, ruminate, muse."

"You're good with words."

"I read a lot."

"What do you read?"

"The Bible mostly. But other books, too. Whatever I can get my hands on." He turned, facing northwest and keeping the Charles River in mind. "Our shop printed Thomas Paine's *Common Sense*."

She brightened. "They printed the booklet in French."

"I know," he said. "We sold one hundred and fifty thousand copies. John Adams said, 'Without the pen of the author of *Common Sense*, the sword of Washington would have been raised in vain.'"

"Powerful words."

"Powerful book—well, pamphlet."

"And you—set the type?"

He nodded. "Me and my employer."

The Charles was in sight now.

"I actually worked with Thomas Paine," Alec said, "before he went off to fight."

"Oh?" Elsie's eyes opened wide.

"A bright man, except he doesn't believe God is active in our lives."

"No?"

"And I don't know how anyone with a noggin couldn't."

"*Moi, aussi.*" She shook her head.

"And what a great God, eh? Look around us." He waved at all about them, the trees and river, and pointed at a flock of chickadees flirting from a bush to a tree, to two squirrels playing tag around the trunk of an oak tree and up through its branches.

Elsie followed his direction.

"There must be a creator," Alec said, "and imagine the fun he must have had doing the creating. Woodpeckers that can pound on a tree like a hammer. Bats that are blind but can fly around without running into anything. Hawks that can spot a field mouse a couple hundred feet away."

Elsie smiled and said, "I wish we were meant to fly."

"Me, too," Alec said. "If I were anything but a person, I'd be an eagle."

"*Oui.*" Elsie giggled. "I'd fly high and spread my wings and glide over the ocean, over the mountains, and dive into a lake to cool off."

Alec pulled his coat tight about him. "Brrr. Not today."

Elsie laughed. "No, not today."

"Try as we might to build something to fly, we couldn't create anything that was as dexterous as birds."

"If I weren't a bird, I'd be a whale," Elsie said.

"Really?"

"We saw some on our way here. Huge creatures, yet they flew out of the water, their tails flipping high into the air. They were playing games."

"Wow."

"*Oui.*"

"More proof there is a great designer."

Elsie nodded.

They were now yards from the Charles, whose waters were flowing inland. The tide was coming in, chilling the air more.

A thought came out of the blue, and Alec turned to Elsie. "Would you like to hear my poem?"

"Your own poem?"

He nodded.

"*Certainement!*" She stopped in her tracks and paid him her full attention. "Speak away, *monsieur de la poésie*."

Alec didn't know what she'd said, but he grinned. "Okay, here goes:

> *Animals on four legs, humans on two;*
> *Birds flying above and bats, too.*
> *Beech trees and birch, pine trees and fir;*
> *Ryegrass and blue, shrubbery and fern;*
> *Flowers of every color in the rainbow,*
> *And myriad creations we don't even know.*
> *Discount the heavens, the moon and the sun,*
> *And you'd still barely scratch the things God has done.*
> *Remove the wind, the waves, and the sea,*
> *And you'd still witness how infinite God can be.*"

Elsie clapped her hands. "*Je l'aime.* I love it."

Alec smiled. "Thank you."

"Do you have other poems, *monsieur de la poésie*?"

"First, tell me what that means."

"Mister of the poetry. Only now I'll call you *maître de la poésie*. Professor of the poetry."

He laughed. "Not quite."

"So, do you have others?"

"Dozens."

"Share!"

"Maybe another time."

"'Another time.' So, I will see you again?"

"I hope."

"*Moi, aussi.* Me, too."

Her brown eyes met his, and he found himself fumbling for words. He decided to buy some time—and himself some embarrassment—by offering her his arm again and walking southwestward along the riverbank. She put her hand on his elbow, and they sauntered for a couple of minutes. A few seagulls flew along the river and cackled at one another, probably sharing the whereabouts of a fish dinner in the tidal water.

Gathering his wits, Alec said, "How about instead of reciting a poem, I tell you about God's poem. Is that *poésie* in French?

"No. *Poèma.*"

"Okay. It's about God's *poèma.* Are you familiar with the book of Ephesians in the New Testament?"

Elsie shook her head.

"The Apostle Paul wrote a letter to Christians living in Ephesus, and he said, 'We are God's workmanship, created in Christ Jesus for good works, which God prepared beforehand that we should walk in them.'"

Elsie nodded.

"Well, the Greek word for workmanship is *poiema*, meaning 'great epic poem.'"

"Ooh. I like that."

"Imagine," Alec said, "each of us is a great epic poem. God is taking the time to 'write' us, so to speak, into something truly wonderful, a poem of beauty that can inspire and encourage those who 'read' us. Paul called believers 'living epistles'—"

"Epistles?"

"Messages," Alec said. "We are messages—as long as we let the Lord 'write' us. If so, we reflect him and his character and integrity."

Elsie's look was of excitement. "Go on."

"There are poems of tragedy and those of victory, poems of great distress and those of abounding joy, and there are poems that run the gamut, the same as all the psalms that begin with anguish and turmoil but end with God's deliverance."

"And God wants us to be poems of honor," Elsie said.

"Right! But to do so, He needs a willing papyrus. Paper."

"So, we are neither the writer nor the ink, but the poem," she said with a nod.

"God is the author," Alec said, "and the Holy Spirit is the ink."

"*Magnifique*, Alec. You know so much of the Bible." Elsie's enthusiasm spread across her face. "The Holy Father says only clergy know what the Bible says and how to interpret the words, so we're not allowed to read the Holy Scriptures ourselves."

"I'm sorry." That was all Alec could manage to say.

"You must tell me more."

They had reached the Rope Bridge. Alec pointed to their left, to a broad grassy area of several acres.

"The Commons," he announced. "We'll pass a line of artillery aimed at the river, but don't be afraid. It's probably unmanned since we don't expect the Brits back any time soon. Hopefully, ever."

Elsie shrugged, and they stepped into the Commons. A marshy area impeded them a bit to the south. Before them was a mammoth elm tree, most of its leaves still intact, obstinate against the coming winter. Beyond the tree rose a knoll to the east and a larger hillock to the left of that, with the barrels of four cannons peeking over its lip. Elsie flinched, and Alec squeezed her hand at his elbow.

As they drew closer, Elsie pointed to a small, stone structure close by the cannons.

"The powder house," Alec answered the silent question.

He led her up the hillock to the battery of cannons. Sure enough, the only people about were an elderly couple, arm-in-arm, looking off in the distance, their conversation muffled. Alec and Elsie walked between two cannons and looked to the river.

"No ship could get past these, could they?" Elsie asked.

"A suicidal mission, that."

They stood silent for a couple of minutes, and Alec thought of the thunder of cannons discharging balls of destruction toward the Charles. War! They were living in history, but which way would that story turn? In favor of the colonists or his majesty?

Finally, they turned and headed back toward Boston proper.

As they walked Elsie looked at Alec, her brow crinkled. "Do you wish you were off to war?"

"I do," he said. "I belong to the militia in Philadelphia. The First Battalion under Colonel William Bradford. They've been called to fight, but I'm not. I feel shame sometimes." He'd been this honest with two people, Calum and Mr. Aitken. Elsie had turned him into a talking machine.

"No," she protested. "No shame."

"Oh, yes. Young men not much older than me fighting and dying for a righteous cause, battling a king's tyranny against his subjects."

She was quiet, thoughtful.

"I'll wait my chance," he continued. "But after we print the Bibles, I will indeed go off to fight, God willing."

"You believe God's will is for you to fight?"

"'The Lord is a warrior. The Lord is is name.' That's in the book of Exodus. God led the Israelites to battle to conquer the Canaanites, Hittites, Perizzites, Amorites, and a bunch of other 'ites' and drive them out of the Promised Land. Sometimes he simply confused the enemy so they killed each other." Alec cocked his head. "Yes, I believe he stands behind the righteous and strengthens men for battle against the unjust. The Bible says he's the same yesterday, today and forever. So ..."

By the look in her eyes, Elsie was trying to fathom all he'd said, slowed down by needing to internalize the translation from English to French, so he stopped right there.

A minute later they reached a granary at the northeastern edge of the Commons, next a burial ground.

Well, that's appropriate to the conversation.

"*Lés morts ne parlent,*" Elsie whispered, almost to herself.

"What's that?"

"The dead don't talk."

"What stories they'd tell," he said.

"*Oui.*"

"You can only hope they went up ..." Alec pointed to the sky "... and not down." He pointed to the ground.

Elsie nodded with sadness spreading over her face.

"I don't want you to die," she said.

He laughed lightly, touched by her response. "Me, either."

"*Je suis sérieux,*" she said, her voice firm, her brow knit. "I'm serious."

"So am I. I've got plans, hopes, dreams. Something beyond a printer's helper. But at least if I die, I know I'm going to a better place."

She shrugged. "Still ..."

"I've got friends who're in battles from Delaware to New York and beyond, I'm sure. When it's time, if I can't connect with First Battalion, I want to join the First Pennsylvania Militia Brigade under Brigadier General James Potter."

Elsie stopped and gulped a deep breath.

"Whatever you do, wherever you go," she said, "you must write to me."

Alec steadied his eyes on her radiant face. "I would be honored, Elsie de La Borde."

She smiled back at him and said, "*Le fait accompli!*"

This expression he knew—so he knew seven words all together—though he'd never heard them said by a French-speaker. He felt a sudden jump to his step and led her out of the Commons onto Commons Street. A minute later, they turned right down School Street, a narrow lane that went straight south and was busy with carts and wagons and bustling men and women.

Alec pointed about fifty feet ahead to their right. A red wooden sign, with a painting of a steaming loaf of bread, hung by the doorway and read: d'Acosta's Bakery.

"Our lunch awaits," he announced.

"Like Lyons. Like Paris," Elsie said. "*Précisément*. Bread fresh from the oven, hot and delicious."

They strolled down the street, hand-in-arm, cobblestones beneath their feet, avoiding two horse-drawn carts—one wagon containing yard goods, which reminded Alec he had a pickup at the docks at four o'clock. Plenty of time.

They entered the bakery and the aroma of fresh-baked bread filled their senses.

What more beautiful smell in all the world? Chocolate? No. Caramel? No.

Alec inhaled and sighed. Elsie followed suit and put the tips of two fingers to her lips.

A plump older lady behind the counter was serving a middle-aged couple, spotted them, and said, "I'll be right with you young people."

Upon the counter were woven baskets filled with loaves of bread and plates holding assorted cheeses.

Moments later, they sat at a small round table by the front window, with two cups of steaming tea and a plate topped with a loaf of bread and cheese between them. Alec bowed his head and said:

> Be present at our table, Lord.
> Be here and everywhere adored.
> These morsels bless, and grant that we
> May feast in Paradise with Thee.
> Amen ...

He noticed Elsie cross herself but did not ask her reasoning. Instead, he said, "Please tell me about yourself."

"What about me?"

"Everything. Your family, your education. Why you're here in America instead of a fancy city back home in France."

He tore a piece of bread from a loaf and handed the portion to Elsie.

"Thank you." She took a nibble. "I love life. I love my father. I love my aunts and uncles and cousins."

She had skipped one mention about which Alec had wondered.

"Your mother?" he asked.

Elsie's demeanor changed, her eyes hooded, and she lowered her head. She was gathering her emotions, her thoughts. Moisture in her eyes revealed tears in the making. Slowly, she composed herself, breathing deeply. She looked at Alec. "My mother died two years ago, not long after my debutante ball."

"I'm sorry," he managed, ashamed and embarrassed he'd asked.

"You wouldn't know," she said with a shrug. "*Ma mère*, she caught pneumonia. There was no saving her. An awful time, seeing her gasp for breath and not being able to help. Prayer was all we could do. But God did not listen. She died in Papa's arms. Theirs was a great love. Papa will live and die unmarried, I'm sure. One reason I travel with him whenever I can."

Alec knew all about losing a parent—in his case two. The ache never subsided altogether.

"At least she was there for my debutante coming out."

He shrugged. "What's a debutante?"

"When young ladies turn sixteen, they are presented to the world." She held her hands apart as if holding a globe. "You're to be your prettiest, your most charming, to speak in the most elegant and delightful way. Rich young men come to dance and look you over like candy on a stick."

Alec stifled a laugh when he noticed she wasn't joking.

She stopped, remembering the night, and added, "The ball meant more to *ma mère* than to me, her thinking a rich young aristocrat would sweep me off my feet."

"He didn't?" Alec took a sip of tea and peered into her eyes.

She laughed and shook her head. "*Non.* Full of themselves, every one of them."

"No one for you, then," he stated.

"I want to be like *ma mère*. To be a force for good, to help the poor. And France has many in poverty. The countryside? The farmers? And even in the city. But the young and rich care not for such as those. *Ma mère*, though, she helped feed them. She confirmed with Papa—a tithe for God, an offering for the poor. She was firm, unrelenting. He was agreeable, always."

Alec was impressed. Monsieur de La Borde honored God. Alec and Calum and Mr. Aitken could, indeed, trust the Frenchman to help their cause.

"Your mother would be proud of you."

Elsie grinned. "Except I chose no rich young aristocrat."

He joined her laughter.

"Where were you educated?" he asked.

"Oh, you don't want this information," she said and snatched a piece of cheese from the plate.

"I do." He dropped a morsel into his mouth.

"Le Maison Royale de Saint-Louis, a boarding school in the town of Saint-Cyr outside Paris. Well, at least for two years. A wonderful school, but so far from home." She smiled. "One of our alumna at Le Maison Royale is Marthe-Marguerite Le Valois de Villette de Mursay, marquise de Caylus, a noblewoman and writer. Her memoirs were edited by Voltaire a few years ago."

"A mouthful." Alec chuckled at the long name. "And impressive," he added, though he'd never heard of the woman, or Voltaire for that matter.

But Elsie read his cluelessness and offered, "I'd assume you know of Voltaire, the nom de plume of François-Marie Arouet. He spoke out for the Lumieres, the Protestants in our country."

"Oh?"

"Yes. Like Catholics in your colonies, Protestantism is illegal in France where our cardinal has banned their books. And when the French courts sentenced to death Lumieres Jean Calas for blasphemy five years ago, Voltaire strongly condemned the execution. Voltaire was lucky to avoid Le Marshalsea himself!"

"Le Marsh …" Alec struggled to repeat the name.

"A prison, most notorious." An eyebrow rose.

"Ah." This was a news bulletin to Alec. But he'd been busy enough keeping up with Britain's tyranny, never mind that of France or other countries.

Elsie sat back in her chair, offered a coy smile, and said, "I did, however, have *le maître de la poésie.*"

He laughed. "A professor of poetry?"

She pointed a finger and giggled. "*Oui!* You're right. Jacques Delille. Young and handsome."

"Handsome, was he?"

"No, actually." Elsie grinned. "Very homely. But brilliant."

"But you studied there for only two years?"

Elsie nodded. "Most of the girls merely wait for their inheritance or for a wealthy suitor to appear. So I returned to complete my schooling at home with *ma mère.*"

"It sounds like your mother loved people."

"'I was naked and you clothed me. I was hungry and you fed me.' *Ma mère* lived this Scripture. My name means 'pledged to God.'"

"She taught you well after naming you well."

Elsie smiled. "Since her death, I have carried on some of her endeavors. In Lyon, she established a *garde-manger* to feed the hungry and a *magasin de vêtements* to cloth the poor. Papa and other prosperous families who joined the cause still fund them.

Alec was growing to love this lady. Beautiful inside as well as out.

He took another chunk of bread and said, "Commendable. Impressive."

"Thank you."

"Your father, a man of the world, obviously trusts your abilities. To continue your mother's work. To bring you here with him to America."

"He does." Her smile warm, she asked, "But what of you? I want to know."

Alec told her about growing up in the lowlands of Scotland, his parents dying, Mr. and Mrs. Aitken paying to bring him to America, and apprenticing in the print shop. He told her about the Aitkens' children and his love for his adopted family.

She nodded, attentive, eyes keen on his, seeming to live his story with him. Wonder at the beauty of Scotland, tears at the loss of parents, joy at his new family.

"When my ma and da died, I struggled to believe in God," Alec said. "I swore at him. I called him dark names. I fought with my friends. I was a tyrant."

Elsie frowned and lowered her eyes.

"And yet I cried myself asleep every night."

She raised her eyes again, seeking the rest of his story.

"And then!" Alec's eyes shot upward.

"Then?"

"Then one evening, while watching a beautiful sunset over Glen Loy turn to deep purple and total darkness, God spoke to me."

"Yes?"

"Well, it was *like* a voice."

"And?"

"The promise of dawn and sunrise," he said. "That was his message. Life, death, and life again—a constant cycle not to dread—that will end with seeing my ma and da again in heaven."

Yes, Elsie believed as him. He could see it in her eyes, feel the connection.

"I've heard Europeans say Philadelphia is every bit as sophisticated as London or Paris," Alec said.

Elsie looked surprised. "Oh?"

He nodded.

"The patriots stripped the city of supplies before the British troops stormed in," he said, "and even carried away the Liberty Bell to prevent the Redcoats from making bullets from the monument."

Elsie interrupted, "But the British did capture Philadelphia. Always in history when one country conquers another's capital, that country accepts defeat."

Alec hesitated and asked, "Is that correct?"

"So I've been taught—" A smile curled her lips, "at the famous Le Maison Royale de Saint-Louis."

Alec laughed with her but ruminated over her comment.

Finally, he said, "Well, Philadelphia is not America's capital. We have no capital. We barely have a country—and maybe we don't have that. Not yet."

He took a decisive final bite of bread and awaited Elsie's response.

Her sip of tea, with pinky raised, was so delicate Alec wondered if the cup ever touched her lips.

"I do hope you win the war," she said with finality. "And I hope you fight with valor but go unscathed by musket ball or blade. I will certainly be praying for you—night and day."

CHAPTER 8

The Atlantic Ocean looked calm as glass through Admiral of the Fleet Richard Howe's headquarters window in Newport, Rhode Island. The older brother to William, Richard was Britain's leading naval commander, former member of Parliament, certain to be knighted, and honored with a host of medals.

But all honors and positions meant little in a world of what-have-you-done-for-me-lately. And the tranquil conditions outside concealed the true state of affairs here in the colonies.

Richard Howe didn't want this war. Like his brother, he, in fact, agreed with the colonists on a number of points of contention. He was still depressed that, though they had won the Battle of Long Island fifteen months earlier, he and William had suffered defeat at the ensuing bargaining table with the revolutionaries.

As emissaries of the Crown, they had brought terms to their American opponents and convened a peace conference on Staten Island on September 11, a year ago. Benjamin Franklin, John Adams, and Edward Rutledge had met with them face to face.

The lightning bolts flashing and deluge pouring down on the hall in which they sat had been omens of the meeting's arguments and conclusion. Despite several hours of, ahem, discussions, they reached no agreement, and the Americans returned to their lines. Since then, William had completed the capture of New York and engaged Washington's army, while Richard was under orders to blockade the North American coast.

Lacking enough vessels, this blockade had proven porous and near useless. But not yesterday. Not along Cape Cod. Not on an especially windy day. A Dutch ship, *Gouden Adelaar,* had been blown off course and straight into the arms of HMS Ariel.

And now, Howe stared at the bill of lading of the *Gouden Adelaar's* cargo and peered across his desk at Andreas Vandermay, captain of the ship. Tall with wavy blonde hair, clean-shaven, handsome. The man spoke English. That was good, since Howe knew little of Dutch.

Two items among all the freight caught Howe's attention.

"Tell me," he said with eyelids narrowing, "with a war going full bolt, with arms and ammunition and essentials at bare bones in the colonies, why on earth are you carrying a large supply of special paper and ink?"

Vandermay shrugged. "I have no idea."

The man seemed sincere. A good liar? Howe's brother William, being a gambler of distinction, could figure him out.

Howe opened the top-right drawer of his desk and pulled out the Most Wanted communique he'd received from England. He looked down the names, and third on the list was "Unknown"—the non-name given to whoever was planning to illegally print the royal family's Bible.

The King's Obsession, Howe called this opaque personage.

"Who's on the bill of lading to receive the paper and ink?" he asked.

"You have the paperwork," Vandermay pointed out.

Howe shuffled through a stack of rough-rag papers. Frustrated, he slammed down the stack in front of the captain. "You find the bill in this mess."

Vandermay rifled quickly through the pile and handed a page to Howe.

"Robert Aitken," Howe read, "of Philadelphia."

Hmm. Aitken may be Mr. Unknown.

"You know anything about Mr. Aitken?"

"This is my first trip to America. I know nothing about anyone, Admiral."

Howe nodded, thought a moment, and quietly, firmly, like Vandermay was his underling, captain of a first-rate flagship in His Majesty's Service, said, "Here's what we're going to do, Captain."

Vandermay's brow raised. He captured Howe's tone and became hopeful. "Yes?"

"Your ship is going to get a new mate and four crew members."

Vandermay's eyes widened.

"Five of my sailors are joining your ship."

Vandermay's expression turned to curiosity.

"You're going to deliver your supplies to Boston Harbor as you intended."

Vandermay's mouth formed a question, but Howe interrupted, index finger in the air.

"That's all you have to know."

Vandermay breathed out, long and heavy. Relief. Or so he thought. He again wished his card-playing brother were here.

"Agreed?" he asked. "A simple operation, and you'll go free as a bird."

"Agreed."

"Don't reveal you were waylaid here. Don't mention me or anyone else in my command, or we will find you out, and you will walk the gangplank—you and your entire crew.

Then we will blow to smithereens your *Gouden Adelaar*. What does that name mean, anyhow?"

"Golden Eagle, Admiral."

"What's Dutch for 'trap'?"

"*Valstrik.*"

"Good. Our secret operation is called *Gouden Valstrik*. Golden Trap. And your cargo is the bait."

When Vandermay left the building, Howe brought in Lieutenant Commander Thomas Clarke and four midshipmen from Clarke's crew aboard the admiral's flagship, *Preston*.

Clarke was ruthless, cunning, the ideal man for the job.

"Take your men and immerse yourselves into the crew," Howe told Clarke. "You're going incognito."

Clarke and the others nodded.

He pointed to Clarke. "You'll be Vandermay's second mate."

Clarke chuckled but nodded. "Yes, sir."

"You others will be on the unloading crew."

"Yes, sir," they said in unison.

"Keep your eyes and ears open."

"Yes, sir."

"Make sure you unload or are near those who unload the shipment of paper and ink."

They nodded but with looks of bewilderment.

"King George wants us to bring to justice the man or men who plan to illegally print Bibles. He is adamant. It's the royal family's Bible, and the king considers such actions theft from the Crown."

They nodded.

Howe scrutinized Clarke, who seemed puzzled.

Insubordination?

"You may consider this a trivial matter, Commander. It is not."

"No, sir." Clarke's expression turned to a crooked grin. "I'm ready to mete out whatever justice you see fit."

"That justice will await my order." He hesitated. "That is, unless you're left with no other course."

"Understood, Admiral."

Howe grunted. "A man by the name of Aitken will pick up the paper and ink. Follow him wherever he goes and report to me."

"Yes, sir."

"If you're spotted as British sailors and can't escape, you'll be imprisoned."

"But can we not fight back?"

Howe considered this and answered, "Yes. With abandon, if necessary."

Once the men had left his office, Howe wrote a message to William:

"'Unknown' on the most-wanted list? Look for Robert Aitken of Philadelphia."

Inhaling the intoxicating aroma one last time, Elsie again took Alec's elbow as they left d'Acosta's Bakery. She had accompanied several young men in various ways—on a dance floor, strolling in a park, to High Mass. But she'd never felt comfortable with the idea. Not until now.

She recalled when her father told her to "hold dear your heart." He'd also warned, "Do not allow their positions, royalty or not, to affect you."

She'd answered, "But, Papa, *memé* wanted me to marry into wealth."

To which he'd chuckled and responded, "She wanted you to marry into love—*hopefully* to a wealthy man."

After a moment, he'd continued, "I know she would advise this—marry only if you have love in your heart for your fiancé as she did with me."

When Elsie asked about their love, he had touched her gently below her left shoulder.

"This is your heart. Second to your salvation, this is God's greatest bequest to you. Don't squander this—this wonder—or fritter away its beauty."

"Of course not, Papa," Elsie had said.

"You know that when you marry, you give an endowment of money to your husband."

"*Oui.*"

"The greater endowment you give is your heart, your love, your affection. Truly, your spiritual endowment." He cocked his head, his eyes going distant. "Your mother's parents thought me a poor match for her. I had no title, few prospects. But she by some miracle had fallen in love with me as I had with her. You know the tapestry your mother embroidered that hangs over our bed?"

Elsie had always loved the flowers and doves on her *memé*'s creation. "*Oui.*" She quoted the words on that tapestry: "Love bears all things, believes all things, hopes all things."

Her father smiled broadly and said, "This is true. And without love—and our ability with that love to bear, believe, hope and forgive—marriage can be the most miserable and abominable life."

So as she and Alec stepped onto School Street and retraced their steps, Elsie wondered what lay ahead for them. Once he gathered the yard goods and rough iron and departed, would she ever see him again? Would she and Papa sail off to France, never to return here? Come the morrow, would this feeling of contentment and cheer dissipate like so much smoke? The thoughts were saddening enough. How much worse the reality?

She looked about them. Children, apparently unaffected by the cold, bustled about kicking a ball along the street. School must be out for the day.

One girl not much older than Elsie trudged along with difficulty, pain on her face, holding a basket full of eggs, and rubbing a belly large with child.

Elsie called to her, "Can we help you with your burden?"

The girl stopped in her tracks, her mouth open in surprise.

"Oh, I'd be so obliged if you'd speak to my babe," she patted her stomach, "and encourage him to come out!"

Elsie and Alec laughed.

"But, truly," Alec said, "can we help?"

"I'm delivering these eggs to the bakery," she said, "in exchange for bread and cheese for me and my little one."

She nodded toward a child Elsie guessed to be about three years old holding onto the young woman's skirt.

"Ahh." Elsie saw the need, pulled a purse from her coat pocket, and gave the girl a fistful of coins.

"I hope this helps," she said.

"Oh, miss!" the girl enthused, "I'm ever so obliged. You're an angel."

"I wish," Elsie said, and her smile went warmer.

The woman introduced herself as Hattie McGraw and said, "You see, my husband's away with the militia. Left right after the Battle of Bunker Hill. Fought in the Battle of Dorchester Heights a year and a half ago. He thought he could remain at home and fight a revolution. Come home, eat dinner, sleep off his exhaustion, and return to war in the morning. Pshaw! Now he's off with Washington. I pray he has boots on his feet and food in his belly."

At that, Alec pulled out his own purse and handed Hattie a paper bill. Elsie wondered how much money that left him.

Thanking them both profusely, Hattie hugged Elsie as best her belly allowed, did a half-curtsy, and excused herself.

"Well done," Alec said as they watched Hattie and her child enter d'Acosta's.

"We all share a common fate, don't we?" Elsie said.

Alec seemed to still be pondering her statement when he motioned her ahead.

They ambled the few yards to the corner and turned right, which was easterly, onto a busier, cobblestoned thoroughfare, a flashback to a section of Paris that Elsie particularly enjoyed for its ladies' fashion stores. She and her *memé* had spent such happy times walking that street. And now she was hand-in-arm with a young man she thought her *memé* would thoroughly enjoy—even if he wasn't titled. If her *memé* had seen Alec give his hard-earned money to that young lady, he would have won her heart as he was winning Elsie's.

In Philadelphia, Robert Aitken kept Jane and Robbie busy helping him with the first page of the Bible. He had finished typesetting the dedication, loving every word.

"Minus all the bowing and bending to King James, 'Defender of the Faith'..." he said with an exaggerated wink, "listen to this, children:

"'We do not know the Bible until we know it thus. The Book comes to us through natural channels, but with supernatural power. In origin it differs from all other books. It is like the Sabbath, made for man; but, like the Sabbath, it was made by God. The sacred volume will never do for us what it can do unless we regard it as sacred, seeing in it God's communication to his children. It took the form of a book, for what other form could it take? It has been marvelously safeguarded through the ages, for the Almighty would not commit his messages to blind chance. It proves its authenticity by its permanence and universality, and testifies its authority by its power over the souls of men.

"'Let us praise God for his Book. It is one of his best gifts to the world. Let us feed upon it, live with it, love it; and let us see that it does for us all God wishes to do for us through its blessed ministrations.'"

"That's wonderful, Da," Jane said.

"I'm considering this for the front of the Bible in place of what the King James Version says."

"What does the King James say?" Robbie asked.

Robert began to answer, but a rustling sound outside the shop door sent a sudden jolt of fear and a shiver down his neck. Both Jane and Robbie scooted across the floor, knelt, and opened and disappeared through a tiny door. Behind the door was a cubby hole large enough to hide two people and some blankets. Robert watched them until they were securely hidden and turned his attention to the shop door.

Two hard knocks were followed by two short knocks, then two hard knocks.

Robert released the breath he'd been holding and opened the door a couple of inches. There stood Jake Tremble, brow wrinkled.

"Soldiers were just here in the pub," Jake said. "They're looking for a print shop."

"Uh-oh."

"They specifically said a printer was breaking the law, or intending to do so, by illegally printing Bibles."

Robert had fought battles in Scotland. He knew the fear of death, had felt the tip of a blade in hand-to-hand combat. But now he had children—indeed, four *wee bairn* and a wife—and this fear? This kind was different.

He swallowed hard. "And?" he managed.

"I told them I know nothing of print shops."

"Did they mention my name?"

"No. No names and no identity for your shop." He thanked God that Angus Rayford had arrived at dawn and taken Janet and the wee ones to the Linnells'.

"And, Robert ..." Jake faltered. Controlling his words, he added, "They're offering an award for capture of the villain."

Robert stammered, "How m-much?"

"Twenty pounds sterling."

Whom could he trust? More important, whom could he *not* trust?

CHAPTER 9

As they turned toward a square that led to Hanover Street, Alec fought off a cold gloom trying to settle over him. The Green Dragon was not far distant, marking the end of their time together. The hours had passed far too quickly. Worse still, he had not nearly discovered enough of the depths of this young lady.

A loud voice split the cool air. Ahead was a disturbance of some sort.

People were emerging from Brattle Street and Wings Lane, heading in the direction of the oratory—Dock Square.

Alec and Elsie quickened their step over the cobblestones and a minute later were at the back of a crowd. Alec was tall enough to see over almost everyone and recognized the speaker—Samuel Adams.

Appearing to be in his forties, Adams was a man of common size, but he stood erect, his blue eyes mesmerizing, his muscular body occupying common garb. He wore a tie wig, cocked hat, red cloak and, on his face, wide-eyed enthusiasm. Confidence filled his voice and the spirit of God his words.

"I stand on free soil today," Adams bellowed from atop a crate. "Boston!"

Cheers greeted him.

"A mere mile from my birthplace on Purchase Street," he said.

Shouts of "Sam! Sam!" came from probable friends and neighbors.

"It's true, we in the Second Continental Congress left Philadelphia when the Redcoats stormed in—"

"Boos" filled the air.

"But what few square miles is that—" he hesitated— "when we inhabit a continent?"

"Hoorahs" rang through the square.

"And what is one defeat behind us when we can see victory ahead?"

Men raised their fists high and cried out, "Freedom!"

The cheer exploded, loud and rancorous. Adams waited.

With a tug, Alec maneuvered Elsie to the left, behind a shorter woman, figuring now she could get her eyes on the man.

"The king and his Parliament have looked at the American like fleas on their dogs, mice in their pantry," Adams said. "They've met us with contempt at every turn when we, like mice, nibbled at their miserly hand to get their attention. They've financially grasped us in their fists, squeezing us dry, taxing us to pay for their wars, yet not giving us a voice, not a whisper in their sacred Westminster assembly."

Boos split the air.

"So why am I here in Boston?" he asked. "To visit friends and family? Yes and yes. To encourage you all? That, too. But more. To embolden the able-bodied among you to take arms to drive the Redcoats back to their little island.

"We need men on the front lines, men in the livery, men in the mess hall. We need them feeding cannons and firing rifles. Driving wagons and marching in the infantry. Join our battle if you can."

Thunderous applause roared and echoed along the streets conjoining at Dock Square.

Alec bowed his head and squeezed his eyes shut.

Turmoil raged within him, wrestling with the ignominy of being vigorous and vibrant, yet without arms or munition. Nevertheless, he knew joining now would disappoint his Lord and Savior, not to mention Mr. Aitken and all the colonists in dire need of Bibles.

Lord, give me wisdom.

Adams had stepped down from the crate and was shaking hands, patting people on the shoulder, always encouraging.

Much of the crowd was dispersing, but a line of men was forming to talk to their hero—perhaps to discover where and how to sign up.

Alec put his hand gently over Elsie's, which rested on his elbow, and led on toward Hanover Street.

He heard "Young man ... Young fellow."

It was Adams's voice and was directed toward Alec, he knew.

Alec turned his attention to Adams, and their eyes met. Oh, yes. Adams was addressing him all right.

"Sir," Alec managed.

"I know you."

"Sir?"

"You were with Patrick Allison, the chaplain of Congress, Reverend Marshall, and the printer, Robert Aitken, and the others."

That stopped Alec short. He had indeed been at Constitution Hall when they petitioned Congress. But Adams had noticed him?

Alec nodded. "Yes, sir."

Adams excused himself from the men in line and stepped up to Alec and Elsie. Alec noticed he hadn't shaven in a day or two and wondered for a moment how the others in Congress had borne themselves since leaving Philadelphia.

"I've been ashamed of my vote since the day we turned you folks down," Adams said. "We should have found a way to print those Bibles. General Washington, in particular, was distressed when he learned of our decision. Our soldiers need those Bibles. Our schoolchildren, too. Every household." Adams extended his hand. "What's your name, son?"

"Alec Craig, sir."

"Master Craig, are you still aligned with Mr. Aitken?"

"I'm his apprentice."

Adams took a half-step back, contemplating. A few moments passed and he asked, "And what do you here in Boston?"

Alec hesitated, then thought his reluctance foolish, considering the man before him. "Getting the printing provisions we need, sir. We'll make do with less than we wanted. Mr. Aitken has decided to make New Testaments small enough to fit into a soldier's coat pocket."

"Ha!" Adams exclaimed. "Good for you."

"But I do want to join the battle as a soldier," Alec said.

"Please, Alec," Adams said, "do not take to heart what I said for yourself. The Apostle Peter said a soldier of the Lord should avoid civilian affairs."

Alec considered this. "I will, but only until we print those Bibles. After that—"

Adams interrupted, "Yours is the greater sacrifice." He put a hand on Alec's shoulder. "We're in spiritual combat as well as military war. Without the Word of God and confidence in his grace and protection, men on the battlefield will lose faith, conviction, assurance, allegiance … you name the consequence."

Alec took note that Elsie was on his arm and stuttered, "M-Mr. Adams, I'd like you to meet Mademoiselle Elsie de La Borde."

Adams flashed a brilliant smile, bowed, took her hand, and kissed it. As if hit by a spit of realization, he repeated, "de La Borde?"

"*Oui.*"

"Are you perhaps related to Monsieur Charles de La Borde?"

"My papa," she said.

"Oh, my! Your father and his partner, Monsieur Beaumarchais, are America's saviors." He chuckled. "I say that militarily, of course."

Elsie smiled.

"You and your father are staying in Boston?" Adams hesitated. "And you're with Master Craig."

Adams was pondering the connection, that was for sure. His mind seemed divorced from the cacophony all about them. Young and middle-aged men were impatient, jostling to gain an audience with Adams.

Adams whispered to Alec and Elsie, "Can I guess your acquaintance is no accident?"

"Oh, but it *is* quite by accident," Elsie said. "Monsieur Craig saved my life."

"Oh?"

Elsie recounted Pope Night, adding that Alec and Calum had dined with her and her father.

"But, sir," Alec added, "*Gouden Adelaar*, a Dutch ship carrying our cargo, was captured by the British, so Monsieur de La Borde is discharging one of his ships to help."

"Ah." Adams nodded and looked at Elsie. "May I ask your accommodations?"

Elsie pointed. "The Green Dragon."

"Do you suppose I could meet with your father there? Perhaps on Monday?"

Elsie shrugged. "I'm sure he'd love to meet you, Monsieur."

"Would you tell him of my visit upon your return?"

"*Sûrement.*"

Adams nodded, bowed a goodbye, and returned to the men awaiting him.

Alec thought he could very well need the man's connections at some point.

He and Elsie turned from Hanover onto another. The Green Dragon was ahead, the morning was behind. Alec dreaded the end to this rendezvous.

Elsie pulled on his elbow to slow their progress.

"What are your immediate plans, Alec?"

He shrugged. "Businessmen back in Philadelphia are expecting me to deliver their goods. I must pick them up at the docks, drive them back home, and await word from your father about delivery of our supplies. I expect to leave at daylight tomorrow."

"I see," she whispered and bowed her head.

Did he detect a tear? If so, he was both sorry and heartened—regret for Elsie's sorrow, yet gladdened for that same regret. The combination generated a strange emotion of melancholy with a shot of elation.

Alec fumbled for something to say. He didn't want to falter, either to fail his own affections, or entangle any prospects for an enduring relationship with Elsie.

He started to form a sentence, but wavered.

Elsie began her own thought, seemed to vacillate, and ceased.

That made him stop in his tracks. They were at the corner of Hanover and Union streets, too close to the Green Dragon to finish a private conversation unless they remained where they stood.

Finally, he turned to face her full-on and cupped her hands in his.

"Elsie," he began, "I am so glad you fell into my arms."

She giggled. "Pulled, you mean... out of the muck."

"Pulled, then." He smiled. Her eyes glistened, either from the sun or tears forming. Yes, tears. "I don't believe that moment was happenstance. God's doing, I'd say."

"How could I feel otherwise?" she asked.

"I don't know the future, what will happen today or tomorrow," he said, "but I do know one thing." He swallowed hard. "I do not want to lose contact with you. I do not want this moment to be the end of the matter."

A tear worked down her cheek and she loosened a hand to pat it dry with a handkerchief. Another tear followed the same course and she grinned and patted that one dry, too.

"I agree, Alec Craig," she said. "We must stay in contact as best we can."

A tingle ran along Alec's back from stem to stern.

"Do you know how long you and your father will be in America?"

"That, I'm afraid, is a mystery. To me and Papa as well."

"Ah." Alec thought for a moment. "Then I will post whatever information I can to you in care of the Green Dragon. But I'm afraid of what I'll find when I return to Philadelphia. The British have a vise grip on the city."

"I understand," she said. "We must leave everything in God's hands."

They walked the rest of the way to the tavern, and Alec left her in her rooms. There was no Monsieur de La Borde in sight to whom to say his goodbyes.

Admiral Richard Howe blew his prodigious nose into a bandana and cursed the blustery cold November wind outside, even if the squall had blown the *Gouden Adelaar* off course and into his hands. He tackled enough disruptions without adding some hullabaloo about an anonymous Bible printer to the list.

He cussed London for not sending him enough ships to blockade the American coast, let alone free up the Delaware River so he could get supplies to Philadelphia.

"England rules the oceans," Parliament was eager to

claim.

Yet we can't spare enough warships to rule over these backwater colonies?

Howe's ships were into their sixth week of a siege on Fort Mifflin on Mud Island in the Delaware River. But American Commodore John Hazelwood and his bothersome little flotilla were preventing the Royal Navy from getting up the river. His brother, William, was livid at the delay.

No, Richard Howe would prefer to simply concentrate on capturing Fort Mifflin and Fort Mercer at Red Bank in New Jersey without this distraction over a book.

Over two weeks before, on October 22, William's Hessian troops had stormed Fort Mercer and failed, taking heavy losses in the Battle of Red Bank. Richard figured days on end, maybe months, were needed for him to assemble enough warships and William sufficient artillery to drive the revolutionaries out of Fort Mifflin. He cursed Hazelwood, Washington, and this coming winter, which always made warfare difficult at best, but especially near shorelines and along waterways where ice caused havoc.

Howe grabbed his quill pen, dipped the hollow shaft into an inkwell, and wrote about what had transpired, including a breakthrough—someone named Robert Aitken was scheduled to pick up the printing supplies in Boston Harbor and Richard's men were infiltrated among the *Gouden Adelaar's* crew to capture the villain.

He ordered a copy written, sealed both communiqués and sent one off by sea and another by land via a sailor dressed as a civilian. One or the other dispatch, preferably both, should find their way to William. If by sea, well, a ship could sail to Philadelphia from Boston in two and a-half days with a good tailwind and no trouble with storms.

A rider? No telling what misfortune he'd encounter. Plus the trip was no racetrack, certainly no Royal Ascot.

True, British troops had broadened Indian paths into the King's Highway during the French and Indian War, but

Howe's messenger would have to beware of colonial militia.

Howe hated unknowns, and the capture of this criminal-to-be would normally not consume his valuable time. But with a warless winter coming on, the mystery intrigued him, and he determined to ferret out the mischief-maker. Discovering the covert operation and placing a traitor behind bars would be a plume in his cap. Perhaps both he and William would win the king's praise.

CHAPTER 10

William White sat at the bedside of his twenty-two-month-old daughter, Elizabeth. He tucked a blanket under her chin and a quilt over that.

Sleeping peacefully in a crib a few feet away was baby Mary, born six weeks ago—seventeen days after the Continental Congress denied the request to fund printing of Bibles and two days after the Brits barreled into Philadelphia.

William had finished reading H. Cooper's *Tommy Thumbs Pretty Song Book*. Betsy seemed to enjoy the rhymes, although she could understand perhaps half the words. At least she comprehended *Ba Ba Black Sheep*, which he converted to "Ba ba baby sheep have you any wool? Yes, sir, yes, sir, three bags full. One for the master, one for the dame, one for wee Betsy who lives down the lane."

When he said the last line, giggles always spilled out of her like the tinkle of tiny sleigh bells.

William smiled at the girl's innocent beauty. She shared her father's blond hair and funny bone but thankfully not his long nose.

He leaned to kiss her forehead, but a loud banging on the front door downstairs disrupted the moment.

Who'd be knocking so loudly at this time of night? Robert Aitken? If so, and there was trouble about. More likely, one of his parishioners had come by in distress. A sickness. A fall. Oh ... or a death.

His wife, Mary, answered the door and loud voices echoed up the stairway. At least two men had entered the three-story Walnut Street parsonage.

William flew down the stairs two at a time. Reaching the bottom hall, he was shocked to see three red-coated soldiers, all broad-shouldered, all solemn. The man in front pushed his way into the house and declared himself to be Major General Henry Clinton, second-in-command to General Howe.

What would a major general be doing here? William thought he knew, and the answer did not bode well. William stepped in front of Mary to shield her.

Clinton, his eyes knit, eyed him suspiciously and read from a paper.

"Reverend William White?"

"Yes."

"Pastor of Christ Church?"

"Yes."

"Born and bred in Philadelphia?"

"Yes."

"Your father Colonel Thomas White, retired British Army living here in Pennsylvania?"

William folded his arms. "Are you getting to a point, General?"

"As a man of the cloth, you tell the truth."

William felt this required no answer.

"Your next-door neighbor is Dr. Benjamin Rush, no? Surgeon general to the Continental Army? One of the signers of the treasonous Declaration of Independence?"

"Yes, yes, and yes."

"Do you know his whereabouts?"

"No."

"His wife, Julia Stockton?"

"No."

Clinton turned to Mary. "You a friend of Julia?"

Mary stuttered, "Y-yes."

"She tell you where she was going?"

Mary shook her head.

"Mrs. White, you're the daughter of Henry Harrison, the former mayor of this city, are you not?"

"Yes."

"As a lady of high society, you should be privy to this information, should you not?"

"Your legions, General, rained down terror on this city with such vengeance and speed that our friends had no time to discuss these matters. And since then, your men have ransacked their homes and stolen their property. You, sir, should have access to more knowledge than I can possibly share."

William's chest burst with pride, then constricted.

Clinton grunted and looked her over, head to toe, lingering in places he should not tarry. Finally, he said, "I'll overlook your baseless charges" and turned to William.

"George Washington," he said.

William waited for the rest of the sentence, which did not come.

Finally, William prodded, "What of General Washington?"

"He's attended your church for years, has he not?"

William nodded.

"What do you say of the man?"

"He's tall."

Clinton couldn't help but guffaw. Once he gained control, he continued, "Tell me your thoughts on the man."

"He's honest. An intelligent military mind. Otherwise, I have no information you don't know."

"He possess family here in Philadelphia?"

"I doubt so. Martha's daughter died four years ago. I don't know about Jacky, her son."

Clinton made a guttural sound, pointed at William's chest, and said, "I'll cut to the quick. Where can we find the man planning to print Bibles?"

William wrinkled his brow and shrugged.

"You must know," Clinton continued. "And as an Anglican pastor, the king is your authority. To him you owe allegiance."

William stiffened. "I owe fidelity to no man but to the Lord Jesus himself."

Clinton raised an eyebrow.

"I serve," William said, "at the bidding of God."

"You're aware that only men with the royal family's permission are allowed to print Bibles?"

"Surely, in the middle of a revolution you have more important concerns than the printing of Bibles," William said.

"This is an intimate concern of his majesty himself," Clinton growled. "He believes such actions to be a personal and impertinent slap in the face."

William shrugged.

"Prison, sir. That's the penalty." Clinton leaned in close to William, his breath heavy with garlic. "Yes, and maybe the hangman."

William flinched and turned his head away. "Does a question accompany your explanation?"

Clinton squared his jaw. "Again, tell me who's planning to print Bibles here in the colonies."

"I have no information to share with you."

"You lie."

William's gaze went distant.

"Where's your desk?"

A tingle flew down William's neck.

"Your writing area, sir." Clinton's voice was firm, his lips curled in a snarl.

William pointed toward to the door of his den at the back of the hallway.

Clinton strode to the doorway and motioned for the two soldiers.

"Scour the place," he barked. "Anything. Any clue."

He stared at William, his eyes torrid, searching for a flinch, an expression of fright. William's mind flew through the possibilities.

Is there something incriminating in there? Or revealing?

He sidled over to Mary, slipped his hand into hers, and whispered, "Pray."

The angst in her eyes was palpable.

The Lord did not give us a spirit of fear. The Lord did not give us a spirit of fear.

Books flew from the shelves of his floor-to-ceiling bookcase.

My Bibles. My commentaries. My theological treatises. How dare they?

Clinton settled into the chair at William's writing table.

Oh no!

Meticulously, the man scrutinized each of the papers on top.

His soldiers' frantic pace made Clinton's calculated leisure all the more menacing.

He scanned each document and methodically returned it to its place. Next, he opened the top-right drawer, one of three on each side of the large oak piece of furniture.

William gulped. What was in there? His mind felt like a big fuzzball—clouded, bewildered. He couldn't remember.

He clasped Mary's hand.

Two are stronger.

Clinton pulled out folders. In them were notes and sermons, and, yes, he'd preached against the king and Parliament and taxation. But not to the level of sedition, right?

Clinton peered at the contents, scowled, looked at William with menace, then tossed them back in the drawer.

The general pulled out the next drawer and filled his hands with small bundles, letters tied together with ribbons.

"Take these," Clinton told one of his soldiers. "I want to scour them."

William's mind spun. What might those letters divulge? Were there any from the Morrises? The Rushes?

At that moment Clinton opened the bottom-right drawer. *Congress!*

William's knees nearly buckled. His thoughts flew into a sudden high rush. He was co-chaplain of the Continental Congress. Certain papers might ...

Clinton snorted in triumph. He snatched a document and held two pages close to his eyes.

He looked over the top of the pages at William. William couldn't see the man's face but guessed a deadly sneer prevailed.

"My, my." Clinton tittered. "What have we here?"

The two soldiers stopped and turned their attention to their superior.

Clinton started reading:

"To the Honorable Continental Congress." Clinton stopped and harrumphed, gazing at William. "Pshaw! United States? You wish, sir."

William fumed.

Clinton continued: "'We the ministers of the gospel of Christ in the City of Philadelphia, because of the scarcity of Bibles, deem it our duty to lay this danger before this honorable house ...'" Clinton released a cruel chuckle. "Honorable? More to the truth: treasonous."

"Treason?" William blurted.

A fine word from a soldier of a king betraying God by not allowing his Word to be freely spread.

Clinton ruffled the papers and, his voice crackling with sarcasm, went on: "'We humbly request that under your care, and by your encouragement, a copy of the Holy Bible may be printed, so as to be sold nearly as cheap as cost.'"

The general muttered, "Ha! The real objective: money. Should've known. Unscrupulous poppycock."

"Not so!" William blurted.

Clinton glanced at William and Mary and asked, "Would you hazard a guess as to who signed this petition to your ... Congress?"

William stretched his arm around Mary, hoping to reassure her, hoping she couldn't sense his own dread.

Clinton shook his head as if reading a distressing tale of mayhem and woe, not a decent, honest plea.

"Hmm. Let's see," he said. "There's Francis Alison, John Ewing, and William Marshall."

Clinton's forehead wrinkled. "Your name, Reverend, does not appear here. Nor the name of any printer."

William turned his eyes upon the large window beyond Clinton. Were those sunbeams bursting through the clouds?

Perhaps this will work out.

"Oh, here, a second page."

Oh, Lord!

Clinton slipped the leaf to the front. "Ah, the committee's response to your friends' petition. Your Congress even has a Committee of Commerce? I'd call that impressive if it weren't so ludicrous."

William dismissed the tease, but he knew a verbal missile was coming.

"... to import twenty thousand Bibles from Holland, Scotland, or elsewhere," Clinton read. "What happened, Reverend?"

"Nothing," William said. "Congress decided the materials were too costly and fled the city."

Clinton brought the paper closer still to his eyes. "Oh, my. This petition was brought to the attention of the Continental Congress by the body's two chaplains. Hmm."

William's shoulders seemed to collapse. Something like a spider ran up his back. He cringed and counted the moments he had remaining with his wife.

The time's been bliss while it's lasted.

"Chaplain Patrick Allison, pastor of First Presbyterian Church, and …" The contempt on Clinton's face was frightening. "And one Reverend William White." Clinton released a rueful chuckle. "Is there another Reverend William White about?"

Willian stuttered, the thought of what would happen to Mary and the children causing a shiver. The vision of a cold prison cell, a hangman's noose, flashed before him.

"That's me," he murmured.

"Well, then. Off you go with us, Willy-boy." Clinton motioned his underlings to take William away.

Mary cried out and raised a hand in protest.

"Back off or you go, too," Clinton said. A glance at her beauty replaced his scowl. "And wouldn't you be fun to, er, interrogate. Right, that's the word. Interrogate. Sometimes we do that sans clothes."

"No!" William hollered and tried to yank away from the tight hold the soldiers had on him. "Leave her be."

Oh, if I could strike this man, I would. His hands shook with anger.

Clinton released an evil laugh and shook his head.

"Wretch!" William said.

Mary spun away, her face pale, eyes large, voice shaky. "Can I expect my husband back?"

"Maybe." Clinton's nose flared and he let seconds pass. "Maybe not." He stepped in front of her. "I might send one of my men here to take his place." He nodded upstairs to the bedrooms.

William shouted, "Enough with my wife! She's a lady!"

Clinton tilted his head, a sudden thought apparent in his mind. He peered at Mary and said, "Mrs. White, tell me where the Bible printer is, and your husband goes free. This very second."

Mary glanced at William. He shook his head.

Her shoulders caved as she returned Clinton's stare. Her voice was barely audible. "No."

Clinton cocked his head. "Subterfuge, aiding and abetting a criminal act, espionage. There's no end to the counts we could levy against your husband."

"It's the Bible!" she moaned.

One of the soldiers at William's side clamped iron handcuffs around his wrists. William clenched his teeth to stifle a cry of pain.

Pay these men no satisfaction.

With a wrenching twist, the two men yanked him through the threshold and out the door, his feet dragging on the rocky pathway to the street.

Mary's cries split the night air.

CHAPTER 11

Andreas Vandermay had slept little as *Gouden Adelaar* sailed with the wind at her back toward Boston Harbor.

He disliked the man Admiral Howe had sent aboard as second mate. Lieutenant Commander Thomas Clarke was demeaning, quarrelsome, irritable, hot-tempered, and he thought he was captain instead of third-in-charge.

The idea of helping capture and imprison men for the "sin" of printing Bibles sickened him. An Anabaptist, he'd spent the night in prayer, his only light a candle and his *Bijbel*, Dutch-language Bible.

He slipped his fingers through his long blond hair and put the finishing touches on what he hoped would foil the British espionage.

A knock came on his cabin door.

"*Binnenkoen.*"

His first mate, Aart Haas, stuck his head in the room. "*Ik kan land zien. Boston Zeehaven.*"

The lookout in the crow's nest had sighted Boston Harbor.

Vandermay slipped Haas a sealed and rolled parchment and whispered to him in Dutch, "Stick to the plan. Let no one see you. This goes to no one but Calum Cameron."

Vandermay had sailed with Haas for thirteen years and trusted him like a brother—more so, a brother in Christ.

"Clarke will believe something's amiss if I leave the boat," Aart said.

"Put him in charge of off-loading. But make him feel it's his keen idea, to keep a close eye on the printing supplies."

Aart put his forefinger and middle finger to the tip of his cap and grinned. "Aye-aye, *Kapitein*."

William White woke from a fitful sleep, a crick in his back, an ache in his head, and fear in his heart. He was in a tiny room with a chamber pot and a cot meant for children, nothing else. The Brits were using the old brick house as a brig.

He'd tried to sleep with his back against the wall and a thin blanket spread over his legs. But the chill of the night and concern for Mary and the babes kept him awake and gnawed at his nerves.

Clinton had allowed him to leave his home with the clothes on his back, boots on his feet, and nothing else.

This whole episode was absurd, no? A charade? What king would stoop to such tomfoolery? William was pastor of an Anglican church, for goodness' sake.

A knock on the wall to his left startled him.

"Anyone there?" a familiar male voice asked.

William replied, "That you, Patrick?"

"Afraid so," answered Patrick Allison.

William knew immediately the parchment Clinton discovered had led the goons straight to his friend.

"Is that you, William?" Patrick asked.

"Oh, yes." William let out a sigh.

"Do I hear voices I know?" That question, belonging to Will Marshall, came from beyond the wall to William's right.

Oh, my Lord. What have I wrought?

"I apologize," William said, loud enough for his friends to hear. "Your being here is my doing."

Silence. They were wondering how.

"General Clinton found the request for Congress to print Bibles in a drawer in my desk. You both had signed the petition." He stopped for a moment. "Is Rob—" he caught himself. "Is the printer here, too?"

"They don't know his identity," Patrick answered. "Only that he's 'a thief and dissident,' according to Clinton."

"He's on a Most Wanted list named as 'Unknown,'" Will said. "I know that much."

"Let's pray for Unknown's continued concealment," William said.

"Amen" echoed from both rooms.

William led the prayer. In mid-petition, a rapid clutch of bangs at his door interrupted them.

The door flew open, two soldiers marched through the threshold and, without a word, grabbed William by his elbows, roughly escorting him to a larger room. Windows revealed a rainy day. Appropriate.

The soldiers forced William down on a wooden chair in front of an empty table.

William had barely settled when General Howe stormed into the building, shook water from his cloak and hat, hung them on a coat rack, and scowled at him. Behind Howe came Clinton, looking as fatigued as White felt.

"You," Howe pointed an accusatory finger. "You will have a place at the gallows, beside the scoundrel who dares print illegal Bibles."

He leaned over the table, his face a mere two feet away from William's. "Your neck will snap at the same moment as his."

William cringed.

"What will your widow and fatherless child think of you leaving them destitute … and for what? To protect a conspirator?" Howe's lip curled. "Will they weep at your grave, or think your life worthless and nonsensical?"

I'm no Judas, nor a frightened Peter in Herod's court. Robert Aitken and his anonymity have nothing to fear from William White.

He detected the steel hilt of the sword at the hip of the man at his right shoulder. Was he ready to suffer the tip of that weapon, or the rough hemp of a rope around his neck?

Howe's fist came crashing down on the table before him, the wood cracking under the thunderous clout. The act was ice water thrown in William's face.

"I want the man," Howe hollered, "and I want him now! Not tonight. Not tomorrow. Now, White!"

"What man?" William asked, his voice hoarse.

"The Biblio-Ghost."

William started to chuckle at the name. but the look on Howe's face stopped him.

Aart Haas stood at starboard atop the poop deck above the stern as the three-masted *Gouden Adelaar* coasted toward Wentworth's Wharf on Boston Harbor.

Aart sometimes struggled with anxiety out on the open sea. When violent storms thrashed the ship about, when massive waves threatened to wash him and his men overboard, and especially in the dark of night when approaching tempests gave no warning, anxiety could easily escalate into morbid fear.

At those times Aart would consider Jesus's disciples in the terrifying storm on the Sea of Galilee. At those times he would pray to see his Savior walk upon the sea and hail him, "Aart. Have no fear. Faith casts out fear. Fix your eyes on me."

At those times Aart knew the devil would remind him of Paul being shipwrecked at Malta on his way to Rome. But he lived through it and then some.

Get thee behind Aart, Satan!

At those times Satan would bring to remembrance Jonah and the storm and the reluctant prophet knowing he'd sinned and asking to be tossed overboard to save the ship and crew.

At those times Aart would wrestle with these thoughts and tell the devil to walk the gangplank, and Aart would do his job and trust.

Trust and live. Lose faith and die. Either way, his life was in God's hands.

This might not be a moment of life or death, but a defining tick in time when he had to be innocent as a dove and wise as a serpent—mostly wise as a serpent.

There was a snake on board: Lieutenant Commander Clarke. And Aart had to be the wiser of the two.

His men had cut the sail. No longer the sound of wind billowing the canvas. Three crewmen stood at equal distances along the length of the *Gouden Adelaar*, with massive ropes in hand, ready to tether the ship to the wharf.

Aart turned to Clarke, who stood a few feet away. "You'll be wanting to direct the unloading, commander?"

"No," Clarke said.

"What of the cargo that interests you?"

"I'll observe. I'm a sailor, not a longshoreman."

Aart wanted to swat the man upside the head. Send him sprawling along the deck. He'd have liked to do a number of questionable things to the foul-mouthed lug. And he'd have done so if Clarke weren't carrying a pistol the size of a hammer and the attitude to pull the trigger.

Instead, he shrugged. "Have your way. I was thinking of you. Wanting not to keep you here any longer than necessary. Our standard procedures, especially when working with American stevedores, put the printing supplies as last to be unloaded."

Clarke cursed and spat out, "I'm not staying here all day waiting for you layabouts."

Aart shook his head. "That's our process."

"Then get out of my way." Clarke shoved Aart aside. "Watch and learn, mate."

Aart motioned him forward and followed, from the quarterdeck to the main deck, from aft to fore. He watched as Clarke pulled his four fellow spies aside and assigned them watch at various pier caps along the wharf. He waited as the Brit verbally bullied the *Gouden Adelaar's* crew into unloading the printing supplies first.

He stayed put until Clarke was totally absorbed in the operation. Once satisfied, he patted the inner pocket of his winter slicker to make sure the captain's message was secure and surreptitiously hustled down the gangplank and off the wharf.

Aart knew Tales of Yore. The old bookstore had served him well in his study of the English language. He simply compared his Dutch version of *Pilgrim's Progress* to the English edition, side-by-side. Like going to school, only better.

He fast-walked from Wentworth's Wharf straight across the way, found Middle Street, and raced along the streets. People were few and far between this early.

Charter Street consisted of storefronts of various sorts, none of them open. Aart sprinted past an apothecary, a haberdashery, a tailor, a mercantile, a cobbler. Finally, standing still and bent at the waist, he put his hands on his knees, and drew a deep breath. Before him was the door to Tales of Yore. A small sign hanging on the door proclaimed "Closed."

Aart rapped on the doorframe. No answer. He knocked harder.

Alec sat across from Calum, a cup of hot tea in one hand, a chunk of buttered bread in the other.

"Thank you so much for your hospitality, Calum. I've enjoyed the lodgings …" he nodded toward the stairs … "the food …" he laid his eyes on the food before him … "and especially your companionship."

"And the companionship of a certain young lady."

Alec grinned. "Hers, too." His face turned grim. "Though I may never set eyes on her again."

"That, son, is in God's hands. If he wants you together, such will happen."

"But she's so grand."

"In God's sight, so are you."

Alec chuckled. "You know what I mean."

"And you know what I mean."

Yes, Alec knew exactly.

"My thoughts are not your thoughts, neither are my ways your ways," he said. He knew he was quoting Scripture but didn't know which book.

A furious knocking on the door downstairs disrupted them.

Calum stood, went to the front window, and peered below.

"Aart!" he exclaimed.

"Who?"

"The first mate of the *Gouden Adelaar*."

"What?"

"He's in distress." Calum hurried to the stairway leading down to the shop, Alec close on his heels.

Calum opened the door and Aart slid inside.

"We heard the British captured your ship," Calum said.

"Captured, questioned, and released," Aart said. "That is, discharged to do their bidding."

He handed Calum the dispatch from Vandermay.

Calum opened the seal, unrolled the parchment, and read the message.

"Uh-oh." He passed the paper to Alec.

Alec read Vandermay's warning and read again what the Brits had put into motion. Spies and subterfuge. The snoops would follow whoever picked up the printing supplies and, when they reached their destination, capture the perpetrators and destroy the print shop.

"But we're in Boston. They've been driven out. How do they expect to do anything here? Follow or arrest or destroy?"

Eyebrow raised, Calum asked Aart, "Is there any way to tell these men apart from your crew?"

Aart shook his head. "Not even Lieutenant Commander Clarke. You'd never know he's not second mate on a Dutch ship."

Alec's chest constricted.

What to do, Lord? What to do?

Benjamin Burdick's face appeared to him, and he blurted out his name.

Calum stared at him, at first not fathoming Alec's meaning. After a moment his eyes went wide. "Yes!" he said. "Let's go."

Alec and Calum rushed to the back of the shop, grabbed coats off racks, and headed to the front door.

"Aart," Calum said, his voice cracking, "thank you. You and Captain Vandermay are lifesavers. Please tell him so."

"What more can we do?"

"Return to ship, keep your eyes and ears open, and if there's anything we should be aware of, let us know."

With that, they all left Tales of Yore. Alec and Calum hustled to the Green Dragon.

CHAPTER 12

SATURDAY MORNING
NOVEMBER 8, 1777
BOSTON, MASSACHUSETTS

The rising sun was creeping over the rooftops of the buildings along Snow Hill Street, then Prince Street as Alec and Calum rushed along. Sleepy Boston was soon to awaken, but right now they had the streets to themselves.

As they turned the corner by the Green Dragon, both slowed to a quick march.

"What do we say?" Alec asked.

"We'll tell Benjamin all we know and see if he'll help hatch a plan."

Calum walked around to the rear of the inn, stepped past several windows, and rapped a door knocker on a red-painted door. He waited and rapped again.

Moments later the door swung open and Sally Burdick stood before them.

"Calum?" she queried, wide-eyed.

"Sally," he said, "we need to see Benjamin."

"Fast asleep," she said. "Late night."

"Rouse him. It's urgent."

Sally backed into the building and motioned them inside. "I'll get the big lug out of bed, but the blame's on you, Calum Cameron."

She winked and off she went, a woman of high energy.

Alec and Calum stood in a sitting room warm with comfortable chairs and a large, blazing fireplace, so high a person could almost walk inside.

A kettle hanging over the fire hissed. A grandfather clock in the corner ticked. A floorboard above them creaked. Someone was moving about upstairs, but the Burdicks' quarters were obviously here on the ground floor, so perhaps the noise above was a guest. The manservant or maidservant of the de La Bordes, maybe.

Alec stifled a cough and pondered the predicament. How would they avoid the spies? Simply leave the cargo on board and wait them out? Distract them while he loaded the goods and then escaped along the confusing streets of Boston? He pictured getting lost himself in this perplexing city.

What Alec was *not* prepared for was what Benjamin Burdick cooked up.

The burly Green Dragon owner roared into the setting room, a huge fist rubbing sleepy seeds from his eyes.

"Calum, so early!" Burdick's voice boomed. "What's up, my friend?"

Sally entered at a discreet distance.

"We need your help."

"Sit." Benjamin waved at the couch and chair. "Speak."

Alec jumped in. "I know mine is not your fight, sir. It's not anywhere near the important matters with which you deal. This has to do with ink and paper and Bibles."

"'Important'? Son, God's Word is of utmost magnitude in our battle for freedom. Act like sheep and you invite the lion. The Israelites found that out with the Romans—to their own demise. Why fight a revolution if your Creator is not on your side?"

Joy slackened Alec's shoulders. On their way here he'd prayed for support, but Benjamin's validation was extravagant.

Over the next twenty minutes Alec and Calum listened and nodded as Benjamin concocted their plan and Sally served them coffee.

Strong coffee and tea within an hour of each other. Bliss!

As they spoke, the sound of feet on the floor above increased, and as they tied matters up, a footfall echoed down a staircase. Seconds later, as Alec and Calum were at the rear door saying their goodbyes, a knock came at the Burdicks' apartment door.

Sally opened the door and said, "Why Monsieur de La Borde, how are you this fine morning?"

Alec spun around. Might there be a chance to lay eyes again on Elsie before he departed?

De La Borde put his fingers to the top of his cap. "Sally, you look, what's the word—chipper?—for so early in the morning."

She smiled.

"I know the hour's early, but I heard voices, so thought I'd check. I hope I'm not intruding."

"Can we do anything for you, Charles?" Benjamin asked.

De La Borde noticed Alec and Calum and his brow wrinkled in question.

"They were saying goodbye," Benjamin said abruptly.

"No, no," de La Borde interrupted. He observed the visitors. "Is there something I should know?"

Not aware that de La Borde was privy to Alec's Bible printing affairs, Benjamin raised a hand to cut him off. But Alec blurted out, "*Gouden Adelaar* has landed," and he filled in de La Borde on what had transpired.

De La Borde told Benjamin and Sally about his involvement with the printing supplies and asked, "Can I offer any help?"

Alec exchanged glances with Calum and Benjamin. No one responded for several long moments. Benjamin broke the silence. "Have you any pistols in the vicinity?"

De La Borde chuckled. "Need you ask, my friend? If you have men to fire them, we can improve your plot."

He stepped toward Alec and Calum and motioned for them all to follow him.

Upstairs in her bedroom Elsie looked out the window. She'd heard muffled voices and thought Alec's was one of them. She pressed her forehead against the pane in a struggle to see below.

Yes, Alec and Calum were with her father. Monsieur Burdick trailed behind, hurriedly shoving his arms into a heavy coat.

She tried to pry the bottom half of the window up, but the frame wouldn't budge. If she could just call out. But what would she utter?

She decided to ruminate on that while hurrying out of her bedroom, through the parlor and into the hallway beyond. The thought that she was in her dressing gown, hardly ready for public viewing, didn't rattle her beyond two on a scale of ten. What prevailed was the idea she could spend one more moment with Alec. Merely one second.

She rushed down the stairs, turned and raced to the Burdicks' quarters. As she knocked, Sally swung the door open. Coincidence? No. God.

"*Excusez-moi, s'il vous plait.*" Elsie hurried through the room.

She reached the back door and stepped through the threshold.

"Alec!" she called.

But he was out of sight. Gone. They all were.

She called again, "Alec!" but her cry faded on the icy morning air.

Deflated, she leaned back against the doorframe, the door open, dead cold air raising goosebumps up her arms.

A whimper lingered on her lips. She swiped at a tear that trickled out of an eye. This wasn't the first time she thought she'd never see Alec's face again. Last night she'd slept in fits at the possibility.

Sally gently put a hand on her shoulder.

"Come inside, dear. We'll sit by the fireside and warm ourselves with a cup of strong tea."

Elsie exchanged looks with Sally, knowing she was an easy book to read.

I'm an elementary school primer. Surely, I'm turning red.

She lowered her eyes.

Sally urged her to sit at a comfortable couch by the hearth and disappeared into another room.

Elsie took a moment to compose herself. This was so unlike her.

Sally returned with a tray carrying a teapot, two elegant cups (must be French), a creamer, and a container with sugar cubes. Holding a potholder, she took a pot from over the flame in the fireplace and poured steaming water into the teapot.

"Only be a couple minutes to steep, Mademoiselle de La Borde," she said.

"Elsie, please."

Sally smiled. "And my friends call me Sally."

Sally laid a pretty shawl over Elsie's shoulders, and Elsie pulled the wool tight about her. They sat quietly, watching flames lick the wood in the fireplace.

Finally, Sally turned to her and said, "Love can be a wild tangle of emotions, reactions, and timing."

Elsie couldn't help but chuckle remorsefully and nod. This sentiment she was discovering. She'd never loved before.

But this must be the feeling.

These emotions were so alien. More than fancy, far above fondness. A foreign experience in a foreign country. She felt raw, as if both emotionally and physically exposed.

But she sensed she could share her heart with this woman. Sally appeared to be in her forties, and she was married. She possessed a wonderful, warm smile, and read Elsie's mind and feelings and, and, and ...

Elsie so wanted her own *memè*. She could cry.

And so she did. Tears flowed unabashed. This, too, was so unlike her. She prided herself on decorum, being in control, demure, reserved. And here she sat—almost blubbering in front of a stranger. So much for pride, *non*?

Sally bent close and put her arm around her.

Elsie laid her head on Sally's shoulder and the sobs slowed, the tears slackening from a torrent to a trickle. Sally handed a handkerchief to Elsie.

"Here, dear."

As Elsie dried her tears, Sally pulled the tray closer to them.

When Elsie'd composed herself, Sally asked, "How do you like your tea, dear?"

"With a bit of milk and two cubes of sugar, please," she managed.

"I don't know Alec," Sally said as she poured the milk and tea, "but he appears to be a mature young man." She dropped in the sugar, contemplated Elsie, and added with a grin, "And quite handsome."

"And a gentleman, though not carrying the weight of proving so, which we frequently see in the young men of France," Elsie said. "And thoughtful. Mostly thoughtful."

"Oh?"

Elsie told Sallie about their walk along the Charles River and through the town and about helping the young woman with the child, and Monsieur Adams's rousing call to arms, and about Alec wanting to fight in the Revolution but placing the printing of the Bible above all else. She paused, not knowing Sally's faith, and added, "Alec knows the Bible so well."

Sally nodded at each revelation.

Elsie sipped her tea.

Fire crackled in the fireplace. Elsie wondered if she'd spoken too freely, assumed too much.

Sally broke the silence.

"Faith," she said, "is indispensable to any successful man-and-woman relationship. And here in America, where wilderness encroaches too close with dangers too many, faith is life itself. The people who settled this continent knew this well."

Elsie nodded.

"The Christian faith, and sharing that belief," Sally continued, "is actually written into the charters of every colony, especially compelling in New England, Virginia and Maryland. The Massachusetts charter, written a hundred and fifty years ago, proclaimed the necessity of inciting the natives to know the only true God and Savior."

This was new information for Elsie. She paid attention to every word.

Sally smiled at Elsie's enthusiasm.

"And now," Sally said, "we find ourselves short of Bibles and know they're nourishment our troops are not getting, our children are missing, and the natives are certainly starved for. Sustenance the king would prefer we not get."

Elsie took another sip and said, "I don't know the English word, but I love how you compare the Word of God to food."

"Without such, we perish." Sally put a hand on Elsie's shoulder. "Your young man has a lofty goal." She hesitated. "A dangerous one. You'll want to be praying for his safety."

"*Oui.*"

Elsie studied the floor.

Alec. So intense, so sold out to his Savior. Would there be room in his heart for her? The way he looked at her, she guessed so. This look was common among the young men who desired to court her. But Alec was not common, that was a certainty.

She looked again at Sally. "You are a woman of faith."

Sally smiled broadly. "Born and raised. Growing up, my pastor was Jonathan Mayhew."

Sally read Elsie's perplexed look and explained, "He pastored the Congregational West Church here in Boston until his death a decade ago. John Adams called him 'the morning gun of the Revolution.' He declared the king must repent of his tyrannies or face the consequences of his subjects forcibly throwing off the chains of tyranny."

"Oh, my! He said this from the pulpit?" Elsie asked.

Sally nodded. "I was there that Sunday morning when Pastor Mayhew quoted, 'All Scripture is profitable for doctrine, for reproof, for correction, for instruction in righteousness' and asked, 'Why shouldn't those parts of Scripture which relate to civil government be directed at kings who are oppressive and cruel?'"

The more Elsie lived here and spoke with these American colonists, the more she grasped the increasing support for the Revolution.

CHAPTER 13

General William Howe fumed. None of these pastors had furnished him a smidgeon of information, nothing worth a pebble. They were so much in lockstep they reminded him of his troops at parade. He stormed back to his headquarters, flung open drawers in search of a bottle of whiskey, filled a tumbler half full, and took a strong slug. He looked out the windows at the cold, gray sky—cold enough and gray enough to match his mood—and drummed his fingers on his desk. On Robert Morris's desk.

What scope of subterfuge had been strategized right here? What snub or poke in the eye of the colonies' sovereign—the head of the church?

Not acceptable!

He had to force these self-righteous theologians to unveil the scheme, to reveal Biblio-Ghost. Do that and they might live their lives unscathed. Resist and suffer the consequences.

He was the supreme commander of British troops over all America. Supreme commander. Supreme! People must answer to him.

So, what maneuver could he use to get these pastors to submit?

In a flash of hope, Howe pictured Sergeant Conrad "Cutthroat" Casey. He wondered where the man got the nickname—from his disposition or success around the poker table? Both, for sure.

Howe had avoided sharing poker tables with his subordinate, but he'd observed him "at work" on the battlefield with a bayonet fixed at the end of his rifle. Darned if the man didn't carry at his hip at all times a fully loaded Sharpe flintlock pistol—a weapon he'd won from a naval officer in a card game. Probably slept with a trade knife in his socks.

If anyone could extract information, Casey could. Howe simply had to devise a plan in which he himself was not complicit in any, er, physical harm befalling the poor wastrels.

But first, a tryst with Lizzy. If she couldn't boost his spirits, nothing would and no one could.

Howe wrote two notes and ordered Lieutenant Brown to deliver them.

The first was to General Clinton to have Cutthroat appear at headquarters at eight o'clock tomorrow morning.

The second note was to Lizzie's husband, Joshua Loring, commanding him to check on the situation at the prison in Delaware.

And keep the lamplight burning at home, Josh, old boy, 'cause Lizzy will be entertaining a paramour.

Howe grinned, a rarity during this sordid war.

Alec and Calum gathered Robert Aitken's horse, Zims, and the wagon from Wilder's Livery on Milk Street across from Jallit's Lane. Calum gave a nod to Nathaniel Ladd, a bull of a man whose blacksmith business adjoined Wilder's.

As Alec snapped the reins for Zims to head off, Calum stayed behind, and Ladd set down his hammer and lowered the handle on the bellows. That much Alec saw. He kept a steady hand on the reins and prayed against fear, wondering if the type he was feeling was akin to that soldiers experienced entering the battlefield.

The simple presence of trepidation made him wonder how much he truly trusted God. If everything failed, would he willingly go to prison for a noble cause? Oh, yes, without question. Would he die for that cause? Hmmm.

He directed Zims to the right down Milk Street toward the harbor close by. There was no sting of salt and marsh in his nostrils, so the tide was in. *Gouden Adelaar* would be well docked and riding high.

People bustled everywhere in all directions, slowing him down, and he prayed again, this time for clear streets after the supplies were loaded. Speed would be a precious commodity. Would Zims be up to the task? True, he was a draught animal, but possessed of an athlete's agility. Having spent the last few days in a stable, the big bay was strutting like a race horse, one of General Washington's Narragansett pacers, or Pastor Asbury's "Spark."

This was good.

Alec visualized the perplexing street map Benjamin and Calum had shown him. In decades past, dairy cows had wandered from barn to field and back, wearing paths men turned into streets as Boston evolved from village to city. And, Alec mused, more than a few of these cows may have taken a drink or two at the Green Dragon before meandering on their baffling way to the milk stand.

This much he knew: Wentworth's Wharf was straight ahead as the crow flies. Problem was, Zims couldn't fly. Alec had to negotiate this spider's web. He directed Zims into the first left, Tanner's Street. He hustled Zims along the narrow way to get past the pungent smell of urine, rotting flesh, and stagnant water at McPhee's Tannery.

When he reached Water Street, two hay wagons crossed in front of him. The winter's supply for someone, perhaps

Wilder's Livery. The men driving the wagons seemed in no hurry, completely unaware of Alec's frayed nerves.

Hurry. Hurry. Hurry.

Alec directed Zims toward the biggest landmark Benjamin had mentioned—Long Wharf.

"She'll be to your right," Benjamin had said. "At that point you're about there. Keep your calm and act normal."

Alec peered down Long Wharf, which extended to a sight-unseen end in the Atlantic. Ships' crews and longshoremen were unloading cargo of various sorts.

Traffic lightened as he passed a swarm of scattered buildings and shops along the harbor to his right. Then Wentworth's Wharf was in front of him.

Alec stiffened and stopped the wagon.

Sure enough, *Gouden Adelaar,* its three tall masts aiming toward the sky, sat docked on the left side of the quay. Across from the Dutch ship, a smaller boat was tied up.

Alec snapped the reins. A minute later, Zims pulled to a halt at the entrance to the wharf. Alec swept his eyes over the scene.

First and second mates calling out orders, men wearing coats against the weather, grunting under heavy loads. These men, with grizzled faces and bulging muscles, were none to tangle with, Alec figured. The enemies among them were impossible to detect.

On the *Gouden Adelaar,* a massive winch hoisted a net filled with three barrels over the side of the ship and slowly lowered the net to the dock. Did those drums contain Mr. Aitken's ink?

Alec sucked in a deep breath and guided Zims to a small space that had opened.

A tall, handsome man stood on the deck, blond hair flowing beneath a cap, oddly not concentrating on the unloading process but scanning the area as if he were looking for someone in particular—perhaps searching for Alec.

Must be the captain, Andreas Vandermay, Alec thought. The man looked as Alec pictured a sea captain, this one with the daring appearance of a man bravely defying the mighty Royal Navy.

Alec spotted Aart on the dock, hopped down from the wagon, and walked to the first mate, trying to maintain an air of ease.

At the sight of Alec, Aart's eyes went wide and he looked with alarm to his left. He hadn't expected this.

Alec handed him the bill of lading.

Aart stuttered something incomprehensible.

Dutch bewilderment.

"I've come for the printer's ink and paper," Alec said.

Aart's eyes darted left and right. Anxious.

Perhaps we should have warned him I'd be coming.

Alec lowered his voice. "We have a plan."

Aart peered at him, grasped the message, and whispered, "Don't look, but Clarke—the man to beware of—is wearing the blue hat and shirt and black trousers." Aart turned to a knot of men in his crew and spoke something Alec did not understand but figured was an order to unload the supplies.

"I'll bring over my wagon," Alec said.

"Right over here." Aart pointed to about ten feet away.

As Alec turned, he could feel eyes on his back. Fierce looks. Scrutiny from British spies who probably judged him too young and inexperienced to present a challenge, too easy to overpower, too tender to stand under interrogation. He braced his back and broadened his step, reminding himself that they didn't know he was the one for whom they were waiting. Not until the ship's crew loaded his wagon.

And then. And then watch out.

In fifteen minutes, the crew loaded Alec's wagon with three barrels of ink and scads of the special, fibrous-cloth rag-blend paper. During that time, Alec kept a stealthy eye out, to spot Clarke and figure out who were the lieutenant commander's minions. They were surely alerted by now that he was their target.

Captain Vandermay had offboarded the ship and approached Alec with a bill.

"You didn't get my message?" he said softly.

"Received and noted," Alec replied as he handed over the money. He caught the captain's eye and added, "If you're a praying man, pray."

"Anabaptist," Vandermay said, "and I will. Know also, young man, that Clarke has rented a wagon."

Uh-oh.

Alec shot a glance down the wharf. Clarke had slid out of sight, likely behind several large wooden crates, readying to trail his prey. But Clarke wouldn't dare capture Alec out here in the open, not in the cradle of Libertymen. The Brit would wait to set upon him in a quiet street or alley.

Alec patted Zims on the nose. "You ready for this, big fella?"

Zims snorted that sound Alec had become fond of and which exuded the quiet strength of the big animal.

Alec climbed aboard, grabbed the reins, clicked his tongue, and off they went, out onto Ann Street heading northeast.

He snuck a glance behind him and saw Clarke and four others hustling off the wharf. Clarke leaped onto a one-horse buckboard with one of the men beside him and the three others in the wagon.

They were in pursuit. The plan assumed they'd be on foot and Alec would ride leisurely.

But with his heavy load, Zims was now at a distinct disadvantage.

Ann Street—named for a reason known only to city planners—became Fish Street. Aptly labeled, Alec thought, as the distinct odor of flounder or cod or some such fish reached his nostrils.

Unexpectedly a huge wagon pulled out of Sear's Shipyard directly in front of Alec. A large rowboat sat atop the wagon.

The fool!

Alec yanked Zims to a dead stop and the horse reeled back and snorted in protest. Alec glanced behind him. Clarke was gaining ground. The man had obviously decided he couldn't inconspicuously follow and spy on the racing Alec.

Change of plan. Alec pulled his left rein and hollered, "Cha!"

Zims again contracted his mighty frame and launched the wagon down a tight little way, Gallop Alley.

Gallop? If only we could.

What now? Alec had to get back to Fish Street, or he'd be truly lost.

Gallop Alley came to a stop at Market Street. And this morning Market Street was true to its name. By the looks of things, a number of men of fighting age were not fighting. Like himself, Alec thought.

Wagon wheels and horse's hooves echoed in the alley behind him. Alec peered behind as one of the men on the wagon hopped off and took off in a run after him.

So much for the idea of them simply trailing me to my destination.

Trying not to panic, Alec pushed his way onto Market Street, turned right and a few yards later right again down Word Street. The spy, his fist raised, reached the wagon and vaulted toward Alec. Alec brought his right arm to his left shoulder and let go a massive blow with his elbow, catching the man square on the nose. A loud crack rang out. Blood spurted. The man screamed in agony and fell to the ground.

Several people on the street stopped and peered at the commotion. Alec shouted, "He's a British spy. Grab him!"

Behind Alec, Clarke hollered. He was bulling his wagon around the corner onto Market Street, evidently unafraid of the crowd knowing his identity.

Word Street was twice the width of the alley. Alec snapped Zims into a sprint back toward the harbor. For a moment they gained against Clarke, but only because they already had the lead. Hooves beat on cobblestones behind him. Sweat tickled Alec's brow despite the cool air. The tiny hairs at the base of his neck tingled.

A half-minute later they reached Fish Street again, and he turned eastward and veered to the right as Fish hugged the harbor.

One after another he passed short wharves—Haywoord's, Halsey's—until Hancock's enormous pier appeared, stretching out into the bay.

Alec shouted out, "Okay, Zims, let her fly. Cha!"

Past Scarlet's Wharf and Hutchinson's Wharf they raced. White Bread Street was to their left.

No, that's not the one.

Clarke was gaining ground.

Past Clarke's Shipyard.

Clarke? Really? How ironic.

Salutation Alley was to his left.

Nope. Why can't this be an orderly city? First Street followed by Second Street and Third Street. Like Philadelphia.

Alec snuck a peek. Clarke was close on his rear, the man beside him appearing to have a pistol in hand. The others standing behind them sported savage looks.

Past Grant's & Greenwood's Shipyard they raced.

Where in the world is—?

There it was: a tiny black sign with white lettering declaring Battery Alley. And "alley" was correct. No highway, no street, not even a lane. Was there width enough for a wagon? Could this be his undoing?

Alec gave a mighty yank with his left arm. Zims objected, squealing, and straining against the forward motion of the substantial load.

The wagon creaked, its sideboard groaning against the wildly shifting weight of its cargo. The right-side wheels must be on the verge of fracturing, Alec thought.

If the barrels of ink fell overboard, this long wait and all this effort and money would be lost, poured out on a muddy alley in Boston.

Alec wanted to holler to the heavens but was too intent on maintaining control of the wagon to muster a sound.

Clarke's lightly loaded wagon had no doubt made the turn with ease. Alec couldn't look. His heart thumped.

Benjamin and Calum stepped out of a doorway and into the alley ahead. A rifle filled Benjamin's hands. Calum's expression could have fired musket balls.

Alec called out, "Whoa! Whoa!" He pulled his forearms tight to his waist and grabbed the brake lever.

Zims felt the unmistakable urgency and in seconds stopped the wagon halfway down the alley.

Alec turned around—both to make sure his supplies were intact and to watch the melee behind him. A dozen men, old and young, rushed into the alley, brandishing rifles and axes, faces crimson.

"Enemy spies!" screamed one.

"Have no mercy!" hollered another.

Alec flinched at the rage.

Clarke and the man beside him scrambled down from the wagon. The two men in the back of the wagon held their arms high in surrender, but Clarke's sidekick fired his pistol. Several gunshots erupted in response and the man crumpled to the street.

Clarke ducked down and pulled a pistol from his trousers.

"Wouldn't be gambling on that, laddie!" The thunderous voice of Benjamin Burdick brought a chuckle to Alec's throat, relief to his mind.

Clarke cursed.

"Wouldn't do that either." That voice was one Alec didn't recognize.

A tall, dark-haired man stepped forward from the Bostonians. His collar gave him away as a minister. His demeanor gave him away as a leader of men.

Speechless, Clarke dropped his weapon to the ground.

Alec's protectors rushed forward and tied Clarke and his men with ropes, treating them with rough disregard for their feelings.

No etiquette here.

Two revolutionaries loaded the dead man's body onto Clarke's abandoned wagon and rode away. No farewell, no word exchanged at all. They knew their job and were doing it.

"Benjamin. Benjamin!"

Three men walked around the corner from Market Street, pushing the bloodied spy whom Alec had elbowed ahead of them. The man's hands were tied behind him, his eyes fearful.

"You may be lookin' for this poor lost fellow," one said, his voice heavy with an Irish accent. He jerked a thumb toward Alec and added with a smirk, "Appears he ran into a formidable young man along the way."

CHAPTER 14

Alec could smell the dread. Dread and its opposite—determination.

Dread from Clarke's three men who remained alive, though seemingly not from Clarke, whose arrogance was unmistakable even as he and his comrades were tied to foot-thick wooden beams in the center of a spacious warehouse.

Determination? That was evident in the tone of voice and body language of Benjamin Burdick, the pastor Benjamin introduced as Samuel Cooper, and a half-dozen, ahem, colleagues obviously loaded for revolution. Among them was the blacksmith, Nathaniel Ladd. Each sported a pistol. What appeared to be hunting knives hung in sheaths at the hips of two of the men.

The building was empty except for a few farm implements, a stack of boxes of unknown contents, and a collection of heavy chains hanging from a wall.

A door swung open and Charles de La Borde, dressed like he was out for a simple walk, stepped inside. He put a hand on Alec's shoulder. "Brave young man."

"*Merci*, sir. But I simply drove my horse and wagon."

"Expertly, I'd add."

Alec grinned. "As my squire would say, practice makes perfect."

"Charles," Benjamin said with a wave of his arm, "again your assistance comes with good timing." He pointed to the captives.

De La Borde tipped his cap. "Glad to help."

"Calum, Alec," Benjamin said, "you don't need to be present for this. Why don't you do what needs to be done, and we'll take care of matters here? One of these gentlemen will tell us what we need to know, and when he does, we'll get in touch."

Benjamin turned to Clarke. "Once our guests answer our inquiries, they'll be sent to jail. If they don't talk, well, all bets are off, right?" The question hung in the air unanswered, but at least one of the sailors winced.

Alec looked to Calum.

"He's right, son," Calum said. "They must learn whether the Brits have discovered the identity of your friend and mine. If so, you need to warn him."

Alec wondered how Benjamin and his men would question the spies. He scrutinized the sailors. A couple appeared ready to spill whatever they knew. Alec might, too, if he occupied their skin.

These rough men were not the Bostonians of the cultured set or the prim and proper Philadelphians. They reminded him of the Scotsmen back home. Not to be fooled with. Not to be doubted. Not to be made enemies.

Calum cupped Alec's elbow in his hand, tugged him in the direction of the door, and they walked out together.

De La Borde joined them.

Alec pointed to his wagon and asked the Frenchman, "Would you like a ride back to the Green Dragon?"

"*Oui. Merci.*"

As they rode up toward the Green Dragon, de La Borde regaled them about the wonders of France, the beauty of her mountains, the brilliance of her art, her grand castles.

The Côte d'Azur on the Mediterranean Sea, its lavender fields and vineyards, and his favorite French town, Colmar, a picturesque village close to the border of Germany.

"You live in Colmar?" Calum asked.

"No, Lyon," Alec interjected. "Where the Rhône and Saône rivers converge."

De La Borde cast Alec a questioning look. "You listen when a lady speaks. That's a good trait, at least in regard to my Elsie. She told you about Lyon?"

"A bit," Alec said. "She said she went to boarding school elsewhere and returned to Lyon to be schooled by her mother."

"Brilliant woman," de La Borde said. "Alyssa taught Elsie more than she would have learned in any school. Expressly about being a woman of substance, of valor, of compassion, and of sensitivity. And of philanthropy."

"That I learned," Alec said. He maneuvered down Union Street.

When he stopped in front of the Green Dragon, de La Borde stepped off the wagon and caught Alec's eye.

"I suppose you won't return home until Benjamin discovers what you need to know," he said.

Alec nodded, then a sudden thought struck him. Today was Saturday. Tomorrow was Sunday. Church. He could attend an early sermon before his journey.

"Monsieur," he said, "would you permit me to escort Elsie to church in the morning before I leave?"

De La Borde, obviously taken aback, hesitated, coughed, and aimed a tight-eyed gaze at Alec.

"You're asking if you can take my Catholic daughter to a Protestant service." A simple declarative sentence, inscrutable in itself, but loaded with innuendo.

Alec hesitated. Had he overstepped? Could this be the end of the man's good graces? Catholics indeed killed Covenanters like his father's predecessors back in Scotland, and some had returned the favor, for sure. The same had happened for centuries in England. That, too, was for sure.

He finally managed, "Yes, sir. By your leave, sir."

"Allow me to consider," de La Borde said. "Are you spending the night at Calum's?"

"Yes, he is," Calum answered.

"I'll send you my answer."

Alec nodded.

"And what time would this be?"

Alec checked with Calum for an answer.

"Quarter to nine o'clock," Calum said.

De La Borde put a thumb and forefinger to his chin, nodded, and proceeded inside the Green Dragon.

Calum chuckled and shook his head. "Bold."

A simple declarative sentence, inscrutable in itself but loaded with innuendo.

By the time her papa returned, Elsie had retired to their rooms and, with Lisette's help, dressed in a brilliant blue dress that startled her when she looked in the mirror. When her papa stepped inside the living room, Elsie sent Lisette and Malcolm on errands and asked him into the sitting room.

They each took a seat in front of the window with a view to the east. The noontime sun had advanced to the southeast corner of the building, leaving her father in shadow and her in a glint of light.

If only we were seated the other way around so I could see his face better, perhaps read his thoughts.

"Papa," she began, "I'm worried."

"About what, *mon chéri*?" He sounded concerned, her dear papa.

"About you helping print Bibles."

"We had this discussion."

"Yes, but are you not violating an edict from Rome? And, if so, wouldn't you face the harshest judgment?"

"Perhaps so, but I must live with myself, and if I didn't help when I could …" He raised his hands at the wrists.

Elsie resumed, "So you believe this is as important as helping the military?"

"Ha!" He thought for a few seconds. "Well, no—and yes. This is the basic question—is the spiritual health of a society as important as its general health and freedom?"

While Elsie mulled this over, he asked, "When we sailed here, was there a priest aboard the ship?"

"No, Papa."

"Here in Boston, is there a priest among us?"

"No, Papa."

He placed a hand upon her own.

"Would the Lord want us barren of his gospel during these months?"

Elsie remembered so often spotting her father in a chair in his bedroom, leaning over his secret Bible, either reading or in prayer.

"No, but there's no Catholic church here."

"You make my point, Elsie. But even if there were a Catholic church on the street next door, and even if we could wander there to pray or seek repentance, would the Lord want us to be without his gospel when at home or here in our apartments?"

Elsie's thoughts went to a classmate at Le Maison Royale de Saint-Louis. The girl had total recall, didn't have to take notes to pass examinations, could recite entire chapters of books. Elsie wished she herself possessed such a gift. If so, she wouldn't need a copy of the Bible to remember God's stories and advice.

She tried to read her father's features. Light and shade. Light and shade. Like her mind, confused and enlightened. Concerned and reassured.

Her worry ended with this thought—*if you were even to be put to death for what's right or for the truth, so what? Isn't that what the disciples did, each dying for sharing the gospel?*

She smiled and squeezed her papa's hand.

Her voice husky with emotion, she whispered, "You're a wonderful man. I love you, Papa."

She stood to take her leave, and her father said, "Elsie, I've been with Alec and Calum."

Elsie's heart skipped three beats. *"Oui?"*

"It's interesting that we're talking about the Bible."

"Oui?"

"Alec asked my permission to take you to church tomorrow morning."

"Church? But where?"

"A church nearby, I'm sure."

Elsie drew a sharp breath and swallowed hard. "And you, Papa? Would you grant permission?"

Oh, to be transported like Elijah in the Old Testament, or Philip in the Book of Acts after baptizing the Ethiopian eunuch, Robert Aitken thought. Puff!

Not to heaven like Elijah, nor to Azotus like Philip, but to Boston. What in the world was happening? Was Alec safe? Had the supplies arrived? Was he on his way home?

To live in these treacherous times is to trust God or go mad. With two children at home and a wife and two babes away, going daft isn't an option.

Floorboards squeaked under his feet as Robert paced back and forth. He glanced yet again at the clock on the mantel.

Impatience, I abhor you. And yet you so often win the battle.

Ezra and Nehemiah must have felt like this before being given the go-ahead to rebuild Jerusalem.

I have the desire, Lord—I simply need the means. The printing press is sitting idle. I know you own the cattle on a thousand hills, but I don't need beef at this moment.

Robert remembered as a boy working the potato fields with his father in the rough countryside outside Dalkeith and his da saying, "We've got the spuds in the ground, son. Now all we need is soft Scottish rain to sprout 'em and the Lord's sweet sunshine to grow 'em."

It's going to be a wee book, Lord, small enough to fit into a soldier's coat pocket, so I only need a wagonful of supplies. A wee book but powerful enough to move mountains. My trust is in you, and you alone. Protect the lad. He's as close to me as a son.

Robert sat at the kitchen table, head down, hands folded. Jane was readying a lunch of potato soup, bread and milk. Robbie was playing pickup sticks in the front room. Robbie's competition was himself, so he was confident he'd always win. Any luck was his own, any misfortune his opponent's.

Robert chuckled. Oh, to have a child's distraction in the midst of calamity.

Noise at the back door broke his contemplation. Two hard raps, a second of hesitation, two soft raps, another hesitation, then two hard knocks. Robert glanced up and, through a window next to the door, spotted William Marshall. His cap was pulled down on his forehead and, with chin to chest, he was obviously trying to hide his sizeable self.

Robert hurried to open the door. Will's lip was cut, his face battered. He slid inside, shut the door behind him, and shot a furtive look back through the window.

"What's happened?" Robert asked. He turned to Jane. "Fetch bandages, girl."

As Jane rummaged through a drawer, Will answered, "I've been released from jail."

Robert straightened his shoulders in surprise.

"Jail?" So many questions swirled about in Robert's mind, he didn't know where to start.

"William White, Patrick Allison and me. They found our names and are looking for you, Robert." Will's face contorted as if in pain. "Soldiers discovered paperwork in Pastor White's desk that revealed the reason the Continental Congress refused our request for Bibles is that the ink and paper are difficult to obtain."

Robert nodded, waiting.

"Well, the report revealed that he and Patrick and I made the appeal. So they rounded us up and threw us in jail."

Robert's eyes went wide with concern.

I'm endangering these men, their families.

"Pastor Marshall, please have a seat," Jane said, holding a can of ointment and a cloth.

Will lowered his bulk into a chair at the kitchen table and, with Jane applying salve to his bruised cheek, told a tale of soldiers crashing into his rectory in the middle of the night last night and threatening his wife and kicking his son and toppling the kitchen table and ...

"*Noo jist haud on.*" Robert used their shared language of old, trying to calm his friend. "Slow down."

"*Keep the heid,*" Will said. "They're looking for you."

Keep the heid? How can I not get upset? Friends jailed and beaten. So much for secrecy.

Robert glanced at Jan. Calm amidst turmoil, the girl made him proud.

"We're doing all we can to remain invisible," Robert said. "Janet and the wee ones are away in the countryside with friends."

Will looked quizzically at him. "How much do you know?"

"Jake Tremble told me soldiers were at Pope's Head, asking the whereabouts of a print shop. They never searched the back of the building."

"But they're looking for you personally, Robert. They simply don't know your name, so they're calling you Biblio-Ghost. Can you imagine?"

Robert harrumphed. "Well, that's silly." He hesitated. "But what happened at the jail. How did you get out?"

"They pummeled me around a bit and just when a soldier pulled out a pair of pliers with mean intention, General Howe entered the room. Phew!" Will gathered his emotions, then coughed out a pained laugh and continued, "Seeing how they were messing with my good looks, Howe lit into them about how they had to improve, not harm, their relations with Philadelphians. The general sputtered, 'If battered clergymen stand before the congregants tomorrow morning, imagine the outrage!"

Robert blew out a breath in relief.

"Five minutes later, they released all three of us. Patrick didn't even suffer a bruise, just a little humiliation." Will shook his head and winced as he put a hand to his cheek where Jane had treated an abrasion. "But, Robert ... beware. From now on they'll be searching any boat, any wagon, anything being transported, to find your supplies."

"Oh!"

"So, we've failed you."

Robert shook his head and managed a smile. *"Failin' means yer playin'.* And if you're playing, that means you're trying like we all are. We're in this together—you, Pastors White, Allison and Alison, John Ewing, me—" Robert pointed at Jane, "my fine young lass here, and Robbie."

"And," he continued, "if they don't know my name, good luck finding me. I haven't left identification on any paperwork, either on Market Street or here. We're still in business."

Will put on a resolute smile. "We are in the right, Robert, and God's with us." He looked at Jane and stood to go. "Thank you, dear girl. I'll take my leave."

"Yes, your wife must be worried sick," Robert said.

Will hesitated, then murmured, "I wouldn't be coming to tomorrow's worship service if I were you."

Once the door closed behind Will, Robert turned his attention to Jane. "I'm sensing you and Robbie should best be going to Reading with your mum and Milly Linnell."

"No, Da!" Jane's eyes were wide in disbelief.

"You heard Pastor Marshall."

"But we've known since Mr. Tremble told you they're looking for a print shop. We were here then. What's different?"

The girl was all spunk and grit, and Robert wasn't so sure himself what had changed. His business had been in hiatus since the Continental Congress fled town, and he'd surreptitiously moved the press into its special hiding place. He'd been going to the shop because that's what he'd done for the past seven years, since immigrating to America and starting his press and bindery. The place was spit shined and the press raring to go. Like a racehorse at the starting gate.

Work was ingrained in Robert. And this project was so far more worthy and vital than any task he'd undertaken—even the *Journals of Congress* and *Common Sense.*

Having the two older children with him had seemed best—especially Jane, because she was already a fine apprentice. So accomplished, in fact, that he would be pleased to leave the business to her control if anything were to happen to him. And danger no longer appeared remote but rather breathing down his neck.

He sat down on a kitchen chair, deflated. If Alec were to arrive tomorrow, Robert would want all hands on deck, Robbie included.

Secondarily, this printing was a calling from the Lord, and he wouldn't want to deprive his own children of the blessing they'd receive for supplying these Bibles.

Jane called Robbie to the kitchen for lunch and set the bread and milk on the table along with bowls of potato soup. The soup was another reminder of Scotland, and Robert wondered if he should have remained in his homeland.

That idea was fleeting, followed by an inner voice.

Who knows but that you have been called for such a time as this. Like Esther, who was in the one place where she could save her people, the Jews. If you were in Scotland, you wouldn't be where the Lord needs you.

Robert blessed the food, still mulling the question of sending the children away.

Jane would not remain quiet. Just as his wife, Janet, was his counterbalance in weighty matters, their effervescent daughter was his appraiser, ever analyzing his assessments and not shy about expressing any doubts.

Jane was Robert's apprentice in the print shop, but she was Janet's trainee in matters of emotions as well as substance.

Robert raised his spoon to sip the soup, set the utensil down, and narrowed his eyes on Jane.

"Daughter, you discombobulate me."

"Discum-what?"

"Baffle. Befuddle. Bemuse."

"All the 'B' words, Da," Robbie said with a grin. "Well, she puzzles me, but I don't know any other 'P' words to add."

"Try perplex," Robert said and winked.

"Hardy-har," Jane said. "Not funny."

"Am too," Robbie said. "But I befud—befud—what was that word again, Da?"

"Befuddle," Robert said with a chuckle. "You're like your ma. She regularly challenges me with—with—"

"With wisdom?" Jane offered.

Robert laughed. "Yes. With wisdom. Indeed, I'll need you here with me when Alec returns—if he returns. But you need to beware of soldiers. We need a contingency plan."

"Conting-what?" Robbie asked.

"We need a way for you two to escape if soldiers come to the house. Like we have with the hiding place at the shop."

"Under God's wing," Jane said.

"Yes, darling. Under God's wing."

As they ate their soup and bread, they discussed their options. And when they were finished, Robert felt one hundred percent reassured.

CHAPTER 15

Saturday Afternoon
November 8, 1777
Philadelphia, Pennsylvania

Sergeant Conrad Casey was a man of numerous talents. He could shoot a pigeon off a clothesline at thirty yards. He could cleave an apple with a knife from fifteen feet. And he was the reigning middleweight boxing champion, including the thirteen cavalry regiments and the 73rd, 78th, 83rd and 95th Foot. And he wouldn't mind pummeling that fool Angus from the Seaforth Highlanders who thought himself the queen's favorite.

If they had been told to follow the Broughton Rules, Casey would have been the first to toss the code aside as so much effeminate foolery meant to emasculate warriors.

Pugilism. He loved the word. He sometimes dreamed he'd lived in Roman gladiator times and was tossed into the arena with a dozen other men of, er, certain abilities. In his dreams, he always won, leaving a carpet of slain bodies, the coliseum audience filled with men cringing at his power and women swooning at his manliness.

Conrad Casey represented the highest summit in men's aspirations. He wore the "Cutthroat" moniker with pride and swagger.

Yet this morning, under orders *not* to "damage" three pansy pastors so badly that they couldn't preach Sunday, he had to admit defeat. Not his personal defeat. That was left at the feet of Howe and the general's own "boundaries." Imagine not being able to yank out finger nails, or twist joints not meant to be twisted, or dunk their heads in buckets of ice water, or myriad other Casey-preferred methods.

Batter and bruise was all Howe allowed him to do. And his superior was upset Casey hadn't gotten better results? Ha!

Given his way, Casey would have resolved matters in minutes. These three jokers possessed none of the guts of, say, the Apostle John who, Casey's granny had told him, survived being boiled in oil without recanting his faith. Granny believed in a lot of myths, but that was one Casey remembered. If true, even he was impressed. He doubted he himself could have withstood such torture for the faithfulness to one man.

"Sarge? Sarge?"

A young soldier ran toward him along Market Street.

"Yes, Corporal?"

"General Clinton wants you to lead a raid."

A trill of excitement quivered up Casey's spine.

"Where?"

"He thinks he knows who'll give us the Ghost's name. Somebody who was a secretary for the Continental Congress. Someone named Thomson."

"Minced Meat. That's what we called the last British spy we captured."

Benjamin Burdick put hands to hips and chuckled as he looked over the four British sailors. "Minced Meat 'cause his face looked more like my lady's mincemeat pie than, well, than the fella did before we, ah, embarked on our fact-finding venture."

The youngest of the sailors—Benjamin guessed his age as eighteen—groaned. The boy glared at the floor—scared to look up, Benjamin guessed. Afraid to make eye contact and risk the ire of his captors.

"Grow a spine, private," said the man they'd discovered was in charge of the little group of Redcoats. A man by the name of Clarke. Clarke with an "e."

Benjamin eyed Darren Holyoke and asked, "Yep. What did you tell that fella?"

Darren stepped beside him and pulled a pair of pliers from his back pocket. "Why, I told him the teeth would come next."

Now two of the spies whimpered, the youngest one joined by a man who appeared to be in his middle-twenties.

"Men, *be* men," Clarke barked.

Benjamin said, pointing to another of his colleagues, "What happened next?"

George Frye joined Benjamin and Darren in front of the spies.

"That fella found his tongue right straight," George said with a laugh, "and a good thing, too."

"Now, we won't admit to any torture," Benjamin said, catching Clarke's eyes in his own, "because, well, gentlemen don't partake of that sort of thing. But, like with making sausage, you want to see the results of a process, not the makings of it. Do you understand, Clarke with an 'e'?"

"Understand, man, that you're speaking to an officer of the king."

"Not my king."

"He is your king, like him or not."

"Laddie, you haven't heard of the Declaration of Independence? Ratified by the former colonies about sixteen months ago?"

Clarke spit on the ground. "That's to your declaration. Declare all you want. Words come easy. You—are—ours."

"Your possession, eh?" Benjamin harrumphed. "That attitude got us to where we're at, Clarke with an 'e.' And we can't print our own Bibles without your ruddy permission."

Clarke nodded. "Consent of the king, you mean."

Benjamin grunted. "I bow to no man, especially one three thousand miles away who cares so little for my well-being and opinion that he allows me no representation in my government."

Benjamin motioned to his men. "Leave the boy-child to me. Take Clarke with an 'e' and the others into the little room in the back and bind their mouths with their own handkerchiefs."

The sailors were taken away, the door closed behind them, and the youngest of the spies fought against the knots tying him to the beam. Sheer fright filled his face.

"Reverend," Benjamin said loudly to Samuel Cooper, "you should go. I'll see you in church tomorrow."

The reverend nodded, his face grim. "What has to be done must be done," he said, voice raised.

Cooper slammed the door behind him. Seconds later, he returned with a jar of pig's blood. He hoisted the bottle and murmured, "Just in from the butcher."

Benjamin tied a cloth over the young sailor's mouth and winked at the older son of one of his best mates. This ruse, pretending to whip the captured spy, would be fun.

"You ready, Jimmy?" he whispered.

"Yes, sir." The boy handed him a switch.

"Then let the festivities begin," Benjamin bellowed.

He set about whipping a nearby canvas bag filled with flour. With each flailing, Jimmy yelled or screamed or begged him to stop.

"Speak up, private. Do you know the name of the printer of Bibles?"

"No!" Jimmy hollered.

More whips, more quickly, more intense. Each was followed by pleadings and yelps and whimpers.

"What do you know? Do you know where the press is?" Benjamin hollered.

"No! Please, no!" Jimmy returned.

Benjamin bawled, "Oh, no! I've gone too far. Check him. Is he still alive?"

Keith O'Halloran called out, "The boy stopped breathing, Benjamin. He's dead."

"Better get the body out of here," Benjamin barked, "and bring in another."

Two men untied the private, grabbed his elbows, and hauled him out of the building, squirming and kicking.

Reverend Cooper unscrewed the cap off the jar of blood and sprinkled drops here and poured more there, all around the beam where the boy had been bound.

Moments later, another sailor was lugged out of the back room, dragging his feet the entire distance. When he was close enough to see the blood, his eyes went wide, his face wild with fear.

"What do you want to know?" he said.

Benjamin smiled. "Glad you asked."

A half hour later, armed with knowledge of Admiral Howe's naval strengths and weaknesses and the location of his vessels (the lad kept a log of the American fleet for the admiral), Benjamin turned his attention to what, if anything, was known about the printing supplies and Alec and Robert Aitken.

Exactly forty-two seconds later, having found the young British sailor a talkative captive overflowing with a will to live, Benjamin had all the answers he needed.

He motioned toward the little room. "Bring in the others, will you, men?"

Before Benjamin had drawn a breath, Harry Morse hustled back out of the little room, eyes wide. "Gone!" he shouted. "Clarke's escaped. Knocked a hole in the rickety wall in there."

"After him, gentlemen," Benjamin said. "Everyone but Jimmy, Keith, and Wilbur. We'll get the others ready for transport to prison. But we need Clarke in our hands, bound up, and behind bars."

A half dozen Bostonians raced out of the building in different directions.

"There's no telling what Clarke could do if he escapes," Benjamin said, half to himself, half to the others.

Oh, how thirty minutes could change the appearances and expectations of man.

Elsie shifted and gazed out the setting-room window. If she craned her neck toward the north, she could see the edge of Mill Pond, and she thought of Alec and what he'd told her about the water-hold and wanting to build a printing press using water power.

People are so ingenious ... and what is the source of that intelligence?

Only in the last forty years, men had invented the mercury thermometer, fire extinguisher, lightning rod, and spinning jenny. And on the trip here the ship's captain had showed her the boat's sextant and navigational clock. That had made her wonder how the sextant-less Christopher Columbus had ever found his way to America, or how Magellan had circumnavigated the world.

Well, the captain would probably be thrilled to hear about the fellow from Connecticut who last year invented a boat that traveled underwater.

Imagine if Alec were successful. He'd be famous like Mr. Franklin and Mr. Fahrenheit and Mr. Watt.

But Elsie didn't fancy fame. At least not in regards to Alec.

He could be a shepherd for all I care.

She settled into the comfort of her favorite chair and wondered what Alec had written. The communication hadn't arrived by Mr. Franklin's postal system, but had been delivered by a boy of about eight years of age, who simply knocked on the door of their apartment and handed two papers to Malcolm—one addressed to her and one to her father.

Elsie had been near enough to see the boy bow before turning and running off, and she smiled. A little bundle of America bowing to a French manservant. Where else would this happen? Not in a place of high society. Not in France or Spain or England.

But, did she prefer any of those countries to America? Any of those people to these rough colonists? She thought again of Alec and of Calum and Sally and Mr. Burdick. *Authentique, reél.* Genuine. No pretense. They didn't dress like her or speak like her. Now she had to stop and wonder if she ever put on airs, acted haughtily—she was sure she did. No, she was far from perfect, no matter what her papa thought. She smiled at the deep, adoring love she felt for her father.

At that reflection, she turned the letter over in her palm. "To the care of Mademoiselle Elsie de La Borde from Alec Craig."

She gently broke the letter's simple red seal, an imprint of Tales of Yore, and unfolded the single page.

"Dearest Elsie," she whispered the words, imagining Alec speaking to her, "from your *monsieur de la poésie.*"

Elsie stopped and grinned. Centered next on the page was the title, *The Morning Search.*

She read on:

> I seek you in the morning.
> I want to know your will.
> I want to feel your tender touch
> And so I sit here ... still.

I fix my thoughts on Jesus—
His love proven on the cross.
And deep tears well up within me—
Of regret and counting cost.
I was a slave to Satan,
In darkness to the nth degree.
But Jesus has released me
By his work on Calvary.
So I seek him in the morning.
I want to know his will.
My first step he is planning,
And I delight to feel the thrill.

Elsie reread the poem, reflecting about how the content revealed Alec, and contemplating her mother. She decided to share the little godsend with her father and found him in his bedroom, reading the other communique.

He looked at her.

"Alec had asked this morning for my permission to accompany you to church with him tomorrow." He held the letter. "Instead, he asks to visit with you later this afternoon. He leaves at sunrise, and so—"

"Yes, Papa?"

"Do you want this meeting?"

"Yes, Papa."

"I will notify him. Four o'clock. Darkness comes early these days."

Darkness. The foreshadowing wasn't lost on Elsie. Would this be their final meeting?

"Papa?" she said.

"*Oui.*"

"You approve of Alec?"

He hesitated, then, "If not, I would not allow a rendezvous with my one and only daughter."

"Even though he is not a man of means?"

Another hesitation. Then, "But he *is* a man of means, Elsie. The most important means—character."

CHAPTER 16

Hannah Thomson stopped in the middle of the cornfield, leaned the snath of the scythe against her hip and removed her gloves. She was certain she'd have blisters by the time she and Donald, a neighbor's son, were finished cutting down the corn stalks. They'd had to sharpen the blade, which neither had done before.

This was one of the chores Hannah was tardy at attacking since Charles, her husband, had gone off to serve as secretary to the Continental Congress. And when Congress had fled to Yorktown, Virginia, Charles was compelled to accompany them.

All of this was to the chagrin of Hannah's father, Richard Harrison, a wealthy antiwar Quaker who had asked her to come and live at his estate on the other side of Philadelphia—at least until this ungodly Revolution was over.

Standing in the cornfield, arms aching, Hannah was weighing her decision to remain on the farm. She wore a middle-weight waistcoat, depending on the hard work to keep her warm despite the chill in the air. Indeed, she needed to wipe perspiration from her brow.

Donald, being the boy he was, merely wore a long-sleeved shirt, no coat, and a big smile, ruminating probably on the wages he was earning. He was pulling a cart filled with stalks into the barn where the Thomsons' three dairy cows were stalled. Thankfully, they had the milk and her laying hens' eggs, so their meager pantry didn't scare Hannah.

She took the minute of rest to pray for God's protection on Charles and the others. This was the first taste of war for Charles. When he and his brothers sailed as boys to America from Ireland, their father had died at sea. Taken into the home of a blacksmith, Charles's life nevertheless had been one of scholarship, teaching Latin at the Academy of Philadelphia, followed by the business world.

When Hannah and Charles married three years ago, and he was asked to scribe for the Continental Congress, he was over the moon about sharing the rarified air around such grand men creating a modern country with new laws, new structure.

When Charles came home at night, he'd shared with her the debates and arguments of the day. The personalities of Adams and Jefferson and, particularly, the Pennsylvanian delegates. He spoke with pride of fellow Irishman Thomas Fitzsimons, whose firm, George Meade and Company, specialized in the West India trade, and glowingly mentioned Scotsman James Wilson, a land speculator and Whig leader.

He'd told Hannah of Robert Morris, whose firm two years earlier had contracted with Congress to import arms and ammunition. Of the quiet, unassuming George Clymer and his interest in commerce and military affairs. Of the wealthy and articulate Gouverneur Morris.

And of course, the man he held at highest esteem for his candor and humor and inquisitive mind—Benjamin Franklin.

But most of all, Charles regaled her about being, as secretary, among those who signed the Declaration of Independence.

Hannah put her gloves back on and wrapped her hands around the grips of the scythe. As she swung back to strike through another two or three corn stalks, a loud shout interrupted her.

"You there!"

Hannah turned and gasped. At the edge of the cornfield, a British soldier on horseback was flanked by a half-dozen soldiers, their muskets trained on her. Their red uniforms stood in stark contrast to the bland dormant grass between them and the barn behind them.

The barn. Donald!

Hannah lost her breath. She'd been half-expecting such a thing, but the reality was too much. A spell of dizziness folded her to the ground. The world went dark, she didn't know for how long. Seconds? A minute?

The dark became brownish and sometime later, a blurred daylight glared like a solar eclipse. Rough hands lifted her to her feet. A man's voice, insistent, sounded as if emanating from the bottom of a barrel.

"Mrs. Thomson. Mrs. Thomson. Woman!"

Hannah thought of feigning unconsciousness. But the hands were groping her now.

"Stop!" she cried out.

The soldier behind her loosened his hold, and she nearly collapsed again. She hoped Donald had seen the commotion and stayed in the barn. Hidden.

At first shaky, Hannah gathered herself. She scowled at the soldier who'd manhandled her and focused on the man speaking at her. He had dismounted and stood not three feet away. Malevolence filled his eyes, a glower his square face.

"Mrs. Thomson?" His voice was brusque.

Hannah took note of him now. He was neither short nor tall—well, taller than her five-foot-four, for sure. Battle-scarred, that was his look.

"Mrs. Thomson!"

He leaned forward, preparing to slap her, for sure.

Finally, she mustered strength and replied, "I *am* Mrs. Thomson. And who, sir, are you?"

"Sergeant Casey. We're looking for your husband." He nodded toward the house.

Afraid, she shot a look in that direction. Soldiers were scurrying around the place, outside and in.

Donald McIntyre, you'd better be hidden!

"Charles—is—not—here." The words hiccupped out of her mouth. Here she was, the church choir director, and she couldn't put together four succinct words.

"Don't lie. You'll make things that much worse for … Charlie-boy …" Casey hesitated a second. "And yourself."

"What do you want with my husband?" Her words shook with fear.

"Simple answers to uncomplicated questions."

"He's a businessman. He deals with imports like tea," she said. Her Quaker background abhorred lies, but this was a truth in a way, just in the wrong tense grammatically. "What could he possibly know that you'd be interested in?"

The sergeant chuckled. "Foolish question." He cocked his head, glared, and dragged out his own succinct words: "Where … is … he?"

That information would endanger all the delegates to Congress as well as Charles.

Hannah shifted her stare to the ground, to the soldier's knees, to the house.

"Woman!" Casey's teeth were grinding. His hands had tightened to fists. "Look … at … me!"

Hannah forced her eyes to him and wished she hadn't.

His eyes were daggers. A smile contorted one side of his face. Not a snarl. Worse.

She struggled for words. "You wouldn't believe me if—"

Without warning, Casey landed a backhanded blow to Hannah's cheek that sent her sprawling. She screamed as she hit the ground. Her cheek was numb as a brick, and her shoulder shrieked with pain where she landed.

Grabby hands again lifted her, again fondled her.
Outrageous!

Hannah flailed with her elbows at the man behind her, and he pushed her forward, staggering upright.

"This, men," Casey addressed his troops, "is an exercise in civilian insubordination."

And now there were two of him, like mirror side-by-sides. Hannah wondered which of the two figures was flesh and blood.

"I've asked nicely," he said. "I don't want to get carried away. That happens sometimes. Sometimes I have trouble controlling myself, especially when facing obstinate—pig-headed—defiant ..." He waited a moment. ... "women!"

Hannah struggled for words and to converge the two images before her into one. But she could not force her lips to form a response. Wham! He released a blow to her other cheek that knocked her straight down.

Again the world went brown for Hannah, and a third time hands pulled her up from underneath her shoulders. This time, a second soldier moved in and two were now propping her up, one at each elbow. They kept their hands off her breasts this time, apparently deciding she'd been embarrassed enough.

Her legs were like noodles beneath her. Hannah would welcome oblivion.

"Your husband's location," Casey said.

Hannah felt blood trickle down her lip.

Casey pulled his hand back as if to deliver another clout when a sudden scream stopped him in mid-swing.

"That's enough!"
Donald!

Hannah looked in his direction and saw two fuzzy *Donalds* running from the barn, a pitchfork held across his chest. "Leave her alone!"

As Donald drew closer he came into focus. He pointed the pitchfork forward like a knight with a lance on a charging horse.

Casey drew a pistol and pointed the barrel at Hannah's head. That stopped Donald in his tracks about eight feet shy of them and about stopped Hannah's heart.

"Drop the pitchfork, boy," Casey commanded.

Donald exchanged glances with Hannah and let the instrument fall to the ground.

"Mrs. Thomson is a lady," Donald said. "She should be treated as such."

"You treat females like ladies, do you, boy?" Casey laughed.

Donald stuttered. "Y-yes."

"Chivalrous, are you?"

Donald wavered, then, "I guess so."

"Well, we want to reward chivalry, don't we?"

Donald vacillated. Hannah could see the boy knew something was coming that neither he nor she would like. But neither she nor he could guess what that was.

Casey took long strides right up to Donald, lifted the pistol to the boy's head, and turned his eyes to Hannah.

"Where's your husband—or the boy dies."

Hannah didn't hesitate. "Yorktown, Virginia."

CHAPTER 17

Alec had been mulling over an idea since Calum told him about Mill Pond, and he wanted to resolve one major question before leaving Boston. Mill Pond's tidal power could generate enough muscle to operate a printing press, that was for certain. But could a printing press be built to harness that energy? If so, such an invention would be revolutionary. He chuckled at the word.

The Delaware and Schuylkill rivers ran along Philadelphia. And if he himself were to build such a press, he could earn the financial means to be able to ask for Elsie's hand in marriage, a proof to Monsieur de La Borde that he was worthy of her affections.

He dropped off Calum and the wagon at Tales of Yore and walked past the ferry to Charles Town and down Snow Street along Copp's Hill to Mill Pond. A small wooden structure stood at the northeast edge of the pond. Behind it a dam hugged the Charles River and stretched beyond sight.

Alec went in search of the master of the pond. In short order, a call came out from his left.

"Oy, there!" An older gentleman walked briskly toward Alec. "Careful, boy, where you go." The warning was good-natured. The man reminded Alec of a deacon in his church. Thinning gray hair, rough cheeks that must have been difficult to shave, dressed like he worked in a bank, not on a dam. Like the crofters back home in Scotland.

The man stretched out a hand. "What can I do for you, young man?"

"I'm Alec Craig, sir. Calum Cameron referred me to you."

"I'm George Leonard," he said. "Bought several books from Calum, I have. Good man."

"I'd like your opinion on an idea of mine."

"Sure enough."

"Could a pond like this, or something like it, power a printing press?"

"Hmm." George put a thumb and forefinger to his chin and repeated, "Hmm."

Finally, he said, "Well, this is a grist mill. But let me give you the royal tour—you know, the one I reserve for royalty, which in our new republic will be our president and Congress."

Alec laughed. "I'd appreciate that, sir."

"George," he corrected.

"George."

George walked with purpose inside the building which stood at land level, overhanging the pond. Once inside, he stepped past grist stones, one of them five feet in diameter, and went to a window directed toward the dam.

He pointed downward and announced, "The gateworks. The sluice wheel—" he pointed to a huge wheel—"opens the sluice gate, which starts the flow of water, causing the water wheel to turn. That's our power to grind the grain."

Alec peered out, following George's index finger.

"The Charles is at full tide and our grist mill is powered by the water we've trapped while that tide was coming in," George said, "so we closed the gate minutes ago. Too bad you weren't here to watch the basin fill up."

Alec smiled at the thought of the chase and capture of the spies. "Yeah, too bad."

George pointed to the southwest corner of the building where several large burlap bags sat.

"The bags contain wheat and rye for the smaller stone over here and corn for the larger stone. My men will be here any minute to empty the grain onto the grinding surfaces of the top stones, and you'll notice they're concave and carved in spoke patterns to—"

"Excuse me, George," Alec said, "this is interesting, but I'm short on time, and I need advice on my question of the printing press."

"Son," George said, "if what you need is the power to press an inked-up type plate onto pages of paper, why not? Those two millstones are fifteen inches thick and weigh one and a half tons each. Three *thousand* pounds. Waterpower is massive. It's extraordinary."

"Phew!" escaped Alec's lips as he thought of the enormity of that force.

"I started refurbishing this mill in 1769 for the city of Boston, so I've been doing this for eight years now," George said. "My only wish is that we were on an inland river with water flowing fulltime, not a tidal river depending on flood tides receding to turn our wheels. We live and work by the changing clock of the tides."

Well, we're blessed with two rivers that flow all day and all night.

"Rotary power is the basic foundation of moving energy. A clever engineer can make any motion a reality," George said. "You simply have to design a system with gears and cams and lever arms and connecting rods, whatever is necessary to turn the rotary power to lineal actuation or cam-operated up-and-down or back-and-forth ... I'm guessing up-and-down for a printing press."

"Right," Alec said. "But what's lever arms?"

George pointed to a rod connected off-center to one of the water wheels.

"When that cylinder," he pointed, "moves against the lever arm, it turns the wheel. Then, bam—" he slapped his hands together, "there's the power generated to operate your printing press."

Alec beamed. He couldn't help himself. His dream was possible. He thanked George profusely, accepted a pat on the back, and returned to Tales of Yore, excited to tell Calum what he'd learned.

"Cutthroat" Casey found General Howe in headquarters with General Clinton, scrutinizing a map spread out over a table.

Howe looked up and asked, "News?"

"Thomson's wife says Congress is holed up in Yorktown."

Howe guffawed. "By the time we catch the miscreants, they'll be hiding away in some hovel in Vermont."

Clinton and Casey joined in the laugh.

Howe turned serious. "And the Ghost?"

Casey lowered his eyes and shook his head.

"Keep up the hunt."

CHAPTER 18

The sky had turned gray, ominous, perhaps portending an early snowstorm. Alec prayed not. The week-long trek back to Philadelphia was going to be difficult enough without Zims hauling the wagon through snow. This was no empty load. He'd spent the afternoon getting the yard goods and lumber on board. Along with three barrels of ink, pallets of paper, and food and grain to last Zims and him through the trip, little room was left. He felt sorry for the horse. Thankfully, he was a sturdy animal.

Benjamin Burdick had delivered bad news. Not only had Clarke escaped, but Admiral Howe had sent a communiqué to his brother, General Howe, in Philadelphia, naming the man he thought was the Bible printer: Robert Aitken. So much for anonymity. That is, once General Howe received the message.

The report raised Alec's anxiety meter. His shoulders caved. He'd have to make haste at the crack of dawn. Meaning he would not hear the Reverend Samuel Cooper speak again. More crushingly, these would be his last moments with Elsi before leaving.

He began singing Charles Wesley's *And Can It Be* in a soft voice:

Amazing love! how can it be
That Thou, my God, should die for me!

Alec's good news, of course, was Monsieur de La Borde allowing him to visit with Elsie after all. One last time, hopefully not *the* last time.

Alec entered the Green Dragon, took the stairs two at a time, quick-stepped down the hall and knocked on the de La Bordes' door.

Malcolm answered and acknowledged, "Master Craig." He motioned Alec inside, where Charles de La Borde stood facing away.

Charles turned and nodded a hello. He held in his hand a small book. Taking long strides to Alec, he extended a hand of welcome. Alec returned a warm grip with his own.

Charles placed the book in Alec's palm, pointed to the volume, and said,

> "If place I choose or place I shun,
> My soul is satisfied with none;
> But when my Lord directs the way
> 'Tis equal joy to go or stay."

Alec raised an eyebrow.

"The lyrics of Madame Guyon," Charles said. "This is her book."

Alec peered at the cover. *A Short and Very Easy Method of Prayer*.

"Madame Guyon," Charles said, "was a lady I consider a treasure of France. And beyond France, for this manuscript was translated to English as you can see."

"I've not heard of her, sir."

"She died sixty years ago. She was a Catholic, but imprisoned for eight years by the church, which called her a heretic. Like St. Augustine and St. Thomas Aquinas, she defended the belief that salvation is the result of grace and not works, that a person's deliverance can only come from God as an outside source, never from within the person."

"Sounds Protestant," Alec said.

"And that's a reason why I stand at your service to help in any way." Charles shrugged. "There are those in our two faiths who agree on most issues. Like this," Charles retrieved the book and flipped through the pages to a passage and read:

> "Prayer is the key of perfection and of sovereign happiness; it is the efficacious means of getting rid of all vices and of acquiring all virtues; for the way to become perfect is to live in the presence of God. He tells us this Himself in Genesis 17:1: 'Walk before Me and be blameless.'"

Charles handed the book back to Alec and said, "I'd like you to have this. From what I've observed, I believe you'll enjoy the reading."

"Thank you, sir," he said in almost a whisper. "I have a long ride ahead of me and I find you can read while riding the smoother lengths of King's Highway—as few as they may be."

Alec cradled the leatherbound volume in his hands. "Mr. Aitken and I bind books as well as print them, but I've never felt a covering like this."

"I had the book re-bound with preservation in mind," Charles said.

"But you're giving it to me?" Alec couldn't fathom the depth of the gift from this near-stranger.

"I believe the Lord wants me to," Charles said. "If you intend a relationship with my daughter, you should be intimate with her faith. I question if she'll ever leave Catholicism."

What to think?

Alec fumbled for words. His mind swirled at the thought of the discord between their religions. But then his heart leaped.

Yet her father is entrusting such a cherished possession to me.

At last he managed, "Then I doubly accept the gift, sir."

A door opened, and Elsie appeared.

Flawless. Always flawless.

Her smile lit something in Alec's chest. Not fire, but more like an exultation. Euphoria.

The world at this moment was too perfect for a printer's apprentice, too jubilant for a young man about to travel a treacherous road to a destination several colonies away, too good for a lad whose Sunday best couldn't get him past the royal guard, let alone into the heart of an upper-class, wealthy girl so perfect outside and in.

Elsie seemed to walk on air to within arm's length of Alec. She flashed a brilliant smile at her father, took Alec's arm, and stepped off toward the door. Lisette held out a knee-length fur coat and Elsie disengaged her arm from Alec long enough to don the garment.

Before Alec regained his head, they were outside the Green Dragon and walking down the street. He paid little attention to their route, only that their bearing was south.

Elsie broke the silence. "I loved your poem, *monsieur de la poésie.*"

"Did you?"

"*The Morning Search*. Good advice to start our day with God."

"I fail my own admonition."

"Admoni—?" Her look was quizzical.

"Rebuke. Warning."

"I doubt so."

"But I do."

They walked on and Alec pulled the Guyon book out of his pocket.

"Look what your father gave me."

Her mouth opened wide in surprise. "My Papa?"

"Yes."

"He loves this book."

"Yes."

"Ma *mère* gave this to him."

"Oh?"

"Papa. He astonishes me sometimes."

"He said if I am to know you, I must know your religion."

"Ma *mère*, she loved Madame Guyon's writings."

"Should I have not accepted the book?"

Elsie wavered for a moment and laughed lightly. "If you do want to better know me, my beliefs, perhaps you should keep this treasure."

Alec caught the mischief in her eyes, smiled, and returned the volume to his pocket. "Then with me, this treasure will go."

"And return?" Concern crossed Elsie's brow. Her big, molasses-brown eyes were wide with uncertainty.

Alec wondered at this question, about his alternatives. Could he not stay in Boston and find a job, perhaps working for Calum; hire someone else to take the printing supplies to Philadelphia; and leave Mr. Aitken to find another apprentice? Couldn't Jane be enough help? But he thought of the strength needed to impress the typeset onto each page of a book. And he thought of his idea to invent a waterwheel-powered system to mechanize that process. This all flashed across Alec's mind in a second or two.

No. Staying in Boston wouldn't do. He owed Mr. Aitken—all the Aitken family—his life and welfare. He couldn't leave them in the lurch. Indeed, the word lurch derived from *lirch* which meant corpse. No, he couldn't abandon any one of his American family to a possible coffin of unfulfilled dreams.

Plus, they'd have difficulty finding someone who could match Alec's output of three thousand pages a day.

Another thing—he'd promised himself to join the war *after* printing the Bibles. And what was more important—love for a woman or love for God? If he and Elsie were meant to be husband and wife, wouldn't God have such a matrimony in his divine plans?

His memory lapsed, Alec turned his eyes upon Elsie.

"What was your question?" he asked with a grin.

Elsie crossed her arms in mock consternation.

"If you want to better know me and my beliefs, does that mean you will return to Boston?"

"Elsie," he pleaded with his eyes, "you must know I have feelings for you. You're the most extraordinary woman I've ever met, ever seen. I hope to fulfill a dream and, if successful, I'm confident I could keep you in the comforts you deserve."

"Comforts?"

"Lifestyle."

There was hurt in her eyes, as if he'd insulted her. Alec gulped and his chin touched his chest in anticipation.

"You believe, Alec Craig, that I am a shallow woman?" Her eyes flashed. "That I must be kept in a style of the rich?" She stiffened. "That I would accept a man's proposal only if he were aristocracy, or at least prosperous?"

"Well—" he stuttered. "Y-you know—your father—" As he struggled to respond, her word "proposal" flashed in his mind.

Did she say "proposal"? Has she thought about me proposing? If I did, would she accept?

Elsie pressed ahead. "You know me little if you believe me thus."

She rolled her shoulders, exasperation etched on her face. This was a woman with backbone. Every time he was with her, he was undone.

But this particular moment demanded an untangling of words spoken.

"I'm sorry, Elsie. I see in you a beautiful young woman of means, of morals, of expectations. I see a woman up here—" Alec motioned like a salute, his palm outstretched and held at the height of his forehead, "and I consider myself a man down here." He moved his palm to chest height. "A man looking to the unattainable."

"Master Craig," Elsie fumed, "you cannot believe this. Why am I here with you if not by my own choice? You are angling for my praise."

"No!" he protested.

"Then be done with foolishness if you wish my continued companionship." Arms still crossed, she turned her back on him.

Alec stammered. He stuttered. He fell silent, wondering how to unwind this tightly wound knot he'd fitted himself into.

Oh. Simple.

"I beg your pardon, Mademoiselle de La Borde."

She remained back to him.

"Mademoiselle de La Borde, I ..."

She remained back-to.

"Elsie," he exclaimed, "I love you!"

The outcry escaped as if the words were butterflies flitting in a breeze. They were unstoppable, unretractable.

He was exposed.

Elsie spun around, her face alive with delight. "Oh, Alec, *moi aussi, je t'aime. Je t'adore.*"

She rose on her toes, threw her arms around his neck, and leaned into his kiss. The moment was tender yet passionate, sweet yet feverish, unforgettable and—

Alert that they were not alone, Alec detached from her lips long enough to look about them. A couple dozen people were on the street, bustling around but all going about their own business. None appeared even to be aware of the young couple.

He returned to Elsie, wrapped his arms around her waist, and kissed her again, softly. These were the first true kisses of his life, and he knew he would never forget them. Ever.

CHAPTER 19

SUNDAY MORNING
NOVEMBER 9, 1777
BOSTON, MASSACHUSETTS

Alec adjusted the harness, tightened the breeching around Zims's haunches, and hooked the leather strap to the shafts.

Calum was at work with a large paintbrush, lathering a thick coat of black paint over the print that identified the contents of the barrels as "Printer's Ink" and the packages of paper.

Alec thanked God no snow had fallen and that the cold weather had frozen the ground, so the sometimes-muddy King's Highway shouldn't cause many problems. All the more important, since he had to make haste over the five-hundred-mile trek to reach Philadelphia before Admiral Howe's messengers.

Short days didn't help. Sunrise at 6:30 and sunset before 4:30 left only ten hours of travel time each day. This did not bode well.

Benjamin Burdick walked in the door.

"Alec, Calum!" he called.

"Ho!" Calum replied.

Alec smiled to see this jovial leader of men.

"Got a surprise for you, my boy," Benjamin said. "Two, actually. Here's the first."

He held out a package wrapped in cloth. "Sally heard you were leaving and was up before sunrise baking."

The aroma filled the air around them.

"Yum," Alec said.

"Besides bread, there's apples and carrots and beef jerky in there."

"Wonderful. Please tell Mrs. Burdick how thankful I am," Alec said and put the package on the seat of the wagon.

"Now for the second surprise," Benjamin said and waved to the livery boy. "Bring out Beau, will you, Michael?"

The boy shot a questioning look. "But, Mr. ..."

Ben cut him off: "Beau's essential for an important mission."

Something stirred inside Alec. Something was afoot, something good.

The boy stepped away to the back of the stable, opened a gate, and came out holding a lead attached to a halter attached to one of the largest horses Alec had ever laid eyes upon. The beast stood eighteen hands at least.

"Meet Beauregard," Benjamin said with a motion of his arm. "Answers to 'Beau.'"

The horse snorted as if acknowledging his name. He even sounded bigger than other horses, bigger than Zims, and Zims was no slouch.

"Give Alec here another harness and a two-horse hitch, Michael." Benjamin said and turned to Alec. "You're in a race to reach Philadelphia before Admiral Howe's man. He's on horseback and with a head start. Time is not your friend. But Beau may help you cut the margin a bit. He won't break any speed records, but he's as sturdy a draft horse as any this side of the Atlantic."

A shiver of thankfulness flew up Alec's back.

"We'll have to move your cargo to my wagon over there." Benjamin jabbed a finger behind him."

The men spent the next half-hour moving the load from Alec's wagon to Benjamin's. When done, Alec stammered a thank-you.

"Your thanks will be those Bibles, including one in my own two hands, okay?" Benjamin said.

"I don't know what to say."

"I do, and they're my own words to say." Benjamin stepped close and settled his big hands on Alec's shoulders. "I'm proud to know you, young man. Proud you're one of us 'rebels.' Proud you're a fellow believer. Thankful you're willing to put your life in danger for God's Word. And I'm glad to help any way I can. Right now, that way is Beau. Take good care of him and when you come back to Boston, bring him back. I love the big ham. And you'll find out his personality's as big as he is."

"So we've got two horses with persona," Alec said with a chuckle.

If they averaged ten miles an hour they should reach Philadelphia in six days, but he had to factor in the ferry across the Hudson River from New York City to Trenton, New Jersey. And what of Brits and battles and other conflagrations along the way?

On the positive side of the ledger, horses' night vision was extraordinary, and Alec could allow them to lead the way when darkness set in. So maybe they could cut the trip to five days.

Alec nodded a thanks to the livery boy and exchanged hugs with Benjamin and Calum.

"Godspeed, me boy." Calum patted him on the back. "But before you go—"

He handed Alec a small book, *Learn French the Easy Way*. "You'll find this handy," Calum said, "you know, in any future relationship."

Alec hefted the volume in his right hand, smiled at Calum, and slipped the book into a coat pocket.

"Thank you, Calum. For the book and for your hospitality, your food and drink, a good warm bed, your help with all that's been happening with this shipment, and for getting Benjamin to capture the spies. He looked at Benjamin. "And thanks again, Mr. Burdick."

"It's Benjamin to you, son. And don't worry. We'll get Clarke."

"With an 'e,'" Alec said with a grin.

"With an 'e.'"

"Probably sleeping out in the cold somewhere on his way back to Rhode Island," Calum said.

"Yep. Defeated and dejected," Benjamin added.

Alec climbed onto the wagon and reached down to shake the men's hands.

"Until we meet again," he said.

"Aye, when you return to visit Miss Elsie," Calum said.

Alec smiled. He remembered with satisfaction that God approved the relationship, proof being the Scripture in 1st John he'd read over his breakfast of biscuit, jam and tea: "Whoever believes that Jesus is the Christ is born of God."

He snapped the reins, and they took off down a silent and empty Marlborough Street and straight past the colonial army's Boston Neck fortification, then off the peninsula-city of Boston and out of town. He was astonished the two horses trotted in synchrony without a hiccup, though Beau was bulkier and a good two hands taller. In a short while, they were rolling along a heavily wooded stretch of road in Dorchester heading southwest toward Roxbury.

Alec was in awe of the power of the horses and watched their muscles work to pull the heavy load. So well-defined, like that British prize fighter, George Meggs, whom Alec had seen in a bare-knuckle match in Philadelphia two years before.

Alec evaluated his right arm, flexed his biceps. Not bad, but hey, he wasn't in training. Well, he was kind of in training, learning a few wrestling moves from Bradley, his best friend in school. Bradley lived on a farm, forking hay, mucking stalls, lifting this and that, and wrestling for fun.

Bradley showed Alec a move he'd put on an angry ram once. Wrapped his arms tight around the sheep's bulky neck and held the grip so long he put the beast to sleep. Something about stopping the flow of oxygen to the brain. At least that's what Alec thought after reading about a Swedish chemist, or maybe he was Norwegian or Spanish, who discovered oxygen a couple of years ago.

When Alec had laughed, implying Bradley was telling a tall tale, his friend promptly spun behind him, put his head in a lock between his massive arms from which Alec couldn't free himself no matter how hard he tried. After a few seconds he felt faint, his eyes lost focus, and he, well, lost consciousness. He'd never doubt Bradley again, that's for sure.

Alec wondered if Bradley could put Zims or Beau to sleep. He looked again at the muscular animals before him. Nah!

This sort of inward discussion was what had kept Alec awake and alert on the long trip to Boston. He supposed that besides learning French and reading Madame Guyon, letting his mind wander would be a temptation on the way home. But being lackadaisical was a danger, especially as he got closer to Pennsylvania.

As Alec left the city, Elsie awoke with a start. She squinted her eyes open, noticed the early hour, and pulled the quilt back over herself in disgust, hoping to return to a pleasant dream. But sleep avoided her.

She saw Alec's face and remembered he was leaving with the rise of the sun.

He's gone!

She pushed herself to a sitting position, sat back against the feather pillow, and folded her hands in prayer.

"Watch over Alec, Lord," she prayed. "Have your angels keep him from harm, and help him to get home safely with all his supplies. If danger lurks, alert him and strengthen him. Be his high tower, Father God.

"You know my heart, Lord. I pray thy plan for my future includes Alec and thou will bring him back to me."

She stopped for a moment and wiped a tear trying to form at the corner of an eye.

Alec's poem occurred to her, and she added, "Jesus's love for you *is* enormous. So is mine."

Vigilance, Alec thought. That was the word, something he'd have to—

A figure dashed out from behind a tree. Clarke! He sprang onto the wagon, raised a heavy stick, and struck Alec with a force that knocked him off the seat. He hit the ground with a thud, landing on his left shoulder. Pain shuddered through his bones from his shoulder down his spine to his hip.

Zims and Beau continued up the road, but Clarke jumped down and raised the sizeable branch to club Alec again. In reflex, Alec copied a Bradley move, rolling toward Clarke. He hit the sailor's ankles as the club came down. Clarke tumbled to the ground and the branch struck the earth inches away from Alec's left ear.

His senses alert, his mind racing, Alec leapt to his feet at the moment Clarke rose to his knees. The club lay next to Clarke and Alec nearly dove to get the weapon, but the sailor beat him there. Rising to his feet, Clarke glared at Alec.

"I'm taking you, dead or alive, boyo." Clarke spat on the ground. "I prefer dead. But surrender and I'll let you keep breathing."

Clarke stood perhaps an inch shorter than Alec's five-foot-eleven but was obviously a roughnecked veteran, probably in his mid-thirties. He'd probably killed men in war. He probably enjoyed the act, by the look on his grizzled face.

"Sounds honorable," Alec said.

Clarke snarled. "Like all in His Majesty's Royal Navy, I'm a man of principle."

"So principled you want to prevent Bibles getting into people's hands."

"Did I say religiously principled?" Clarke laughed. "You can believe in your God, I'll believe in mine. And that would be …" He waited a second. "Me."

The sound of the wagon wheels stopped. Zims whinnied. The horse sensed trouble.

"Well, Clarke's god," Alec said, drawing out each word, "you know I can't submit to an idol."

Clarke guffawed and swung the branch. Alec ducked and felt the breeze over the top of his head.

Carried off-balance by missing his mark, Clarke grunted.

I muffed my chance to attack. "Get 'em when they're off-balanced," *Bradley always says. Gotta be quicker.*

Clarke steadied himself and swung the stick backhanded at waist height.

Alec jumped back in the nick of time. He took a long deep breath through his nose and released it—a trick Bradley had shared to steady the nerves.

Clarke tossed the branch aside.

"Hell with it," he said and pulled a knife from a sheath at his waist. This was no ordinary knife. This was a dagger of Goliathan proportions.

And I don't have a slingshot.

Alec's astonishment pushed the air from his lungs, and he repeated Bradley's breathing trick.

Clarke smiled. "More than one enemy's died by this blade," he said. "Another won't bother my conscience none."

Like murdering the Queen's English with a double negative. Ha!

Alec stumbled backwards. "You have a conscience?"

Clarke snarled and jabbed the knife at Alec's chest. Missing by an inch, he swiped horizontally. Alec felt a sting at his abdomen. Saw blood on his shirt.

Looks worse than it feels.

Clarke lunged again, trying to spear him like a piece of meat.

Alec slipped sideways.

As Clarke went at him again, Alec shoved him on the shoulder.

Alec put his hand to his wound. Sticky blood wetted his palm.

This is not good.

Clarke cursed, growled and swung again at an angle. This time the knife found more flesh, on Alec's upper right arm below his shoulder.

He yelped in pain.

Not good at all. Is this how I die, Lord?

He scanned the ground around him for something to defend himself. He grabbed a rock and threw the missile at Clarke but missed. Clarke chortled, a laugh of death obvious in his eyes.

Alec grabbed a fallen branch at his feet and held it in front of him. It was little more than a twig. He tossed the scrawny thing aside.

Clarke flipped his knife from one hand to the other and back again, enjoying his coming triumph. He was right-handed, for sure. Alec recalled Bradley mentioning that fighting lefthanded confused pugilists who weren't used to lefties. He took a left-handed stance and raised his fists like Meggs had done.

Clarke chuckled. "Lesson number one: don't bring your fists to a knife fight, boyo."

He took a step toward Alec as if deciding which limb to slice off first. Two more quick steps. Alec retreated—and tripped.

A tree root?

He staggered upright.

You are Jehovah Naheh, the God who smites, right?

"Say your dying prayer, boyo," Clarke said, moving in for the kill.

Out of the blue, Zims neighed like a war cry. He and Beau had pulled the wagon around in a circle behind Clarke. They were so close, Zims's whinny startled the sailor. Clarke spun around at the sound, and Alec seized the moment.

Moving in fast, he grabbed Clarke from behind and squeezed his biceps around the man's neck, his left elbow beneath the sailor's chin.

Clarke flailed with his arms, trying to stab Alec. Zims rose on his haunches, bracing against his harness, and the startled Brit dropped the knife. He pushed his full weight against Alec and they both fell to the ground on their backs, but Alec maintained his hold.

Clarke jabbed his elbows at Alec, striking him in the ribs near the stab wound. Alec winced but held on, tightening his grip. Clarke kicked backwards, booting Alec in the lower leg, but Alec was relentless. Clarke swore with words beyond Alec's vocabulary. Alec constricted his grasp.

With each passing second Clarke's thrashing lessened. Alec leveraged his feet against a rock in the ground and pushed himself to a sitting position.

Squeeze water from the stone. The voice was from heaven.

Finally, Clarke went completely limp and sagged to the ground.

Exhausted, yet thinking the sailor was possibly trying to fool him, Alec slackened his left arm enough so he could slap the man's face. No response.

His strength depleted, Alec barely managed to flip Clarke over on his stomach. The sting of pain reminded Alec of his knife wounds, but he grinned.

A warrior after all.

He looked at Zims and said, "You, my friend, deserve a treat. Both of you."

Zims's big brown eyes were intent on Alec's as if the animal understood the sentiment.

"Count it done."

Alec retrieved a rope from the back of the wagon, tied Clarke's arms behind him, hauled him to the back of the wagon, and bound him to the rear frame. Then he tied his feet together and strapped them to the side frame.

"Neat as a pin," he said.

Hopping up, he rummaged through the package Benjamin had given him and came out with two large carrots and two apples.

"Courtesy of Mrs. Burdick," he said.

Zims and Beau snorted their approval and made fast work of both.

Only now did Alec contemplate how to stem the bleeding. He pulled a handkerchief from a pocket, pressed the cloth against the wound over his stomach, and held it there for several minutes until the bleeding slowed.

Retrieving a rag from the wagon and using his teeth and left hand, he tied the material around his shoulder wound which he figured was superficial.

Simple enough. Now to dump Clarke.

The Brit groaned awake at the back of the wagon. Alec smiled and silently thanked the Lord—and Bradley—for his deliverance.

Before jumping onto the wagon, Alec walked around to face Clarke, who rattled off a string of expletives.

Alec took the blood-soaked handkerchief from his abdomen and stuffed the cloth into the sailor's mouth.

Donning a crooked smile, he said, "I've got no soap to wash out your mouth, so suck on that awhile." He dropped his smile and added, "Boyo."

Ten minutes later, they approached the Colonial Army barricade called 1st Parallel, which stretched in both directions horizontal to the highway.

Soldiers waited like a roadblock for Alec to reach them. When they asked his name and business, Alec showed them his prisoner, told them Lieutenant Commander Clarke was a spy captured along with four others in Boston, that he'd escaped, and Benjamin Burdick and others were searching for him.

The soldiers eyed Alec like he was an unlikely victor in a scrum with the scruffy veteran sailor. The younger one, whom Alec guessed was his own age, grinned and asked, "How about joining the fight?"

"I will. I will. But first I have a job ahead of me."

The younger soldier joined Alec atop the wagon and accompanied him around a bend to the Roxbury Meeting House, which served as the regiment's headquarters.

"You oughtta get a medal for this," he enthused.

Alec shrugged.

A sergeant there agreed to inform Benjamin and added, "We'll keep the prisoner here until he's transferred to jail."

Noticing Alec's blood-stained shirt, the sergeant motioned for him to wait. A minute later, another soldier entered the room carrying a satchel. A doctor.

"Fought a good fight, I hear," he said.

Alec smiled. "I guess."

Before long, Alec was mended and on his way.

CHAPTER 20

Today was a strange Sunday for the Aitken family. Not only was Janet away with the two youngest children, but Robert and his charges were unable to attend worship services because of the danger of being captured.

He had sequestered Jane, Robbie, and himself in their home.

First, he'd considered rising with the sun, hurrying off to the print shop, and making doubly sure the typeset was in order when Alec arrived with the supplies. But today was the Lord's Day, after all, and he commanded rest.

So they sat around the living room, Jane and Robbie playing Jackstraws and Robert reading the hefty *History of the Decline and Fall of the Roman Empire, Volume 1*. He wondered how on earth the author, Edward Gibbon, had the energy to write more than this tome. The Englishman deserved his place in Parliament, probably more so than the rest of the quarrelsome throng. He could probably talk circles around the bunch. At least reading this book made the notion appear so.

What fascinated Robert were Constantine, the first Christian, and Julian the Apostate, who had returned the empire to paganism. He wondered how King George would stack up against those two. The king considered himself pious, that was certain. But how could a practicing Christian treat his subjects with such disdain? Well, that was a question to be resolved between George and God.

After a while, the children tired of their game and Robert read them the story of Jonah and the whale.

When he reached the part where Jonah refused God's calling to warn Ninevah of its sins and instead fled to a sailing ship, Robbie interjected, "Da, if you decided not to print the Bibles, could we live like normal?"

Robert eyed his son. "Normal?"

"Yeah. Like Ralphy and Ezekiel. I'm sure they're at church right now, and afterward, their da's and ma's will let them go out and play."

"Ralphy's parents operate a haberdashery and Ezekiel's dad is in the lumber business. Or at least Ezekiel's dad was until he went off to war."

"Yeah, but they're normal, ordinary. We can't be normal 'cause you insist on printing those Bibles."

Robert laid the Bible on his lap and squeezed his lips together.

"Tell me, Robbie, what do ya think of King David?"

Robbie didn't hesitate. "He was fearsome."

"And how did he get there—to fearsomeness?"

Robbie put his thumb and forefinger to his chin like he was contemplating the origins of the universe. "Hmm."

"Put yourself in David's place when he was a boy not much older than you."

"A-huh."

"Well?"

Robbie turned his eyes to his sister for help, but Jane offered none.

He thought a bit longer, then, "He began when he said he'd fight Goliath?"

"Right. Was that offer normal?"

"No." Robbie's eyes went wide. "It was kinda crazy."

Robert chuckled. "Well, crazy if he didn't believe in God."

"Yeah!" Robbie said. "But he'd killed both a lion and a bear when protectin' his sheep, right?"

Robert nodded. "So?"

The boy harrumphed. "So he wasn't scared of no giant."

"Ha!" Jane interjected. "I wondered where you were heading."

Robbie looked again at his sister. "Whattaya mean?"

Jane raised a hand. "No, this is Da's moment."

Robert laughed. "No, Jane, go ahead. What do you see?"

"I see we don't achieve everything God wants from us unless we step out of the ordinary, reject fear, and go for greater challenges. Like Jonah. If he'd simply done what God wanted, that is, warn the people of Ninevah to repent, he would've avoided the whale altogether. God had a job for him to do."

I love this girl. So much like her mother.

His wife, Janet, was a wise woman, a lady who'd bravely accepted the challenge of moving across an ocean to a new world with two children in tow, who taught Sunday school, helped plan camp meetings each summer, and never turned down a challenging task.

And when he'd asked Janet about printing the Bibles despite the danger of prison, she'd replied, "How will we ever accomplish the thrilling, wild-hearted greatness God wants from each of us if we live lives of restraint and moderation?"

Robert had quickly written down the statement so he wouldn't forget its deep substance. He repeated her words to himself now.

The thrilling, wild-hearted greatness God wants from us.

Jane angled toward Robbie and put a hand on his arm.

"If I were to say to you, 'Little brother, I've got a jar of candy upstairs. You can have that, or—'" She dragged out the little two-letter word. "'—you can have a bucketful of one-dollar coins that could buy enough candy to fill an entire house. A lifetime of candy. But to get those coins you have to swim all the way across Lake Sansom. Now, you've never swum farther than across Schuylkill River. What do you do? Go for the big prize or settle for less?"

"A nice challenge," Robert said, looking at Jane, "but the test works better when the prize is something in God's bailiwick, a task that will please him."

He turned his attention to Robbie. "What say you, Son?"

The boy hesitated and with a sly look asked, "What sort of candy?"

CHAPTER 21

MONDAY MORNING
NOVEMBER 10, 1777
WICKFORD, MASSACHUSETTS

A cup of tea and warmed-up tin of baked beans in his belly, having removed feed bags from Zims and Beau and strapped their harnesses in place, Alec was ready for the day's journey.

From Roxbury, King's Highway went directly south, as a crow would fly the route, to Newport, Rhode Island, then hugged the ocean all the way to New York City.

But because Admiral Howe had established temporary Royal Naval headquarters in Newport, Alec had decided Sunday afternoon to "cut the corner." Instead of riding all the way south to Newport, then due west along the ocean, he'd turned off King's Highway at Plimoth. A young woman hanging clothes on a line outside a farmhouse told him of a road that skirted Newport Sound altogether.

"It's a jumble-gut road, and'll shake yer bones 'til you're silly," she said, "but it'll get ya where ya wanna go."

Alec laughed and accepted the challenge. The road went west a few miles at the most inward tip of the sound and from there south along the west side of the waterway.

The countryside was desolate. All the men off to war, perhaps? All the women indoors tending children and household chores? He wondered about the strength and endurance of these ladies.

Storefront placards and handmade road signs told him he passed through Warwick and eventually Bule, where he lit a campfire and bedded down for the night under the canopy of a mammoth oak tree in a pasture beside the road.

Alec had considered traveling through the evening, but thick clouds meant an ink-black night that would challenge even an eagle-eyed horse. He'd weighed the chances of a wheel hitting a rut deep enough to break a spoke and, urged by the referee in his mind, decided not to challenge the odds.

He'd pulled out his Bible, turned to Psalm 31, and read verse three: "For thou art my rock and my fortress; therefore for thy name's sake lead me and guide me."

Guide my steps, O Lord.

He reached into his pocket, pulled out *Learn French the Easy Way* and found "the Lord God,"—*le Seigneur notre Dieu*—and "Lord God Almighty"—*Seigneur Tout-Puissant*. He wished to hear Elsie's voice repeating these greetings, certain they would carry a flair befitting the Creator.

Alec sighed.

Here he was on Monday morning, greeted by a sunrise made for a king. That would be Louie, not George. *Ce qui sera sera.* Ha!

Perfect traveling weather.

Off they went, the brawny Zims and Beau never faltering under the load.

Since Zims had saved his life, Alec had showered ever more attention on him, depleting his supply of sugar cubes.

Nevertheless, he drove hard for Philadelphia, fighting the clock, alert to avoid enemy troops. He had to beat Admiral Howe's messenger to Philadelphia to warn Mr. Aitken.

By ten o'clock, he'd reached Wickford. By noon, he'd passed New London, or at least that's what the sign said over the empty wagon station. He stopped there to let the horses drink their fill at a public trough.

"Hey, there, young man." The friendly voice belonged to an older woman, probably in her sixties.

"Hello," he said. "Mind if my horses have a drink and rest a bit?"

"No. Where're you off to?"

Alec paused.

A secret mission. One that must remain a secret.

"South."

"That's vague."

Alec smiled stupidly. Better she think him dumb than hazard an answer.

"Yep."

He pulled himself back onto the wagon.

"Thank you, ma'am." He nodded and tipped his cap.

They could rest further along the roadway.

"No need to rush." The woman took a step closer, peering at the barrels. "Take your time. I'm not expecting any visitors. Not today."

"Nevertheless." He snapped the reins.

Once he was a mile down the road, he stopped the horses and hung grain bags on their necks.

He stepped out into a meadow to deliberate.

Why did that woman put him on edge? What about her, precisely, troubled him?

He hurried back to the wagon, removed the feed bags and settled again on his seat.

"Zims, Beau," he called, "Cha!"

The horses took off at a good clip, sending Alec back on his seat.

Samuel Adams was a confident man. His presence had filled Dock Square, and here his magnetism overwhelmed the de La Bordes' living room as Elsie looked upon the man who'd come to visit her father. Monsieur Adams had flashed a broad smile and taken her hand for a light kiss, as he had when they first met.

"Your young man?" he said. "Alec?"

"He left yesterday for Philadelphia," she said.

"Minus his printing supplies," Adams said with a frown.

"No, sir. No," she said. "With Papa's help and that of Mr. Burdick and others, they have the supplies."

"A story that must be told some day," Elsie's papa said. "I'd like to hear such a tale."

"Please," her father said and directed Adams to the window seats.

"I'll have Lisette prepare tea and biscuits," Elsie offered.

"Thank you, sweetheart," her papa said.

The next hour or so the two men sat in secretive discussion, voices low, with sporadic nods of agreement.

At one point Mr. Adams's blue eyes went bright with something more than satisfaction. *Délice*. Delight.

Her papa took that opportunity to pull a chair to the table and wave her to them. "Sit with us, *mon très cher*."

Like her mother, always asked by her papa to join the men's conversations. Elsie nodded demurely and took a seat with them.

"I was telling your father," Adams said, "America's Constitution shall never be interpreted to prevent her citizens, those who are peaceable, from keeping their own arms."

"Of course I agreed," her father added.

"And I pushed the idea forward—"

"Straight into my province," her father said.

Elsie filled the following moment's quiet. "By that you mean to arm the individual people, Papa?"

He nodded.

"I'm indebted to you, Charles. Personally as well as for the good of our country," Adams said.

"Oh?"

"Two years ago, King George promised his most gracious pardon," Adams held his arms high as if to welcome home a long-lost friend, "to all persons who would lay down their arms and return to peaceable duties."

"I recall," said Elsie's father.

"That is," Adams added, "with two exceptions: John Hancock and—"

"Samuel Adams?" Elsie guessed.

Adams nodded. "To the king, John's and my offenses were what he termed 'so grossly wicked' that we could not escape punishment, even from his, ahh, divinely inspired leniency."

"America's response?" Elsie's father asked.

"Disdain. His tender was a token of despair from a deceived and weak administration. The 'gracious offer' only spurred me on to prepare our country for the last and most solemn resort—war."

Elsie asked, "You believe King George a man without morals, Monsieur Adams?"

"I believe all men are entitled to just and true liberty, equal and impartial freedom." Adams's face was intense. His eyes seemed to see straight through Elsie. "By denying Americans this independence, this autonomy, King George is rejecting an immutable law of God and nature—a law the nations have borrowed from the Creator Himself.

"So, to answer your question, Mademoiselle de La Borde, I think the king deceives his subjects and himself as the Church of England's ambassador to God. I see no morals in the man."

Samuel Adams and her father could have been nurtured in the same womb.

Her father spoke up, his voice firm, emotional. "I've told Samuel any American who wants arms will have arms, and Monsieur Beaumarchais and I will not profiteer from them."

"If only we had such assurances for our army for food and clothing," Adams said. "Our men are woefully ill-fed and wretchedly clothed, not to mention poorly paid."

Elsie's papa shrugged. "I wish I could do more about that. But we're shipping what we can."

"I know, my friend." Adams looked out the window, perhaps gauging the time, and said, "Thank you for your time, your assurances—and, yes, I am one of those who would like personal arms when the time comes—and your continued friendship with our government. I'm afraid it's time I take my leave."

Adams stood, bowed to Elsie, and extended a hand to her father.

Elsie's papa took Adams's hand and led him to the door.

As he opened the door, Adams caught Elsie's eye. "I'll be praying for Alec and his mission. There's no nobler cause than his, and especially during this Revolution."

His words stirred something in Elsie's breast, and she smiled with thanksgiving.

She, too, was in prayer—hourly.

CHAPTER 22

General William Howe cursed. Roused from bed by Aide de Camp Lieutenant Brown at an unsavory hour, he had to leave Philadelphia for who knew how long. The blasted Americans continued to hold on to that tiny plot of land on the Delaware River from which they were blasting his brother's ships and preventing them from delivering supplies to William's troops.

His soldiers' daily ration included one-and-a-half pounds of bread, a pound of beef or a half-pound of pork, a quarter pint of peas or an ounce of rice, an ounce of butter, and one-and-a-half gills of rum.

But such indulgence was in peril. His supply was running dangerously low.

Howe fingered an ear, brushed the seeds of sleep from his eyes, looked out a window, and tried to focus on the world outside. Bad idea. The inky blackness only confirmed he'd prefer to remain in the comfort of the feather bed and down comforter.

This river battle was the last thing he needed. He'd suffered a cascade of ill news. After the disastrous British defeat at Saratoga came a Pennsylvania campaign that had exposed General Burgoyne's troops in upper New York, then Howe had failed to destroy Washington's shabby bunch of renegades.

Next came the failure to capture even a remnant of the Continental Congress. Now his new nemesis, the Biblio-Ghost. All this to boot, his crucial supply line was in jeopardy.

Another blow to his prestige was unacceptable. Blast! He was returning to England next spring or summer, and his homecoming would be one of celebrated hero. London's arms would be open wide. The king's court would be festooned. Knighted, General William Howe would be ensconced in his seat in Parliament, a tidy fortune at his fingertips.

This was his dream, soon to be his reality.

"Sir?" Brown's annoying and urgent voice bristled at him.

"What?!" he bellowed.

A hesitation followed, then, "Your horse is saddled, a regiment at the ready."

Minutes later, Howe and his escort, one hundred soldiers, set off toward the Delaware River. He'd left a message for Cutthroat to continue his search for the Ghost in his absence.

Howe glanced over his shoulder. Behind him was a contingent of the world's most skilled, experienced soldiers, their long blood-red coats disarming enemies the world over—the kind of fright that would gladden even Longshanks.

Here in the colonies? Twenty-two thousand strong, including skilled German, Swedish and Scottish recruits. And aligned with, what, another twenty thousand Loyalists, that should be enough to beat back any rebellion, let alone the scruffy bunch holed up on the Delaware.

The idea of all this agitated Howe. Not only was the enemy shabby, but they were also belligerent and had no reverence for the Crown, no respect for the king's soldiers, no regard for the rule of war or British law. Totally without veneration.

He recalled the Boston Massacre seven years earlier. Accounts he'd read gave credence to the British soldiers firing on the crowd of commoners. They were goaded by the jeering challenge, "Come on you rascals, you bloody backs, you lobster scoundrels, fire if you dare."

What did the Americans expect? A turn of the cheek? Such a response would have only encouraged further badgering.

A sailor would blush at the words that escaped his lips.

Alec had finally seen the end of a cold drizzle that had fallen from a steely sky and slowly drenched him and the horses. He'd tugged his cap down on his forehead, taken a canvas off the rough iron, and draped the covering over his shoulders and head. The protection had helped, but though the rain had ended, his legs were soaked.

He shivered and dreamed of a blazing campfire, a warm chair before a fireplace, a steaming bowl of Mrs. Aitken's chicken soup. He hunkered down to his reveries.

Elsie permeated his musings. The design of a water-powered printing press filled his deliberations. He envisioned the gears, horizontal connecting to vertical, hinged to a lateral, waist-high press. In his vision the waterworks was so powerful the gears had to be slowed some way. More hands would help, but would they be enough?

And who would build the machinery? Who *could*? The rough iron behind him came to mind. Mr. Bradford! He could build anything, and he had the muscle to hammer a shank of molten iron into whatever shape you dreamed up. Gears? Cams? Lever arms? Connecting rods? No problem. And if he didn't have enough iron, Alec recalled being told a Philadelphia grist mill's gears were made of oak and when a tooth broke, they simply knocked out and replaced the broken appendage.

Alec was elated at the thought. He came out of his daydream in time to notice a sign.

They were in Connecticut. They'd traveled through Seabrook and Guilford, past Brandford and were now, the sign announced, in Newhaven. Ever since a few rough goings Sunday and Monday morning, Zims' and Beau's strides were back in sync. Two peas in a pod, them.

Had they been bothered by the rain? No. The drizzle seemed to invigorate them. Perhaps horses, too, had visions—theirs being of a warm bed of straw in a cozy barn. Ha!

Alec thought of stopping to light a fire and dry off, but wondered if he could risk losing the time. Indeed, how at risk was he at this moment?

He had no idea who was in control of Connecticut. The Continental Army or the Redcoats? The war was so fluid you'd have to be omniscient to know the particulars.

"Cha!" Alec snapped the reins to push the horses into a gallop. His stomach was grumbling and he wanted a bit of shelter, if only long enough to eat.

A crack sounded behind him. A gunshot?

Alec turned to look. A troop of British horsemen approached, not more than twenty yards away.

Oh-oh.

"Yo there," one soldier hollered against the din of the rain. "Halt!"

Alec blew out a long breath and pulled back on the reins. The heavy load squeaked. He prayed these men weren't on the lookout for him.

The soldier at the front—a colonel by a look at his bars and the hat on his head—rode to him while the others stopped at the rear of the wagon.

"The woman at the New London wagon station told us we'd find you. Looked like you had a large supply of paper.

You bound for a newspaper spouting propaganda against the Crown, fella? Like *The Connecticut Courant*, maybe?

Alec thought quickly.

Work, brain. Work.

"No, sir. *Rivington's New York Gazetteer*." He'd heard about James Rivington being the Royal Printer of New York with a newspaper located on Wall Street.

The soldier was caught short by the remark, thought about Alec's response, and asked, "So why not get your supplies delivered at the New York docks?"

Alec stammered, not ready for that inquiry.

"Off the wagon," the officer demanded, pointing a pistol at Alec's chest, and cocking the lock.

Alec nodded, tossed aside his covering and hopped down, both boots on the ground. Drenched, he considered his options. He had no alternative but prayer.

"Let's have your bill of lading, boy."

Alec reached over the sideboard into the wagon and rummaged through his canvas luggage. The document would reveal Mr. Aitken's name. If the colonel hailed from Newport, Admiral Howe's headquarters, he surely was aware the supply was meant for illegal Bible-printing.

Here is where faith meets fact, where dreams go awry, where ...

As Alec pretended to search for the paperwork, a shot rang out from the southern forest. He whirled. The musket ball had struck the colonel in the chest. A look of shock filled the soldier's face as he stared at the hole in his bosom, at the blood spurting out of his body, focused incredulous eyes in the direction of the gunshot, dropped his pistol, slumped forward and fell headfirst off his horse.

A cheer rose from the forest. "Liberty or death!"

Alec dove under the wagon and rolled to the other side, up against the right rear wheel as salvos of musket balls resounded. Zims and Beau spooked and started forward. For the first time Alec thanked God for the wagon's heavy load because the horses took a couple of seconds to establish forward momentum. The wheel nudged his shoulder and he bolted out of the way. The wheel caught the fabric of his pants, and Alec fell into a watery ditch.

From his stomach, Alec watched as the British soldiers, now leaderless, charged at their enemies. But who were those adversaries?

Alec rose on his knees, watched his wagon pull away, and spotted a number of rifles behind trees that bracketed the road. Another volley of musket balls sounded, smoke rose from the barrels of the rifles and three of the Redcoats fell from their horses. Another volley sent the last three to the ground.

Again the shout rose up: "Liberty or death!"

A man leaped into the middle of the road in front of the runaway horses, raised his arms high and hollered, "Whoa!"

Zims and Beau stopped the load in short order.

Alec rose to his feet, looked heavenward, and whispered, "How can I continue doubting you?"

Two dozen militiamen hustled around the fallen Redcoats, stripping them of their arms and bullet pouches. Others gathered the British horses. A young man about Alec's age ambled toward him like he was out for a Sunday stroll.

"Hi ya," he said. "Don't mind our showing up and spoiling your party, do ya?"

Alec couldn't control the laugh that erupted, deepened by his relief. Moments ago he'd faced prison, even death. Now he was free to go.

"Who are you, anyhow?" he asked.

"We're Cook's Regiment of Militia. And I'm Joseph Stafford." The fellow offered his hand. "Call me Joey."

Alec shook his hand and introduced himself.

"We all live in or around Wallingford, a ways north of here," Joey said and chortled. "A shorter ways for some of us now that we've got horses."

Alec laughed with him.

"Yeah," Joey said. "We fought in the Saratoga Campaign. About a month ago, Burgoyne surrendered, but General Gates didn't disband us until a couple days ago."

"Well, you saved my skin."

"How so?"

Alec proceeded to tell Joey and the others about his mission.

"So, you're headed to Philadelphia," Joey said.

"Yep."

"I've got a friend in Philadelphia."

"Really? Who's that?"

"Alice Alfond. Her parents are Bruce and Carliene Alfond."

"Ahh." Alec didn't know the Alfonds, but was this a coincidental encounter?

"I haven't seen Alice since they moved away from Wallingford."

"Oh?"

"A year ago. I'd like to see her again."

Alec nodded.

"When your life comes this close to ending ..." Joey held his thumb and forefinger an inch apart "... you start mulling over what you'll miss if you die."

"I'm sure."

"I'd miss Alice. I've missed her since the day they left."

"What about your family here?"

"I have none. Dad's dead—died in the Battle of Bunker Hill. Mom's dead—died of a strange fever. Got an uncle, but no brothers or sisters."

"I'm sorry."

"Not your fault."

"Still—"

Joey scratched the back of his neck and peered at Alec. "Mind company?"

Company? No problem.

203

Alec took the measure of the young man. Unruly red hair tried to escape his cap at all angles. Freckles covered his cheeks. His blue eyes had a shine to them, perhaps dreaming of Alice. He was as white as a sheet, maybe whiter. The sun sure must wreak havoc with his skin.

"I'd love to have a friend come along," Alec said.

Joey raised his index finger and took in his companions. "Fellas, I'm going with Alec here. Please give my goodbyes to Mr. Keene at the farm where I work. Worked, I should say. I may or may not return." He turned to Alec and lowered his voice. "That all depends on Alice."

"Wait a minute," said a militiaman whose full beard covered a weatherworn face. He handed Alec a rifle. "Better take Charlie here with you."

"Charlie?"

"She's a Charleville Model 1766, courtesy of our French friends. There's two of you. Two weapons seems right."

Alec hefted the rifle, noticing the weapon was slick with water. Only then was he reminded his clothes were sopping wet. But at least he was alive.

CHAPTER 23

A knock at the rear door startled Robert Aitken. He was so on edge. Increasingly so. He snuck a look out his second-floor bedroom window to spot who was there.

Below, Douglas Bradford appeared to be trying to shrink his massive presence. As if narrowing his thick shoulders would turn the trick. Robert couldn't resist chuckling to himself. The blacksmith was probably visible from across the river, if anyone was keeping watch on the house.

Douglas was a close friend and had done work for Robert at his printing shop. He was one of a handful of confidants who knew where Robert had moved the press.

Must be important for him to risk a visit.

Hushed voices sounded downstairs. Jane had opened the door.

Douglas disappeared from sight, his substantial bulk barely squeezing through the door.

Robert hurried down the stairs, almost tripping over a miniature horse-drawn wagon fashioned from straw and wood, one of Robbie's favorite toys four years ago or so.

"Douglas," Robert acknowledged, "everything all right?"

Douglas removed his cap and, extending an index finger, winked at Robert. He handed Jane two pieces of hard candy, saying, "A reminder of when you first arrived, and I could win your smile with one of these."

"You still can." Jane beamed.

"She inherited the famous Scottish sweet tooth," Robert said.

Douglas grinned, then his countenance turned serious.

"You may have to reconsider your decision to remain here in the city," he said.

Robert gulped air. "Go on."

"You're aware Howe has his troops searching for the illegal printer of Bibles."

Robert nodded.

"They're now knocking on the doors of merchants or businesses that provide products related to printing. Book stores. Paper goods. Mercantile. They bullied their way into my barn late yesterday afternoon. That is, they acted like bullies—until they laid eyes on me." Douglas chuckled and Robert joined him, imagining the expressions on the soldiers' faces when they appraised the giant before them.

"What did they say?" Robert asked.

"First, they offered the carrot—the handsome reward they've put on your head. Then the stick—if they discover someone knows your identity after denying so, they'll be slammed in prison. Maybe worse."

"Worse than prison," Robert repeated. He considered turning himself in and calling off the whole idea of printing Bibles.

No one should be imprisoned for protecting me.

"But." Douglas's husky voice made the three-letter word sound like an oratory from heaven or the Mount of Olives. "We who you do business with, Robert ... we all, to a person, refuse to submit to these henchmen. I'd go to the gallows before standing in the way of God's Word being spread to our soldiers and families."

"It's not that there are *no* Bibles out there," Robert offered, feeling somehow smaller saying so.

"Paltry compared to the need." Douglas's eyes bore down on Robert. "A trifling number. My brother, you must—must—proceed. But—" There was that three-letter proclamation again—"I advise you to reconsider keeping your press here in Philadelphia. Reflect on a hidden, less precarious site."

"Considered and declined," Robert said. "Even if we could load the entirety on a wagon and ride out in the dead of night, with all the soldiers watching the streets we'd be so obvious, so transparent as to invite our capture. Besides, every page has been typeset, the plates clamped and stabilized and stacked in place where we are. Moving all those type plates right now is, well, not a consideration."

"Even with a lot of helping hands?"

"Helping hands can move them, but ..." he shook his head, "too risky."

Douglas balled a massive fist and rested his chin on its bulk.

"They still don't know my name, right?" Robert said.

"No. To them you're the Ghost."

"Ghost? Ha. I only wish."

"But, despite all us businessmen remaining mum, someone in the city may well give you up. I don't know who or when. But someone and probably soon. There's a Loyalist behind every bush, and the soldiers are bound to find one who knows your identity."

"Then they'll have to find me."

"Changing houses hasn't made you invisible. I noticed you hurry out of your place down Market Street to the church the other day."

"Oh?"

"Yes. And answer this: Are you named in the *Journals of Congress* on that particular day you gentlemen requested financing to publish the Bibles?"

Robert nodded. "Yes."

"You suppose they haven't yet found any copies of the *Records* or the *Journals*?"

"I don't know. Maybe they haven't thought to read through them. They interrogated William White, Patrick Allison, and William Marshall. If they'd learned my name from them, we'd know by now."

Douglas crossed his arms over his chest.

"Actually," Robert said, "you yourself must be careful. You've stayed in Philadelphia only to spy for Colonel Bradford, right?"

"Hey, he's my cousin. Figured since I can't shoot worth a darn, I could put my ears to better use than a rifle."

Robert laughed, but he knew the spying business was a deadly affair. This was wartime, not the spy game played by school children.

Alec guessed that over the next several hours, as they passed through Stanford and Fairfield, he and Joey learned more about each other than most people do in a year.

Alec shared why they needed to make haste, how he hoped Admiral Howe's messengers by land and sea had been waylaid or stopped completely, maybe caught in a skirmish or battle, maybe captured. And he told how the Bibles Mr. Aitken and he wanted to print were like lifeblood to the recipients. Spiritual health, physical healing, all one's needs and questions answered and encompassed in the pages of Scripture. They sure changed Alec's sorry self once he read them, believed them, and tried his best to live by them.

As they rode along, Joey told Alec about his boyhood, the tough times on his parents' farm, helping his father with chores in the field and his ma milking their two cows. The family struggled but got by. The war came and his father died. Illness came and ma died. His story mirrored what Alec had lived an ocean away.

Two orphans now. Alec felt like he had a good friend and brother—all at once.

They talked about girls. Oh, yeah. Elsie and Alice. And the girls' families, the de La Bordes and the Alfonds. Elsie's wealthy French father, Charles—Alice's rock-solid mercantile-owning American parents, Bruce and Carliene. Parents all wanting the best for their daughters—the finest lives, highest aspirations, and worthiest husbands.

Joey appeared as smitten with Alice as Alec was with Elsie. There was one difference—Alec thought Monsieur de La Borde's assessment of Alec was positive. Joey was unsure at best, worried at worst, about the Alfonds' regard for him.

Alec and Joey wondered aloud how the young women in their lives would get along.

"Like best friends," Joey guessed.

Then Alec asked the crucial question: Was Joey a Christian? So much of their relationship hinged on his answer, Alec had hesitated to ask.

Joey looked him directly in the eye, thought over his response and said, "Am I a believer? Let me tell you about my believing. I lost two close friends at Saratoga."

Alec cringed at the revelation.

"Mikey took one in the chest, and I held him in my arms. And he was frantic. He was scared. His eyes were huge and dark and fearful and tears poured out. He knew he was dyin', and he didn't know what would happen. When he took his last breath, his eyes pleaded for me to do somethin'. Me! What could I do?"

A tear worked its way down Joey's cheek and his face contorted a bit more with each disclosure.

"Joey, I'm sorry."

Joey shook off the comment, tried to regain his composure, and went on, "Two days later, Frankie, my best pal in the whole wide world, took a slug in the belly. I held him in my arms like Mikey. But Frankie? He was calm. He was fearless. His eyes were huge, too, but with brightness, with light, as if he were expecting somethin' beautiful, somethin' extraordinary. Remarkable even. And when he took his last breath, he looked me keen in the eyes like he was tryin' to grab me by the collar and, and—" Tears poured down now. "—and he said, 'I see Jesus!'"

Alec pulled the horses to a halt as a young couple in a carriage passed by going the other direction.

"Wow, Joey."

Right, Alec, some theologian you *are.* "Wow, Joey?"

Joey swiped at his wet cheeks. "Yeah, and that's when I saw Jesus, too. Almost like he was right there standin' over us. Almost like I could touch his cloak. Almost—"

Joey's voice faded away.

"But Jesus was just a vision? Imaginary?"

"Not imaginary, but in a different form than you'n me." Joey's eyes were wide with the memory, and he grinned almost mystically. "That's when I became a believer."

As they approached New York City, Alec and Joey faced a decision.

"This is where things get risky," Alec said. "I was scared enough going north to Boston with an empty load. Now?" He let the inference fade.

They shared looks of concern, then Joey brightened and snapped his fingers. "There's another way," he said.

"Oh?"

"Turn to the right up ahead."

A hand-written sign with an arrow told them Fort Washington lay in that direction.

"But the Brits took over Fort Washington a year ago," Alec complained.

"Right," Joey said, "a year ago next week, to be exact. But I know someone."

"You know someone?"

"Peter Bourdette. But you can never ever reveal his name."

"Who is he?"

"His dad, Stephen, ran the ferry from Fort Washington on this side of the Hudson River to Burdett's Landing by Fort Lee on the New Jersey side. Mr. Bourdette gave General Washington use of his house for his headquarters back before the Brits stormed in. Actually, they were a few thousand Hessians." He spit out the word. "Hired killers."

"But the Hessians *did* storm in, so ...?" Alec questioned.

"Mr. Bourdette's off to war with Washington, I think. But Peter has a secret barge."

Alec leaned in toward his friend. "And?"

"And young Peter possesses the guts of a warrior. The week before the Redcoats drove Washington out, Peter rowed back and forth across the river, giving Washington information on British troop movements."

"And ..." Alec continued to push.

"Well, General Howe controls the Hudson, but not one hundred percent of it. If we can connect with Peter, he'll surely get us across."

"You know where they live."

"About a mile south of the landing in an old brick house."

"So our plan is to cross the Hudson south of Fort Washington. Then what?" Alec asked.

"We ride south. By noon tomorrow we could reach Guttenberg, New Jersey. From there we go over the Hackensack River at New Bridge Landing and the Passaic River where Acquacanonk Bridge used to be before the Redcoats tore her down."

"Brilliant."

"That's me. That's what I call myself."

Alec guffawed and slapped Joey on the shoulder. "Let's go!"

The journey was sluggish. Like molasses.

Only a sliver of moon lit the way. Alec lamented the darkness.

"But the dark is what'll protect us when we get to the Bourdettes'," Joey reasoned.

More and more as the two rode on, Alec confirmed their meeting had surpassed fortuitous. Someone else's hand had guided their steps, starting before Alec loaded up in Boston and Cook's Militia marched out of Saratoga.

At one point, they stopped on a pasture alongside the road. They shared a couple of pieces of bread, cheese, a carrot, an apple, and water.

Zims and Beau scarfed down bags of grain, and they were off again.

Sometime around midnight, Joey urgently pointed to their left and said, "There. There!"

The tiny bit of moonlight lit a puff of chimney smoke. A narrow path, barely wide enough for the wagon to pass through, led them to a clearing. The silhouette of a home sat in the middle of the meadow.

"The Hudson's directly behind the house," Joey said.

They jumped off the wagon.

"Better let me talk," Joey said.

"Okay."

They hustled along a walkway to the house.

Joey knocked on the door. No answer. He knocked louder and waited.

Alec heard noise inside. A voice. A second voice. Scuffling.

And the door opened wide. A tall, skinny man, his thinning gray hair in disarray, stood before them, aiming a rifle at Joey's head.

"Oh!" Joey howled.

"Your business?" the man demanded.

"Mr. Bourdette?" Joey asked.

A young fellow appeared behind the older man and held a lantern high, its dim light exposing Joey and Alec.

"Étienne. Who's asking?" The man looked directly at Joey and Alec, then beyond them toward the horses and wagon.

Before Joey could answer, the young man called out, "Joey!"

Joey breathed a sigh of relief and responded, "Peter."

"Grampa, this is my friend, the one who shared with me the best beef jerky I ever tasted. Joey …" he hesitated.

"Stafford," Joey finished. "From Wallingford, Connecticut, Mr. Bourdette. From Cook's Militia."

Étienne's eyes widened, and he flashed a furtive look toward the road.

"Come, come," he said, hurrying them inside.

Once all were in the house, Étienne closed the door.

"You realize the time?" he asked.

"I'm sorry, but it's crucial you help us," Joey said. He turned to Alec. "Tell them."

Alec recapped a short version of his story and the need to get his supplies past the British troops to Philadelphia.

Étienne harrumphed. "Good luck with that."

"I can get them across the Hudson, Grampa," Peter said, "on the little barge."

Étienne slowly shook his head. "I don't know, Peter."

"How little?" Alec asked.

"More like a large float, with fifty-gallon barrels along the edges for buoyancy. Big enough for your horses and wagon and the *four* of us—no more." Peter hesitated. "The tide's probably going out right now. That'll help 'cause we sure want to be south of Fort Lee.

"As a matter of fact," he added, "the guards have started midnight rounds along this side of the river."

"We'd better get crackin' or you'll get captured before

you board the float," Étienne said.

"We?"

"You're not doing this without my help." His voice indicated argument was futile. "Peter, you take the canoe across to hitch the pull rope and I'll help these boys load the barge. By the time you get back with the rope, we should be ready to go."

"Right, Grampa." Peter chuckled.

Alec noticed the young man's freckled face matched that of his grandfather.

"Cut from the same cloth," Mrs. Aitken would say. Like Mr. Aitken and Jane.

CHAPTER 24

Within minutes both the Bourdettes were fully dressed, their muskets loaded.

Lifting a lantern before him, Peter ran ahead while Étienne held another lantern high and led Alec, Joey, and the horses around the house and down a path to the Hudson River. Rays of moonlight revealed swift-flowing water.

The river's speed took Alec's breath away, and he wondered about the wisdom of the endeavor. In daylight, this crossing would appear precarious.

He prayed Peter, in his canoe, could navigate the river. But the young man was out of sight, so—

"Hurry, boys," Étienne encouraged, holding firmly to Zims's harness as they approached the riverbank.

No time to consider or debate. Only time to pray.

Étienne touched a long stick to the flame in his lantern and lit a hurricane lamp atop a long post at the corner of a dock.

The barge was tied tight to the wharf which obviously floated up and down with the tide. At this moment Alec guessed six inches separated the barge and the parallel dock. They'd take the horses and wagon onto the dock and cross onto the barge for the trip over the river. A false step and they might lose the entire load. Mr. Aitken's ink and paper, the yard goods and the rough iron. Everything.

Alec dropped down off the wagon. Joey did the same.

"Perhaps we should take the load off the wagon," Alec suggested. "Make two trips, one with the horses and wagon, another with the load."

Silence ensued as they considered the idea.

Finally, Étienne said, "Consider the time unloading, going over and back, then reloading, then over and loading again. Besides the tide ebbing out, the time constraint's a big problem. Regardless if the British patrol spots you, by the time you start the second trip across, daylight will be upon us and we'll all be dead in the water—literally."

Alec bowed his head. Étienne understood what he was doing and joined him, hand on shoulder. Joey pulled close and they prayed.

Let your heart be the arbiter. Let your heart ...

"We go now," Alec blurted out. "If God is with us what tide can be against us?"

"Right, son," Étienne said with a broad smile.

They took positions, Alec by the horses, at their left, Étienne at the right-front of the wagon. The light from his lantern prevented the darkness from overwhelming the group.

With caution, Alec tugged on Zims's cheek-piece, and Zims and Beau stepped toward the dock. Then another step, then another. At length, they were on the dock. An agonizing minute later, the front wagon wheels rolled on. Finally, the horses took their first precarious strides onto the barge. The barge swayed with their weight. They stopped—skittish, panicky. Alec wobbled, widened his stance, and placed his hands on Zims's and Beau's noses, trying to calm them.

"There, there, boys," he said. "Everything's all right."

He waited several long seconds for the horses to grow accustomed to the fluid motion. Then, he pulled again on the nose band. Zims resisted. Alec insisted. Zims relented, and he and Beau took their second steps onto the barge, which seemed to sway less this time. The heavier weight helped quiet the barge's motion.

Another slow step and another and a third, and ultimately the front wagon wheel was at the precipice of the dock. Those crucial six inches still separated the dock and the barge.

Alec gulped a deep gutful of air and said to Étienne, "On the count of three you pull Beau and I tug on Zims. Lightly."

Étienne nodded an affirmative.

Alec checked with Joey. "Ready," he said.

"One, two, three—"

The three did their jobs. Zims and Beau pulled the wagon forward, and the front wheels both clicked as they boarded the barge. Again the barge rocked precariously, but Alec was better prepared this time.

"Shh, shh," he said and scratched behind Zims's left ear. "You're doing good." Zims whinnied and Beau followed suit.

"We've got to strap these horses to the barge," Étienne said. He looked fretfully toward the shoreline, probably concerned about the British patrol. "A rope fastened to each side will help stabilize them in the middle."

Alec nodded.

Étienne pulled two long, thick ropes out of nowhere and handed one to Alec. They went about tying their ropes, one end to a metal loop near the front corners of the float, the other end tethered to the terrets, the metal loops on the horses' breast collars.

"Should we do the same to the wagon?" The question came from Joey, who stood behind Alec.

Alec looked toward Étienne for an answer.

Seconds later the elder Bourdette handed a rope to Joey. "You take this side, I'll take the other, and you, Alec, stay here and keep the horses calm as possible."

Alec nodded and while the others were fastening their ropes to the barge and rear of the wagon, he looked eagerly out into the river for a sign of Peter.

There was none. Each second that clicked by seemed like ten.

Once the ropes were tied, Joey noted Beau's heavier weight tilting the barge to the north, so they moved some of the iron to the left on the wagon.

All the while, Alec prayed for Peter's safety and peered into the darkness. Still no sign.

Alec breathed out and sucked in a chest full of cold November air.

Is Peter in danger? In distress? Has he been captured?

He squeezed his eyes tight, unable to muster any single verse other than the totality of Scripture, all declaring God watches over the faithful.

He opened his eyes and there a few yards away, the bow of a canoe was cutting through the Hudson waters.

"Hey, there," came a low call. "You guys ready?"

Alec turned to look behind him. Joey gave him the thumbs-up. On the other side of the wagon, Étienne said, "By the time you're out of the canoe we'll be untied at the dock. You got the pole?"

"Two poles, actually. One for you, one for me. It's rough out there."

Peter reached the barge and handed the thick rope to Alec. "This is attached to a pulley on the other side. We pull, we pole, and we get there eventually. But don't—that is, do not—lose hold of this rope or we're doomed."

Étienne came to Alec's side, grabbed hold of the rope, and chuckled. "Peter oversimplifies sometimes. We put this rope through a loop at the front of the barge so she won't blow in the wind. But do hold tight and tug with all your strength. This is a heavy load indeed."

Peter paddled past them, tethered the canoe to the rear of the barge, and moments later was on the barge with them.

He handed a long pole to his grandfather and grasped a second pole in his own hands.

"So Joey and I will do the pulling?" Alec asked.

"Better you than Grampa and me," Peter said with a laugh.

A flickering light caught Alec's eye.

"Uh-oh," he exhaled and pointed toward the house.

A light bobbed and moved.

"The patrol," Peter said with a tinge of anxiety. He hustled back onto the dock, removed the lantern from the pole and shut off the oil supply.

"Hurry up," Étienne urged.

As Alec and Joey rushed to the front of the barge Peter raced back and took the rope from Étienne.

"Push off," Étienne said, blowing out his own lantern, and Peter heaved his weight into thrusting the pole against the dock.

Ever so slowly at first, the barge shifted. Peter again drove the pole into the side of the wharf and shoved. The barge stirred. Its wooden flooring creaked. Then the current took hold with such force the rope nearly escaped Alec's hands.

With a gasp, he clutched the line. The rope filled his palms. Joey was at his side.

"With a heave?" Alec asked.

"With a heave."

"Okay, heave!" As soon as the word left his lips, Alec realized he spoke too loudly.

Voices from through the woods exclaimed something unintelligible.

"Uh-oh," Joey wheezed.

"Hurry, boys," Étienne whispered, and out of the corner of Alec's eye he spotted the older man putting his weight into his pole.

Alec lowered his voice. "Heave … Heave … Heave."

With each pull, they propelled the vessel further into the middle of the river.

"You, there!" a voice called from the shoreline.

"Don't answer," Étienne warned in a low tone.

"Stop or we shoot!" The declaration was uncompromising.

"Respond or beware!" A rigid demand. Must be a lieutenant, Alec thought. A lieutenant full of himself and his power.

"Heave … Heave," Alec whispered.

"I'm heaving," Joey said with a hint of exasperation.

"I know. Heave."

A gunshot rang out and Alec cringed. There was no way to know where the slug went, but apparently astray, missing them and the horses.

"How far across the river?" Alec asked, hoping Étienne could hear him.

"Shh. Just pull!" was the response.

Incoherent shouts dissipated with the distance they'd put between them and the dock.

Another gunshot and Alec could swear he heard a *plunk* sound in the water to his left. Imagination? The river was splashing against the righthand side of the barge, its noise adding to Alec's anxiety.

A salvo of gunshots followed. All apparently missed their mark, and Alec thought this barge was a sizeable target compared to the dart boards he was used to. They must be out of range for the Redcoats' rifles.

Ha!

"Heave … Heave."

Alec's palms were raw, maybe bleeding. Good thing he couldn't see well enough to find out.

He pulled a handkerchief from a pocket and wrapped the fabric around the rope. Joey did the same.

"I'd like to shoot back at the varmints," Joey said.

"Another time. Heave ... Heave."

Several seconds elapsed.

"Halfway, boys," Peter announced. Another gunshot rang out, and he grunted in pain.

Startled, Alec glanced behind him and saw the faint silhouette of the young man disappear.

A splash followed and Alec sprang away toward the back of the barge.

"Help!" Peter called. "I'm ..." a second or more elapsed "... overboard!"

Alec swiftly untied the right-rear rope attached to the wagon.

Étienne appeared at his side, welcomed by another barrage of bullets. A couple hit the back of the barge. The horses whinnied and moved about uneasily and the wagon tipped sideways several inches, nudging Alec's hip as he heaved the rope in the direction he guessed Peter must be.

Oh, no, my aim was off.

But he managed to call, "Rope's coming your way," and pray, "O, Lord. O, Lord. O, Lord."

"Got it!" Peter gurgled. "I got it."

Alec had only a split second to wonder how an ill-fated toss could go aright when Étienne ordered, "Pull."

Alec joined him in hauling Peter toward them, one giant reach of rope at a time. The tide was forceful against them, but Peter was moaning and grunting, apparently pulling himself toward the barge as well.

Another volley of gunshots. Alec heard none land.

Yes!

His heart pounding against his chest from exertion, Alec allowed a moment to encourage himself with the importance of this task.

"Here!" Étienne exclaimed. He had knelt down and was reaching over the side of the barge. "Grab me."

A glint of moonshine off the river revealed Peter lifting an arm out of the water, his hand seizing Étienne's.

The older man groaned. Alec leaned down and grabbed Peter's other hand and they both pulled him up and onto the barge, one leg at a time.

Drenched, Peter flopped onto the boards, gasping for breath.

"Where were you shot?" Étienne asked.

Peter touched his upper arm and grimaced. "A flesh wound, Grampa. Ain't nothin'. Patchin' me up can wait."

The wagon shifted again, edging toward the side of the float. Alec grabbed and retied the rope to the wagon.

"Some help here!" Joey called.

Alec glanced down at Peter, who managed, "You'd better get up there, or we could all be lost still."

Étienne also left Peter's side. "I'll man the pole but necessarily on this side of the barge to control against the tide."

"Yeah, my pole's out there somewhere." Peter pointed behind them into the darkness and struggled to his knees. "I'll help with the rope."

Alec shook his head at the young man's doggedness.

Moments later, Alec was beside Joey. Several seconds elapsed before Peter joined them.

"Heave ... Heave," Alec said.

Seconds passed by, then minutes as Alec and the others fought through utter fatigue. At last, exhausted, they reached a dock on the western shore of the Hudson. The pier was covered with evergreen tree branches.

Peter jumped from the barge to the wharf with surprising vigor. Alec and Joey joined him, and they all hauled the branches off to the side.

"I'm exhausted," Joey said.

"I'm energized." Alec laughed. "Naw. I'm exhausted,

too."

"I'm pulverized," Peter said with a chuckle.

"You're all crazy." Étienne shook his head, a smile fixed wide on his face. "And you can't stand around waiting for a dose of get-up-and-go. You gotta be gone before those troops get back to Fort Washington and ferry over to Burdett's Landing on this side."

"Will you be able to go back to your home?" Alec asked.

"Let us worry about that," Étienne said.

"Just finish the race," Peter exhorted.

They hurried to untie all the ropes and unload Zims and Beau and the wagon onto the dock and ride up a slight hillock onto a beaten path. All was done with a miraculous lack of glitches.

Alec finally prepared to jump back on the wagon and said, "We can't thank you enough."

"Our honor, young man," Étienne said.

"Funny that whenever we meet, somethin' strange's going on," Peter said, elbowing Joey.

Alec tossed a questioning look at Joey, and his friend said, "Tell you the story later."

Alec and Joey both hugged Peter goodbye.

They jumped aboard and Alec took hold of the reins.

"Your next stop's Guttenberg, New Jersey," Étienne said. "Named for Johannes Gutenberg."

"Ha!" Alec said. "That's appropriate."

CHAPTER 25

Elsie had slept fitfully since laying her head on the feather pillow. Not only did slumber avoid her, but she did not feel well. Her heart was skipping beats, her nerves were on edge, her thoughts relentlessly focusing on Alec. A vicious circle with evermore increasing intensity.

Mon Dieu, mon Dieu!

Sometime in the middle of the night, she sat up, thinking what she needed to do—go to church and pray to the blessed Mary, entreat Saint Christopher. Plead for Alec's protection. But Elsie had no Catholic church for comfort, no priest for wisdom, no Christ on a cross for humility and inspiration.

She mentally threw her hands high—she physically lay down again and sulked, pursing her lips in displeasure. The inspiration struck her, and she spiritually sought God in the utter darkness. What better time and place to inquire of the Almighty? No distractions. None by other people, by demands for this and that, by dining needs and drinking wants and whatever other minutia that fill people's lives.

Merely her and God. No priests. No saints. No Mary. Solitude with her Lord.

Help!

One word was all she could manage, all she wanted, really. Her request did not address her fitful heart, or her on-edge nerves. Her appeal was not for herself at all, or her father, or her friends back home, or her homesickness, or any of these common affairs. No, her petition was totally *not* of this world.

Though she knew this fact, the realization struck her— God did not operate like men. He was not constrained by time nor space. He was not controlled by emotions and sentiments. Neither was he limited by inabilities.

All and all it was God's discretion. Elsie simply should trust him. This didn't mean to leave him be—no prayer, no repentance. No. She remembered the story of the persistent widow who continued to entreat the judge until he finally acquiesced to her request. Since God was a great and loving Father, how much more would he listen intently to his children's prayers and answer them?

So, she returned to her one-word plea.

Help!

At last, she fell into a quiet, consuming rest. Not until Lisette knocked on her door and entered the room did Elsie open her eyes. Her maidservant threw open the drapes to reveal dawn had passed, the day was upon them. Her nerves were calmed. Whatever had troubled her in the night had been resolved.

She looked out the window and muttered, "Thank you."

"*Qu'est-ce que c'est, mademoiselle?*" Lisette asked.

"*Oh, ce n'est rien.* It's nothing."

Later, their breakfast eaten, Elsie's father said he was going to Griffin's Wharf for business and asked if she needed anything and what were her plans.

"*Se promener. Se <u>réfléchir</u>.*"

"In English," he scolded.

Elsie sighed. Would she always be the student? Then translated, "To walk. To think."

"What is filling your mind? Your young man?"

She nodded.

"I approve of him, you know."

She looked up, perplexed. What, exactly, did her papa mean? That he approved of Alec's mission? Alec as a man? Alec as a match?

Was his approval simple support, or maybe admiration? She thought him sometimes too free with his esteem as well as his scorn, a man who embraced extremes.

Whatever, Elsie knew his meaning was a good thing.

She examined the countenance of the man who had loved her without condition since she could remember, the man who had taken on the job of father-mother with all his heart irrespective of her care obstructing his work life.

My papa. My protector.

More to confirm than to quiz she asked, "You do? Approve of him?"

"A young man of courage and integrity, who puts his personal desires secondary to those of the Lord. That's my type of person." Her papa smiled. "Add to that, a man who treats a lady—my daughter—with utmost respect while honoring her father's patriarchal position of authority."

Elsie's heart was full at his response.

Soon after her papa left, Elsie stepped outside the Green Dragon with Lisette at her side. Cold air met them, and Elsie pulled her fur coat close around her.

An east wind was coming off Boston Harbor, so at the corner of Union and Hanover streets she turned westward, putting the breeze at her back. They strolled along Hanover Street, the cobblestones crackling beneath their feet.

The briny sting of ocean air assaulted Elsie's senses. Tide was out. *Assurément.*

She thought she'd retrace her walk with Alec and let her mind wander. But before long she found herself on Brattle Street.

A clothing store, darkened inside, stood at the corner. At 58 Brattle Street, a sign announced Shelton and Cheever Imports and Manufacturers.

A massive home with English-looking landscaping followed. A flatstone sign at the front door was meant to impress passersby that the mansion belonged to William Brattle. Ahh, therefore the name of the street.

Next, a handsome yellow house that looked like an Italian villa. Another sign, this one bronze, perhaps competing with the Brattles' for boastworthiness, declared the owner of the manse to be John Vassall.

She recalled her papa telling her the Continental Army headquarters had for a time been in the Vassall home, and General Washington had lived there for a few months.

Elsie's gaze settled on a tall church. What a juxtaposition, a church so near an army headquarters. What would God think?

She stopped and read the sign on the side of the substantial stone structure—Brattle Street Congregational Church—and in smaller letters, Reverend Samuel Cooper.

Before she could think, her feet were hurrying along the brick sidewalk to the church, and up the stone pathway to the front door. Lisette's petticoat rustled behind her.

Seconds later, Elsie stood on the top step and hesitated. She had never entered a Protestant church before. Never considered the idea. Never needed to ponder such a notion. Holy Roman Catholic churches dotted the cities and villages of Lyon, Paris, Orléans, everyplace in France. What would Father Bellerose say?

She drew a deep breath and bowed her head in prayer. She did not want to offend her Lord. But she remembered her dream about being excommunicated by the tribunal of cardinals, and recalled Father Bellerose's look of satisfaction. She again heard the conversation as if the exchange were real:

"You've broken our rules, child," said the cardinal in the center.

"But your Eminence—"

"But nothing!"

Elsie straightened her shoulders, squared her jaw with a look of determination, and tugged on the bulky wooden double-door. Opening the two-inch-thick door was a test of strength, but she prevailed. And now what?

She ushered Lisette inside with her and pulled the door shut with a groan. The noise echoed through the high ceiling, along the mahogany pews, past the lectern, to the back where a massive wooden cross hung on the wall beside towering, beautifully painted organ pipes.

Something was missing from the cross. Someone, rather. Jesus.

Oh, my ...

She scanned the vestibule, looking for votive candles to light in prayer. None.

She searched for a statue of the Blessed Virgin. None.

She glanced around for any icons of the saints. None.

So strange, this. And yet she felt a warmness, a welcoming, a comforting despite the vast size of the place.

Elsie vacillated and looked again, mesmerized by the Christless cross.

Again, the gentle push at her shoulder impelled her forward. She motioned for Lisette to take a seat and walked slowly down the center aisle. Halfway to the raised altar, she stopped, genuflected, methodically crossed herself, sidled into the pew, and loosened her coat so she could sit with comfort.

At her feet, she noticed a cushioned prayer bar. She knelt on the bar and rested her forehead on the back of the pew in front of her.

There she stayed, her prayer list so long she lost track of time.

With no saints before her, no Mary, Elsie implored God for Alec's safety, for her papa's protection and favor, for all the men on both sides of this murderous war, for her Aunt Desiree and Uncle Andre, for her friends back home, for Monsieur and Madame Burdick, for King Louis to make a wise decision as to whether to truly join the Americans in fighting the war, and for so many people and circumstances.

The Bibles? She prayed for God's perfect will to be done—whatever that was.

Her knees throbbed and she pushed herself back on the pew seat, but kept her head bowed, her eyes closed.

A minute or so expired, and footsteps echoed from the sanctuary area. They were coming her way.

When they drew near, Elsie opened her eyes and looked up. A broad-faced, smooth-skinned man approached her—a man she'd seen in the Green Dragon, speaking boldly to others who appeared gathered for revolt. His black clothing and white collar gave him away as the church's pastor.

He nodded.

She returned the salutation, expecting but not experiencing tension. His look was kind.

"May I?" he asked, motioning to the pew seat.

"*Oui.*"

"I noticed you genuflect upon entering the pew. You're Catholic."

"*Oui.*"

"You're welcome here, of course."

"*Merci.*"

"I'm Reverend Cooper."

"Elsie," she offered.

"You've no church or priest here, but if there is indeed anything I may help with, any prayer or ..."

"I entered because I simply wanted to feel closer to my Lord," Elsie replied. "I found that intimacy here."

"Mmhmm."

"I'm surprised a bit."

"Oh?"

Elsie thought she should explain. "Father Bellerose says there is one true church—that of Rome. All others are pretenders. So, I wouldn't imagine the home of a 'pretender' would possess such tender communion with God as I've found in my few minutes here."

The man chuckled. "Few?" he said. "Child, you've been here more than an hour."

Elsie's eyebrows rose.

An hour? But such a sweet hour.

"Truly?" she asked.

"Indeed."

"Then I must go."

"Tarry if you'd like." He smiled. "Is there a particular concern at the center of your prayers?"

"Oh, so many," she said, "but, yes, one in particular. I'd ask St. Christopher for safe travels through dangerous territory for my friend, Alec Craig."

Reverend Cooper straightened up. "St. Christopher?"

"The saint of travelers," she said in way of explanation.

"But St. Christopher is dead, is he not? About fourteen hundred years now?"

The question was sincere, not hostile.

Elsie was taken aback. "But of course."

"He's in heaven with his Creator?"

"*Oui.*"

"Worshipping his Lord, perhaps?"

She hesitated a moment, then, "*Oui.*"

"You believe he's in heaven worshipping God ... but listening to prayers from people down here on earth for hundreds of years, his job on earth not yet complete?"

Elsie crinkled her forehead, thinking over the question. A query so simple, yet one she had not contemplated.

Reverend Cooper continued, "And listening, he is able to perform your request and the requests of numerous people around the world concerned for loved ones traveling?"

This flustered Elsie. Finally, she answered, "Well, St. Christopher can join us in our prayers, no? Just like the Holy Mother?"

Reverend Cooper peered at her, his kind brown eyes sparkling despite the lack of sunlight in the sanctuary.

"Well," he said, "that's a revelation I've not yet received. I do think, however, we can agree the best person to lift our prayers to is Jesus Christ, our Lord and Savior, no mere human but divine and part of the godhead."

Elsie brightened, tilted her head, and smiled.

He extended a hand, inviting her to join him. She wrapped both her hands around his, feeling as if she'd known this man for years—his demeanor so gentle, his inquiries so discreet and unintimidating, his offer overflowing with good will.

"Our Lord, our Savior, our Mediator," Reverend Cooper began, "we ask that you send angels to watch over Alec's comings and his goings, with their swords unsheathed, to be his front and rear guard, to defeat any who would try to stop him. I know this young man. His mission is yours, the goal to get your true and perfect Word into every American's hands. Cover Alec in your precious blood. Amen."

Silence followed along with a tranquility Elsie knew she'd treasure. She determined to return to this refuge, perhaps not for a Sunday service but for prayer and reflection.

CHAPTER 26

Soldiers changed their shifts at eleven in the morning. That much Robert Aitken had determined. Now he had to figure if Robbie could safely "pretend" his way right out of the city to the Brackett farm, where they'd visited several times.

The odds were oddly good. Robbie weeks ago had befriended the Redcoats, pretending to admire their courage and honor, saying he was sorry they had to be away from their families, maneuvering them to trust him, perhaps reveal a secret or two.

Thus far, he'd been unsuccessful in garnering any inside information. So, partly in retribution, partly for fun, Robbie said, he had stuck a sign on the back of a soldier, the message being "I'm a swill-bellied pickthank."

Yes, there were heavy drinkers and certainly a few were gossiping telltales, so perhaps some filled both descriptions. Robert had released a guffaw that caught in his throat. Janet, announcing her alarm, had admonished the boy.

Later, though, Robert acknowledged to his wife in private that watching their son in action was astonishing.

Another positive sign was there were certainly fewer soldiers in the city to beware of right now. Word was General

Howe had taken a large contingent to the Delaware River to again try to blast open his supply route.

Hallelujah for Commodore John Hazelwood and his ships fending off both Howe brothers for this past month or so.

Ha! Keep her up, boys.

He wondered if Hazelwood's men could hold the waterway until winter and force General Howe to retreat all the way to the Atlantic. As things stood, Philadelphian Loyalists were perhaps on the verge of terminating their goodwill after so much of the British troops' thievery and debauchery. More than one Loyalist had returned home from a day of work and found his place ransacked. More than one Philadelphian woman had been harassed by a Redcoat when walking down a public street or private walkway.

Sure, Howe had tried to stem the negative opinion by ordering the execution of two of the most odious offenders. But one could only pray the cost of the trespasses would outweigh Loyalists' allegiance to the king.

So here stood Robert, staring out the sitting-room window, deep in thought, determining whether Robbie's gregariousness, combined with his neophyte thespian skills, could help in a way Robert had never before considered.

The boy simply had to get out of town to the Brackett farm and find out if Maurice or Madeleine had heard any word from Alec. If so, Robbie could return with the information without arousing suspicion. If there was no word, the Bracketts—good friends from brave Welch stock—would keep Robbie until Alec, or a message, arrived.

Robert had struggled with the idea of attempting an escape but decided against putting Jane in a such a precarious position for a young lady.

At the moment, as he decided to send Robbie on his mission, the boy tugged at his elbow, startling him.

"Please let me go, Da," his son said. "I want to find out about Alec, too. He's like my big brother, and I love him like you and Ma do."

"I know, Son. Yes, you can go."

Robbie's face lit like a streetlamp at midnight.

"Besides," Robbie said, "Alec owes me a game of marbles. He beat me last time. So I want to be waiting at the Bracketts' to challenge him to a game of Cherry Pit as soon as he arrives."

"I'd say Dropsies would be your better bet," Robert said with a chuckle. "You can't take any extra clothing or the soldiers may expect something, but I'll bet you can sneak out a pocketful of marbles."

The boy's eyes twinkled.

Robert clicked his tongue and said, "As soon as you can, hurry back, even if you must postpone that game. With a price on our heads, we don't know how soon soldiers could be knocking down our door."

Robbie squeezed his lips together and nodded. His eyes were now ablaze.

Adventure, Robert thought. The boy was far too young for battle but was primed for adventure. Anything to rile or bamboozle an enemy.

After General Howe had, in effect, arrested and imprisoned Robert's friends in the clergy, his resolve had grown stronger. Censorship should itself be expurgated. Suppression threatened free thought.

Whenever Franklin, Jefferson, Monroe and the others were freed to write the new republic's laws, they'd better include freedom of worship and freedom of assembly in addition to freedom of speech.

As for Bibles? How many in the world could read Latin or Hebrew or Greek? Ordinary English-speaking people needed Bibles written in ordinary English, regardless of who owned the copyright—king or commoner.

Had not the taxpayers' money funded the King James translation? Had not that entire counsel of fifty translators been housed and fed and paid by money raised on the backs of British subjects, both in the homeland and the colonies?

Did not James undertake the translation in order to produce a single, popular version that all English-speakers could rely on "to be read in the whole church" as James himself phrased it?

The work was a miracle. The Old Testament was produced over a fifteen-hundred-year span and completed four hundred years before the 1st century AD. Forty men wrote the New Testament and sixteen hundred years later, fifty men translated it. Yet its structure, rhythm, cadence and imagery were so profound and harmonious as to have shaped civilizations and cultures for generations.

"Da!" Robbie's exasperated call interrupted Robert's thoughts. "I asked if I could take Roger with me."

"Roger?"

Robbie pulled a frog out of his rear pocket. "Somebody has to feed him, and no one will if I'm gone."

Robert shook his head and laughed. "Of course, Robbie. Take Roger with you."

"Maybe I can use him to coax information out of a soldier."

"And how would that work?"

"I don't know. I'll think of somethin'."

"Okay, Son. You do that, but don't overdo your questions and get in trouble. I want you gone at eleven o'clock when the soldiers change guard."

When the big hand reached eleven Robbie ran down the stairs, walked straight to his father, shoulders straight like a soldier—for certainly he saw himself as one—and put forth his hand.

Robert covered the small hand in his own, drew his son close to him, and laid a kiss on his forehead.

"Da," the boy protested, raising himself on his toes to appear older. "A spy doesn't get a kiss to send him on his mission."

"Oh." A child so young, yet enjoined in conspiracies—was the world upside down? Thirteen colonies, poor in money and arms and overwhelmed in manpower, were at war with their king whose lands extended around the world—were they gone mad?

Robert was glad he wasn't the one building coffins these days. Still, mass graves were more in order for the chaos of the battlefield. He'd seen enough of the killing in his younger years in Scotland and thought he'd never again witness such calamity.

He shivered at the thought. His arm recoiled at a distant memory. He was a boy, about Robbie's age, a flag bearer. Sitting cross-legged, head in hands, weeping himself dry on the shore of Duddingston Loch near Edinburgh. So much blood the water turned red as men had tried to escape on boat only to be cut down in the attempt.

The beach around Robert was littered with bodies, including those of his father and two uncles. The mostly Presbyterian Covenanters were pummeled that day by the mostly Catholic Highlanders. Scotsmen killing Scotsmen. A nation's history brimming with all the emotions and exploits of mankind—love and hate, loyalty and tyranny, kindness and cruelty.

All in all, Scotland contained more spies and turncoats than any land should claim.

Right up there with the history of the Jews, loaded with unholy kings and wicked usurpers and, every once in a while, a righteous leader like King Josiah or King David.

What tragedy.

Scots, Irish, Welsh, Brits—would they ever be at peace? Robert released a rueful chuckle at the question.

The answer—only in heaven.

And what about today here in America?

Robert sighed with deep emotion. His own son, a flag-bearer's child, walking out a generation later into a battlefield of sorts. For surely this Revolution was in part not merely a fight against flesh and blood but against the rulers, authorities, and powers of this dark world and against the spiritual forces of evil in the heavenly realms.

"If God is for you—" Robert said.

"Who can be against me," Robbie finished.

"Greater is he who is within you—"

"Than he who is in the world." The boy puffed out his chest, proud he knew the Scriptures.

"Good man."

Robbie's face broadened.

There was a sound behind Robert, and Robbie looked over his shoulder.

"Sis," the boy said.

Jane hurried to her brother and wrapped her arms around him.

"You'll be in our prayers," she said. "You and Alec and the Bracketts."

Robbie nodded, said thanks, and walked out of the house, heading north.

Robert went to the sitting room window and Jane joined him. They watched Robbie stroll up the lane northward toward Race Street.

Robert noticed something in his son's hands.

"What's that?" he asked, pointing.

Jane peered out the window, her eyes squinting. "His wooden rifle."

The boy lifted the rifle skyward, leaned the toy against his shoulder, and marched like he was in a column of soldiers.

"What's he doing?" Jane asked.

Robert stared out beyond Robbie and answered, "He's spotted a soldier. He's playing a part." He shook his head. *What a lad.*

Robbie had read the great books of adventure—*Gulliver's Travels, Robinson Crusoe,* and his favorites, *The Adventures of Peregrine Pickle* and *The Adventures of Roderick Random.*

Of course, everyone knew *Robinson Crusoe* was about a Scotsman, Alexander Selkirk, a castaway who lived for four years on a Pacific island.

Maybe he liked the adventure books the most because the author, Tobias Smollett, was his Da's friend back in Scotland.

Robbie's heroes inhabited the pages and illustrated the qualities he desired to emulate and those from which to flee. True, Peregrine was self-centered and disdained authority, but right now Robbie was about to disdain "authority," was he not?

And true, "Rory" Random was bitter about losing his parents and living under the controlling lordship of a brutal schoolmaster; but he was honest and trustworthy and relied on his own wits. And wasn't Robbie about to do that right now?

Robbie had recognized the Redcoat standing erect at the corner of North Third and Race streets like he was guarding His Majesty the King. Corporal Mason Mason. Who'd burden their son with a double name like that? When Robbie'd learned the soldier's name he'd almost doubled over in laughter, thinking the man was joking with him. But he'd proven to be a nice enough fella.

Robbie figured Corporal Mason was, in fact, bored to tears, probably missing his lady friend back in London, or Cardiff, or from wherever he hailed, Robbie forgot where. He guessed Mason was glad he'd been left behind when General Howe marched out of the city into a bitter November morning.

Robbie decided to draw the corporal's attention and so, as he marched along, he barked out the cadence, "Left, right, left … Left, right, left."

He only wished the wooden rifle at his shoulder was real and that he was marching along with General Washington or General Cadwalader. Probably Cadwalader 'cause not only was he in charge of Pennsylvania troops but Robbie liked the way the name tripped over his lips. Cadwalader. Cadwalader. Plus, Cadwalader was yet another Scotsman like his family.

Boy, Robbie wanted to travel. Like Rory Random, go to South America and Africa and the West Indies.

"Left, right, left … Left, right left."

He reached the corner, performed a perfect left-hand turn in front of the soldier, then—bam!

Corporal Mason Mason's rifle came down hard on the ground right next to Robbie's right foot.

"Master Robbie!" he said.

Robbie studied the hidden grin, the smile Mason withheld to pretend sternness.

"What are ya doin'?"

The Welsh accent reminded Robbie—yes, Mason was from Cardiff. Once Robbie had cajoled him into speaking that strange Welsh language for him.

"Corporal Mason?" Robbie answered.

"I asked what ya're doin'."

"Marchin', sir. Practicin'."

"Oh?" Mason allowed the grin to work its way out onto his pockmarked face. Even though Robbie wanted to dislike the man, he couldn't. But he could keep up a charade. He could dupe his acquaintance.

"Practicing like I'm a fencible," Robbie said. "A fencible in the first line of foot soldiers right behind General Howe and the horsemen."

"Fencible, huh?"

"Yeah, like the Argyll Fencibles back in Scotland."

"Ah, that's right. You're Scottish."

Robbie nodded, keeping eye contact, knowing that avoiding so would make him appear suspicious. Eye contact. Something spies used to such advantage, to ensure people they were to be believed.

"I got nothin' against Scots. Got a couple in our regiment."

Robbie nodded but wondered how a good Scot could fight for King George. Maybe they were like Robert the Bruce fighting for Longshanks, biding his time, hoodwinking his enemy before he fought against the tyrant. Hmmm.

"Goin' off to war, are ya'?" Corporal Mason pointed at Robbie's wooden rifle.

"Off to fight Cadwalader."

"Aim straight—" Mason stopped mid-sentence and asked, "What's your last name?"

"Wallace."

"Aim straight, Private Wallace." He winked and motioned for Robbie to get going. "Sure you know your way?"

Robbie considered an appropriate rejoinder but thought better of the idea and also figured his da was watching the whole exchange through binoculars.

"Which way did General Howe take his troops?" he asked.

"To the Delaware." The answer was offhanded as if Corporal Mason cared not their destination.

Robbie pulled Roger out of his front pocket and held him up for the corporal to see. "Good, 'cause my friend can always find water and needs a good swim before the river ices up."

Mason chuckled.

Robert laughed to himself as he watched his son return his rifle to his shoulder and resume his march out Race Street on his long trek outside Philadelphia.

"Your brother," he said, turning to Jane, "is a right Falstaff."

"The comic?" Jane asked, smiling.

"The charismatic."

Jane tilted her head. "He reads so much he probably knows all about Falstaff and is impersonating him."

"Or his beloved Rory."

"Right." Jane straightened. "We should pray for his safety and quick return."

Robert took her hands in his and began.

The walk was several miles to the north, but Robbie was up to the task.

Once he got out of eyesight of the corporal, he hightailed past Drew Street, broke into a stroll as he approached and passed a packet of soldiers on the south side of Strawberry Road, increased the pace, and didn't slow down until he reached Cohoquenoque Stream.

Here he stopped for a breather. He'd covered more ground than he'd ever run.

So, he walked right on over the bridge, his head high, making eye contact with the soldier standing there eating a chicken leg while pretending to be vig ... vigil ... vigilant.

CHAPTER 27

"Papa," Elsie asked directly, "is the statement true there is no salvation outside of the Church?"

She had returned from Brattle Street. Her papa was back from his business dealings, and both were seated in the first-floor dining area of the Green Dragon.

Malcolm and Lisette were installed at a table in a corner, ever watchful to the needs of Elsie and her father. The room was half full and everyone seemed to be involved only in their personal conversations.

Her father tilted his head. "From where does this question come, *ma chéri*?"

She told him of her experience.

"Reverend Cooper," her papa said. "An impressive clergyman. So, you're asking if a non-Catholic can be saved? A question not only about the reverend, but most everyone in this room, this city, this entire country. Even Alec."

Elsie dropped her eyes. "*Oui*."

"I believe you know the answer."

In a voice low enough that only her father could hear, she said, "Father Bellerose would say they're all bound for hell."

He nodded. "He would. But others in the church would disagree."

"Including you." A statement, not a question.

"Including me."

"The Holy Father, is he wrong, also?"

"My darling, God is love, is he not?"

She nodded.

"And does he not want all men to be saved?"

She flashed him a questioning look.

"The Apostle John said, 'For God so loved the world that he gave his one and only Son, that *whoever* believes in him shall not perish but have eternal life.'"

Elsie knew this Scripture.

"Did he say only *Catholics* who believe?"

She shook her head.

"Did he say 'only those who belong to a church'?"

She shook her head.

"He said 'whoever' believes in Jesus."

She nodded.

"Is Alec a 'whoever'?"

She laughed lightly. "*Oui,* bien sûr. Of course."

"Are Monsieur and Madam Burdick 'whoevers'?"

"*Oui,* especially Sally."

Her papa chuckled as if he knew something she didn't about Monsieur Burdick.

He leaned forward and looked keenly into her eyes. "The thief on the cross next to Jesus. The one who asked the Lord to remember him when Jesus came into his kingdom—"

"*Oui?*"

"Did not Jesus say to him, 'Today you will be with me in paradise?'"

Elsie nodded.

"So the thief was not baptized, did not repeat any prayer of repentance, did not take the sacraments?"

She shook her head.

"He simply believed in the Christ." Her papa folded his hands and asked, "What would the Pope, or Father Bellerose, say to that?"

A young server Elsie knew as Harriet arrived with two steaming bowls of beef stew, and as the appetizing aroma wafted to her nostrils, Elsie knew she would be satisfied, physically and spiritually, from hunger and fretfulness.

Robbie wished he hadn't eaten his chunk of bread and cheese so soon. What he'd give for an apple. Somethin'. His stomach was growling.

He was mulligrubs—down in the dumps—that was for sure. He reached inside the front of his coat where he'd tucked Roger to keep the frog warm. He pulled him out and held him high.

"Look around, Rog. What do you think? How close are we?"

The frog croaked.

Robbie'd been praying for Alec. Alec, his big, strong protector—like when that bully Paul had tried to pick a fight. Alec, his partner when time came for reading adventures or discovering interesting insects in the marshes outside town.

Alec, the funnest guy in his life. Alec, always crackin' jokes and making homework fun, and asking questions about the books Robbie was reading. Forever encouraging him to "expand your horizons."

Besides caring for Alec and his safety, Robbie knew his return from Boston was critical. No Alec, no materials for printing. No printing, no Bibles. No Bibles ... he didn't want to consider that outcome.

Robbie had to reach the Bracketts'.

God, don't let me get lost.

His thoughts went straight to Robinson Crusoe—when the castaway washed onto the shore of the island.

Yes!

Robbie scanned the horizon for the tallest tree. Climb that and he could get bearings on his location.

"Aha!"

There was a giant oak. Too giant, maybe.

But Robinson does not panic. Neither does Rory.

Robbie tucked Roger back in his pocket, approached the tree, set his wooden rifle against its trunk, grabbed hold of the lowest branch, and scurried up the tree like a squirrel.

As he neared the top he could make out a road ahead that curved out past a pasture. In the middle of the pasture stood a weird-shaped pine tree—one he'd wondered about when traveling to the Bracketts' with his parents.

"There!" he yelped. He pulled out Roger and pointed. "You see it?"

Twenty minutes later he turned off the road into the Brackett property.

He searched for his da's wagon. For Alec and Zims. No sign of any of them.

Darn.

Not that he expected to see them. He'd hoped, he'd prayed, but he had a feeling Alec hadn't yet returned. Alec was trustworthy. Not only that—he was as adamant as Da and Ma about getting the Bibles printed—and fast. Alec wouldn't go muckin' around wastin' time.

Nope. If Alec were back, he'd already be home.

Madeleine Brackett stepped out of the door at the side of the house, drying her hands on an apron, her eyes expectant.

"Robbie! What on earth are you doing here alone, my darlin' boy?"

Oh, how he loved Madeleine Brackett. She made the most delicious soft molasses cookies and smiled the best of smiles and hugged the warmest of cuddles and always smelled of somethin' sweet. Vanillary.

All Robbie could manage was the question: "Alec?"

"We've not heard a word," she said. "All of you must be terribly anxious."

Robbie nodded, trying to suppress his fears. He knew if he spoke his voice would shake like a boy. He wanted to show courage. Like Robinson Crusoe.

"Mr. Brackett and I've been praying daily," Mrs. Brackett said.

Robbie held back a tear at the thought somethin' awful had happened.

Somethin' unmentionable, maybe.

She put a hand on his shoulder and guided him toward the kitchen door. "I had a dream the other night, and Alec was driving two horses, not one. So I thought he'd get here earlier. But—" She shrugged.

Robbie didn't know much about dreams. He was always runnin' away from monsters in his, but his feet were forever stuck in mud to his ankles. And then—

Maybe Alec had two horses but they were mired over their hoofs in mud. Somewhere near Boston. Or Cancut. Or maybe mud in a dream meant somethin' slowin' ya down.

Alec had been slowed—of that Robbie was as sure as his da, who was never wrong—well, hardly ever.

Robbie followed Mrs. Brackett and stepped onto the porch that swept around the front of the house and into the kitchen. Before he knew, he was sitting at the kitchen table with a molasses cookie in his left hand and a tall skinny glass of fresh milk in front of him.

Before he finished the milk, Maurice Brackett came through the doorway, lugging two buckets filled near the brim with milk.

"Straight out of the cow and warm if you'd like a fill-up, Master Aitken," he boomed.

Robbie loved being called "Master Aitken." Made him feel older. And boy did he like Mr. Brackett, too, maybe 'cause he always addressed him this way upon first encounter, maybe 'cause he'd let Robbie milk the cows a couple times, and maybe simply 'cause he told funny stories about growin' up in someplace called Angels See in Wales.

Robbie'd said somethin' about angels seeing you play ball and swim and everythin' in that town and Mr. Brackett had gotten a great chuckle about that.

Robbie smiled at him. "Thank you, sir, but this'll do." He nodded toward his glass.

"Well, milk and a cookie oughta hold you over 'til supper," Mr. Brackett agreed. "That is, if you're staying with us."

"Robbie's here looking for Alec," Mrs. Brackett said.

"Hmm," Mr. Brackett acknowledged. "A bit worried, are we?"

Robbie nodded. "Expected him a couple days ago. And now General Howe's men are searchin' for Da and the print shop, but they don't know his name or where the shop is. They wanna find whoever's gonna print Bibles and stop 'em. Put 'em in jail."

"Mm."

"Is there anything we can do, Maurice?" Mrs. Brackett asked.

"Not a thing unless I were to saddle up a horse and ride King's Highway in search of the lad. Maybe the wagon's broken down. Maybe Alex's been—" He swept a quick glance at Robbie and fell silent.

But Robbie knew the rest of the sentence.

"Your riding out is something to be discussed later," Mrs. Brackett said. "But the idea is worth considering."

"And praying about," Mr. Brackett added.

"Aye."

"Robbie says Janet has taken the two young'uns with her to help Milly Linnell with her baby. Robert and Jane are back at the home they're renting."

"Hiding out," Mr. Brackett said. "Brave. But I wish he'd been able to get that equipment out here. He could've set up in that empty stall in the barn."

"Not enough room," Robbie ventured. "Da wants to print hundreds of Bibles. Thousands."

Mr. Brackett nodded slowly, perhaps thinking over how much space was necessary for the operation.

"Your father's a brave man," Mrs. Brackett said.

"And so are you and Jane," Mr. Brackett added.

Robbie smiled, then, "Jane and me've got a hidin' place in the print shop."

"Oh?" both Bracketts responded.

"Yeah. A secret door in the wall. Big enough to squat down in, get comfortable, but not too much."

"So what are your marching orders, son?" Mr. Brackett asked.

"I was to come and see if Alec was here, or if you'd heard from him. If'n not, I was to ask to stay with you until he arrives."

"You're welcome for the rest of the war if need be," Mrs. Brackett said.

"You can be my farm hand," her husband added. "You're as strong a ten-year-old as I've ever met."

Robbie grinned and took the last bite of cookie, finished off the glass of milk and stretched the glass out toward Mr. Brackett. "Maybe I will take a fill-up, Mr. Brackett."

"You can call me 'Boss.'" The man's smile was genuine, that was for sure and certain.

CHAPTER 28

Wednesday Evening
November 12, 1777
New Jersey Countryside

"King's Highway's pretty well maintained around these parts," Joey said. "Back home the roads would rattle this wagon around like a dead man's bones."

"Like two gears out of whack." Alec glanced at his companion and cracked a smile.

Joey caught his drift. "Like a cat chasin' a mouse."

"In the attic."

"Yeah, in the attic."

"Like dice in your hand."

"Like popcorn on the stove."

"We're getting silly. We must be tired," Alec said.

"Yeah."

Alec inspected the cloud-laden sky. Dusk was going on dark, the winter sun far over the treetops. They were somewhere between Brunswick and Princetown, New Jersey. So far, they'd been fortunate. No Redcoats. Only a few other wagons here and there.

But they seemed to be approaching some kind of affair. More than a dozen carriages and a scattering of horses were tethered outside the barn on a farm and scores of heavily clad people were braving the cold to get inside the large structure.

A dance perhaps? Alec doubted so. No one had been in the mood for a dance since the Revolution blasted everyone's plans to Timbuktu, which he thought was somewhere in Africa.

"What do you suppose is going on in there?" Joey wondered.

"Don't know." Alec pulled his coat tighter. "But I'm cold, Zims and Beau appear exhausted, and I'm curious to find out. What about you?"

Joey raised an index finger and called out to an elderly couple walking past.

"Say, sir, ma'am, can you tell us what the 'do' is all about?"

The man's face was wide with excitement. "Francis Asbury," he said. "He's here!"

"Asbury," Joey repeated. He shrugged and cast a look at Alec.

Alec couldn't believe his ears, or his continuing good fortune.

Asbury!

He turned to Joey. "The only British preacher in all the colonies to defy his church and stay in America after the Revolution broke out. The Methodists, Baptists, Presbyterians, all the denominations who'd sent preachers to America, called them back home. Asbury's a Methodist, so he even defied John Wesley."

Joey nodded. "Guts."

"More than that. Said he agrees with our cause and refused to leave behind people in need. He's been in hiding for a year or so."

"Why's that?"

"Refuses to pledge allegiance to anyone but God. Including America whom he supports. Or England, for he says there's only one King—Jesus—and his loyalty is to him alone."

"Where's his church?"

"Has none. Plants 'em and travels on. Thousands of miles each year on a horse."

"You've seen him? Heard him?"

"Once. In Philadelphia." Alec blew out a breath, his decision made. "We're staying here tonight."

"The whole night?"

"No one will want to leave. Believe me."

Hymns sung with no hymnals or organ, prayers said with no prayer books, a collarless preacher with no pulpit to stand behind. This was different.

The barn was big and square, lit by lanterns hanging from rafters and walls.

A loft above encircled the four walls so people on the floor could see straight to the roof. Bales of hay, their aroma intoxicating, filled most of the loft and what room was left was occupied by boys and girls. Sitting hip to hip, their feet dangled above the crowd. People were packed together so tightly one could barely sit if they wanted.

The farmers must have moved their cows or sheep or horses out into a corral or pasture to make room.

Asbury stepped onto a small crate before them. At five-foot-nine, he was a handsome man in his early thirties, much too young to hold such a reputation. He possessed a prominent nose and large mouth, as if purposely made to preach life to the dead. His dark hair flowing, eyes searching, he seemed concerned.

"Outside, minutes ago," he said, "a man asked me if I feel the pastors who boarded ships back to England and Europe were like Jonah. 'Did they flee,' he asked, 'from the duties to which God had called them?'"

Asbury's gaze roamed the barn. "These are difficult times. Add a measure of fear to these pastors' inclination toward submission to authority and you find good reasons to act as they did.

"They're fine men, all of them in a strange new world, called to duties for which many were unprepared." Asbury shrugged. "I can judge no man in reference to whether he has done what God has called him to do. I can only answer for myself, and I *would have* felt like Jonah if I'd left. I *would have* known that I'd violated God's plan for me. I *would have* been constantly looking over my shoulder, fearing God was chasing me and at the same time afraid he would never try to use me again.

"Jonah was truly fortunate the Lord didn't let him sail away to who-knows-where and use who-knows-who to prophesy to Nineveh. The prophet's entire eternity would have been squandered."

A shiver went down Alec's back.

"Some here may have a calling that promises to take them away from their dreams for a time." Alec was certain the preacher's eyes were fixed on him. "But who's in charge of time?"

"The Lord!" the answer came from several scattered voices.

Asbury nodded.

"You know Jonah was three days in the belly of that fish before he called out to God. Three days."

"A stinky three days," a boy called out from the loft.

Everyone chuckled, including Asbury. Looking at the youth, he said, "Jonah's story teaches us several lessons, but one for us in particular tonight.

"Riding along Pokomoke River in Delaware, Silver Fox and I were on our way to Annapolis, where I intended to preach. That is, if the authorities would allow me. I'd heard Joseph Hartley and Freeborn Garrettson had been imprisoned for not taking an oath in support of the colonies."

Asbury put a snap to his voice. "Suddenly, I heard the sounds of at least several horses ahead on the trail. Quick and quiet, I turned Silver Fox toward a thicket of evergreen trees and retreated behind them as a half-dozen men rode by, two wide and three deep. On the left front, a rough-looking character was speaking to the man beside him. 'If Asbury's speaking tonight at Gumboro he'll be passing this way, Davey. We grab him, get him to sign an oath to America, denounce England, and he can be on his way. If not, we fine him. If he doesn't pay the fine, we jail him. No question.'

"When the men were out of earshot, we escaped eastward but found ourselves in a swamp. At first the water was a few inches high, then knee-high, and then reaching my stirrups until we discovered a small piece of dry ground.

"Oh, the smell was pungent," he said, "like mold and dirty rags constantly wafting up into my nostrils."

"Yeow!" several children from the loft cried out.

Asbury peered at them. "'Yeow' is right, but what could we do? We'd found refuge. We were anxious to move on, but an ominous feeling told me we must remain there."

"But the Holy Spirit warned me to stay there. Three days! For three days and three nights, with only a few carrots and grain to sustain us."

Moans in response.

"Then," Asbury said, "I noticed the nasty smell of the swamp no longer bothered me. I'd become used to the stench."

Asbury shot a disarming look about him and continued, "That's when the Lord taught me the lesson. 'Frankie,' he said, 'I wanted you to see the lost for who they are, what spiritual condition they're in. I wanted you to realize you cannot expect them to act as if they're saved. They're not. Do you smell the swamp now?'

"No," I answered aloud.

"'Correct,' He said, 'because you've lived in this place, you cannot smell the decay. Consider the people in the wilderness of these colonies—and in the towns and cities.

Many have lived not days, but years, decades in the 'smell' of their sins. They're used to those sins, so much so that their iniquity does not hold a nasty odor for them anymore.'

"'I see, Lord,' I replied.

"'And so you see that once they do know me, the stench of those sins will be too much for them to bear ...'"

The message took one second to settle into Alec's mind, a split second for him to join the raucous response around him.

Joey "whooped" and jabbed him in the ribs with an elbow.

CHAPTER 29

A commotion broke out behind Alec. He turned and peered through the crowd. Several soldiers of the Continental Army burst into the barn, their rifles at chest height, shoving people aside as they advanced directly toward him.

The man in the lead—supposedly an officer since telling any one of them from the farmers and other townspeople gathered in the building was so difficult—pointed over Alec's head.

"You Francis Asbury?" he demanded.

Alec turned to see the response.

Asbury shrugged. "Since birth."

"Then you're preaching illegally, sir!"

The barn exploded in commotion. Shouts of objection from all corners.

"Who do you think you are?" an elderly man asked.

"Sergeant Thomas Wells of the Continental Army," the leader responded, "and we've come to do our duty."

"We're Americans, your countrymen," blurted a lady.

"This is a service of God. No rifles allowed!" growled a giant of a man who took a long stride to confront the leader.

At the same time two older men stepped in front of Asbury, to protect him. They planted hands to hips with no small measure of resolve in their visages.

Wells kept pushing his way forward, leading his men like the point of an arrow. He elbowed Alec in the ribs and Alec shoved him away with force. Fierce eyes turned to Alec, and he met sternness with sternness.

Asbury extended a hand to silence everyone and asked, "How can one preach illegally?"

Wells turned from Alec to Asbury, a snarl curling his lip, and demanded, "Have you sworn the oath?"

"I don't swear," Francis replied, "either by the heavens, which is God's throne room, nor by the earth, which is his footstool. I swear not. But my 'yes' will be 'yes' and my 'no,' 'no,' sir." His blue eyes pierced Wells as the soldier approached him. "I affirm America's struggle against England. And I favor the proposed motto, 'Rebellion to tyrants is obedience to God.' But I will never raise a hand in anger against either side in this Revolution."

The soldier was unaffected. "With no oath, you're fined five pounds."

He walked forward, continuing to bully people aside until he reached the two men standing firm in front of the haybale on which Asbury remained. He set the butt of his rifle on the floor, extended his palm over the shoulders of Asbury's two guards, and said, "I'll have the money now, or to jail you'll go."

"Five pounds? That's a king's ransom!" Asbury objected.

"Yes, and the king has been holding us up to ransom for years, has he not?"

"What have I to do with the king? And who has five pounds?"

"You'll have it, or you'll be behind bars this day, sir."

Francis threw up his hands. "Then to jail I go."

Alec listened in disbelief and blurted, "Five pounds? Have we not five pounds among us?"

"I've got some coins," Joey said and dug in his pocket.

All around, those gathered scrambled for their money pouches. Alec took off his hat and dropped his own coins into his cap, which he held forward as he walked around the barn. People tossed in coins from all sides.

As Alec neared the large door, Silver Fox stretched her long neck through inside and nudged him, knocking him sideways a bit. Everyone laughed, even the soldiers.

Finally, Alec finished the offering and counted out the money into a pouch someone gave him. "One pound. Two pounds. Two pounds five. Three pounds. Three pounds six. Four pounds. Four pounds five, seven, eight..."

He looked up, puzzled and disappointed.

"We're twenty pence short," he said softly. A collective moan answered the news.

As men and women around the barn turned their pockets and purses inside out looking for another coin, one of the Army patrol, a skinny young fellow, stepped over to Alec's hat and tossed in a coin.

"Higgins!" Wells screamed. "What are ya doing?"

"Why, topping off the collection, sir," the young man replied and winked at Alec. The entire congregation rang out a round of applause.

Asbury looked down at the lad and smiled.

"God has his hand on you, my friend," he said.

"Top off the collection!?" Wells bawled. "We came here to arrest this man for preachin' without swearin' allegiance—and you give toward his fine?"

Higgins straightened his shoulders and answered, "Yes, sir. And proud to contribute, I am, sir."

"We'll see how proud you remain, Private!"

With that, Wells turned to Alec. "I'll take that money." He grabbed the pouch and, looking at Asbury, barked, "You're a marked man in these parts, Parson."

"I can only pray you're wrong," Asbury replied.

"No more preachin' for you."

"Best to stop me from breathing," Asbury said, "for life and God's Word can never be parted."

"Don't believe I can't do something about your breathing," the soldier returned, menace in his tone.

"You answer to a higher authority, a colonel or general perhaps," Asbury said. "So do I, but mine is higher still. I submit to the one and only king, Jesus. I have relinquished the throne of my heart to Him alone. You would be wise to consider the same, sir, or face losing more than your own breath. Think of your eternal salvation."

"Pshaw!" Wells threw an arm upward toward Asbury. "Nonsense."

"It's the highest of sense," Asbury retorted, "the supreme decision of anyone's life. And the Lord's offer is both guaranteed and free of charge."

"Free of charge?" Wells harrumphed. "Money is all you preachers are after."

Asbury laughed. "To ask me, a Methodist preacher, for five pounds is as astounding, and unlikely to be fulfilled, as asking me for the country of Brazil."

"And yet," Wells hollered above the din, "and yet here I have five pounds, eh?"

One of the two men protecting Asbury stepped chest-to-chest with Wells. "Five pounds of our money. I call such a thing theft."

"Extortion," the other protector cut in. "Be proud of your accomplishment tonight, Sergeant."

Wells turned away from his two adversaries and motioned for his men to leave. People parted to make a path for them, and Alec thought it odd there were no jeers, no taunts. As if the crowd amassed in this barn had swiftly forgiven the intrusion. As if they were proud to have given of hard-earned treasure to keep a man of God from prison. As if they were part and parcel of a thing greater than a sermon. A thing to tell their children and grandchildren about.

Alec thought of the young soldier who had tossed the last twenty pence into the hat and smiled.

I'll bet he's one of those who'll get our Bibles to hold dear.

Asbury dove into a sermon on warfare, declaring, "We're in the midst of a revolution, but first of all the Lord wants *revelation.*"

He pointed skyward. "When you're fighting against the devil, you'd best be wearing the helmet of salvation, the breastplate of righteousness, the belt of truth, the gospel of peace about your feet, holding the shield of faith to quench the fiery darts—and the musket balls and bayonets—of the enemy, and brandishing the sword of the Spirit which the Holy Spirit wields."

Roars of agreement echoed around the barn.

Asbury straightened his shoulders. "God Almighty wants us to go into spiritual battle with fervor. Passion. Zeal! You may not carry rifle or sword, but without your fervent, zealous prayers, this revolution will not be won."

Alec lost track of time. Had an hour expired? Two? No, worshippers lingered through midnight.

At first, teenaged boys and girls sailed down the ladders from the loft, joining dozens of adults responding to Asbury's altar call. Faces were drenched in tears of repentance and joys of deliverance—an almost contradictory mixture of emotions and revelation Alec recalled from his own salvation four years before.

Old men sobbed in contrition for lifelong sins, leaving the barn with arms wrapped around their wives' shoulders. Young women, two of them now war widows with children, accepted comfort and encouragement.

Alec slumped to the floor, right there in the middle of the barn, thanked God he was still alive, and pleaded with him that he would get the supplies safely home.

To ask for anything personal seemed far too self-absorbed. What more did he need? A future with Elsie? His new dream of a water-driven printing press? Some success and honor and recognition? Save for Elsie, the burning desire of his heart, these were wants, not needs, and as such they would all fade away when he'd lived his life's span.

No, his prayers had to revolve around this immediate calling. He felt God had commissioned him to deliver his wagonful of supplies.

Alec's eyes shot open. Had enough time elapsed for Zims and Beau to gain strength for the final leg of their journey? Could Joey and he stay awake through a night of travel? Outside, the moon was supposed to be close to full. He knew the direction to take, could keep the wagon on the King's Highway, wouldn't be concerned about enemy soldiers like he was in the daylight.

He looked up. Joey had gone forward to publicly proclaim his faith. At this moment he and Asbury were speaking in hushed voices. Joey shared something and the preacher's eyes went wide and sought Alec out.

Alec pushed himself off the floor and rose to his feet while Joey led Asbury toward him. Alec met them halfway.

"I told Mr. Asbury, Alec," Joey said.

Asbury locked his attention on Alec and declared, "If God be for you, who can be against you?"

Alec smiled in recognition of the Scripture.

"And the verse before that?" Asbury said. "Those He predestined, he also called. Those he called, he also justified. Those he justified, he also glorified."

"I seek no glory, sir," Alec said.

"And that lack of ego pleases God no end. Can I pray for you?"

Asbury was renowned for his prayers. Alec nodded with enthusiasm.

Laying his right hand on Alec's head and his left hand on his shoulder, Asbury prayed: "Lord God Almighty, giver of all good things, bless this young man with the true faithfulness of another young man, King David; with the wisdom of Solomon; the faith of Abraham; the zeal of Peter. Bless Alec to overflowing with the talents and abilities he needs to fulfill your task. Lavish him with the ability to use his gifts to further your kingdom.

"At a time of revolution your people need revelation and for revelation they need your word, Father—in their hands, in their hearts."

Asbury squeezed Alec's shoulder and his eyes narrowed. "In the days ahead, especially this day, today, may you discern wisely, judge righteously, and act faithfully. And may angels watch over and shield you with supernatural protection."

Asbury took a half-step back and withdrew his hands. As Alec thought the prayer was over, the preacher grabbed his right hand.

"And, Alec?"

"Yes."

"At the right time, may you be blessed with a virtuous spouse. May your children be as olive trees in the house of God and may you have health, wealth, and success. Godspeed."

Alec had a difficult time catching his breath from the entire prayer, but especially the final bit. That was like an addendum, an epilogue. And as a final word, the idea fueled an excitement that sizzled up his spine. He was wide awake, revitalized. Today, this very day he could go to the ends of the earth and beyond. He simply knew so.

CHAPTER 30

Thursday morning found Elsie back inside Boston Congregational Church's nave several pews back from the sanctuary, Lisette several pews behind her. She and her father had learned from Sally and Benjamin Burdick about Alec capturing the British sailor who'd tried to assassinate him. Proof the danger was real, tangible, lethal.

Elsie had grabbed her Latin prayer book and hurried out of the Green Dragon straightway here. The cold had invaded Boston, a blistering wind coming off the harbor. She needed refuge, a quiet place to seek God.

She huddled, pulling her coat tight about her, seeking physical comfort as well as spiritual. A clutch of women gathered about the pulpit, discussing decorations or some such thing. Maybe Christmas a month from now. Maybe a memorial for a dead soldier or soldiers. There were plenty of fatalities on both sides.

Elsie wished her little bound leather book of prayers was written in French, or English or Spanish. She'd admittedly struggled with Latin and Greek, perhaps because the men teaching those classes were, well, boring as a flowerless garden, stale as week-old bread. During those classes, she'd found herself sketching cabins in the mountaintops of the Vosges and boats on *la Rivière Seine*.

But regardless of her scholastic carelessness, she'd been able to translate a portion of Virgil's *The Aeneid* for her final grade in Latin and Homer's *Iliad* to finally finish her studies in Greek. And so she was tolerable if not comfortable with her little book.

Her thoughts at the moment—the notion that even the *Iliad's* great warrior Achilles had a weakness, a flaw in his armor. Alec surely would have a vulnerability as well. And that weakness must be protected. He couldn't do that. She couldn't. Only God ...

She opened her book at random and read: "Dear glorious St. Michael, guardian and defender of the Church of Jesus Christ."

Right there she stopped and recalled Reverend Cooper's words on her first visit.

If St. Michael is in heaven worshipping God, his job on earth must be complete. And isn't Jesus, our Lord and Savior, the one to whom to pray?

Old habits.

Elsie set aside the prayer book and went to her knees, her hands on the back of the forward pew, and rested her forehead against her knuckles.

Her whisper aloud was for her own good, she knew, for God knows our thoughts.

"Lord, I pray you protect Alec from all the evils hiding between him and Philadelphia, for there are many who would do him harm—the devil among them. Put your hedge of protection and safety around him. Father, grant Alec discernment to see things happen before they do, yet keep his heart free of fear and full of your perfect peace. Be his ever-present help in time of trouble, accompanying him all the way."

She breathed a deep sigh—did she discern a sweet aroma in the air?—and added, "Amen, Jesus."

Elsie felt a release to return to the Green Dragon, thinking she would retrace the steps she and Alec took on their stroll. A cup of tea and biscuit, perhaps. That would be a nice treat for her and Lisette. A smile curled her lips as she rose to her feet and walked toward the foyer.

Lisette joined her and as they reached the front of the church the door opened. Standing before them, eyebrows high in surprise, was Reverend Samuel Cooper.

"Mademoiselle de La Borde!" he exclaimed.

She bowed her head slightly. "Monsieur Cooper."

"Perhaps you've heard your young man captured a spy who was on the loose?"

A wide smile played across her face and she nodded. "We heard."

"Brave fellow. Tenacious. A man after my own heart. After God's heart, I'd venture."

"I hope to write to him soon, and I'll mention your kind words."

"Thank you."

He stepped aside to let her and Lisette pass.

"Visit any time," he said. "Our door is always open."

"*Merci bien, Monsieur,*" she said and stepped back out into the outdoors.

Rejuvenated, Alec hitched up Zims and Beau in the middle of the night. Zims twitched his tail and nickered, and he stroked the big horse on the nose and said, "Not long, big fella. We'll be home soon."

He took the reins and guided them along King's Highway while Joey lay down on top of the pile of yard goods and snored away, contentment painted on his face. Dreams of Alice, no doubt. At one point he giggled and sighed her name.

Good dream, that.

A cloudless sky hid none of the waxing moon's beams, so they made good progress. Past Monmouth and Princetown they traveled.

The farmhouses and homes were sleepy as if mesmerized and war-free. Indeed, if an Indian were planted here from Canada, he'd have no idea a war was afoot.

After a time, they passed Trenton and reached Coryell's Ferry. New Hope, Pennsylvania, lay across the river. Alec smiled to himself. He had a newfound friend here, Moses De La Warr, the ferry master who had transported him across the Delaware on his way to Boston.

As soon as they met, Alec had decided he wanted to know Moses forever. In the span of time they took to load Zims and their empty wagon and ferry from New Hope across to New Jersey, Moses had told Alec his brief life story. A Lenni-Lenape Indian with a name Alec could not pronounce, he'd been saved by the white man's Savior, Jesus, and renamed himself "Moses."

When Alec told Moses he'd made that spiritual leap himself and was on a mission to print Bibles, they grabbed one another in a hug that had cemented their relationship.

Over a cup of tea, Moses said, "Last December, Lord Cornwallis arrived with his troops at the ferry on the other side of the Delaware to cross the river. But you know what?"

Alec went along. "What?"

"I'd helped the revolutionary troops destroy all boats on the New Jersey side of the river."

"Ha!"

"Those Redcoats were so miffed, so frustrated, they shot volley after volley over the river into New Hope," Moses said. "They pelted a few trees, but missed us. We simply laughed at 'em."

Chuckling and shaking his head, Moses had pulled a musket ball out of a pocket and held the pellet for Alec to see.

"A significant crossing, this," Alec said.

"Yes, and our side'll use the ferry again for yet another triumph," Moses had said, "... 'cause God is with us as he was with the Jews against the giant Amalekites."

Heartened by Moses's faith, Alec had gone on his way to Boston. And now he was back with his own tale to tell.

And as fortune would have it, Moses was on the New Jersey side of the Delaware. The Indian stood in the doorway of a little brick toll house, his head down, reading a paper.

"Yo there, Moses!" Alec called. Moses looked up, broke into a wide grin, waved and hustled outside. Joey woke behind him as Alec pulled the horses to the toll house.

"Where're we at?" Joey asked.

"Coryell's Ferry. The Delaware."

"Ahh." He wiped his eyes with the back of his hand.

Alec introduced him to Moses, whose face was a mixture of joy—at their reunion—and concern.

Not sure what the concern's about.

Alec jumped down from the wagon and the two exchanged hugs.

"Success?" Moses asked.

"Success." He motioned toward the wagon.

Moses took the cue and walked around the dray, inspecting the cargo.

Patting the noses of Zims and Beau as he came around, Moses said, "Gained a horse, too, as well as a passenger."

Alec nodded.

"Good. Now to get you the rest of the way safely." He waived the paper he'd been reading. "Something you gotta see."

"Oh?"

"A friend who'd been in Philadelphia handed me this dispatch from General William Howe to his troops. Howe decrees a 'general alarm' and warns about you, my brother."

He handed the paper to Alec.

"What's it say?" asked Joey.

Alec scanned the document.

"An alert to be on the lookout for any payloads, on boats or wagons, that include printing materials. Ink, paper, typeset. King George the Third is distressed that barbarians in America dare to parse God's Word without his permission. That said, General Howe is offering a fifty-pound reward for information leading to the capture of anyone plotting to print or distribute illegal Bibles."

"Fifty pounds!" Joey blew out a breath and looked behind them at the wagon. "Talk about having a price on your head."

"Let's get you loaded up," Moses said.

Turning his attention to the horses, Moses said, "Zims, good to see ya', fella."

Zims stomped his foot and bowed his head.

"That one there's Beau," Joey said, pointing.

"Ahh. Handsome he is, too. He yours?"

Joey shook his head. "Belongs to someone in Boston."

"Long story." Alec grabbed hold of Zims's breast strap. "I'll tell you on the way over."

Reaching the opposite shore, they unloaded the horses and wagon.

Alec pulled out his money pouch, but Moses raised a hand, "No charge. My contribution to the cause."

Moses hustled to a house across the road while Alec and Joey hung grain sacks over the horses' necks.

"They're famished. I'm famished," Joey grumbled.

Moses returned with an enormous loaf of bread that smelled fresh.

"Sustenance," he announced. "My wife, Nayeli, pulled that out of the oven moments ago. She invited you to lunch if you can spare the time."

"Time is one thing we don't have. We've been pushing Zims and Beau hard, but, well, Admiral Howe discovered Mr. Aitken's name and sent messengers to General Howe by land and by sea."

"Won't get there by water." Moses laughed. "British ships're jammed up at Mud Island. But by land? He didn't ride this way. Maybe hugged the coast to the sand barrens and headed inland to Philadelphia from there. That route would certainly take longer."

"I pray."

"And I pray with you. Nayeli'll fry bacon and eggs and bring them over for you. With milk." He hesitated, then: "You get all the printing supplies you wanted?"

"Sure did. Possibly more'll be coming." Alec explained Charles de La Borde's actions.

"A Frenchman," Moses said.

"*The* Frenchman," Alec said. "Without him and his partner we probably would have lost the war by now."

"And without him Alec'd still possess his own heart," Joey said with a good-natured slap to Alec's shoulder.

Alec answered Moses' questioning look with a redacted version of his romance with Elsie, words spilling out of him like floodwater over a dam.

Somewhere in the midst of his recollections, Moses stated matter-of-factly, "Ya love her, then."

Alec nodded and wondered what Elsie was doing at this precise moment. Looking beautiful was all he knew. Exquisite. Sublime. Probably sipping tea and reading a book by a French poet. Someone who could write a whole lot better than him. He hoped she was thinking about him, too.

Minutes later they'd finished the task and Nayeli called out for them to join her in the cabin for lunch.

In the midst of their meal a baby cried in a back room, and Nayeli excused herself to go to the child.

"Little Daniel," Moses explained, turning his head toward the upstairs. "Named for the prophet. Lions. Kings. Nothing's gonna stop that boy."

Alec smiled and wondered what he'd name a child. If ever ...

CHAPTER 31

Their stomachs full, their thanks given, and with a promise provided to return with Bibles, Alec and Joey headed out Aquetong Road past a Presbyterian church, a post office, a barber shop, and a blacksmith's forge. People were scarce, maybe because so many had joined the fight after Saratoga.

Once out of town, the highway toward Philadelphia was known as York Road. They'd ride this until they could turn off toward Germantown and the Brackett farm.

Beautiful fieldstone houses dotted the landscape.

They rode past barren fields that two months ago were filled with cabbages or corn. Before their defeat, the Redcoats had sacked all they could, all that hadn't already been willingly given to the Continental militia.

Or perhaps the whole thing was vice versa. Oftentimes you didn't know which side a landowner supported. For instance, the Pennsbury Manor they passed—who did the current owner support?

And the neighboring land they rode through in Bensalem Township? For sure, Joseph and Betsey Galloway, who owned that huge tract and Growden Mansion, were loyal to the crown—despite having Washington, John Adams, and Benjamin Franklin as guests in their home.

When they reached Manor Moreland, the little hairs on Alec's neck stood up. His back stiffened and he tightened his hold on the reins.

"What's the matter?" Joey sensed something himself, since he reached behind him to grab his rifle and "Charlie," the Charleville given to Alec.

"Somethin'. Don't know what."

Joey had loaded his Brown Bess with cluster shot to fire multiple projectiles. Alec's "Charlie" was ready with single shot.

"Pray you'll never have to fire her," Joey said.

Someday I will ... Probably ... Maybe ... We'll see.

They came around a bend in the highway straddled by fir trees and where the road straightened out a British soldier, a corporal, stepped out from behind a large oak tree to their right. He shouldered a rifle aimed directly at Alec.

"Better lay down those rifles, fellas, and stop your wagon," he said. "You've the look of rebels to me."

Alec wanted to slap the disdain off the soldier's face. He pulled Zims and Beau to a slow stop, Zims snorting a complaint.

"What do we have here?" the corporal asked, striding forward and nodding toward the wagon.

Alec wondered if he was alone or had a comrade nearby. A one-man British roadblock was unusual. He glanced to his left. No one was in sight, but perhaps Howe had sent his troops elsewhere and was thin on patrols.

He shrugged. "A load of yard goods and rough iron."

"Yard goods and rough iron in barrels?" The soldier scoffed and pointed to the ground in front of him. "Put your rifles on the floorboard and step down here."

Alec stared at the barrel of the rifle pointed at his midsection. He calculated the distance between him and the soldier's rifle, the speed with which he could leap away from the musket ball's trajectory, the moment's time to spin and kick the soldier's legs out from under him. Another maneuver Bradley had taught him.

Alec exchanged looks with Joey. This soldier had one shot so he could only take out one of them. What was their response? Joey was the soldier, so Alec would acquiesce to his decision.

Joey's mouth twisted. Alec couldn't read his thoughts. To gamble or not? Gamble and he'd be putting Joey in danger, too.

Get off the fence, Joey!

At the instant of decision another soldier, a rifle at his shoulder, stepped into the roadway from the fringes to their left. "Sorry," he said, "trouble with my buttons." His eyes went to his britches.

Alec let go a sigh, hung his head, and stepped to the ground. Joey sidled over and leaped down beside him.

"Let's have a look at yer cargo, eh, boys?" the corporal said.

Prodded by the rifle barrel pointed now at his head, Alec turned to walk to the rear of the wagon. Joey began to follow, but the soldier said, "No, you stay here." To his comrade he said, "Watch this fella, Private."

The private nodded and Alec continued alongside the cart. Its wooden sides angled upward from its spine, making for difficulty seeing inside. But the rear, where the barrels were tied down, was open.

"Stop right there," the corporal said and pointed to the barrels. "What's in these?"

"Syrup," Alec said.

"Not a yard good, not rough iron?"

"No, sir."

"So, you lied."

"I thought it nothing to concern you."

"I didn't ask you to think."

Alec squirmed.

"What kind of syrup?"

"Maple."

"Three barrels of maple syrup?"

Alec nodded.

The corporal's voice rose an octave. "You expect me to believe you have three huge barrels of maple syrup?"

Alec hesitated, wondering what was wrong with his answer.

"A couple of young dirty-beaus like you are in charge of a fortune?"

"Ah—"

"Open one up!" The soldier poked Alec in the ribs with the barrel of his rifle.

"Open a barrel?"

"What are we talking about, boy? Of course the barrel."

"But—"

"But nothing. Take the lid off."

Alec looked heavenward.

What to do now, Lord?

No answer came.

"Open or I put a musket ball in all the barrels and watch your syrup bleed out." He hesitated. "Or maybe I'll take them off your hands and earn a tidy retirement."

Now that might not be a bad idea. He'd be without a loaded weapon.

"And I'd pike you with my bayonet." The corporal leveled the dagger at Alec's belly.

There goes that solution.

Alec climbed aboard and stood next to the barrels. "What do I use?" he asked.

"Forget it. I'll open the casket myself."

The soldier jumped close to Alec and took a long knife from his waist while holding his rifle firmly pointed at Alec. Eyeing the tip of the barrel, he took the point of his knife and pried at the lid.

Alec held his breath, hoping against hope the soldier would stop.

But with a deep echo, the lid popped up. The rich aroma of ink rose to their nostrils. The corporal's eyes shot wide, he aimed a glare at Alec, and peered into the dark liquid.

"I know maple syrup. I was stationed in Canada. And this ain't no maple syrup." He let the lid drop, holstered his knife and prodded Alec's chest with his rifle. "I also went to school through the fifth grade, and I know ink."

The corporal raised his eyebrow and called out, "I believe we've earned ourselves fifty pounds, Private. We got the Biblio-Ghost, or the Biblio-Ghost's underlings."

"Biblio—" Alec frowned.

The corporal motioned for Alec to climb down.

Seconds later they were at the front of the wagon.

"The prize is ours!" The private's face was full of glee.

The corporal was smiles ear to ear. "Now to get these mumbleskins to General Howe and prison."

Alec stole a look at Joey. He'd led his newfound friend straight into the arms of the enemy … maybe into the hangman's noose or a firing squad, depending on the mood of General Howe, the judge and jury.

He shrugged and peered at the ground. Perhaps an opening for escape would present itself on the way to Philadelphia. Right, and perhaps a lightning bolt would—

A crack of wood on bone rang out and the corporal crumpled facedown, grabbing his shoulder and groaning in pain, beside Alec.

Alec stood straight and looked to the private. His rifle was on the ground and his arms in the air. A tall-as-a-tree, stern-looking older man stood beside the private, a long rifle in his arms.

Alec spun about and there before him stood Maurice Brackett, the stock of a rifle cradled in his fist, a broad smile on his face.

"I'd say these fellas aren't going to collect that reward," Maurice said and winked. "More like going to prison themselves—a Continental Army prison." He turned to the older man. "Right, Carlton?"

The man nodded.

Maurice motioned to his friend. "Carlton, meet Alec. Alec, Carlton."

They nodded to each other and Alec turned a thumb toward his companion. "Joey."

Alec picked up the fallen corporal's rifle, stepped heavily on the man's leg to keep him from slipping away, and stretched his arms wide in question. "What are you doing here?"

While Carlton took charge of the private, tying his hands behind him, Maurice took Alec and Joey aside and spoke softly to avoid being heard by the soldiers.

"Janet and the two little ones have gone to Reading to help Milly Linnell with her newborn, leaving Robert and Jane in the city," he said. "Sitting, waiting, stewing, praying for you, laddie. So, finally, Robbie arrived looking for any news about you, and Madeleine insisted I come looking. I enlisted Carlton here ..." He nodded to the older man "... to help. We figured you should be on the York Road, King's Highway. So, well, here we are."

"Impeccable timing, by the looks of things." Carlton was now beside Joey.

"'Tis that!" Alec exclaimed. He studied Joey's face and grinned. "Another prayer answered, eh?"

Joey shrugged. "Hard to explain otherwise."

"Mr. Brackett," Alec said, "we're in a race."

"Oh?"

"Admiral Howe discovered Mr. Aitken is the recipient of the printing supplies, and he sent messengers by land and sea to General Howe. We've gotta warn him."

Maurice's forehead creased. "Robbie didn't know this, or he would've said." He thought a moment and motioned to Carlton. "Take these young men and our prisoners to my place. I'll ride to Philadelphia and warn Robert."

With practiced hands, Carlton strapped the wounded corporal and the speechless private in sitting positions behind the ink barrels at the back of the wagon.

"Stop your crying," Carlton said to the corporal. "It's only a flesh wound. I suffered worse than that fighting for the king years ago."

Alec shook his head and chuckled. *Poor fellas were counting their fortunes. Now they've got none.*

They started off behind Carlton, whom Alec learned was a veteran of the French and Indian War when he fought for the British with the Virginia militia under Washington. How many former British soldiers like Washington and Carlton were fighting for America?

Good hands to be in.

Still, he had to pray without ceasing. Germantown, where the Brackett farm was located, was an area of contention between the armies.

In early October, British troops had been housed in Germantown. When the Continental Army launched an attack on the garrison, more than six hundred colonists had died in the fight, but the British also lost close to that number. The battle, combined with the victory at Saratoga, was a major victory for the Americans.

Carlton led Alec off King's Highway onto a narrower path.

Alec scanned the woods and fields as they traveled.

The battlefields of America were such a mishmash, how could one tell who controlled what land? Which farmer was a loyalist or revolutionary?

Alec stiffened as they passed the Coenders and Hendericks farms.

At the Updegraeff place, he relaxed a moment. A giant wooden cross was driven into the ground by the driveway to their large two-story house, and a man there gave Carlton a friendly nod.

They continued along, Zims and Beau animated, seeming to sense they were near the finish line. Anticipation rose in Alec's chest.

A man with a hoe in one hand and pitchfork in another—making Alec wonder how the two utensils could work together—stepped out of a field and motioned for them to stop.

They did so and Carlton bowed his head in greeting. "Abraham." The acknowledgement was affable.

Abraham peered past Carlton, catching Alec and Joey in his sights.

"I have word, Carlton." His voice denoted stealth, secrecy.

"Yes?"

"On the good side, General Howe has been away this week and was unsuccessful in opening the Delaware to British supply ships. On the bad, he has returned and, not winning on the battlefield, is determined to win elsewhere."

Carlton shrugged. "Elsewhere?"

Abraham laid down his instruments, reached into a rear pants pocket and extracted a paper. "This!" he said and handed the document to Carlton. "I'd heard he'd offered a reward to his troops and another to local citizens, but I'm inclined to believe the general is losing his mind over the mere printing of Bibles." He threw up his hands. "During a war? It's demented."

Carlton peered down at the dispatch, then back at Abraham.

As he read, his mouth twisted downward. Finished, he said, "The general must be looking for a substantial reward back in London."

He sidled his horse back to Alec and handed him the paper.

Large, bold type declared Howe had doubled the reward for information leading to the capture of:

> *Any Enemy of the Crown who defies God and His Servant, King George III. Who demeans the Bible by Printing copies in Violation of the Law of England, which declares in undeniable terms that the royal family holds all Rights Foreign and Domestic to the English version of the Lord's Word.*

> *Any Violator Shall Be Placed in a Stock for Three Days, Shot, Hung, and Their Body Thrown in the Delaware River where No Miscreants Can Esteem Them a Martyr.*

Alec felt his heart constrict but kept his demeanor. This he had to downplay, put from his mind. If threats could frighten him to inaction, he didn't deserve to serve his true King.

He handed the decree to Joey and said dispassionately, "We're famous."

Behind Alec the corporal had regained consciousness and groaned something about his head being in a vise.

Too bad, poor sod.

As dusk turned to dark Carlton said, "Not far now."

Alec snapped the reins and turned to Joey with a nod toward Carlton. "We owe our lives to that man.

"And Maurice."

"Mm-hm." Alec flexed his stiff shoulders. "Sure will be glad to get a good night's sleep."

"Can you sleep?"

Alec thought this over. "Well, if we find out the Aitkens are all right."

Joey nodded in agreement.

"The Aitkens and the Alfonds," Joey said.

"Them, too." Alec gazed at his friend. "Thinking of Alice?"

Joey released a sly grin and patted his chest.

A faint moon tried to brighten the way as Carlton led them along lanes and through a couple of pastures.

Alec thought back over the last five days. After the chase along Boston Harbor on Saturday came the ambush sprung by the British spy, Clarke, on the outskirts of Boston on Sunday in which Zims had saved his life; the skirmish where Joey and his comrades from Cook's Regiment of Militia rescued him from capture on Tuesday morning; the narrow escape on the ferry crossing the Hudson River at Burdett's Landing with the help of Peter and Étienne Bourdette that night; and the near-capture this afternoon from which Maurice and Carlton bailed them out.

In all this, God had been watching over him and his cargo.

Timing had been perfect at every point. A minute earlier and Cook's Regiment wouldn't've been there to rescue him. A few minutes later and he and Joey would have been caught at Burdett's Landing. A minute in either direction, and today's rescue wouldn't have happened.

What a trip!

Not to mention meeting and praying with Samuel Adams, the evening with Francis Asbury and his prayer for safe passage, the blessing of meeting Moses De La Warr.

And how easily the barrels could have slipped off into the ditch along the jarring, rutted detour he'd taken to avoid Newport, or into the roiling Hudson River with musket balls sailing overhead and everyone diving for cover.

So here they were finally, in Germantown, all those dangers in the past for him and Joey. Or were they?

Did either of the messengers make their way to General Howe? Alec said a silent prayer for Maurice, for Robert and Jane. He looked about him as they rumbled along.

Here and there thickets of evergreen trees encroached on the path, perfect places for evil to lay in wait. After all, Satan had legions at his behest, right? Not to mention Howe's troops.

Howe's troops!

Slowly the daydream he'd had of bright-faced welcomes, of hallelujah hugs awaiting him turned into a misty gray veil of doubt. An ominous feeling crept in.

"Get your rifle at the ready," he whispered to Joey. Joey did so without question.

Darkness seemed to further constrict the narrow road. And the cold seemed colder still.

Probably imagination.

He pulled back on the reins. Carlton noticed and laid back, too, letting Zims and Beau catch him. Seconds later, Carlton rode beside Alec and Joey.

"A problem, son?" Carlton asked.

"A feeling," Alec replied.

"Since the skirmish, folks around here are keeping an eye out for Redcoats. Shadows may be our friends."

"Still—"

Carlton nodded and put his rifle close to his chest with one hand while fingering his reins with the other.

"Slowly," he said.

"My rifle, Joey." Alec gestured toward his Charleville behind them.

He pulled the weapon close and snapped the reins. The horses responded and on they went at a slow and steady gait.

"What do you think's happened to the Aitkens?" Joey asked at last.

"I can only hope God's watched over them as he has us."

The hoot of a night owl broke the silent woods.

"Someone's out hunting," Joey said.

"I hope that owl's the only one."

Ten minutes passed. A short alder in a field seemed to move. Joey tapped Alec on the shoulder and brought his rifle to ready position.

"Nope," he said at last.

Another ten minutes went by. Nothing.

A whistle startled Alec and he shivered until he realized Carlton was the source. Carlton was getting their attention. He pointed, his body a dark silhouette.

Alec followed the direction of Carlton's finger.

There was movement in a clump of trees to their left. A lot of movement. Bodies. Bodies with rifles!

Alec pulled the horses to a halt and put Charlie to his shoulder. Carlton dismounted his horse. Joey jumped to the ground and took cover alongside the wagon.

Tension filled the air. Alec's shoulder twitched at the weight of the rifle butt. He took aim at the form of a man stepping into their path.

"Halt there!" the fellow called in a baritone voice. "Not one of you move."

Carlton called back, "And who's doing the commanding?"

"Lawrence Telner, lieutenant, Continental Army, and a troop of veterans you'd not want to skirmish with, friend."

"Ha!" Carlton exclaimed. "Larry, it's me. Carlton Webb."

Carlton turned to Alec. "You can relax, boys."

Telner and Carlton approached one another, and Carlton said, "We have a load you could take off our hands."

"Oh?" Telner replied.

Carlton escorted him and a couple other soldiers to the rear of the wagon and pointed to the two Redcoats.

"Two hog-tied lobsters?" Telner remarked. "Looks like the job of a friend of ours."

The corporal grunted and spat on the ground. The private whimpered.

"We'd be glad to take these disagreeables from your custody," the lieutenant said. "Perhaps teach 'em manners on the way to the brig."

A couple of minutes later, Alec, Joey and Carlton were on their way.

Shortly after that, Carlton announced, "The Brackett place."

Lamps lit two rooms of a sprawling farmhouse.

A minute later they pulled the wagon to a stop in front of the large, two-story barn.

Madeleine opened a door at the side of the house and Robbie scurried past her.

"Alec. Alec!" he hollered and raced to the wagon.

Alec hopped to the ground and took the boy in his arms.

Madeleine hurried to them, alarmed. "Where's Maurice?"

"He left us to hurry to Philadelphia and warn Robert and Jane," Carlton said.

"Warn them?"

"The Brits have his name."

"And Howe has a fifty-pound reward for anyone leading them to Mr. Aitken," Alec added.

"Fifty pounds!" Madeleine's hand flew to her mouth. "Oh my."

Robbie squiggled out of Alec's embrace, his eyes flashing fear. "What do we do?" he asked.

Alec looked first at Madeleine and next Joey and, finally, Carlton.

Carlton shook his head. "This is probably the best place for all of us to be—not scattered everywhere from here to Market Street."

"What about you?" Joey asked.

"Son, I'm a fatherless widower. No family outside of my Christian brothers and sisters—like Madeleine and Carlton ... and you. I'll stay here as long as you need." He patted his rifle. "This may be a long, vigilant night."

"But I have to go and find—" Alec began.

"No, you don't." Madeleine held out her hand, palm up. "But—"

"You don't know where Robert and Jane or Maurice are," she said. "None of us do. Carlton's right. We should all stay here on the farm."

"Well, then, we have to store the supplies," Alec said.

"In there." Madeleine pointed to the barn. "Maurice has kept an open stall waiting for you. First one on the right. It's big enough for your cargo. The horses can take the next two stalls."

Alec breathed out. "Okay."

Robbie's face twisted into a knot, his eyes red. He swiped the back of his hand across his cheek, drying a tear.

Alec climbed back on the wagon and took the moment to introduce Joey.

"Saved my life, Joey did," he said. "More than once, probably."

Joey shook his head. "My militia the first time. My friends at the ferry the second."

"Deflect all you want. I owe you."

Alec turned to Madeleine. "By the way, do you know an Alfond family?"

Madeline pondered the question.

"Moved here a few months ago," Joey prodded.

"Have a pretty daughter named Alice," Alec chuckled with an elbow to Joey's ribs.

Joey grinned and corrected, "A very beautiful daughter."

"Some who know her would say stunning," Alec added.

"Most," Joey corrected. "Most would say stunning."

Madeleine laughed.

Alec had accomplished his purpose. Lightened the stress and anxiety. His own and the others'.

Soon everyone was inside the barn. Lanterns lit the vast space, the huge front door was closed, and Carlton helped Alec and Joey remove the halters and other strappings and harnesses off the horses.

There was an aisle down the center of the building, with stalls on either side. Three cows lowed from one stall and a handful of sheep bleated from another. A dozen or so hens of various colors had scattered into the air upon their arrival and, perched upon stall doors, looked on curiously.

"I'll get Zims and the other horse water," Robbie offered.

"And grain?" Alec asked, his eyes on Mrs. Brackett.

She nodded and brought two full nose bags to hang behind Zims and Beau's ears.

"These two," Alec patted their heads, "carried this heavy load—"

"Day and night," Joey added.

"From Boston to here—"

"In five days," Joey finished.

"As fast as a mail run," Carlton said.

"I'll go in and bake a dinner fit for a king," Madeleine said.

"No kings but Jesus honored here," Carlton said with a smile.

"Fit for heroes," she corrected and headed out.

"These barrels aren't light," Alec said. "Maybe we should keep them on the wagon until we know what we're doin'."

"Can we move the printing press from the city out here?" Joey asked.

Alec shrugged. "We considered that before the Redcoats stormed Philly. Guess we should have done so. But Mr. Aitken thought keeping the paraphernalia in the city was easier. Besides, he didn't want to endanger the Bracketts."

"Too late for that now."

Alec cringed.

"What about this other stuff?" Carlton pointed to the rough iron and yard goods.

Alec pushed hair back off his forehead, wondering. After a few moments, he said, "I need to deliver them to Mr. Bradford and Mr. Hinckle. That could be my entry into town and—

"And loading the press your exit!" Joey exclaimed. "I'll be your assistant."

Alec nodded. "That's *if* Mr. Aitken decides to move the press out here."

"This way you don't have to worry about soldiers spotting the barrels and guessing what's in them. Like the guy back in—"

"Moreland Manor," Alec said.

"We've got to stop finishing each other's sentences," Joey said with a smirk.

CHAPTER 32

General William Howe looked askance at his adversaries around the card table. This was as soon as he could gather them. None of these men could come Sunday, a day of worship.

Sheep.

He himself had been deployed through Wednesday to oversee new battle plans along the Delaware River and had returned in the afternoon, leaving Clinton in charge at the river. He simply must free up the river to get supplies delivered. The rebels were ensconced into battle works on Mud Island, and British ships were set ablaze at every attempt to get upriver with supplies to Philadelphia.

His army couldn't operate with no supply line, whether in a city or not. Thankfully, many Loyalist farmers around Philadelphia were selling meat and canned vegetables to Howe's quartermaster.

And of course, Friday was always reserved for his evenings with Elizabeth Lloyd Loring.

So here they were, at Robert Morris's—well, Howe's— home now.

Howe put his earlobe squarely between thumb and forefinger, squeezed, and assessed the three gentlemen seated around his dining room table. All Loyalists. Two of them had been heavily involved with the Continental Congress but had had their eyes opened by reality and good sense.

To his left, the forty-something Joseph Galloway, former speaker of the Pennsylvania Assembly and member of the Continental Congress until he decided he could not accept independence and became a leader of the Loyalists. Last month Howe had appointed Galloway Philadelphia's civilian commander under the city's occupation.

Directly across the table sat rotund, seventy-something, London-educated former Philadelphia Mayor William Allen, who had become the wealthiest man in Philadelphia through investments in trade, land, agriculture, industry—oh, yes, and a bit of privateering on the side. Allen supported a number of public interests and had built the state house, Independence Hall.

To Howe's right, his back straight and stiff in his chair, was forty-year-old Jacob Duché, a professor of oratory, Anglican rector of Christ Church, and chaplain to the Continental Congress from 1774 to 1776, delivering the prayer at the first opening of that body.

All three were defectors to what Howe considered an honorable cause—England's. All three had joined Howe for Brag, his favorite game of cards. And "brag" he could because he was as accomplished as they came.

As-nas, the Persian card game? Well, he was superb at that as well.

But Brag, with a fifty-two-card deck where the game came down to two final players and where the best three cards won, this match separated men from boys. And Howe? He was a man's man as well as a general's general. He'd pick their pockets and their brains tonight and perhaps discover the name of Biblio-Ghost.

Opponents thought Howe's earlobe twisting was a "tell," and imagined they could read his thoughts by his habit. Those who thought so were the ones he fleeced the most.

But his first goal this particular night—Biblio-Ghost's identity. Second—sending his guests home lighter in the money purse but thankful they were among the elite at the general's table. Each man had a snifter of liquor at his side, each a reason to seek Howe's favor.

Howe looked again at the hand he'd been dealt and decided to divert attention around the table.

Looking at the diminutive Duché, he said, "So, Jacob, you and Elizabeth are sailing back to England, I hear."

Duché nodded, looking troubled.

"How soon?" Galloway asked.

"Soonest." Duché pushed his wireless glasses up his thin nose.

"Something about a letter," Howe pressed.

Duché waved a hand, trying to focus his attention on his cards and his decision.

The ante was ten English shillings and by the time the bid reached him, Duché'd have to put down two pounds and ten pence of his cherished trove. Despite his inherited wealth, the man was stingy, but in certain ways that trait made him a crafty card player.

"A letter *you* wrote." Howe felt like he was riding a stubborn horse that refused the hunt. If he had a spur on his boot, he'd use the barb.

In a controlled fit of pique, Duché placed his cards on the table face-down and said, "I'm out."

Good. Consistent with your character. Now the hand's down to three of us.

"Tell us the circumstances," Allen urged. A lawyer by education, the man commonly cut to the chase. One reason he was a bad card player; the other flaw being the quiver in his jowls when deceiving his mates.

"The missive the general refers to is one I wrote to Washington."

"Yes?" Howe said.

Duché removed his eyeglasses, peered at the lenses, and wiped them with a linen handkerchief. He was obviously gathering his thoughts. He was, after all, in the presence of gentlemen, and aristocrats were rue to entrust more personal information than necessary.

Finally, Duché placed the palm of his hands on the edge of the table as if to keep himself from tilting left or right, and blurted out, "I pleaded with Washington to end the Revolution because of the dire mood here in Philadelphia, the division among friends and family and business partners and church brethren and every soul, apparently, in our fair city."

"Sounds common enough thinking to me," Galloway said.

"I agree with the Quakers and Peace Germans," Duché said. "God alone has the right to overthrow a legal government, so how can you swear loyalty to a revolutionary authority?"

"Well," said Galloway, "reading the so-called Declaration of Independence confirmed my suspicions—the radicals deceived the people from the beginning. Notwithstanding all their solemn professions to the contrary, independence was always their goal."

"I'd say," Howe agreed. "They turned down our peace offering without a glance at the document when Richard and I met with them at Staten Island, and that was fourteen months ago. And I say 'met' in the least connotation of the word. As far as Franklin, John Adams, and Edward Rutledge were concerned, we—and, by extension, the king and England—were objects of disdain."

Howe cast his eyes upon Duché. "I'd say, Jacob, there is no reason to sail off to London."

"I fear charges of treason," Duché said, "if the British army were to lose this war. Otherwise, I will return. I was born here. I hope to die here. London? Cambridge? Though I lived there while in college, they never replaced this city in my heart."

"But victory is ours, no doubt," Howe said.

Now he himself had lost concentration on this blasted card game.

He folded the cards in his hand and continued, "I've word from Brigadier General Cortlandt Skinner, who himself was a New Jersey Assembly speaker—like you, Joseph. He says our overwhelming Mid-Atlantic campaign convinced five thousand New Jersey men to take oaths of allegiance to King George. We believe more New Jersey men are serving among our ranks than in the Continental forces."

Galloway leaned forward and said, "A lot of them, no doubt, initially supported the revolt against parliamentary taxes. But inciting war and demanding formal independence? Well, that was nonsensical. Folly."

"The economy drives war," Allen said, "Even such a slight as over-taxation."

"You think not power?" Galloway asked. His eyebrows rose and he turned his eyes to Howe. "You've fought wars on two continents and off the Brittany coast, William. What say you?"

Howe considered the question a moment and weighed in.

"You, my friend," he said, eyeing Allen, "ought to know about finances, eh?" Howe switched his focus to Galloway. "And you, Joseph, as speaker of the Pennsylvania Assembly for eight years and as a delegate to the First Continental Congress, ought to know about power."

Galloway shrugged noncommittally.

"Don't deny the truth—you had that power right up until your Plan of Union flopped." Howe referred to Galloway's plan for the colonies to have their own parliament whose Grand Council would interact with its British colleagues and have the power to veto laws the Council opposed.

"My Plan of Union was a grand idea," Galloway objected. "The Crown would appoint a president-general of the Colonial Parliament while the colonial assemblies would appoint delegates to three-year terms. We'd remain under the British Empire but have a bit of say over our affairs."

"Lost by a slim six-to-five vote, I recall," Howe said. "So close."

Galloway flashed a remorseful smile.

The three colonists sighed in regret.

Howe fingered an ear and continued, "Back to the question of what drives war. I'd say equal parts money and power, two elements often mixed together. Like a good stew in a hotchpot. Wealth is the venison and partridge. Power is the carrots, parsnips, beets and onion.

"Wealth and power. Fine alone but brilliant together."

His companions all nodded agreement, and Howe thought of his three decades fighting battles, planning campaigns, leading assaults and defenses. Now was the time to leave nostalgia behind and begin a new chapter.

"I'll plainly enjoy my seat in Parliament," he said, "more than ordering cannon fire on a city."

"Words over musket balls," Duché said.

Howe grabbed the opportunity to change the subject.

"Speaking of words," he said. "I have a question regarding God's Word, the Bible."

Quizzical looks all around reflected that he was not thought of as "a man of God."

He peered at Galloway and asked, "Were you, Joseph, present the day the request was brought before the Continental Congress for printing Bibles?" Then to Allen, he asked, "Or you, William?"

Galloway's forehead wrinkled and Allen's eyes sought the ceiling.

Howe waited and counted the seconds. After three, Allen responded, "No, I was not there."

At six seconds, Galloway raised a forefinger. "But I was."

"And do you recall who brought the request?"

"Certainly. The two pastors, William Marshall and Patrick Allison, and the two from the University of Pennsylvania: John Ewing and Francis Alison."

"No one else?"

One eyebrow raised, his mouth screwed up, Galloway was certainly searching his memory banks. Two seconds, three...

At five, he blurted, "The printer. The printer was there."

Howe nearly leaped from his chair. But kept his bottom on the seat and leaned in. "And who might—"

A knock on the door interrupted Howe and before he could respond, Lieutenant Brown rushed into the room. His face was animated, his right hand holding a sealed parchment.

"Urgent. From the admiral," he declared.

Howe rose from his chair and motioned to Galloway, saying, "Hold that thought."

Brown strode to Howe and handed him the document.

Howe tore open the scroll. His brother Richard's personal handwriting seemed to speak to him: "William, take notice!"

Howe's eyes ran down the brief note. Richard had intercepted a ship sailing to Boston with printing supplies. The name on the bill of lading: one Robert Aitken. And Aitken's address followed his name.

Howe felt a thrill down to his toes. Accolades from London awaited. An invitation to dine with the king. A knighthood, perhaps.

He turned to look at Galloway. "The name?"

"Aitken," Galloway said. "Robert, I think."

The prey's in sight.

Howe brought his full attention to Brown and commanded, "Lieutenant, get Cutthroat. And dispatch this name to every barracks."

He handed Brown the communiqué.

Facing his guests, he said, "I'm afraid duty calls."

As the three men gathered their money and their coats, Howe mustered his thoughts. Apprehend this miserable malcontent Aitken, lock him in the stocks of the public square for a good day or two of pelting with rotten tomatoes and spoiled eggs, toss him in the dock for a quick open trial for trying to make a mockery of the King's Bible and English law, then dangle the blackguard from a rope too lax for a quick death. Because a good public firing squad would be too painless for such a loathsome rotter.

First things first: seize him.

Robert Aitken thanked God for the foresight to secure his personal and business finances from prying hands before the Redcoats stormed Philadelphia.

He'd been able to send Alec north with enough Spanish coins to pay for the printing supplies.

He'd also had the prescience to cash in the Continental currency before the savings had depreciated to the point that "not worth a Continental" had become common parlance.

If only Congress and the states had coordinated their monetary policies, the Brits wouldn't have found counterfeiting so easy. Their forgeries were so exceptional they'd driven the genuine money into oblivion.

If only Congress had called on Robert Morris or another person with financial acumen to organize that aspect of the new country.

If only they'd prepared a vast arsenal of weapons before declaring independence.

If only.

There was a vast mine full of "if onlys." Yet without the "if onlys," God would not have shown himself the architect of the new republic—like Gideon's army.

Most of Robert's modest fortune was in the form of specie—silver and gold coins that were the main types of commodity in the colonies. Coins that couldn't be imitated.

Laying down his ledger, he walked over, slid his bed a foot to the left, knelt, and with a penknife pried up a floorboard.

He drew up a large metal box, rose to his feet, and laid the box on the bed.

When, Lord? When?

Sergeant Conrad "Cutthroat" Casey led three dozen soldiers double-timing down Market Street.

General Howe and Lieutenant Brown joined them at the Morris house.

"Forge on, Sergeant," Howe said. "You're the point of the spear. I'll hold the shaft. You know the address."

"Sir!" Cutthroat saluted and dashed ahead, his scabbard thudding at his thigh, a rifle strapped to his back.

Cutthroat didn't try to conceal his joy for the hunt. Deer, bear, wild boar. Great stuff. But humans? They were the ideal. In a way, Cutthroat wished he were alone. One-on-one, man-to-man confrontation was a thrill. But to take a company of men and full-bolt crush the enemy with utter abandon? Such was the crown jewel of conflict.

The evening's bitter cold only fueled his enthusiasm.

Light from a lamppost signaled the street he sought. He glanced behind him. His men were keeping up well, their rifles held at chest height. General Howe and that waster, Brown, were on horses behind them.

Cutthroat signaled his men to turn up the street.

A furious knock rattled the front door, catching Robert's attention. His hackles rose. Who could that be at nine o'clock in the evening?

This could not be good. This could be danger.

He replaced the money under the floorboard and descended the stairs two at a time.

The door cracked at the insistent blows.

He reached the living room and stepped toward the door.

The hinges shook under thundering raps and a man's deep voice called out, "Aitken! Open!"

Not "Robert" but "Aitken." That didn't bode well. And he didn't recognize the voice.

Answer? Don't answer? Hide?

The sheer fear Robert felt at this moment wasn't for him but for his daughter.

He twisted toward the stairway and called, "Jane! Jane!"

The girl was in bed, probably reading a book.

"Aitken!"

This moment had drawn closer and closer with every passing day, Robert knew. He had fought the idea of being caught. He'd pretended such a thing couldn't happen, not to stop the Lord's work. No. He'd prayed God would confound Howe. That he'd blind the Redcoats like he did the men from Sodom in Lot's doorway. That he would deliver Robert, Jane, Robbie, the entire family.

But now, at this second in time, his faith wavered.

"Open the door, Aitken. If you're in there, you'll want to open up!"

Spittle clung to Cutthroat's chin as he pounded away. He knew someone was on the other side. No candle light glowed from within, but he knew. His instincts never failed him.

His troops surrounded the two-story wooden home.

"Aitken!" He cursed and shouted, "Aitken, open the door, or I swear I'll—"

He put his shoulder into the door and the wood cracked.

Again and wooden slats would splinter, he was sure of that.

He motioned for two of his soldiers to barge through the structure.

The noise was almost deafening.

Robert sucked in a breath, figuring things would go better for him and Jane if he didn't force this soldier to break his way in. Cooperation could earn him a tiny bit of coinage, so to speak, in the courtroom. If there were a courtroom.

Meantime, he prayed perhaps Jane could get to her hiding place before being discovered.

He reached his hand toward the door knob, breathed out, and ...

Cutthroat stood aside as two privates piled into the door, which seemed to open by itself under their brawn.

A smile of satisfaction spread across his face. He followed a squad of torch-bearing soldiers inside. Then his face went slack. The place was shrouded in darkness. He bulled his way past the men and into an empty room. No furniture. No drapes. Nothing.

The words that left his lips hadn't been uttered by a human being since Pontius Pilate's soldiers found an empty tomb. Cutthroat was sure of that.

A British soldier, breathless and his face ashen, a corporal by his insignia, stood before Robert. He was the soldier Robbie had spoken with at the corner when he left for the Bracketts'.

"Mr. Aitken?"

Robert hesitated. He could lie.

"They know your name, sir. You have to leave. Now."

Robert was stunned.

Why was this soldier warning me?

The question of how they'd discovered his name would have to wait for a future answer. If he had a future.

He stammered.

"Now!" The soldier's eyes were wide with alarm.

Robert stepped back and motioned the soldier inside.

"No," he protested, standing firm. "Get Robbie and escape. While you can. General Howe and Cutthroat are leading a company of soldiers to what they're told is your house. They'll find out soon enough that you're not there."

"Where are they?"

The corporal nodded to his left. "North Fifth Street."

"Thank you, Corporal—" He wondered the man's name.

"You shouldn't know," the soldier said. He spun on his heel and hustled away.

Ahhh, Robbie's friend.

CHAPTER 33

About an hour later, Maurice Brackett, his horse lathered and himself winded, heard the commotion from a distance. As he approached the Aitken home at North Third and Arch streets, he noticed lanterns waving in the night and men's hoarse voices hollering orders back and forth.

His heart caught in his throat, but he realized the hubbub came from two streets to the west—somewhere around North Fifth Street.

He stroked his horse's nose.

"Easy now, Goldie," he said to the mare and ambled down Race Street. He kept his eyes out for the three majestic oak trees that marked the corner of North Third Street. The city's lampposts down Market Street were too distant to light the way. But moments later he saw the trees and turned down the street. The Aitkens' home fifty yards away was dark. He tethered Goldie to one of the oaks and hurried toward the little house.

The front door was slightly ajar. Maybe they'd left in a hurry. He drew a breath and stepped inside.

"Robert?" he called in a loud whisper. More insistently, "Robert."

The room was so dark he couldn't see his hand in front of his face.

"Robert, you here?"

Silence did not speak volumes, he thought. Silence was, well, merely that. Maurice could only guess the circumstances, so guess he did.

Admiral Howe's messenger had arrived, unveiling Robert as the printer they'd been calling "Biblio-Ghost."

The uproar Maurice had heard came from the vicinity of the Aitkens' former house, meaning Howe had assembled a force to overpower and arrest the lawbreaker.

But Howe had the wrong address.

Meanwhile, Robert had somehow learned he'd been unmasked.

Ha!

Maurice hustled back to Goldie, lifted himself onto the saddle of his tired horse and turned her handsome head westerly.

He'd ride parallel to Market Street to Robert's close friend Douglas Bradford and his livery stables. That would be the wrong direction but the right move. For surely a horse would be Robert's quickest means out of town.

At least that was what Maurice guessed. What he hoped. What he prayed.

Three minutes later he'd covered the three-quarters of a mile to the livery at the corner of Race and North Eighth Streets. The livery was dark and so was Douglas's cottage to the rear of the smithy.

Maurice slid off the saddle, tethered Goldie to a railing outside the livery, and hurried to the cottage.

Before his second knock, the door opened and Douglas yanked Maurice inside.

"What are you doing here?" he asked in a low, strained voice.

A woman in the next room called out, asking Douglas who was at the door.

"Go back to sleep, darlin'," he responded and looked again at Maurice.

Maurice took the cue. "Howe's men are all over Robert's old house and he's gone from the new place. I thought he and Jane would be escaping the city."

"They are. They're headed to your place."

Praise God!

Maurice was upset he'd missed them but exhilarated they'd fled away.

"So they're on horseback. How long ago did they leave?"

"They can't be two miles away. Hustle and you'll catch 'em before you know."

"Yeah, well, Goldie's pretty tired after what we've been through today."

"Leave her with me. We'll saddle you up one of my stable."

General Howe leaned forward in his saddle and cursed beneath his breath.

What had happened to Aitken? The man had a wife and brood of brats. They couldn't simply vanish. And why was this address on the *Gouden Adelaar's* bill of lading if the scoundrel lived here no longer?

Cutthroat, rage in his eyes, stalked toward Howe, the troops behind him scouring an obviously empty house. To Cutthroat, missing Aitken was like waving a red rag at a bull.

He held a pistol in his right hand, appearing eager to expend a ball of lead on the first person to look at him sideways or speak to him—idly or otherwise.

Howe admired the man's zeal. Certainly not a character of whom to make sport. Absolutely the predator Howe wanted on this hunt. For a "hunt" it was.

Aitken's head mounted on my wall. That would satisfy.

"Scour the area," Howe groused, teeth grinding. "Knock on every door. Someone in the neighborhood must know their whereabouts."

Cutthroat nodded and half-turned on his heel when a man and woman stepped out of the home across the way and walked with purpose straight toward them.

Howe took account of the couple. Both middle-aged. The man was clean-shaven, the woman homely as a hedge fence but neatly attired.

The man raised a hand in greeting.

"General Howe," he said, "I'm Hugo Nesbitt. This is my wife, Helen."

Howe nodded.

Cutthroat, snarl in place and pistol still in hand, stepped between them and Howe.

"Your business?" he asked, scowl firmly in place.

Nesbitt looked askance at Cutthroat and made the wise decision to look over the soldier's shoulder and train his eyes on Howe. He pulled a piece of paper out of his pocket and waved the page in the air.

"The reward," he said. "We can lead you to the man you call the Biblio-Ghost: Robert Aitken."

Howe's senses were heightened.

Money always speaks loudest.

"I'm listening," he said. Cornering the prey, this was called. How close were they to the Ghost? How thankful would King George be? "Go on."

"You know his name, then?"

"Yes."

"But you don't know where he lives now?"

"Apparently not."

"The reward still stands?"

"Yes."

"Well, the family up and moved awhile back," Nesbitt said.

"We figured that, numbskull," Cutthroat cut in.

Howe raised a hand toward his underling to preclude ill will when there need be none. Cutthroat growled, perhaps thinking his own reward pinched.

Howe kept his voice calm and sociable. "Exactly where did they move?"

Nesbitt raised a finger and pointed east. "Heard they were two streets down. Corner of North Third and Arch."

Howe peered down at Cutthroat and repeated, "North Third and Arch."

"Painted green," Nesbitt said. "Owned by a Mr. Carlisle, who lives on Chestnut Street."

Cutthroat swiveled around and hurried off, yelling orders to his men.

"So—" Nesbitt began, a question coming.

"You'll get your reward," Howe said. "The double amount."

Helen Nesbitt blurted, "Better than us, they thought."

Her face was contorted—with what? Hate? Disdain?

"Everyone round here was all agog about the Aitkens, they was. Oh, how godly they were." She shook her head, feigning praise. "Oh, how beautiful Janet was, how nice the kids acted, so respectful to their elders. Oh, how smart Jane was, how cunnin' the little 'uns were..."

A true back biter.

"Oh, they had everyone bamboozled, they did," Helen Nesbitt went on. "Then they turned on their king. Our king. Yours and mine.

This caught Howe's interest. "How, exactly, did they turn against the king?" he asked, wanting to end this conversation but curious to know the answer.

"Said religious freedom could only be secured through independence," Helen said.

"That meant through this horrible war," Hugo added.

"Said the British had violated the natural rights of the American colonists, in particular the right to property."

"Well," Hugo put in, "Aitken never said that, but his friends did."

"Yes, and his friends claimed the Parliament was tyrannical and illegitimate."

Hugo harrumphed.

"One of the pastors declared failure to support the Revolution amounted to treason against God. Called us Tories 'agents of Satan,'" Helen said, her chin lifted in indignation.

"Pshaw!" Hugo remarked. "Scotsmen and Irish and Welsh. This war is not so much an American rebellion as an Irish-Scotch-Welsh Presbyterian rebellion."

Howe thought of Pastors William White, Patrick Allison and William Marshall. And there were others. Like that damnable John Witherspoon. Not a decade after immigrating to America, the Scotsman took over as president of the College of New Jersey and had turned the campus into a center of revolutionary sentiment.

Howe's opinion of this husband and wife changed. They were incorruptible in his eyes now. Salt of the earth. Loyal to the king. Outspoken. He wondered how opinionated they'd been when they heard all this codswallop from the lips of Aitken and his pals.

Well, he'd heard enough to fill a bowl with pig swill. Now was the time to move on.

Curtly he gazed at the couple and said, "Come to my office tomorrow. You'll get your reward—*if* they're there."

And off he rode, hoping to reach Cutthroat before the soldiers broke through the door at North Third and Arch.

Robert was as adept at riding horseback as he was making horseshoes, which was to say, "not at all."

The same for Jane, his young bookworm-slash-assistant-slash-typographer.

In Scotland you'd be lucky to have a highland pony. Rugged and inexpensive, but more than Robert's family could afford. And in America he and Janet and the children had been city-dwellers from the day they'd landed seven years ago.

So, hobbling along a country road in the middle of the evening was no simple trick. Or trip. Or trundle. And none of this was made easier by leaving behind so much.

As soon as the British conquered Philadelphia, he and Janet had discussed the possibility—perhaps the inevitability—of what had happened tonight. Besides the money, they'd packed necessities into satchels to carry on their backs.

They'd secreted the printing press, type, what paper they had in stock and other paraphernalia necessary from the print shop to the hidden space behind Pope's Head.

Robert thought they'd done all they could except altogether leave the city. And yet here they were. As his da would say, "Tatties o'wer the side." Or, in today's word: "Throw the potatoes overboard. Disaster has struck."

Perhaps they'd failed to totally keep the particulars of their moves away from prying eyes, neighbors who didn't share the same faith and values.

Thank God only Jane and he were left to avoid detection. He took a moment to thank the Lord for moving on the heart of that soldier to warn them of their imminent arrest.

He turned to Jane, riding to his left. "You okay, sweetheart?"

"Sure, Da." A girl of many words, normally, she'd been quiet as a graveyard since saddling up.

Not like her at all, my little intellect-in-a-bundle.

"What's on your mind?" he asked.

"Ma, Euthan and Maggie in Reading. Alec. Robbie. My friends. The church. Those who're in danger. Maybe Pastor Marshall at Seceders. Pastor White." She released a mournful laugh. "Not much, huh?"

Robert shrugged. "You love people. Makes sense you're concerned for them."

"Well, yes, and not to forget." She hesitated, then, "My favorite boots, the brown ones. I left them at the print shop."

They laughed and Robert leaned back and patted the saddlebag Douglas had given them. Yes, the money pouch was still in there, and he felt a bit paranoid for checking.

The old Scottish saying—"*Mony a mickle maks a muckle*"—was true. "Look after the pennies and the pounds look after themselves."

With the finances secure, he figured if they could reach the Bracketts' safely he'd have three worries: Alec, his press, and everyone's safety.

Except for Janet and the children being secure in Reading, the rest was a debacle. Alec was who-knew-where. And the press? Well, all his equipment was in one place: the wrong one, encircled by the enemy.

Could he and Maurice have even a gamble at moving that gear out of the print shop and to the Brackett farm? Maurice had offered a portion of the barn. In fact, he'd considered the move before the fatal September British invasion. He shook his head. Surely he'd missed that spurring by the Holy Spirit.

Robert peered around, trying to get his bearings. He could discern forest but nothing distinct.

They didn't have far to travel, he was sure. But their exact location? Forget that. If only—

"Hey, there!" A voice behind them cut through the darkness. The timbre, the tone, the accent belonged to Maurice Brackett.

Yes! Maurice to the rescue.

Relief shed trepidation from Robert's shoulders. He breathed out a thanks. Maurice being out on the roads looking for them meant news.

Maurice rode between Robert and Jane, shook Robert's hand, and leaned over to plant a kiss on Jane's forehead.

"Can't believe I found you," Maurice said.

"Had to leave in a hurry," Robert said.

Maurice jabbed his thumb toward Philadelphia. "'twas a ruckus back there."

"You know?"

"I was coming to warn you that Admiral Howe had sent a message to his brother naming you as the Biblio-Ghost." Maurice tittered. "Biblio-Ghost? I must say, Robert, that sounds like a lot to live up to."

Robert frowned and shook his head.

"I'd like to be a ghost tomorrow," he said. "We need to get my printing gear out of the city. You and me, Maurice."

"And me, Da," Jane objected.

Robert shrugged. "If we're caught, you'll be caught. And if Howe doesn't kill me, your mother will."

Maurice announced, "You can add Alec and his friend, Joey, and maybe Carlton Webb to the crew."

"Alec?" Robert asked, and at the same time Jane yipped an exclamation of joy.

Alec's back. Alec … is …back! My boy! Praise the Lord. Yes, praise you, Lord!

"Oh, Da, Alec made it," Janet exclaimed. "God answered our prayers!"

"Yep," Maurice said. "He and Joey arrived with all your supplies earlier tonight. They brought the warning your name had been discovered up in Boston. I rode off to warn you while they kept going to the farm."

Robert's shoulders dropped, like they no longer carried the weight of the world of worry. What relief!

"Alec's got tales to tell you," Maurice said. "I wanted to get to your place post-haste. There was riotous goings-on at your *old* house, so I went and found your new place abandoned. Figured you'd want a quick getaway out of town, so I went down to Douglas's and he said you'd come and gone. Switched horses there and here I am. And, boy, will Madeleine be happy to see you two. She's been worried sick. Prayin' morning and night. Robbie arrived yesterday and filled us in on Janet and the children."

Robert gathered his thoughts. "Your offer for us to stay at the farm still stands?" he asked.

"Ha! Of course. No want for fowl in the pot, eggs in the pan, milk in the glass, warm beds—"

"And hospitality," Robert added.

"So let's head on home," Maurice said, and with a twitch of his horse's reins, he was off, Robert and Jane on his tail.

CHAPTER 34

When Robert, Janet and Maurice rode into the Brackett driveway, Alec ran out to meet them, with the others in the house trailing behind.

Robert read the joy on the young man's face from ten yards away. His own emotions were about to bubble out of his skin. He heaved a thank-you heavenward and came down off the horse to a wild embrace that lasted long moments.

"We did it," Alec said, taking a step back. "We got the load. Three barrels full and plenty of paper stock."

Robert nodded, feeling speechless, or at least without words worthy of the moment.

"Couldn't have done it without Joey," Alec said, motioning toward a freckle-faced young man standing with Madeleine, Robbie and Carlton.

He motioned toward Joey and introduced him.

"Well, Maurice said you had tales to share. We'd better get settled and hear a few."

Later, the group gathered around the Bracketts' kitchen table, eating the treat and drinking milk—"straight from the cow," Robbie had announced.

Robert smiled at his son's exuberance.

Farmer or printer. Printer or farmer. Your choice, Lord.

Robert's eyes swept around the table. "The question is how to snatch the printing press out from under the eyes of the Redcoats and haul the equipment here without detection."

Silence followed. Milk was drunk. Cookies were chewed.

Then Alec blurted, "Disguises. We can put on fake beards, powder our hair ..."

Robert pondered the idea.

"You've got make-believe beards?" Robbie asked, his eyes big as saucers. "Boy, I want one of 'em."

Everyone laughed.

Alec shook his head at the boy's question and smiled at him.

"We don't have them yet."

"I don't need any disguise," Joey said. "Never been here before. No one knows me except the Alfonds, and what are the chances of seeing them? As much as I want to see Alice, that'll have to wait 'til we get the press loaded out here."

"So, Alec, you in disguise, and Joey can ride into town with the supplies for Douglas and Henry," Robert said. "In broad daylight, acting like everything's normal and you're merely doing business."

Alec nodded. "A sprinkle of flour in my hair and I'm a passable forty, right?"

Robert looked Alec over. "I've known you since you were so tall," he said, lifting his palm to his shoulder, "so you're not fooling me. But the Brits shouldn't recognize you. Simply keep a distance from any Loyalists we know—Mrs. Nesbitt in particular."

Jane piped up, "Maybe Mr. Bradford would lend a hand with the press."

"Surely," Maurice said. "That fellow could lift the press all by himself."

"He's an ox," Carlton added. "Shod my stallion one time and when the horse kicked him, Douglas gave that boy an elbow that took his breath away. No more kicks."

Knowing chuckles circled the table.

Robert laid out the rest of the plan and suggested they all get sleep to be alert for the day ahead.

Elsie was alone in her room, waiting for her papa. He had not returned after hurrying off in the afternoon when he'd received notice a ship full of armaments for the Americans had arrived unexpectedly early. Along with the notice was a dispatch from his partner. The letter was posted in France, which Monsieur Beaumarchais reported was on the verge of allying with the colonists. The king was sending Foreign Minister Charles Gravier to negotiate an alliance with the Americans and draft a treaty recognizing the United States.

"A breakthrough," her father had called the news. "There'll be a celebration in the Green Dragon tonight."

He'd kissed her on the cheek and rushed out to inform Major General Artemas Ward and Mr. Burdick.

Elsie had pulled a shawl over her shoulders and prayed the rosary, prayed the rosary, prayed the rosary. After a while she simply held the beads in her hands, having received no answers from her heavenly Father but feeling a sense of comfort at least.

Before her, a fireplace—so tall she could step inside—blazed bright and warm.

Outside her window snow fell in oversized fluff balls. Sally had said snow arriving from the north, from Canada, was unusual, even bizarre, this early in the winter.

Elsie wondered how difficult this place was to live through the winter. Was Boston like home? She'd certainly prefer to be here right now, at least until she heard from Alec. If indeed she heard from Alec.

CHAPTER 35

The aroma of bacon cooking and the distinct warm smell of a wood-burning stove wafted up the staircase and awoke Alec. After several days of cold meals or no meals at all, Alec's stomach growled, wakening him fully. He turned and elbowed Joey beside him.

"It's time," he announced.

Joey grumbled and pulled the heavy quilt to his neck.

Alec shook his friend's shoulder.

"Joey!"

"All right, all right." Joey lifted his head, rubbed his eyes, opened one eye, then the other. "Felt so good sleepin' in a bed after more than a month on the cold, hard ground and then in the back of a wagon."

"I'll bet it did."

They scrambled to pull on socks and boots, threw cold water on their faces from a basin on a bureau, and stumbled downstairs to the kitchen.

Janet was setting plates and silverware around the table, while Madeleine Brackett stood at the woodstove, scrambling eggs, flipping pancakes, and frying slices of bread. The bacon was in the oven.

A feast.

Robert entered the kitchen a few steps behind them, appearing anxious.

"Have a seat, everyone," Madeleine said. "Breakfast will be ready in a jiffy."

The back door swung open and in walked Maurice, holding a bucket full of milk and Carlton holding another. As the door swung shut behind them, a small hand appeared, pushed the door open and Robbie stepped inside.

He held high a ceramic pitcher with a stopper plugging the top and announced, "Syrup! The best thing God ever made." He hesitated, "Well, trees, but—"

"We know what you mean, Son," Robert said.

Maurice set his bucket on the cupboard and said, "Robbie was dressed before me this morning, raring to go 'do the animals.'"

"I milked a cow," Robbie said.

Alec smiled at the boy's enthusiasm.

"I could use a farmhand." Carlton eyed Robbie.

"Oh, thanks," Robbie said, "but I've got a job with my da."

Carlton chuckled. "My loss."

"Set the syrup on the table, Robbie," Madeleine said. "Breakfast is ready."

Moments later, everyone was seated, grace was said, and all mouths were busy eating.

"Even have dried blueberries in the pancakes," Alec noted. "This is a treat."

Maurice plucked a Bible off a nearby shelf and said, "A double portion. Food for the body and sustenance for the soul."

He started reading:

> The plans of the heart belong to man, but the answer of the tongue is from the Lord. All the ways of man are clean in his own sight, but the Lord weighs the motives.
> Commit thy works to the Lord and thy plans shall be established.

"Proverbs 16:3," Maurice said.

"I'd say our work *is* committed to the Lord," Robert said.

"Amens" echoed around the table.

Alec knew the Word of God was as unchangeable as God himself was. Yet the question formed in his mind: *So, you're convinced your plans today will succeed?*

Always asking yourself the tough questions, eh, Alec Craig? Confident about your plan, are ya? Assured you're not going to your grave, laddie? Positive Elsie won't be receiving any devastating news of your demise?

Even as the questions rambled about in his head, as accusations came that he was a small and foolish young man with a high opinion of himself, Alec knew they came from the enemy. As soon as God's Word was read, the devil came in to steal that truth, to kill and destroy God's people, to spoil any plans he deemed too righteous to bear fruit.

Alec shook his head as if to toss overboard the incrimination that he possessed doubts.

"You all right, son?" Robert asked.

The question broke Alec's reflections. He turned his attention to Robert and decided to share with everyone his idea for a water-driven printing press.

He told about his visit to the Mill Pond in Boston, the power of the water turning the huge stones, how they might harness that force to pressure type plates onto an ink-soaked surface of some sort.

"The process is all gears and levers," he said. "The printing speed would be extraordinary."

"Fascinating," Robert said, interlacing his fingers and, by the look on his face, conjuring an image of the press.

"A grand idea," Maurice added.

"That's my brother!" Robbie exclaimed.

Alec looked across the table to observe Jane's reaction—since soon after he'd arrived in America, she'd been his looking glass into all sorts of ideas they'd shared.

Jane grinned. "It's a marvel."

"And we have a river not a mile away from home," Robert said.

Chills tingled up Alec's back, the thrill of a challenge brightened his eyes. Satan's accusations were forgotten.

As they ate, they spoke about who could design the gearworks, where they could go to have iron or wooden gears manufactured, who had the expertise to assemble the invention. And, as importantly, how'd they finance the work.

"Mr. Franklin," Alec said. "He's always inventing things. Do you suppose he'd back us financially?"

"Won't hurt to ask," Robert said.

Alec squirmed in his chair, thinking of the possibilities.

"Of course," Robert said, "this is your brainchild, Alec, so she shall be your success, financially and professionally."

Alec sat back. He'd thought of the ramifications before, but now they seemed so much more—more real. More tangible.

He could barely wait to write Elsie about his trip, the possibilities surrounding the printing press, everything.

If I'm not captured first.

When finished with breakfast, Robert gazed about the table, prayed, and said, "We leave in five minutes."

Enthusiastic nods answered him.

Standing with Jane at her side, Madeleine said, "Tonight, when you return ... it's a venison celebration."

General William Howe swung his feet out of bed and lifted his six-foot frame to his feet.

He rubbed his stubble, straightened his shoulders, and fingered an ear.

"*Look* like a general. Carry yourself with aplomb," his father, Emanuel, the 2nd Viscount Howe, would chide.

William knew self-confidence and composure were crucial. State of mind was all-important. His father had raised four sons, and three had achieved high military rank. Besides Richard, an admiral, William's oldest brother, George, had earned the rank of general before being killed in the French and Indian War. Youngest brother Thomas commanded ships for the East India Company, probably earning more money than any of the other three, if not the fame.

The Howes were born and bred to be leaders. Success was expected, whether the job was little or large. Leading British troops in all of North America? Large. Finding this pipsqueak Aitken? Little—at least on its face. But King George saw the publication of Bibles without his sanction as a reprehensible—blatantly and worse, public—slap in the face. That strike, coming from a commoner, had put a premium on this capture.

And so, Aitken's seizure would in fact have large implications when Howe returned to the British Isles. Yes, besides putting a smile on the king's face by winning this deplorable war, if the general could also put Aitken's head on a platter, he would in essence kick open the palace door for a grand "welcome home" gala. Icing on these new cakes the wealthy were eating for dessert nowadays.

The immediate problem was capturing the bugger.

Howe shook his head. He'd slept little, plagued by the seething anger of missing the Biblio-Ghost last night. By all accounts, Cutthroat had missed Aitken by a mere few minutes at the second house. Cutthroat had been as peeved as Howe, who'd ordered the place thoroughly searched for clues to Aitken's whereabouts and burned to the ground once the sun rose this morning. He stepped to the window and looked eastward in the direction of 3rd Street. Sure enough, smoke billowed high above that neighborhood.

You'd assume the flames would bring a smile to his face. But merely the name Robert Aitken made his brain hurt. He'd given the feeling a name: The Aitken Ache.

Well, he'd soon relieve the ache. He was giving himself nine-to-one odds to catch the miscreant. He compared his chances to holding a pair royal, the best hand in brag. And, true, this ordeal felt more like a flush but, hey, you can't have everything.

Howe turned from the window and stepped to his wash basin to shave and prepare for the day. His aide had readied his uniform and filled the basin with water that still steamed in the cool air.

First thing: Howe'd order stocks built right out front of his headquarters.

Nothing like a front-row seat for the public outrage before what he expected to be a highly publicized hanging. Everyone would be invited. Allison, White, the whole bunch. They'd all be shepherded to front-row seats. That is, after they were forced to throw rotten tomatoes at Aitken's bare head while in the stocks.

Second order: A door-to-door search of the city. Man-to-man confrontation with every single one of the Seceders Church members. More carrots with another reward. More sticks with threats.

He put straight razor to beard.

Who says November is always dreary in Pennsylvania?

"First to the livery where we'll drop off Mr. Bradford's rough iron and recruit him to help," Alec repeated the plan as he snapped the reins. "Then to Henry Hinckle's mercantile to deliver the yard goods."

Several bales of hay covered the rough iron and yard goods packaging, but Zims and Beau pulled the load along as if the wagon were empty. A major change from five days tugging a cart loaded with barrels of ink and stacks of paper.

They were approaching the outskirts of Philadelphia.

Joey peered at him and chuckled.

"What's so funny?"

"I don't recognize you. The Alec Craig I know is about twenty years old. A handsome *young* guy."

Alec smiled. Mrs. Brackett's flour-in-the-hair trick worked well. The beard, too. In case someone recognized him who shouldn't.

They'd lost sight of Robert, Maurice and Carlton, who'd ridden ahead on horseback.

When the group had left the farmhouse, the sky was heavy-laden with clouds. Ominous.

Alec looked up. Splat! A large snowflake landed square in his right eye with a sting.

Ouch!

"Man!" he exclaimed, rubbing his eye.

Joey held out a hand and watched as another large flake landed on his palm.

"Kinda early for snow, isn't it?" he asked.

"Yep. But I'm young yet. Those men," Alec pointed in the distance, "probably have tales to tell."

Joey mimicked, "When I was a boy, I walked waist-deep in snow to go to the schoolhouse."

"And the snow was to my da's chest." Alec held a hand palm-down to heart height and laughed. "But I do remember the winds in Scotland would knock you over."

"Sure," Joey said, skepticism dripping off the word.

Alec said. "Well, I admit I was a bit puny."

"But, really, in Connecticut we've had snow a few times by the end of November. The thing is, those storms always come from the west or southwest. These clouds here are bearin' down from the north-northwest."

Alec looked again, protecting his eyes with a hand, and watched the clouds for a minute.

"I believe you're right," he said finally. "I hope no storm prevents our plan."

Shortly afterwards they approached the Schuykill River. Two Redcoats guarding the bridge eyed them wearily, causing Alec's heart to flutter and he glanced behind him into the wagon to make sure Charlie and Bess were handy. But the soldiers let them pass.

A half-hour later they were circumventing the city, traveling counterclockwise toward the west end of Market Street. Alec looked south and spotted a plume of smoke slowly circling skyward, carried away in the direction of the wind.

"I wonder what's afire," he said.

Joey shrugged. "Got a firehouse, don't they?"

"Yeah."

Alec blew warm air into his hands, pulled his hat down to his ears, and snapped the reins.

They entered the city at the north end of Seventh Street and hurried down to Race Street.

When they were within fifty yards of Bradford's Livery, Alec pulled on the horses, hand to brake lever. Then he put a hand over his brow to fend off the snow and peered around the store and adjacent cottage.

No Redcoats were in sight. Besides that, he and Joey were simply delivery men bringing Mr. Bradford necessary supplies. If approached and questioned, that was their straightforward story.

"See anything?" he asked.

"Snow," Joey deadpanned. "A coupla guys haulin' firewood. A few kids playin' fox and hound. Otherwise, no."

Alec looked directly at the livery and squinted. In spite of the weather, Douglas Bradford kept the outside door to the blacksmith's forge open. Yellow and red light blazed within. Inviting. But dangerous?

Now or never.

He took a deep breath and snapped the reins. As they drew closer the sound of hammer on anvil was unmistakable.

Alec stopped the wagon directly in front of the door, jumped down, and walked inside, motioning Joey to join him.

Douglas was hammering molten iron on an anvil and didn't hear them enter. But when he spotted them out of the corner of his eye, he swung around, astonished.

A cautious smile crossed his face and he asked, "Can I help you, gentlemen?"

"Mr. Bradford, it's me. Alec Craig."

A look of doubt crossed Douglas's face, he stared closer, and finally exclaimed, "My boy! It *is* you!"

With a set of tongs, he grabbed the rod of iron he was forming, dipped the sizzling metal in a bucket of water, took two giant steps to Alec, and bear-hugged him as if he were a long-lost child.

As tall and lanky as Alec was, he couldn't put his arms around the burly blacksmith.

"Laddie, laddie," Douglas said, "we've been so worried." He looked over Alec's shoulder and spotted the wagon. "You brought the goods and an assistant?"

Alec nodded and introduced Joey.

"Glad to meet ya, Joey. My wife and I've been praying for your friend here. Have you connected with Robert and Jane?"

Alec gave Douglas an abridged version of what had transpired and their plans. Done, he pointed toward the smoke.

Douglas shook his head. "I hadn't noticed. Haven't heard. That's close to Christ Church."

Alec pondered for a moment. "And near the Aitkens' home."

"Oh, no!" Douglas stepped back, concentrated on the smoke, and squeezed his hands into giant fists. He locked Alec with a set of steely eyes and said, "Soldiers are out in force looking for Robert. Came by here again this morning, demanding his whereabouts."

"And?"

Douglas scoffed. "Think they got anything out of me?"

Alec chuckled. "Guess not."

"Biblio-Ghost, they've been calling him. Until now. Until they learned his name." Douglas scowled. "No one's taken the reward as far as I've heard. Maybe last night they did."

Alec considered this revelation. The man he considered his second father was liked throughout the city. Well, mostly.

Maybe not by Mrs. Nesbitt and other outspoken Loyalists, like the Knights, but by the people who mattered most. The pastors and Messrs. Monroe, Adams, and Jefferson. And men like Douglas Bradford.

Had they burned down the house? What of my clothes? My books? My poems?

Alec's brow furrowed and he shook his head in anger and then resignation. He couldn't let any fire, even to the house where he and the Aitkens lived, slow down their timetable.

He gazed at Douglas. "We need your help."

"Anything."

Once the three men had unloaded the rough iron, Douglas said, "I'll shut down the forge, tell Tessy I'm leaving, and hurry over there."

Back on the wagon, Alec again blew warm air into his cold hands.

The snow was thickening, the large flakes turning to medium-sized.

They continued on and turned left down North Ninth Street to Hinckle's Mercantile on Filbert Street.

At the store, Henry Hinckle was startled, both at Alec's looks and that he had finally arrived from Boston.

"Is that truly you?" he said. "Boston must age a person, eh?"

He chuckled and Alec and Joey joined in.

"I hadn't heard you were home," Henry said. He lowered his voice, "You shouldn't be here. It's dangerous. For you, for Robert and Janet and Jane and the wee ones."

"Don't worry, Mr. Hinckle. We've got a plan."

"I hope you do! What times we live in, eh? A war's going on and there's all this upset about Bibles." Henry shook his head. "God's Word scares people, doesn't it?"

"And rightfully so," Alec replied.

Henry nodded. "Rightfully so."

"Well, my friend Joey here and I'll unload if you're ready.

Henry took a measured look at Joey before responding. "Sure enough. Good to have an extra hand helping, eh?"

Finished, Alec and Joey again climbed onto the wagon. Alec brushed a good inch of fluffy snow off the bench and sat down. Looking at Henry, he asked, "You wouldn't happen to know what's burning, would you?"

Henry shook his head. "Didn't hear a fire alarm. Maybe they want whatever it is to burn."

CHAPTER 36

As they headed east toward North Eighth Street, Joey elbowed Alec and asked, "Suppose this snow'll put a kink in everything?"

Alec shrugged. The storm couldn't be good, right? He had no answer. He swiped the back of his hand across his eyes.

"At least we've only got about a mile to the print shop."

At the corner, they turned south, riding right across Market Street.

As they crossed the street, Alec looked eastward and noticed a knot of men hammering away on lengths of lumber. They appeared to be in front of Robert Morris's home.

"I wonder what they're building in the middle of the street," he said.

Joey shook his head.

The shortest route was straight down Market Street, past the Morrises', Independence Hall, and Mr. Franklin's house. Surely more Redcoats would stand between them and the print shop in that direction. So, Alec chose a route down South Eighth Street to Chestnut Street, where they headed east again, parallel to Market, until they reached South Second Street.

The north wind was whipping swirls of snow around them. The flurry had turned to near-blizzard.

"The heavens have busted open," Joey declared, tucking his chin into his coat. "How close are we now?"

"Close," Alec said, turning the horses north across Market Street again. The steeple of Christ Church—so near he could throw a stone and hit it—was barely visible through the snowfall to their left. "One more minute."

The thought struck him. "You notice there haven't been slews of Redcoats up and down the streets? They're supposed to be searching for Mr. Aitken."

"Ha!" Joey said. "The snow ain't no curse. It's a blessing."

"Right." Alec knew he shouldn't be surprised. *Never doubt God. Ever.*

Loud voices rang out ahead of them. Alec pulled Zims and Beau to a stop and threw out his right hand in front of Joey.

"Pope's Head," he said.

"A pub?"

"Coffee shop-slash-pub. All according to the time of day. Morning it's a coffee shop; night, a pub. Our print shop's hidden in the back of the building."

"Too early to be drinkin'."

"You'd be astounded." Alec guided the wagon down an alley to the right, turned left into a narrower alleyway, and pulled to a stop at the rear of the wooden building.

Four horses were tethered to a couple of small trees.

Alec hopped to the ground and knocked on a door. Two hard taps, two soft taps and two hard ones.

No answer.

"Can't hear you with all the noise in Pope's Head," Joey guessed.

Alec rapped harder. Tap-tap... tap-tap... tap-tap. The door creaked open a sliver. Maurice's face peeked out.

"Boys," he whispered and opened the door wide.

Wind and snow blew in along with Alec and Joey. Alec shivered but the difference between the room inside and cold outside was welcome.

Douglas and Carlton stood nearby. And there behind them was a bearded man, leaning over a wooden frame, busy with a screwdriver. Wait. The stranger was Mr. Aitken.

"Aha. Sir!" Alec exclaimed.

Robert's smile was broad, his eyes alight. "Even fooled my third son," he declared.

Alec looked about. They'd disassembled the wooden press to the point that its bottom half, the body, was unattached from the top half, including the press plate and roller and handle. Set apart were the platen and ink table.

"We've got to be quick and quiet," Robert said as rowdy shouts sounded through the wall to Pope's Head.

"They're off the caffeine and on the sauce already," Carlton noted.

This was a good thing, Alec thought. The noise from the Redcoats and the snow and wind from heaven would provide protection from detection.

Alec and Joey joined the four men in loading the printing press aboard the wagon, moving all the paraphernalia to the front, and maneuvering the bales of hay to hide every bit and piece.

As they loaded Robert said to Alec, "I've told Douglas your idea for a water-driven press."

"And I can help. I'd be blessed to lend a hand," Douglas said hefting the roller carriage on his shoulder. "I'm certain I can fashion the gears and pulleys, most everything you need. Give me the design and we'll make her happen."

"Wonderful." Alec blew out a breath, smiled broadly.

"All for future discussion," Douglas said.

Alec nodded. Further encouragement, further confirmation.

A blast of snow knocked his hat off.

Joey laughed, looked skyward, and said, "Someone, with a capital 'S,' wants a snowball fight."

"A friendly one, I hope," Alec said.

Robert stood outside and looked about him. Thanks to the snowfall, the operation was going smoothly. The storm had driven most soldiers from their duties to the warmth and camaraderie of Pope's Head.

When he, Maurice, and Carlton had arrived, Maurice had gone to the pub and informed Jake Tremble they'd be moving out the printing press.

Maurice returned to the shop and told Robert that Jake had flashed a grin filled with mischief.

"Let me help," Jake had said.

"We've got enough hands," Maurice had replied.

To which Jake had said, "Naw. I mean in other ways. The hour's never too soon to break out the beer and liquor. Combine that with a bit of competition at the dart board and, well—"

The snow and cold, the beer and the darts had all made for success ...

"What have we here?" The question, its words dripping in inebriation, was bellowed by someone behind Maurice. Robert looked in that direction. That someone was a soldier, and that soldier had a musket aimed in their general direction—as if he wasn't sure at all what he was observing. Well, he wouldn't be, would he?

A shiver quivered down Robert's spine and he glanced around him. Despite the storm, a quiet encompassed everyone as they assessed the danger.

Go boldly, Robert. You're innocent as can be.

Robert spoke light-heartedly, saying, "Suspicion always haunts the guilty mind."

The soldier shot him a vacant look.

"Shakespeare," Robert said. *"King Henry the Sixth."*

A frown seemed to extend from the soldier's hat to his chin.

"A bit sozzled are ye, my friend?" Robert said. "We're moving a lady's, er, spinning wheels and braiding tools."

"Pshaw! In a storm?"

"Had to be today," Maurice interjected, catching hold of the ruse, "or my wife would skin me alive."

The soldier lightened up and chortled. "Women!"

All the men nodded as if the soldier had offered a milestone of wisdom.

"Aye," Maurice said. "But the spinning keeps her off my hands. So the joy works both ways, eh?"

"Eh," the soldier repeated. He lifted the rifle to his shoulder, mumbled, "Carry on, then," and disappeared around the corner, staggering toward the front of the building.

"What was he doing back here anyhow?" Douglas asked.

Carlton pointed toward a yellow circle in the snow at the corner of the building.

"Oh" was the collective response.

Sleet mixed with snow and pelted them like little metal spikes.

"We've got to keep the type plates dry," Robert said.

"I've got canvas back at the livery," Douglas offered.

Robert scratched his chin. "Too far. Too much time."

"I can check with Jake. See if he has something we can use. Blankets, maybe."

"Blankets," Alec said, eyebrows raised. "The cubbyhole."

"Right." Robert hustled inside to the cubbyhole he'd created for his children to hide in case of a raid.

He knocked on the wall at the right spot and a latch popped open. Inside were four blankets.

Yes! That'll be enough.

"We'll use these," Robert said, pulling them out. "Be careful, Alec, to keep every type plate covered."

He handed Alec one of the blankets. "I'll pass each blanket out as needed."

Alec nodded.

The metal type plates were stacked in several piles along the back wall near the door, each precious plate filled with hundreds of individual letters, tightened like a vise to prevent spills.

The older men formed a line while Joey stood atop the wagon and Alec a few feet forward.

One by one—as careful as they could be swift, as swift as they could be careful—they moved the plates onto the wagon.

Alec was quick with the blankets and stacked the plates in order.

"Don't want to confuse Jeremiah with Isaiah, or Luke with John," he said.

When they finished Douglas brushed his hands together, eyed Robert, and said, "As quick as you can say Jack Robinson."

Robert couldn't help himself but chuckle.

"Wouldn't have happened without you—" he swept his eyes around to the others, "all of you."

"Well, we're not done yet," Maurice said. Looking at Robert, he added, "You have to get out of town unseen. Carlton and I will accompany the boys back home."

As Robert closed the print-shop door, he handed Jane's beloved brown boots to Alec, hugged them all, and swung up onto his saddle which was covered with snow and sleet.

Leaning forward to sweep the snow from his horse's eyes and nose, he said to Douglas, "I'll get her back to you, my friend."

Douglas nodded. "Get yourself free from this city and print those Bibles. That's all I ask."

As he rode away, Robert lifted a thank-you to God, remembering a prayer from *Piercing Heaven: Prayers of the Puritans*:

"God of my end, as the sun is full of light, as the ocean is full of water, as Heaven is full of glory ... so let my heart be full of thee."

The heaviest snow in his life pummeled the earth as Alec guided Zims and Beau north toward Germantown. Maurice rode on ahead, Carlton behind. The soldiers who had been at the Schuykill bridge when they'd ridden into the city had sought refuge. Probably huddled in front of a warm fire, Alec reckoned.

Can't wait to get front of the fireplace at the Bracketts'.

His ears felt like icicles, and he wished he'd worn one of those hats someone invented with flaps down over the earlobes. Alternately he wrapped his one hand in a handkerchief, keeping the other in his coat pocket, and swapped when one hand or the other was capable of holding the reins.

Alec turned to Joey. "I sure am glad you joined me back in Connecticut."

"Yep, you couldn't have done all this without me."

Joey was looking for a rejoinder, but what he'd said was the truth, so Alec simply nodded assent.

"You admit as much?"

Alec nodded again.

No argument here, my friend. Freely stated, freely thought. A God-sent helper.

Following a moment of silence, Joey continued, "Truth is, there was nothin' for me back home. And bein' part of this ..." he waved an arm toward the load in the wagon "... well, I believe our meeting was God-ordained. Heck, I may sign up to work on your printing press if you'll have me."

"I'm still an apprentice myself," Alec said.

"I'll be an apprentice's apprentice if there's such a thing."

Alec pondered the idea of being an employer instead of an employee. That's exactly what would happen if his brainchild became reality. If ...

First things first, he thought as he blinked and wiped snow from his eyes, trying to keep Maurice within view. Although Maurice was no more than ten feet ahead, he appeared like an apparition.

Alec couldn't tell where the road was. No other wagon-wheel or horseshoe tracks betrayed the way. The edges of the road weren't visible. The blanket of snow was fully two or three inches now. The wind had already caused small drifts here and there.

Move a couple feet off the road and we could lose the whole load.

He quaked at the thought.

Maurice turned and said something, but the wind and snowfall muffled the words.

"What'd he say?" Joey asked.

"Redcoats?" Alec responded.

"I said, 'we're close,'" Maurice bellowed with a laugh, obviously able to hear them.

Relief. Joy. What do you say when you combine the two?

"Hallelujah!" Alec exclaimed.

Five minutes later they arrived at the barn and the door swung open.

Robert, still in full-bearded disguise, opened his arms wide. "Come on in, fellas."

Robbie stood behind his father and called out, "Alec! Alec! You did it."

"*We*, Robbie. *We* did it," he replied.

"With a well-timed blizzard," Joey added.

Alec pulled the horses into the barn, stopping the wagon next to the stall where they'd print the Bibles.

He jumped down and hurried to unhitch Zims and Beau.

Robbie hauled over a couple of heavy towels and Alec and Joey wiped down the horses and led them to a warm stall filled with hay and water while Robbie hurried off to help his father.

By the time Alec and Joey shut the stall gate, the older men had put their horses away and were unloading the wagon.

The satisfaction, the joy ...

CHAPTER 37

The Brackett barn was a whirlwind of activity.

Though the early winter snow had startled Pennsylvanians, the storm ended that night. Nothing had prevented Robert, Alec, Jane and Robbie from getting to work. With Joey, Maurice and Madeleine pitching in, printing was proceeding smoothly.

The three barrels of ink were a good beginning as was the supply of special paper.

Carlton and Maurice had hauled over a Franklin stove from Carlton's home and continually stoked it to keep the barn moderately warm.

Robert sighed a deep thankfulness as he surveyed the process. Jane covered ink balls with ink and pressed them to the type plates, Alec put his muscle into pulling the lever that pressed the ink-covered type plates together with paper, and Robbie collated, keeping each precious page of paper in order.

Robert sat at a table, binding each Bible, using covers he had printed while in Philadelphia. He was proud of the quality of the covers--that they had turned out so well. They would be a good cover for the newly printed New Testament.

HOLY BIBLE
Containing the NEW TESTAMENT
Newly translated out of the
ORIGINAL TONGUES
And with the former
TRANSLATIONS
Diligently compared and revised.

At the bottom of the page was the Pennsylvania crest that declared: "Virtue. Liberty. Independence."

Binding was a task Robert loved, having learned the skill as an apprentice while a lad in Scotland after all his chores on the croft were done.

Robert had always enjoyed prose, admired how authors strung words together into phrases and sentences and entire stories in sometimes extraordinary fashion. But the Bible and all its sixty-six books held highest esteem in his pantheon of favorite books, so far above man's attempts at wisdom, at beauty.

Soon he hoped to print its entirety—both Old and New Testaments—the magnificence of the creation story, the poetic splendor of the Psalms, the wisdom of Proverbs, the hidden nuances and meanings in Song of Solomon, the precision of the prophets, the life-changing power of the gospels, the inspiring stories of the lives of Job and Elijah and Moses and Ruth and David and Daniel and Esther and Paul and numerous others.

Most of all, the poignancy of the cross toward which both the Old and New Testaments pointed. The totality of the Bible displayed the overwhelming love of God the Father, Jesus Christ his Son, and the Holy Ghost.

The book defied natural explanation. Forty authors—from shepherds to fishermen to kings to scholars, a cupbearer and a military general—writing from prisons to palaces over a span of two thousand years and yet the narrative was defined in seamless harmony.

And the theology?

Of all the religions in the world, Judaism and Christianity were unique, their prophets foretelling events that came to pass, most particularly more than one hundred prophecies concerning the birth of the Messiah.

But when considering the claim Jesus was the Savior, the Jewish Messiah, Robert came upon the one supreme fact that secured Christianity's veracity: While many people had willingly died for causes in which they believed, none had freely died for a cause they knew to be false. If Jesus had not been resurrected, none of the twelve apostles would have laid down their lives to preach his divinity. Not one.

The Resurrection was an inescapable truth, a life-changing certainty, a message of hope in time of despair, healing in a time of pain, an anchor in any storm, and a guide to life everlasting.

And Robert's calling was to place the message of that reality into as many hands as possible. On the battlefield, in the home and school and throughout the churches of America.

A cough shifted his attention to Joey, who was loading a wooden box full of the pocket-sized Bibles onto the wagon. The lad from Connecticut had proven invaluable. Already he'd transported a supply of the Book to General Washington's men in Valley Forge.

Joey had reported back about deplorable conditions at the encampment. They redoubled their prayers for the troops, and sent Joey back, this time with food and clothing from the Bracketts' Germantown neighbors.

At that moment General William Howe stood at the front window of the Morris mansion, not hearing a word from the mouth of Sergeant Conrad "Cutthroat" Casey. The man had proven a deep disappointment. He'd made no progress finding Robert Aitken. The printer had vanished along with his wife and toddlers. The Biblio-Ghost was an apparition indeed. A ghoul. A phantom.

Howe bellowed to his new aide de camp, Lieutenant Victor Ham. In a fit of pique Howe had demoted Ham's predecessor, Lieutenant Brown, the day before. No good reason. Only irritation at the circumstances. His troops were stymied, his lover was unavailable, and this feeble search was gnawing at his nerves.

Feels like death's head upon a mopstick. Poor and miserable.

"Ham," he said when the soldier arrived before him, "get rid of that thing."

"Sir?"

Howe pointed out the window.

"Have those blasted stocks torn down and burned."

He'd have no constant reminder of his disappointment.

"Yes, sir."

Howe turned to Cutthroat, who was still rambling on about a grand idea of tracing Aitken. The plan involved a circular search pattern whose epicenter would be this headquarters. Day by day his squad would fan out further and further.

More soldiers would be used because more doors would be knocked down, more citizens and clergy interrogated. Oh, and yes, more money was necessary for a still higher reward. More. More. More.

"Sergeant Casey," Howe said abruptly, raising his palm.

Cutthroat, whom Howe knew was as frustrated and aggravated as he, stopped in mid-thought.

"Yes, sir."

"I'm resigned to your failure."

Cutthroat's brow furrowed and his face turned shades of crimson. Howe had seen that look one day in the battlefield when the man was about to slice open an enemy's throat.

So, despite his superior rank, Howe decided to relent. He coughed. "That is, *our* failure."

The crimson softened to hues of pink, but the dark eyes were as intense, menacing.

Howe chose his words with care. "Aitken's out of the city, I'm sure. And who knows where? We don't have a clue what direction he's gone, do we?"

Cutthroat shook his head. "Too many friends," he said. "But if I could only use a bit more—" he interwove his fists and turned them in a twisting motion—"persuasion."

Howe shook his head.

"My kingdom for a rack, or rope and pulley, or thumb screws," Cutthroat pleaded. "We'd have the answer like—" He snapped his fingers.

"And if the word got out? We'd undergo the same maltreatment on our return to England," Howe said. "No, Sergeant. No more troops for the search. Keep those you have and continue. Hunt down whatever clues you find. But when the spring thaw comes and the Delaware flows freely, we'll need every soldier we can muster for battle."

"But until then—" Cutthroat began.

"Dismissed, Sergeant," Howe said curtly.

Despite Elizabeth's warm and expert companionship, he'd be more than happy to return home. Even without Biblio-Ghost in shackles, or his bones in a box.

Taking a break for lunch with the others, Alec found his favorite spot in the Brackett home, a window overlooking fields that stretched a hundred yards or so. In the summertime, corn grew on the entirety of this piece of land.

He pulled a paper from his rear pocket and flattened out the sheet on a table.

Before him was the rudimentary diagram of a water-powered printing press.

Alec wanted to return to Boston for another look at the Mill Pond operation. Perhaps Mr. Leonard, the mill manager, could tell him the appropriate size and weight of the wheels needed in Alec's plan.

He knew this—his innovation would happen, and he wanted to be the one at the helm.

And, yes, while in Boston he'd again see the young lady who'd made his heart flutter.

Flutter away, heart. This is no mere infatuation.

But such a trip must wait.

He'd had Joey stop by a postal station on his friend's first Bible delivery and post a letter to Elsie. He'd told her about his travails getting here, the hand of God on him, his hopes for the printing press, his new address should she be able to reply.

So many demands on his life, he thought. Printing and distributing the Bibles, followed by his joining the fight in the Revolution, followed by creating a printing press. And in the midst of all this, there was Elsie. When and how did she fit in?

He prayed to God, who certainly had his life's timetable arranged.

Protect Elsie and Monsieur de La Borde, keep them in America. Boy, are my prayers selfish!

Back to his illustration, Alec had a good picture in his mind's eye of how the press would work. First the entire operation would have to be in a spot where the current was fast.

One large vertical wheel would start a smaller, geared horizontal wheel in motion, turning another vertical wheel that was hooked to a double-armed lever. The arms of the lever were connected to an ink plate and would pressure that plate onto a platen, or type plate, causing the impression.

Voilà. A printed page.

His obstacle might be keeping pace with the speed of the press. Now that was not a bad problem to have.

Robbie's voice interrupted Alec's thoughts. The boy shook what sounded like a bunch of marbles in his hand.

"Time for that game of Cherry Pit?" Alec asked.

A mischievous look, a gleam in the eyes, and Robbie's

response: "Naw. Dropsies. And watch out 'cause I've been practicin'."

Sally Burdick knocked on the door to the de La Borde rooms, and Lisette ushered her inside.

"A letter for Mademoiselle Elsie," Sally said.

Elsie appeared from another room, her face brightened at seeing Sally, and she hurried to hug her.

They'd become close despite the age difference. Elsie was such a beautiful spirit. If there was one person who could lift you out of the doldrums, Elsie was Sally's choice.

Sally held the letter out to Elsie. "For you," she said, conspiratorially, "from a certain young suitor."

Elsie snatched the message from her fingers and tore open the envelope.

As the girl read, her face told myriad emotions. Anticipation followed by fear then joy, surprise then relief. Finally, exhilaration.

She turned her look upon Sally, eyes bright with excitement.

"He's safe. They're printing the Bibles somewhere outside Philadelphia. And—" Her arms swept toward the ceiling. "—he plans to come back to Boston!"

Sally cheered in shared joy and noticed a second sheet of paper. "Is that more news?"

Elsie flashed a bashful look. "It's a three-stanza poem ..." she held the page close to her bosom "... which I feel I should keep to myself."

"As you should, dear," Sally replied with a bright smile. "A love poem, no doubt. One of many, I expect."

CHAPTER 38

Low on ink and out of paper, Robert hung his head.

He and his crew all stood in the barn's workspace.

Exhilaration and depression struggled against one another—two emotions at loggerheads.

On the one hand they had printed hundreds and hundreds of New Testaments, distributed them to military encampments, homes, churches. On the other hand, they were forced to stop.

Robert's money had run dry, and well, you couldn't print when you didn't have paper and ink.

"What now, Da?" Jane asked.

"Yeah," Robbie chirped, "whatta we gonna do? Can we go see Ma?"

Robert shrugged. For once he had no answers. But seeing his beloved Janet after all this time would be a blessing.

The words of Scottish poet James Thomson came to mind:

> Give a man a girl he can love,
> As I, O my love, love thee …

The barn door flew open. In burst Maurice Brackett, and with him came a frosty wind. The winter had been bitterly cold, and their prayers had gone out doubly every day for General Washington's men. But oddly, there had never been enough snow to prevent Zims and Beau from hauling the wagon or a sleigh over the countryside.

"A post," Maurice said, holding high a brown packet. "From Boston. From Charles de La Borde."

Maurice handed Robert the envelope. Inside were two letters.

"One's addressed to you, Alec," Robert said and handed Alec the note. "The other's to me."

"Read on," Maurice said.

"Out loud, Da," Jane added.

"Of course," he replied and read:

"'Dear Mr. Aitken,

'On hearing of your need for printer's ink and special paper for printing Bibles, I asked my business partner in France, Monsieur Beaumarchais, to search for your needs and ship them to Boston.

'He found those materials in Italy, and they arrived today, 9th of March. They are being stored in the Green Dragon and await your arrival to pick them up.

'If for any reason I am unavailable, contact Mr. Benjamin Burdick, proprietor.

'It is my deep pleasure to offer these materials without charge. Indeed, I consider being able to assist as a blessing from our Lord and God.

'If ever you need my assistance in any matter, please feel disposed to communicate with me at my commercial enterprise, Roderigue Hortalez Company, at One Fleet Street, Boston.

'Yours sincerely,

'Charles de La Borde'"

Robert scanned the faces around him. Eyes alight. Heads shaking in disbelief of the timing of God.

"He's given us time to take a break before getting back to work," Robert said.

"I'll travel to Boston," Alec volunteered and motioned toward a stack of freshly completed Bibles. "Matter of fact, I'll take a batch with me."

"Count me in," Joey said, "and we can drop off a few to my militia."

"But Alice—" Alec objected.

"You remember just last week Alice gave me her blessing for the entirety of this work. She'll wait. If nothing else, I'm sure of that."

Robert eyed Jane and Robbie. "And we can go and visit your mother in Reading. That'll give Maurice and Madeleine an escape from having all of us under foot."

Maurice simply shook his head. "The more the merrier— forever and a day. Our tithe goes to our church, but this is our offering, freely given."

Madeleine stood by Maurice's shoulder. She had walked into the barn while Robert was reading the letter, and she nodded. "You're all a pleasure to have as long as you like. Bring Janet and the bairn back with you."

Alec stepped away from the others, leaned against the stall door behind which Zims and Beau peered out. Both horses came over to him and Zims nudged his shoulder.

Alec patted them both on their cheeks. Zims nickered. Beau shook his massive head.

Alec turned away from his friends. This was as close to "alone" as he was going to get in the barn. Across the center aisle were the horses, cows and sheep.

He opened the envelope. Inside was a letter from Elsie.

"My dearest Alec," she began and already tears formed at the corners of his eyes. Elsie told him how she missed him, how she hoped he would come quickly, how she wanted to hold his hand and stroll along the Charles River, snow or rain, how she was growing closer to the Lord and ... and ... and reading her papa's Bible.

She ended with "Hurry, please."

He brought the letter to his lips.

"I will. I will."

After supper Robert went out on the front porch of the farmhouse, heavy coat pulled tight around him, and stood looking at the brilliant night sky.

Creator God is amazing, he thought. What an adventure he has led us on.

He stepped off the porch and strolled to the barn. Slipping inside, the fragrant aroma of cedar still burning in the stove met him and he walked over to Robbie's collating table. An entire King James Bible lay there and he found his way to Isaiah 52:7.

"How beautiful upon the mountains are the feet of him that bringeth good tidings, that publisheth peace; that bringeth good tidings of happiness, that publisheth salvation; that saith unto Zion, 'Thy God reigneth!'"

Robert shook his head in wonder that his dream to be one of those publishers had come true.

To think, a dirt-faced boy from a croft in Scotland, fortunate to have survived childhood, weeping himself dry and covered in the blood of Covenanters after the Battle of Duddingston Loch, now a grown man here in America publishing the Word.

Thank You, Father, for watching over us in all of this, for protecting us and directing us in Your plan to bring Your written Word to this new land.

Robert was truly the Lord's Biblio-Ghost and printing His Word for the people here was indeed bringing Americans, so embroiled in war, true freedom.

(Dear reader: If you enjoyed this book, please take a minute to write a brief review at Amazon.com and Barnesandnoble.com as well as check out the other books on my website: www.markalanleslie.com.)

AUTHOR'S NOTES

- Robert Aitken went on to print the New Testament again in 1778, 1779 and 1781, then the entire Bible in 1782. The Bibles measured 7.25 inches tall by 4.75 inches wide by 2.5 inches thick.

On September 1, 1782, Congressional chaplains Rev. Dr. William White and Rev. Mr. George Duffield told the US Congress that Aitken "undertook this expensive work at a time when, from the circumstances of the war and the English edition of the Bible could not be imported, nor any opinion formed how long the obstruction might continue. On this account particularly he deserves applause and encouragement."

Nine days later Congress recommended Aitken's edition of the Bible "to the inhabitants of the United States ..."

In 1783 Dr. John Rodgers of the First Presbyterian Church of New York suggested to General George Washington that every discharged soldier be given a copy of Aitken's Bible. Since the war was nearing an end, and Congress had already ordered the discharge of two-thirds of the army, the suggestion came too late. However, Washington said, "It would have pleased me well if Congress had been pleased to make such an important present to the brave fellows who have done so much for the security of their country's rights and establishment."

When Robert died in Philadelphia in 1802, his daughter Jane carried on his work and became the first woman in the United States to print an English translation of the Bible.

- The power-driven printing press was indeed invented, but not by Alec Craig and not on the American continent.

The first working water-driven printing press was built in the 1800s in Germany and replicated by William Hughson Golding (1845–1916) in the Fort Hill area of Boston, Massachusetts, in the 1870s. Golding also built three printing presses at the Mount Washington Hotel which were unique to New England, with a huge water tank supplying water to the hotel as well as the presses.

- France formally recognized the United States on February 6, 1778, with the signing of the Treaty of Alliance that called for France's direct participation in the war.

- Charles de La Borde was chief aide to Pierre-Augustin Caron de Beaumarchais and stood at Beaumarchais's side as an early French supporter of American independence.

- General William Howe was finally notified in April 1778, that his resignation was accepted. On May 24, the day Howe sailed for England, General Sir Henry Clinton took over his post as commander-in-chief of British armies in America. There is no record of Clinton searching for Aitken or the printing press.

- The Philadelphia occupation ended within nine months. On July 27, 1778, General Clinton evacuated his fifteen thousand troops from the former US capital back to New York City to increase that city's defenses against a possible Franco-American attack. They were harried all the way across New Jersey by General George Washington's troops.

- Guy Fawkes Night memorializes what became known as the Gunpowder Plot, executed in 1605. Fawkes and seven others rented a cellar that extended beneath Westminster Palace. They planted more than thirty barrels of gunpowder and were about to blow up the entire building during the opening of Parliament on the night of November 5th.

The reason behind the plot: After the pope excommunicated her, Queen Elizabeth I heavily subjugated Catholics for years, and they'd hoped that once King James I took the throne he'd be more lenient. But when he condemned Catholicism as a superstition and ordered fines for refusing to attend Protestant services, that was too much.

The British discovered Fawkes' scheme in the nick of time.

Guy Fawkes Night was also called Pope Night because most assumed the Vatican had ordered the plot for the mass. That allegation was never proven.

Guy Fawkes's band was not the only Catholic gang to be caught. Two years before, a group of British priests plotted to kidnap King James I but was turned in by fellow Catholics. The next year there was a plot to kill James and install his cousin on the throne.

In 1715 and 1745 Catholics James III and James IV, called the "Pretender," both tried to retrieve the English throne by invading Scotland, providing more fuel for the anti-Catholic fire.

- King James I—who was Scotland's King James VI before succeeding his cousin Elizabeth in England—instructed the Bible translators that the English Bible needed revision because existing translations "were corrupt and not answerable to the truth of the original." The Great Bible authorized by Henry VIII in 1538 contained several inconsistencies. The clergy favored the Bishops' Bible, published thirty years later, but that version failed to gain Elizabeth's official authorization, or wide acceptance, for that matter. And the Geneva Bible, released in 1556, though popular with Puritans, was less so among more conservative clergy.

So King James had commanded that, unlike the Geneva Bible, his translation would contain no marginal notes except to explain Hebrew or Greek words. Let the people decide what the Lord meant by his plain Word. He wasn't a God of confusion.

King James had established an elaborate set of rules to prevent individual penchants and ensure the translation's scholarship and nonpartisanship. He'd insisted that familiar terms and names be used and the Bible be readable in the idiom of the day. Thus Yonah became Jonah and Yacob was Jacob.

- The city now known as Plymouth, Massachusetts, was originally known as "Plimoth" and "Plimouth." English spelling rules were inconsistent when the settlement was first established.

- The book cover shows America's first flag, the Grand Union—also called the Continental Color, Congress, or Cambridge flag—which predated Betsy Rose's famous thirteen-star version that was unveiled in June 1777.

A banner needed to be distinct from the British Red Ensign flown from civilian and merchant vessels. Since the British Red Ensign was readily available (being the official flag of the colonies), the unknown designer simply needed to sow on six stripes of white cloth so that it alternated red and white stripes representing the thirteen colonies.

That Grand Union flag was first hoisted by First Lieutenant John Paul Jones December 3, 1775, on the US Navy's first flagship, the USS Alfred, on the western shore of the Delaware River at Philadelphia, Pennsylvania. This is why it is sometimes called the "First Navy Ensign."

General George Washington most likely raised the Grand Union flag at Cambridge, January 2, 1776, and it was given a thirteen-gun salute.

OTHER BOOKS
BY
MARK ALAN LESLIE

HISTORICAL NOVELS

• *Midnight Rider for the Morning Star: From the Life and Times of Francis Asbury*, published by the Francis Asbury Society Press, Wilmore, Ky., 2007

• *True North: Tice's Story* (Publishers Weekly Featured Book), available through Amazon.com and Barnesandnoble.com, 2015

• *The Crossing*, published by Elk Lake Publishing, Plymouth, Mass., 2017

CONTEMPORARY NOVELS

• *Chasing the Music* (Thrill of the Hunt Book 1), published by Elk Lake Publishing, Plymouth, Mass., 2016

• *The Three Sixes* (Thrill of the Hunt Book 2) published by Elk Lake Publishing, Plymouth, Mass., 2017

• *Operation Jeremiah's Jar* (Thrill of the Hunt Book 3), published by Elk Lake Publishing, Plymouth, Mass., 2018

• *The Last Aliyah*, published by Elk Lake Publishing, Plymouth, Mass., 2018

• *Torn Asunder*, published by Elk Lake Publishing, Plymouth, Mass., 2020

DEVOTIONAL

- *Walks with God*, published as an e-book and available on Amazon.com and Barnesandnoble.com, 2010

SELF-HELP

- *Fired? Get Fired Up!*, published as an e-book and available on Amazon.com and Barnesandnoble.com, 2009

GOLF INDUSTRY

- *Putting a Little Spin on It: The Design's the Thing*, published as an e-book and available on Amazon.com and Barnesandnoble.com, 2013
- *Putting a Little Spin on It: The Grooming's the Thing*, published as an e-book and available on Amazon.com and Barnesandnoble.com, 2014

ABOUT THE AUTHOR

The winner of six national magazine writing awards, Mark Alan Leslie has written thirteen books, including four historical novels, four modern-day mystery/adventures, one end-times thriller, two golf books, a devotional, and a Christian self-help book. His career as a newspaper and magazine editor and writer spanned thirty years before he began writing books full-time.

While AFA Journal called Mark "a seasoned wordsmith" whose contemporary novels are "in the class with John Grisham," Midwest Book Review cited his "genuine flair for compelling, entertaining, and deftly crafted storytelling."

He and his wife live in Maine and have two adult children and four granddaughters.

Leslie may be contacted at:

gripfast@roadrunner.com, www.markalanleslie.com

www.ingramcontent.com/pod-product-compliance
Lightning Source LLC
Chambersburg PA
CBHW051129030726
47504CB00004B/774